The
CHRISTMAS
KEEPSAKE

The
CHRISTMAS
KEEPSAKE

ANNIE RAINS

FOREVER

New York Boston

Forever
Hachette Book Group
1290 Avenue of the Americas, New York, NY 10104
read-forever.com
@readforeverpub

First edition: October 2025

Forever is an imprint of Grand Central Publishing. The Forever name and logo are registered trademarks of Hachette Book Group, Inc.

The publisher is not responsible for websites (or their content) that are not owned by the publisher.

Forever books may be purchased in bulk for business, educational, or promotional use. For information, please contact your local bookseller or the Hachette Book Group Special Markets Department at special.markets@hbgusa.com.

Library of Congress Cataloging-in-Publication Data

Names: Rains, Annie, author.
Title: The Christmas keepsake / Annie Rains.
Description: First edition. | New York : Forever, 2025. | Series: Love in bloom ; book 2
Identifiers: LCCN 2025020684 | ISBN 9781538768075 (trade paperback) | ISBN 9781538768099 (ebook)
Subjects: LCGFT: Romance fiction. | Christmas fiction. | Novels.
Classification: LCC PS3618.A3975 C47 2025 | DDC 813/.6—dc23/ eng/20250602
LC record available at https://lccn.loc.gov/2025020684

ISBNs: 9781538768075 (trade paperback), 9781538768099 (ebook)

Printed in the United States of America

LSC-C

Printing 1, 2025

For Lydia, my beautiful daughter (inside and out)

And for mothers and daughters everywhere.

This special relationship is made with love
and meaningful memories, not blood.

Chapter One

All the world's a stage,
And all the men and women merely players;
They have their exits and their entrances,
And one man in his time plays many parts.
—William Shakespeare, *As You Like It*

Thanksgiving was supposed to be all about relaxation and guilty pleasures, along with counting your blessings and loving on friends and family.

Not this year.

Mallory Blue audibly sighed as she plopped into a chair behind the nurses' station for the first time in hours. Her legs ached, her temples throbbed, and her throat was dry. She'd had no time to quench her thirst during this eight-hour ER shift. No time to hit the restroom either.

Finally, the halls were quiet enough for her to hear herself think, which might not be a good thing. She took a steadying breath, inhaling the sterile aroma of bleach mixed with lemon. This wasn't home by any means, but she spent more time in this hospital than she did in her own house. Especially lately.

Popping open a can of Dr Pepper—her favorite vice when working long shifts—she reached for her iPhone and checked her messages.

Maddie: Have you considered what I said?

Mallory's momentary peace fizzled like the carbonation in her soda can. Her younger sister was referring to a conversation they'd had last week. Ever since Nan had gone to live at Memory Oaks, the bills had been piling up. These extra hospital shifts were the temporary answer, but Maddie was pushing the idea of selling their grandmother's beloved community theater as the permanent solution.

Another text came through with a loud ping.

Maddie: You're skipping Thanksgiving dinner tonight just to work overtime. You can't do this forever. Sam and I miss you.

Sam was Maddie's husband. They were newlyweds. This afternoon, they were having turkey and all the sides with Mallory's paternal grandpa, Charlie, who also happened to be a newlywed. Mallory's best friend, Savannah, might even stop by with her new husband, Evan. Love seemed to be all around Mallory, and she felt like the Grinch choosing work over Thanksgiving with loved ones.

Her phone dinged a third time.

Maddie: The show must go on!

It was Nan's favorite expression, which she had used at every opportunity.

A boyfriend broke their heart? *The show must go on.*

Their dog died unexpectedly? *The show must go on.*

Their absentee mom failed to show up for Mallory's sweet sixteen birthday party, even though she promised? *The show must go on!*

In this circumstance, Maddie wasn't implying that the theater doors remain open. Instead, the show she was talking about was their lives. She'd made it clear in their last conversation that her vote was to sell Bloom Community Theater. And promise or no promise, Maddie also voted that Mallory not put on Nan's annual Christmas play. In fact, Maddie didn't want to do any of the things she'd promised Nan. They were supposed to go through the box of keepsake ornaments and read Nan's journal, sharing the special memories that explained them. *"I don't have time rolling around in the past, Mallory. In case you haven't noticed, my present is pretty different these days,"* she'd remarked, talking about the fact that she had been recently in an ATV accident and was now paralyzed from the waist down. *"My future is far different from the one I imagined. That's what I need to focus on."*

Mallory empathized, of course, but Nan had raised them when their mom had walked away. Shouldn't Nan's wish be granted?

Maddie: Nan won't even know if we keep our promise to her. She doesn't remember us anymore.

It was true that Nan's clarity of mind had been slipping away over the past year. It was rare that she even recognized Mallory's face, much less knew her name. The "now" Nan wasn't who Mallory and Maddie had made a promise to though. They'd promised the Nan who'd been a mother to them all their lives. The theater was Nan's passion, and this play meant everything to her. And the town.

Nan had written the script herself, and the annual production of *Santa, Baby* had become a beloved town tradition. Last year, when subtle signs of forgetfulness had started to set in, Nan made Mallory and Maddie swear to carry on, no matter what.

It wasn't even a huge ask. The cast was the same year after year except when cast members were sick or moved away. The set was already built, requiring only minor touch-ups each season. The script had evolved over the decades, but, like a fine wine, only for the better. Everything was in place. All they needed to do was step into Nan's shoes and make it happen.

Mallory: Ruby Corben dropped out of the play yesterday. There's a part for you.

Maddie's response was quick and expected.

Maddie: NO.

All caps with no pretenses or apologies.

Maddie: I don't recall a wheelchair ramp leading up to the stage anyway.

Mallory: We could make one.

Maddie: My answer is still no. Theater was never my thing and you know it.

Yeah. Nan knew it too. Maddie liked the great outdoors. She loved long hikes, mountain climbing, and cycling, anything that required sunshine and adrenaline. Or, at least, she had enjoyed those things. Since the four-wheeling accident had left her using a wheelchair, life had changed. Maybe it was wrong of Mallory to expect Maddie to get onstage in front of the entire town right now when she was still adjusting to her new normal.

Mallory reached for her Dr Pepper, preparing to take a long sip when the sound of a woman clearing her throat stopped her.

"Sitting down on the job?"

Wanda Boswell stepped up to the counter with a snide expression. Wanda was also a nurse at Bloom Memorial, and she loved to catch others doing things wrong. Not that taking a break after eight hours of walking up and down the halls, delivering medication and helping patients to the restroom, was wrong.

Mallory offered a reluctant smile. "Actually, my shift was technically over half an hour ago. I never had a break or lunch. So yes, I'm sitting down on the job, technically, but the floor is quiet right now." For the first time in hours. The Thanksgiving shift was notorious for cooking injuries. Turkey fryer burns. Family brawls. The winner of this holiday shift went to the man who'd actually been attacked by the turkey that was supposed to be today's guest of honor. And by the looks of the guy when he'd come in, moaning, the turkey had won.

Wanda glanced around. "I love working the holidays. It makes me grateful that I don't have family to worry about. It all seems so unnecessary, if you ask me." She looked at Mallory a moment. "I guess we're the same in that way."

Mallory's lips parted as she tried to decide if Wanda was insulting her or paying her a compliment.

"You volunteered for this shift, right? There's no ring on your finger." She shrugged. "No judgment from me. I think you're a smart girl."

Overtime pay and feeling like a third wheel weren't the main reasons Mallory had chosen a shift over dinner at Maddie's. Her main reason was Nan. Thanksgivings were never small with Nan in charge, even after Grandpa Mickey died. Nan cooked enough for an army, inviting anyone who needed a place to go. With Nan at Memory Oaks Nursing Care this year, the holidays would be different. While Maddie didn't want to entertain the past, Mallory was stuck there.

"We just got a new arrival in curtain 12," Wanda said. "I got him settled while you were checking on the hypoglycemic in curtain 2."

Mallory nodded, taking note and wishing her coworker didn't call patients by their diagnosis.

"And since it's quiet on the floor and my back is killing me," Wanda continued, "I think I'll clock out early. You don't mind, do you?"

Wanda didn't wait for Mallory to argue. Instead, she continued walking down the hall, whistling loudly, which would undoubtedly wake the patients and ensure that Mallory was back on her feet until the next shift's nurses arrived.

Picking up her phone, Mallory tapped out another text to her sister.

Mallory: Happy Thanksgiving. Save me some turkey and...

The sound of barking erupted down the hall, grabbing her attention. *Barking?* Either someone had the TV volume too high or one of the patients had a therapy dog. Therapy dogs were typically quiet. Well trained. They knew not to bark unless...something was wrong.

Mallory got up and moved quickly in the direction of the sound. While it was usually a patient's buzzer that alerted her that a patient was in distress, maybe this time it was a loud, barking dog. After ten years of nursing, nothing surprised her anymore.

She followed the yellow-tiled hall to open curtain number 12 and yanked it back, pausing as her brain tried to make sense of the sight in front of her. Wanda hadn't mentioned that the new patient was Hollis Franklin or that he had his dog with him. Hollis was lying on the hospital bed, his face pulled in a painful grimace as he clutched his left leg to his torso. On the floor beside him was his chocolate lab, Duke, barking anxiously.

"Hollis? What's wrong? Are you in pain?" *Stupid question.* "Where's your pain?" Her gaze moved to Hollis's shin, where a long, open gash poured blood.

"I don't think this should hurt as bad as it does, but..." He groaned. "I think I must have hit a nerve with my fall. That dog knocked me right off my feet."

Mallory eyed his gentle giant dog suspiciously. "Duke hurt you? Do I need to call security? Animal control?" She didn't even think hospital policy allowed a dog in the ER, but Hollis had a charm about him that made it hard for people to tell him no.

He cracked his eyes open just enough to look at her. "Not Duke. One of my rescues. It wasn't the dog's fault. I scared him."

Mallory quickly gathered astringent and dressing. The wound didn't appear to be a dog bite. "Duke stays within the confines of this curtain, and as soon as I get you all fixed up, you've got to take him out."

Hollis nodded. "Promise."

Mallory pulled up a stool and sat. "I can get you clean and bandaged, but after all these years, I can't fix this hopeless need of yours to save every dog you meet."

Hollis's grimace shifted to a tiny grin. "You know that's the pot calling the kettle black, right?" He relaxed his hold on his leg and lowered it to the bed. "Says the nurse who cares for everyone around her except herself."

Mallory and Hollis had known each other since they were kids, and Hollis was best friends with Evan, who was married to Mal's best friend. Over the years, they'd had their fair share of feuds, but they were on friendly terms now. "Tell me what happened?"

"I'm not one to startle easily, but the dog lunged at me. I stumbled backward into a pile of lumber, one piece of which had a six-inch nail bent at the perfect angle to rip my leg open."

Mallory flinched. "Ouch."

"Ouch is an understatement."

"I'll try to be gentle, but I can't promise this won't hurt," she said.

He grinned some more, which wasn't the response she normally got when she warned a patient of pain.

"Then I won't promise not to scream."

"This hall has been a mixture of screams all evening." Her shoulders slumped. "Forget the pumpkin pie. All I want for Thanksgiving is peace and quiet... Are you up-to-date on your tetanus shot?"

"I've been working construction since I was eighteen. Do you realize how many times I've been in this ER?"

Mallory laughed at the question. The ER wasn't her regular department, but she knew that Hollis had been all-boy and was now all-guy. "If I had to guess, you probably have a bench named after you somewhere."

He watched her intently as she worked, swiping the wound with alcohol wipes and dousing it with antibacterial ointment. "Rehearsals for *Santa, Baby* start this weekend, right?" he asked as she applied the bandage.

Her gaze flicked up. "Yep. Please tell me you're not backing out too."

Hollis hadn't held an acting role since he was fifteen, but he managed the stage props and did a lot of the heavy lifting. If he backed out, she swore she'd scream.

"Too?" he asked, narrowing his eyes as he tilted his head.

Mallory kept her focus on his wound. Now that it was clean, she reached for a bandage. "Mrs. Corban messaged me yesterday. I tried to get Maddie to take the open spot, but she's got other priorities right now."

"The newlywed life," Hollis said with a nod, absently scratching the side of his beard. "Sam mentioned to me that Maddie missed being active, so I reached out to a friend of mine from my juvie days and connected her with Maddie."

Juvie meaning when Hollis had been locked away in juvenile detention during his late teens.

"Renee is heavily involved in adaptive sports, and she runs a group here in Bloom and the surrounding communities," Hollis said. "I think she could help Maddie find her groove again."

Mallory looked up from his bandage. It had never occurred to her, but of course Maddie would be missing the outdoor activities that she'd always enjoyed. "That is so nice of you. Do you sleep?"

His brow lifted in question.

"You're doing construction, rescuing and training dogs, doing stage work for the theater, and helping my sister find a new outlet. And," she said, lifting a finger, "every time I visit Nan, you're there visiting Pop." Pop was Hollis's foster grandfather.

"I can sleep when I'm old and gray. What about you?" he asked. "Why don't you take that role in the play?"

Mallory shook her head. "I'm the director. I feel like I'm doing enough without taking on an acting role too." Too much actually. Standing from the stool, she turned and started to walk toward the small metal rolling cart along the wall. She didn't need anything specific, just space because the weight of responsibility on her shoulders was heavy, and sometimes it felt hard to breathe.

Hollis touched her hand before she stepped out of reach. "Hey. I know how hard you work, and I've seen how often you visit Nan when not many others do. I've watched how much you've supported Maddie since her accident, and even Savannah with her autoimmune condition. You're everyone's rock."

Suddenly, she felt seen in a way she hadn't been in a long time. Not since Nan had a clearer mind. "Then why are you questioning me about acting in the play?"

"I just remember how much you used to love being onstage, until I ruined it for you." He looked down and then flinched, reminding Mallory that he was in pain.

"I'm going to need to glue this gash of yours."

"It's that deep?" he asked.

"Yep, and you'll have a nice, new scar to match all the others. It's not fair that men get sexier with scars and women have to cover ours with makeup." The realization that she'd just called Hollis sexy hit her with a quick surge of heat through her cheeks.

He was kind enough not to call her on it, but the look he was giving her somehow felt worse. "Let's get this over with. Matt and Sandy invited me over for Thanksgiving dinner."

"That was nice of them." She pulled the tray of medical items closer and got to work, tending to his wound on auto mode.

"Wanna come with me?" he asked, avoiding looking at his wound. She found it comical how many men came in and got woozy at the sight of blood. "I'm sure Sandy made more than enough."

The suggestion took Mallory by surprise.

"You're about to get off shift, right?" he prodded.

Now she regretted telling him that because it would be awkward when she rejected the invitation. Some part of her wanted to say yes though. "That's okay. It's been a long shift, and I'm exhausted. But thank you." She applied a bandage in a quick movement, pushed the metal tray aside, and smiled back at him. "All done."

He finally looked down, his brows lifting. "I'm impressed."

She shrugged a shoulder. "If you knew how many times I've glued up a gash like that one."

"Probably as many times as I've hammered a nail into a piece of lumber and constructed a basic frame. If you change your mind about dinner with Matt and Sandy…" When he stood, so did Duke, wagging his tail anxiously.

"Thanks." She led him out of the closed curtain and down the corridor. "I think I'll actually swing by Memory Oaks and visit Nan though."

She hadn't planned on doing that, but it seemed like a good idea now. Then she might head home and open Nan's box of keepsakes afterward. She had been waiting for Maddie to join her, but now that it was clear Maddie wasn't interested in a deep dive into her family's past, Mallory was eager to discover exactly what was so important for Nan to show them. Mallory had assumed her grandmother was an open book, but everyone had secrets—little things they wanted to keep hidden from the world. Even Mallory.

As Mallory approached her small, one-story brick house later that evening, she slowed her step when she noticed an insulated bag hanging on her front doorknob, and a faint smell of delicious food wafted under her nose. Undoubtedly, Maddie had sent Sam to drop off a dinner plate from their earlier meal with Grandpa Charlie and his new wife, Eleanor.

Regret threaded through her, but without Nan, she couldn't fathom sitting down to a turkey meal with all the sides and a slice of pumpkin pie, pretending everything was fine.

Even though Nan hadn't known Mallory from the nurse who worked her hall, Mallory was grateful for the half hour she'd sat with Nan tonight.

After unlocking her door, she took the bag inside and kicked off her shoes—her feet practically sighing with relief. She was hungry, but the food could wait. She left the insulated bag on her kitchen counter and headed down the hall toward her bedroom, flipping on the light and veering into her closet. In the very back corner was the large plastic box that Nan had given to Maddie and her last Christmas.

"This is my Keepsake Box. Just a few treasured items that might not make sense if you don't know the memories behind them." She held up a small, brown journal to show Mallory and Maddie. "That's why I'm also giving you this. Inside this journal, you'll find the meaning of all the items. I've numbered them because they're meant to be hung in order, according to the time line."

"Hung?" Mallory had said, shaking her head slightly. "Hung where?"

Nan's smile was warm, as always. "On the Memory Tree." She didn't wait for them to ask what exactly that was. Nan had been showing subtle signs of forgetfulness, and part of Mallory wondered if it was related to that. "A Christmas tree except this one tells a story. My story."

She'd made both Mallory and Maddie promise they'd wait until this Thanksgiving or after, pulling each item out in their proper order and reading whatever she'd written for that memory.

"*I promise,*" *Mallory agreed, ignoring the fact that Maddie had said nothing.*

Nan's shoulders seemed to slump in relief. "*I have one more request. If I can't make it happen next year, promise me that you'll run my play. The town is depending on us. The show must go on.*"

At the time, Mallory thought Nan was making a mountain out a of molehill over little things like losing her keys or getting lost on the way to the grocery store where she'd been shopping for decades. No part of her really thought that she was agreeing to put on Nan's play on her own.

Dragging the Keepsake Box to the side of her bed, she sat on the floor while leaning against the side of her mattress.

I wish Maddie was here.

She understood why Maddie wasn't. After months of living moment to moment, Maddie was finally focusing on the future. Maybe getting involved in adaptive sports would be fulfilling for her. Mallory couldn't be prouder of her younger sister's strength and determination. Maybe next year, she'd be ready for Nan's full story.

Lifting the lid, the first thing Mallory saw was Nan's journal lying on top of several small boxes, all numbered. The journal was a small brown book with tiny white flowers, and the word *Memories* was indented into the leather. Hooking the tips of her fingers beneath the cover's edge, she opened to the first page.

Nan's familiar cursive handwriting felt like a hug, reaching out of the book's binding and squeezing Mallory's heart. It felt good, but also left her heart aching because, deep inside, she knew things had changed and would never be the same again.

Blinking past her blur of tears, she focused on the words that Nan had written.

My dear sweet Granddaughters…

If you're reading this, I'm probably gone, in one sense or another. No man (or woman) lives forever, and I don't think I'd even want to. The best that one can hope is that we live on in our loved ones who remain.

As a girl, I watched my grandmother forget. First her address. Then things like her last name. Then she forgot me, which I couldn't comprehend at such a young age. As an adult, I watched the same thing happen with my own mother. Then, it started happening to me.

I told myself that I was just being paranoid. When

you're young, you assume you're invincible. That you'll live forever and remember every moment. But those moments of forgetfulness increased, month by month, year after year.

I've always thought of a Christmas tree as a sort of memory album. Each keepsake ornament in this box will probably seem like random things that have no worth, but they're priceless to me. In the journal, you'll find the story behind each and every one. I hope that you'll remember me as you hang these keepsakes on what I like to call the Memory Tree.

You may be surprised by what I tell you in these pages. People have different sides to themselves. Different faces. Different masks. I was so many people in this lifetime. A daughter. An actress. A writer. Friend. Wife. Grandmother. But first and foremost, I was a woman who lived, loved, and made a million mistakes.

When the time comes, I may not remember or be capable of saying so, so allow me to say it here. I'm sorry. I always did what I thought was best for you, and for your mother. Maybe my best wasn't good enough. Maybe I should have done things differently. All I can say is that life doesn't have a dress rehearsal. It's all improv on one big stage.

Dearest granddaughters, memories are the secret to living forever—because even after you're gone, they live on in the hearts of those who love you most. Some good, some bittersweet, and too many the kind that break you piece by piece. All of the memories are necessary to understand the final product, however, which I hope ultimately will be a life well-lived.

Thank you for being a part of my story. The mind may forget, but the heart never will. I love you always.

Nan

Chapter Two

You gotta have a dream. If you don't have a dream, how you gonna have a dream come true?
—Oscar Hammerstein II, *South Pacific*

Hollis swiped his shirtsleeves across his sweaty brow and looked out at the work of the day. His foster dad's construction crew had made a lot of progress building the frame for the Maynard Farm's new barn, but it wasn't quite finished, and Hollis wouldn't be able to see it through to the end. Since he was seventeen years old, Hollis had been working with Matt's crew ten and a half months out of the year. The other six weeks, however, Hollis helped Matt's father, who had a business of his own, Popadine's Tree Farm.

When Pop went to live at Memory Oaks, Matt had tossed around the idea of selling the farm. Construction was Matt's passion, not Christmas trees. Hollis had always loved the farm though, even before the Popadine family had taken him in at seventeen. Prior to that, Hollis would trespass on their property and get himself into trouble. That's what he was well-known for back then. Matt himself had been the one to call the cops on Hollis the last time he'd gone to juvenile detention. But when Hollis was seventeen, the Popadines took him into their home and treated him like a son.

And Pop had treated him like a grandson. Even though Hollis had never been legally adopted, they were his family.

"Looks good, heh?" Matt clapped a hand along Hollis's upper back.

Hollis offered a nod. "Yeah. Real good."

Matt's gaze dropped to Hollis's leg, where the bandage that Mallory had placed there had soaked through, leaving a dirty, brown stain. "Better get that cleaned up before it gets infected. I don't know why you deal with stuff like that." That "stuff" being anything dog related. "I get that you enjoy training 'em, but some dogs aren't rehabilitation material."

"That's what folks said about me." Hollis reached for his bottled water on his truck's tailgate and drained the last sip. Then he looked at Matt. "And look at me now."

It was meant to be sarcastic, but Matt had a shine in his eyes. Matt Popadine hadn't just taken on the role of Hollis's foster dad at seventeen, he'd also given him a job.

"Look at you now indeed," Matt went on. "I'm proud of you, son."

Son. Hollis used to hate the term of endearment. Loathe it even. The word was akin to nails scraping along a chalkboard. Now it ran over and through Hollis like a spoonful of thick honey. That was the effect of unconditional love. Back in his young adult years, he hadn't trusted that it was possible for him to be loved by anyone. It'd taken him a while to understand that the Popadine family weren't going anywhere, regardless of what he did or didn't do.

"Want to come over for dinner?" Matt asked. "I'm sure Sandy would love to see you."

"Thanks for the offer, but I'm actually going to get cleaned up and take Duke over to Memory Oaks to visit Pop."

"He loves you and that dog of yours. Sometimes I think he loves you and that dog more than he does his own son," Matt joked, referring to himself.

"Not the case," Hollis said, even though Pop recognized him more often than Matt these days. That was because Hollis made time to visit. In February, Hollis had moved in with Pop, hoping that a roommate would be enough to keep Pop at home where he belonged. Hollis couldn't be there around the clock though, and it had quickly become apparent that's what Pop needed to ensure his safety. "I'll tell him you said hello."

"Please do. See you tomorrow." Matt started walking toward his blue Chevrolet truck in the gravel parking lot.

"No, you won't," Hollis reminded Matt, stopping him in his tracks. "It's the Monday after Thanksgiving. Tree season." Matt already knew this, of course. "And, if you remember, now that Pop is at Memory Oaks, that's where I'll be from here-out." That was the plan Hollis and Pop had made in August, and they'd already let Matt know.

"Oh, come on, son. I need you on the crew. The other guys don't have your grind. And the Maynard's barn isn't even finished. You start a job, you finish a job."

"The crew will be fine, and so will the Maynards' barn," Hollis said, feeling an uneasiness through his chest. "We have loyal customers, and I've already secured seasonal help."

Matt put his hands on his hips and blew out a heavy breath. "Can't the seasonal help run the farm? And what's this talk about staying on afterward? What for?"

Hollis had told Matt all this information many times. So had Pop. "The barn."

Matt chuckled. "That barn has been sitting empty for years. Turning it into some location for events is a pipe dream of Pop's. You really think folks want to have their weddings in a barn when they can recite their vows in Eleanor and Charlie's garden?"

"Yeah, I do." Hollis was also hoping to take in more rescue dogs. The farm was the perfect location. He didn't want to argue with Matt right now though. Matt was a great person, and Hollis owed the man beside him a lot. But the way Matt's voice changed when he talked about Hollis and Pop's "plan" felt dismissive. Was Hollis imagining that?

Pop had acres of land in addition to the tree farm, and he'd been open about his desire to see it used for something good. For years, Hollis had been saving every spare cent he made working on Matt's construction crew. In his mind, he'd created plans for a place that was more than just a tree farm. He imagined it also being an event location. A dog rescue. He'd even considered opening a little general store with food and gifts. And hayrides pulled by Pop's old unused tractors. There was so much potential, and Pop had always loved hearing Hollis's ideas. *"As long as we keep it in the family,"* Pop always said. Then he'd make sure Hollis was looking at him before he'd clarify, *"You are part of this family, Hollis."*

"I'll call you tomorrow," Hollis called over his shoulder as he headed toward the driver-side door of his decade-old Chevy Tahoe. Duke barked as he chased after him. *Don't forget me*, is what Hollis imagined his dog saying. "You know I wouldn't leave you, buddy. Where I go, you go." And that was because Duke was a well-mannered and trained therapy dog. Hollis had taught him himself.

Hollis opened his truck door and let Duke hop in first. Then Hollis slid behind the steering wheel and pulled the door shut.

Duke let out an excited woof as Hollis cranked the engine and the radio came on. Then, reaching into the middle compartment, Hollis grabbed a treat and tossed it on the passenger seat at Duke's paws. "You get a bone, and I get a jerky stick."

They had a routine, and for the most part, he enjoyed life. Some might say "Why mess with a good thing?" Hollis had everything he needed. Why leave Popadine Construction? Especially now that

Pop was at Memory Oaks? Maybe Matt was right, and transforming the barn into anything remotely attractive to the public was a pipe dream. Hollis loved the trees as much as Pop though. He could see himself filling Pop's shoes, or trying his best, and adding on to what Pop had already built. Maybe Matt didn't want his father's dream, but Hollis did.

Pushing his frustration aside, he drove home and took a quick shower. Then he applied a clean bandage to the injury on his leg and put on a fresh change of clothing and prepared to go to Memory Oaks. The residents ate an early dinner, and the hours of five to eight were for visiting and recreation. As Hollis headed out the door, his phone buzzed in his pocket. He recognized the number for the local animal shelter. Tapping his screen, he placed his phone to his ear. "Hello?"

"Hey, Hollis," Amanda Jasper, the animal shelter's manager, said. Her tone of voice already had him bracing himself. "I have bad news. I wanted to tell you first."

His stomach clenched. "What's going on?"

"The dog that injured you yesterday…?"

"Whoa. No, he didn't hurt me. I fell on my own," Hollis argued, worried about where this conversation was going. Some part of him already knew what Amanda was going to tell him.

"He growled and lunged at you, Hollis. Those are aggressions. We don't keep dogs like that here. We're going to send him to Chesterbrook, and I just thought you should know."

Chesterbrook was a rescue in a town about sixty miles away. Hollis had gotten Duke from Chesterbrook, and at the time, Duke had been all bones and scared of everything. Hollis wasn't sure what took place at that rescue, but he was sure he never wanted to see another dog go there again.

"No! No, you can't do that!" Hollis leaned against the porch railing, clutching his phone in one hand and clenching a fist with the other.

"It's our policy. I'm sorry."

"He only lunged at me because I put a demand on him before he was ready. Because he was scared. Not because he's an aggressive dog."

"You know we can't take that risk, Hollis. This rescue is barely holding ground. We can't afford one misstep. Sending an aggressive dog home with one of our foster families and risking having someone get hurt would be bad for our rescue."

"Fine. Then I'll take him," Hollis said, without thinking.

There was a silence on the other end of the line. Hollis could almost hear the thoughts moving through Amanda's head. "You can't save every dog, Hollis," she said gently.

That truth stung even though he'd learned it long ago. This was a truth that every rescuer had to accept. Otherwise, they became the hoarders who tried to do good by animals but ended up being unable to provide for them. Animals needed food and fresh water. They needed bathing and exercise. The more dogs a person took in, the more workload. For some, it became a full-time job. One that didn't pay. "No, I can't save every dog, but I can save this one. Please." Helping this dog felt personal somehow, and it didn't take a psych degree to know why. For his entire childhood, he had felt like that "bad dog" that no one wanted, and Matt and Sandy had taken a chance on him. If they hadn't, Hollis might be locked up somewhere by now. That's the path he was on when he was a broken, angry, scared teenage boy.

"Are you even allowed to have a second dog at the place you rent?" Amanda asked.

"Actually, I moved in with Pop last spring when he started having memory concerns." Now Pop was at Memory Oaks, and Hollis was still living at his house with Pop's blessing. Pop said Hollis staying would be doing him a favor and keeping kids from breaking in and looting, which was funny because Hollis had been one of those kids at one time.

"Wow. Rent-free life," Amanda said. "Maybe you can afford to take more dogs," she teased.

"At least one more dog. So? Can I come get him?"

Amanda sighed into the receiver. "You'll have to sign a waiver releasing us of any liability if he attacks."

Hollis didn't believe for a moment that the dog he'd met yesterday would harm him. "I'll be there in ten minutes."

Amanda let out a resigned laugh. "I don't know whether to call you stupid or a saint."

"I've been called worse," Hollis joked. "By you, if I recall," he told the shelter manager.

"Well, I was wrong to suggest you were stupid," Amanda said. "Hopefully, I'm wrong about Buster too."

Chapter Three

The show must go on.

—Circuses in the 1800s
—Theaters throughout the 1900s to the present
—And Nannette "Nan" Wilder

Mallory pushed through the front door of Memory Oaks Nursing Care.

"Long time no see, Mal!" Francis Hemby called out from behind the front desk.

This was always how Francis greeted Mallory when Mallory stayed away for more than twenty-four hours. It was some sort of guilt trip that Mallory suspected Francis gave all the visitors when they'd gone without seeing their loved ones for too long. "Work has been busy," Mallory said.

Francis nodded. "Everyone's lives are busy, aren't they?"

Mallory cleared her throat. Maybe other families used that as an excuse, but Mallory was busy because of Nan. All the extra hours were to keep Nan here. "How's Nan today?" she asked, changing the subject.

Francis's facial expression shifted. "Bright-eyed as usual. And her day is always better when she gets a visit from her favorite person."

"Well, it depends on the day if I'm Nan's favorite person or not." And it depended on whether Nan remembered who Mallory even was.

Francis rolled her lips together, her expression sheepish from behind her thick-framed glasses. "Of course, you're Nan's favorite visitor. I just meant her favorite *non*family member."

"Oh." Mallory realized that Francis wasn't even referring to her. "Nan has another visitor?"

"Mm-hmm. Hollis is here with Duke. You know the folks here just love him and that dog," Francis gushed.

Hollis had done what few ever achieved—changed his reputation in a small town. Small town reputations were like granite headstones. Once they were planted in the ground, they stayed put. But somehow Hollis had gone from the rebellious bad boy that no parent wanted their daughters to even look at, to the big, lovable, burly teddy bear that every woman over the age of sixty pushed their single loved ones on. Even Mallory's paternal grandpa, Charlie, had made a bid for Mallory and Hollis to go out a few times.

She and Hollis were just friends though, and she was happy with that. Once upon a time, she'd been one of those people who'd despised him but with good reason. It wasn't easy to like the guy who'd shown up to Mallory's first starring moment at the Bloom Community Theater drunk as a skunk. Hollis was supposed to be starring alongside her, which was Nan's first mistake because, back then, Hollis wasn't the stand-up, trustworthy guy he was now.

He hadn't shown on opening night, which meant the understudy had taken his place. And if that wasn't bad enough, as Mallory made her first appearance onstage, Hollis burst into the audience, swaying on his feet and booing her. He'd made people laugh, and he'd made Mallory cry, which wasn't an easy thing to do. Mallory could count on one hand the number of times she'd cried in front of someone, at least since being a kid. One of those times was the evening she'd watched her mother leave her daughters' luggage in their grandparents' living room. Then she'd hugged Mallory, kissed her temple, and said she was sorry.

"Funny thing is, Nan didn't even like dogs before," Mallory told Francis. No explanation was needed for the word *before* at Memory Oaks. Before memories faded for the residents here, leaving behind a fog of confusion and upset. Before Alzheimer's hit like a storm destroying everything in its path for the person affected and their loved ones.

"All I know is there is a special place in heaven for people like Hollis Franklin, volunteering his time and talent for the folks here," Francis went on. "Half the time our residents' own family doesn't come regularly, but that man is like clockwork every Friday night. I wish I could say the same of my own husband," Francis said. "There's nothing regular about him." The corners of the older woman's mouth quirked in a subtle frown.

TMI, Francis. "Interesting." Mallory cleared her throat. "Well, hopefully Hollis is done visiting Nan. I don't have long to stay."

"I thought you were off-shift for the night," Francis said.

"I am, but I have some work to do at the theater."

"Before the big Christmas production?" Francis's eyes lit up as she brought her hands together at her chest. "Oh, the play is always my favorite part of the holidays."

Mallory's stomach tightened. "That's right."

"Your grandmother would be so proud of you and Maddie. Some part of me worried you'd both be too busy to put on the community play."

"It's just me, actually," Mallory told Francis. "Maddie is pursuing new things these days."

"I'm happy for her," Francis said with a nod. Then she looked at Mallory. "You have a busy life too, but look at you. You're a good granddaughter," Francis said. "Even if you missed the Thanksgiving dinner here the other night."

Mallory's lips parted, and no words came out.

"It's fine. Our residents might be forgetful. But they still sense when something is missing."

Something meaning "family." Meaning Mallory specifically.

Maddie's husband, Sam, could have gotten a day pass for Nan. He could have picked Nan up for the celebration at their house. Why hadn't he?

"Well, perhaps you can join us for some of the Christmas festivities over the next month to make up for it." Francis winked. "There's even a holiday dance next week to kick the whole season off."

"A dance?" Mallory repeated, looking at the flyer behind Francis's head.

"Our recreational therapist, Nancy, plans so many fun activities for the residents. Your grandmother doesn't feel quite as comfortable coming to the activities though. Sometimes it helps for family members to come by and go with them. It gives them confidence."

"You're talking about the dance?" a woman asked as she walked by.

Mallory turned to face Nancy, whom she'd already met on prior visits.

"It'll be fun. We're not trying to play matchmakers here at Memory Oaks, of course. Just trying to get the folks up and moving. Movement and laughter are good medicine."

As a nurse, Mallory could attest to that. "I agree."

"So, you'll come?" Nancy asked.

"Thank you." Mallory gestured down the hall. "I'm going to go check on Nan."

"Of course."

Mallory watched the tiled floor pass under her feet as she walked, hearing the sounds of patients inside their rooms. In some ways, being here reminded her of working at the hospital. Some of the sounds were familiar, but also distinctly different. Someone was crying somewhere, and Mallory knew it wasn't because they were in pain, which would have been the case at the ER or even the pediatric floor, where she typically worked. The cries here were emotional, mostly due to frustration and confusion. Loneliness. Suddenly, a familiar holiday tune blended into the mix.

"Barely past Thanksgiving, and now we can't escape Christmas tunes," Mallory muttered before stopping a foot short of Hollis's chest.

"Never pegged you as the Scrooge type." He grinned ear to ear as he stepped out of Nan's room with Duke on a leash.

"Hi." Mallory had forgiven Hollis a long time ago for what had happened when she was fifteen. They'd returned to being good friends, and that was all Mallory wanted out of their relationship. Except sometimes, in a moment like this, when her guard was lowered, a wave of attraction rolled over her.

She wasn't blind after all. What all the matchmakers said was true. Hollis was handsome. Her kind of handsome. Not the pretty boy, polished type. No. Hollis was solid. He was tall, wide, and muscled. He also had twinkly eyes and the kind of stubbled jawline that made women want to lean in and rub cheeks. *Or some women.*

"How's my grandmother?" Mallory gestured toward Nan's door. "Looks like you visited her and your grandfather tonight."

Hollis nodded. "She's still got it."

"Got what?" Mallory tilted her head.

"That spitfire meanness that puts me in my place with a single cut of her eye."

"Yes, I know exactly what you mean." Mallory checked the time on her Apple watch. "I better go on in. I can't stay long tonight. I'm working on the theater. Doing a little cleaning out of things." More like packing, but Mallory wasn't ready to share her intentions for the theater.

Hollis nodded knowingly and shrugged his broad, quarterback-esque shoulders. "Big job. You're doing that alone?"

Mallory nodded.

"Need help?" Hollis asked. "You know I don't mind heavy lifting. I'm not busy this evening."

She lowered her brows. The truth was that Mallory felt like she'd been doing everything alone lately. Everyone was too wrapped up in their own lives, and years of therapy had taught Mallory that her MIA biological mother had left her with not only abandonment issues but also a hesitance to ask for help and an inability to trust people to follow through with their promises. Mallory had long ago decided she'd rather be overwhelmed herself than disappointed in someone else. "No, that's okay. I actually don't have much to do," she lied.

Hollis's expression revealed that he wasn't buying it. "If you change your mind, let me know. I'll just be at Pop's place, working with the new dog, Buster."

Mallory's gaze flicked to the bandage on his leg, instinctively knowing exactly what he'd done. "You didn't."

Something vulnerable flashed in his brown eyes. "It wasn't the dog's fault."

"You are unbelievable, Hollis Franklin. Well, I hope I won't be dressing any more wounds."

"I kind of enjoyed it. I thought we had a moment." He winked in a completely platonic way. There was nothing flirtatious, but her heart still betrayed her with a subtle skip as she watched him continue down the hall. Catching her breath and returning to her senses, she turned back to Nan's door.

Nan had always been the one Mallory turned to when she was feeling out of touch with who she was. Nan would always remind her. *You are my Mallory.* Four simple words, but they gave Mallory purpose and belonging. Ever since Nan had come to live here, Mallory had missed hearing Nan say those words to her.

Maybe this time.

Mallory stepped inside Nan's room and waited for Nan to look at her. It had been weeks since Nan remembered her. A small fear was growing inside Mallory that maybe Nan would never remember her again. Maybe Mallory would forever be a stranger to her own grandmother.

"Who are you?" Nan's thin brows lifted shakily on her forehead.

Mallory wanted to respond "I'm your Mallory," but instead she swallowed back an onslaught of tears that tightened her throat. "Hi, Nan. How are you today?"

"Fine-fine. Did you see that dog out there?" Nan asked, looking delighted. "So cute. His owner ain't bad to look at either."

Mallory took a seat in the chair by Nan's bed. "You think?"

"Oh, yes. If I were your age, I'd be getting that man's number." Nan's gaze fell to Mallory's left hand. "You're not married?"

It was amazing how someone could remember the significance of a left ring finger but not the face of their own family member.

"No." Mallory laid her purse on Nan's bedside table, accidentally letting it topple to the side and letting Nan's diary slide out. Mallory had brought it with her, wondering if she should show it to Nan. Anytime Mallory brought up the past lately, however, Nan got agitated. When Nan couldn't recall what Mallory was discussing, Nan became angry in a way that wasn't like her at all. The Nan of old was slow to anger and quick to laugh.

Nan's gaze fell on the brown leather-bound journal. "What's that?"

"A journal." Mallory approached the subject with caution. "Have you, um, ever seen that book before, Nan?"

Nan studied the journal and gave a slight head shake. "No, I don't think so. It's a book, you say?"

"More of a diary than anything." Or like a series of letters to Mallory and Maddie.

Nan looked thoughtful. "I used to have one of those. Does it belong to someone you know?"

Mallory nodded. "Yes, but she gave me permission to read it."

"To read her diary?" Nan looked at Mallory. "She must trust you a great deal to give you all her secrets."

"I guess she does." Or she did. "I'm sure she wouldn't mind if I share it with you as well. Would you like me to read it to you?" Mallory held her breath. This could either go very badly or it could be no big deal.

Nan sat stiffly for a moment before relaxing into her pillow. "I'd like that. And I promise not to share whatever we find out."

Mallory didn't think Nan was the type to keep secrets. She had a flare for theatrics, but otherwise, her life was kind of boring. At least from Mallory's vantage point.

"Okay. Maybe just a few pages." Picking up the leather diary, Mallory opened to the first page and smoothed her hand over the lined paper, feeling the dips and grooves of Nan's handwriting cross her skin. Then she pointed her index finger and trailed each word as she read them aloud. "The Santa Hat." Mallory glanced up at Nan, who seemed to be hanging on Mallory's words.

"That hat was part of the first play I ever took the lead in, a monumental moment for a budding actress. We performed in the school cafeteria," she said, lowering her voice to a hushed whisper. "Mickey played Santa until an unfortunate accident happened during the dress rehearsal." Nan's gaze reached to a far-off place. "That's when Ralph, the Santa understudy, stepped up, and little did I know."

"Know what?" Mallory asked. Mickey was her grandfather, but she had no idea who Ralph was.

"Well, I fell for him," Nan said, looking at her again.

Everything inside Mallory froze except her heartbeat, which seemed to echo through her body. "*Who* did you fall in love with at that time?"

Nan's blue eyes suddenly blinked. Whatever memory she'd been wrapped in had unraveled, disintegrating like moth-eaten fabric. "Hmm?"

Mallory knew Nan wasn't talking about the Santa in the script that Nan had written herself—*Santa, Baby*. The first play Nan starred in must have been a different Santa story. Probably a *generic*, *happy one. The kind everyone expects.* Nan's script had gone against the typical Santa grain though. "Nan?" Mallory leaned forward, wondering if Nan was confused.

Nan's confusion was visible as the skin between her eyes crinkled into a deep divot and the lines around her eyes became more pronounced. "Who-who did you say you were again?"

Mallory's throat squeezed so tightly that it was hard to take a deep breath. This too would pass. *The show must go on.* If Nan were here, that's what she'd say. She wasn't here anymore though. At least Mallory couldn't seem to find her.

"Who are you?" Nan said more forcefully, her cheeks flush.

Closing the diary and setting it down, Mallory patted Nan's frail hand. "I'm a friend, Nan. A good friend."

Nan gave her a slightly uncomfortable smile. "I think it might be Christmas soon?"

It was a question.

Mallory swallowed thickly. "It's just a month away." Nan's favorite time of year.

"I've always loved the tree farm. Did you know that?" Nan's smile widened, giving her a girlish appearance. Mallory couldn't remember Nan ever visiting the local farm, but Nan was confused right now.

"Yeah?" she asked, toeing the line and trying not to further aggravate her grandmother.

"Do you think you could get me a tree for my room?"

"Oh." Mallory's mind raced, trying to determine how to respond. She wasn't sure Francis would allow that.

"Not the fake kind either," Nan pressed. "Illusions are for the theater, not real life. I want a real tree for my room."

Mallory stared at her grandmother. She'd heard those words a million times in her lifetime. Right now, Nan sounded like her "old self" again. It gave Mallory hope that Nan was still here, even if she was hard to reach at times. "I'll see what I can do."

The Santa Hat Tree Topper

The Santa Hat Tree Topper is where we start this story because I feel like I wasn't truly alive until I met the other half of me. Sure, there are memories before Ralph, but he was the jump start. Everything before him was just pouring the foundation for what was to come.

Mickey Whaley was originally cast as Santa in the little school play our high school put on. Secretly, I was excited, because I thought Mickey was cute. No one else knew about my tiny crush though. I kept it to myself because I didn't want my friends to tease me during my scenes with him.

Anyway, it was the night of the dress rehearsal. There was a celebratory mood in the air. We'd put something together that we would present to the town the next night. Something wonderfully merry.

I'm still unsure of what exactly happened. All I know is that some of the guys were roughhousing and the laughter quickly turned to chaos. Because of his unfortunate injury, Mickey had to step back from the play the day before opening night. Since Ralph was the understudy, he stepped up and became Santa to my Mrs. Claus. I'd never wanted to kiss Ralph. He wasn't my type. I didn't find his jokes funny. To be honest, he annoyed me.

The theater director at my school, however, adored Ralph. Most people in town did for a reason I couldn't comprehend. So, even though the original Santa was unavailable, the show went on.

The show must always go on in theater, and in life.

When the curtains opened that next night, I delivered my lines as Mrs. Claus. Nerves made my voice shake. Then Ralph came onstage, dressed in his red suit, his eyes twinkling just like Santa himself, and I felt this tiny spark inside my chest. And when it was time for him to kiss me, that spark ignited into an inner explosion.

I'd underestimated the tall, thin boy with the goofy grin and Santa hat. When I'd been focused elsewhere, he'd swooped in and stolen my heart. No one finds their true love at seventeen though. Young love derailed lives. My mother had made sure I knew that. Whatever sparkles and fluttery feelings I had would be fleeting.

Even so, this is where the story starts, where the Memory Tree starts, with a Santa Hat at the tip-top.

Chapter Four

Laughter is much more important than applause. Applause
is almost a duty. Laughter is a reward.

—Carol Channing

Hollis stepped into his grandfather's room at Memory Oaks and paused to watch Pop resting peacefully with his eyes closed. At least he looked peaceful. As soon as Hollis pulled in a full breath, however, Pop's eyes opened with a start, pale blue and just as clear as they'd ever been.

Patients at Memory Oaks struggled with various ailments related to aging, including Alzheimer's or other forms of dementia. But most days Pop was clear-minded and could tell you anything, including every address and phone number he'd ever had.

It didn't seem to bother Matt, Pop's own son, but Hollis hated seeing Pop lose his independence. "Hey, Pop." Hollis slid into the visitor's chair next to the bed. Before moving here, Pop had been an active guy. Spending any time during the day in bed was an atrocity, according to Pop. Yet here he was, lying in bed, presumably napping. "How's it going?" Hollis asked again when Pop didn't respond immediately.

Pop scoffed. "How do you think it's going in here?" His tone was answer enough. Using his arms to push himself up into a sitting position on the bed, he looked over at Hollis and his resentment began to visibly melt away. "How—how's the farm?"

Hollis knew Pop was okay if he was talking about his business and lifelong passion. "It's doing well. The trees are more beautiful than I've seen them in a long time."

"You're making sure they get the right amount of water?" Pop had trained Hollis about the business the same way that Matt had trained Hollis in construction.

"Measuring it to the drop, exactly as you taught me. The crew is nearly finished up working on the Maynard Barn, so I'm switching gears and prepping to open the tree farm for holiday hours. The season is upon us."

"Good. That's good," Pop said with the slight nod. "That was always my favorite time of the year. Preparing for the customers." He rubbed his old, leathery hands together.

"No more talking in past tense, Pop. You're still here," Hollis reminded him.

Pop shook his head. "No. I'm *here*." He pointed at the bed he was lying in. "And I don't see that changing."

"You say the word. I'll get a day pass, and we'll work the farm together anytime you want."

Pop's eyes seemed to glow. "Yeah?"

"Of course."

"I'll slow you down," Pop argued.

"Life at the tree farm isn't fast-paced, you know that." The only issue would be making sure Pop was supervised at all times. When Pop became confused, he'd taken to wandering. Add hundreds of Christmas trees and customers searching for the perfect one for their living room, and he could easily get lost.

"I'd like that." He waved a hand. "This place is nice. The food is good. And we played bingo on Friday. Next Friday, there's going to be a holiday dance."

"Yeah, I know. Francis mentioned it." Hollis waggled his brows. "You going to sit against the wall or make a move on one of the ladies?"

Pop offered a sly grin and broke into a soft chuckle. "I stopped looking for love a long time ago." Pop had become a widower in his early fifties. He held up a finger. "But there's nothing wrong with a little flirting. There's some advice for you, boy."

"I think I missed the lesson on flirting," Hollis admitted. "When I flirt, women think I'm either weird or rude."

Pop looked at him with interest, narrowing his pale eyes. "Oh, if you can care for trees, you can flirt, son. It's easy."

Hollis disagreed. "I somehow say the wrong thing. Every time."

"Doesn't matter what you say. You could be talking about dog poop on the sidewalk. The key to flirting is the way you say something."

As Hollis listened, he wondered if he was getting the clearheaded version of the man he considered to be a grandfather or the foggy version of Pop. "Can you explain exactly how one would discuss dog poop in a flirty way?" Hollis glanced around to make sure no one was overhearing this ridiculous-sounding conversation.

"It's in the eyes. First, you look at your lady friend for a long moment. You lock eyes just long enough to think in your mind, *You are beautiful*. Then you break eye contact. Flirting is in the pacing. It's in the tone. You may be discussing a pile of dog poop, but your tone needs to be the same as if you were telling her with your words that she is the prettiest woman you've laid eyes on.'"

Hollis had to admit, this was compelling advice. "You always said math was easy too, and you and I both know I got all Cs." Honestly, he was more of a D+ student, but grades didn't matter after getting his GED. Hollis hadn't gone to college because he'd had employment with Matt.

"Watch and listen…" Pop cleared his throat.

As Hollis watched, the older man's expression changed.

"Watch your step. There's dog poop on the floor." Pop's voice dipped low and turned gravelly. He looked at Hollis and counted off his next words on his fingers. "You. Are. Beautiful." Then his gaze swept toward the window to watch the birdfeeder momentarily. "Any respectable pet owner would clean up after their pet."

Hollis wasn't sure what was going on right now.

Returning his attention to Hollis, Pop pointed a finger in his direction. "I bet you're a respectable pet owner."

Hollis's jaw hung slack, and he honestly didn't know what to say until Pop started laughing, slapping a hand against his own thigh. "Pop, were you just flirting with me?"

The older man with light blue eyes and sun-speckled, weathered skin seemed to work hard to catch his breath from laughing. "My first lesson in flirting. I should have taught you a long time ago, Matt."

Hollis's heart dropped into his stomach.

Pop seemed to realize his mistake as well. The look on his face, fear and shame, broke Hollis's heart.

"Come to the dance, and I'll give you another lesson."

Hollis laughed. "I'm already planning on attending. I'm bringing Duke."

"You're bringing your dog?" Pop rolled his eyes. "You don't bring a dog to a dance. You bring a woman. Or you go and meet a woman."

Hollis absently rubbed his fingers along his beard. "You'd be surprised, Pop. Dogs are lady magnets."

Pop grunted and waved a dismissive hand. "Maybe a woman will walk over and pet your dog, but their focus is on the dog, not you. You just told me you need practice flirting. Trust me, all the ladies here will line up to dance with you."

Hollis imagined the line, full of women with canes and walkers. He loved the people here, but he wouldn't call Memory Oaks a hotspot to meet a romantic partner.

"Leave your dog at home and come sweep some ladies off their feet." Pop grimaced. "Well, keep them on their feet. A lot of us aren't as balanced as we once were."

At least Pop's humor was still intact. Sharper than it ever was, in Hollis's opinion.

Someone cleared their throat from Pop's doorway.

"Nancy," Pop said, greeting the facility's recreational therapist. "How are you?"

"I'm good, Pop. I was walking by and I overheard you saying there was...dog poop...somewhere? Do you need assistance?"

Hollis suppressed a laugh.

"You must have misheard me. I do need your assistance with something though. Convince my grandson here to come to our dance—sans his dog."

The recreational therapist's grin stretched wider. Hollis wasn't good at estimating age, but he guessed Nancy was probably in her forties. She was a beautiful Black woman with shoulder-length hair and big brown eyes. "I didn't know you had a grandson, Pop. That means you're Matt and Sandy's son?" she asked Hollis.

Hollis started to give the long explanation that, no, he wasn't really Matt and Sandy's son or Pop's grandson. He was a foster that they had taken in like a stray.

Before Hollis could say anything though, Pop answered. "Yes. He's Matt and Sandy's boy."

Nancy nodded. "Well, it's nice to meet you. I'm new to Bloom, so I don't know everyone here."

"Bloom is a small town," Hollis said. "Give it a few months and you'll know everything about everyone here, down to their Social Security number."

"Good to know. And yes, you should come to the dance. In fact, Nan's granddaughter will be there too."

"To take Nan?" Pop asked. "Nan hardly ever comes out of her room. Is she coming to the dance?"

"I hope so," Hollis said. "Maybe you can refine your own flirting skills. But, uh, perhaps choose a different topic than the one you just used on me."

Pop's eyes grew a bit brighter. "You can ask Nan's granddaughter to dance with you."

"My guess is her dance card will be full."

Pop looked at Hollis and offered a wink. "Maybe you can sweep her off her feet. And discuss dog poop."

Nancy's smile bottomed out. "I'm sorry?"

Hollis shook his head. "Inside joke."

"I'm not joking, son."

Hollis loved it when Pop called him "son," even though he had never felt worthy. Glancing over at Nancy, he wondered if she was mentally chalking up this peculiar conversation as a symptom of Pop's dementia. Hollis knew this was on-brand for his grandfather though.

"Do you think that tactic will work on Nan?" Hollis asked.

Pop shook his head. "No. No, I don't think it will. I've never been at a loss for things to talk about with Nan though."

"Well, first you'll probably need to reintroduce yourself to her, Pop."

The corners of his eyes crinkled. "I don't think so. Far as I know, Nan has never forgotten me."

After leaving Memory Oaks, Hollis drove home and fed the dogs, taking a few extra minutes to work on his bond with Buster, the scraggly lab-mix who offered scared, brown eyes when Hollis slid a bowl of kibble in his direction.

"It's all right, buddy. I'm not going to let anyone take it away from you. The food is all yours." Hollis wanted Buster to feel safe with him. Having another dog in the vicinity might be threatening, but Duke was well trained and Hollis was keeping them crated in separate areas of the house as Buster adjusted.

Slowly, Buster edged toward the bowl and sniffed before lowering his head and snapping up the food pebbles hungrily.

Hollis's injury on Thanksgiving hadn't been Buster's fault. Hollis had moved too quickly, forgetting all his dog training skills that he'd gotten during his seven months of juvenile detention as a teen. The program was a way to build job skills as well as confidence in the young juveniles. Hollis hadn't expected to gain anything from those seven months, certainly not a lifelong passion.

He loved working with dogs, but his mind had been on other things Thanksgiving Day, like opening season for the tree farm and his hope of moving forward with the plans that he and Pop had made together. Not many knew about what Hollis and Pop were planning. Hollis had hoped to leave Matt's construction crew next year and start working full-time at Popadine's Tree Farm with Pop's full blessing. Did Pop's decline in memory change that prospect? Hollis had even entertained the possibility of inviting some of the teenagers at the juvenile detention facility to learn under him. There was a lot of satisfaction in learning how to teach a dog the obedience skills that made the dog more appealing to prospective owners and often led to the dog being adopted.

"You'll find your forever home," Hollis promised Buster as he watched the dog continue to eat. The food was nearly gone.

Buster's gaze lifted to watch Hollis as he continued eating, showing a bit of territorial food behavior. It was easy to see that Buster wasn't quite comfortable around humans. He also needed to get used to being around other dogs and possibly cats. Animals who could tolerate other pets and the loud, unpredictable behavior of children were more adoptable.

The gash on Hollis's leg ached at the memory of what had

happened on Thanksgiving when Buster had lunged at him. He needed a bandage change, but it'd have to wait until after dinner because he was hungry too. After Buster finished eating, Hollis led the dog outside where there was a small fenced-in area. Pop never had pets, but when Hollis came to stay with him last year, Pop had insisted on getting a fence for Duke. Out of respect, Hollis hadn't taken in any other fosters. Respect and a lack of time, because Hollis had shifted his focus to Pop for a while. Things were different now though. Pop lived at Memory Oaks, and Hollis now lived here alone.

Leaving Buster in the fenced area, Hollis headed inside and placed a Hot Pocket in the microwave. Living alone equaled convenient dinners that usually tasted like cardboard. As long as it extinguished the hunger. Three minutes later, Hollis dropped the steaming Hot Pocket on a paper plate, grabbed a canned soda, and headed toward the back door that led to the porch. Before he could step out, the doorbell rang.

Who would be visiting right now?

He wasn't expecting anyone, and there weren't any neighbors for miles. He peeked through the peephole before opening the door. "Mal. What are you doing here?"

Mallory wrung her hands as she stood on the wood plank porch. "Sorry for stopping by so late."

"It's fine. Everything okay?" He'd just seen her earlier at Memory Oaks, and she hadn't looked as shaken as she did now.

"Something happened earlier," she said. "Can I come in?"

"Of course." He gestured her inside and closed the door behind him, leading her to the sofa. He took a seat in the recliner across from her. "What's going on?"

"Something happened when I was with Nan this afternoon. After you left."

"Okay." Hollis had no idea what she might tell him. "Is she okay?"

"Yeah, yeah. She's fine. I mean, as fine as she has been." Mallory reached inside her purse and pulled out a leather-bound book that Hollis had never seen before. "This is Nan's book."

"Nan wrote a book?" he asked.

"Well, kind of. It's a journal obviously, but she wrote the story behind each of the ornaments for her Memory Tree."

Hollis nodded. Nan had mentioned her Memory Tree to him last year, briefly explaining its purpose when he'd helped her pick out the perfect tree on the lot, which just so happened to be the smallest.

"Tonight, I read her one of the journal entries, and she remembered," Mallory said excitedly. "It was only for a brief second, and I'm not sure if the memory was real or fake. That's why I'm here." Mallory rolled her lips together, looking uncharacteristically nervous. "Do you know anything about the first play that Nan was in?"

Obviously, Hollis hadn't been alive when Nan started acting. He'd grown up going to the Bloom Community Theater every day after school though, and Nan had always told him stories of her younger theater days over milk and a plate of cookies before giving him chores at the theater. As he grew older, he helped construct the stage sets.

"The first play your grandmother was in? You mean in high school?" Hollis asked, trying to think back to all the black-and-white photos from past productions that hung on Nan's office walls. "The first play was *Merry Little Santa*, I think." He shrugged. "Or something like that."

Mallory leaned forward, and when she did, Hollis caught her floral scent.

"Who played Santa? Do you know?"

Hollis had rarely ever seen Mallory, typically so composed, so worked up. She was normally professional. At least since being an adult. The younger Mallory that he'd grown up with, though, had been energetic, and she'd loved the theater just as much as Nan. "I couldn't tell you. Why? What's up?"

Mallory was glowing, visibly trying to contain her excitement.

"I'm not sure. This evening when I was reading Nan an entry from her journal…" Mallory shook her head. "I can't confirm that any of what she said is correct, but she seemed to remember something."

"Wow. That's great, Mal."

"The entry talked about her first love, and I don't think that person was my grandfather." Mallory pressed her lips together. "Hollis, I came here tonight to ask you for a favor."

Hollis already knew, whatever Mallory's request, his answer would be yes.

"I need a tree for Nan's room."

"In Memory Oaks?" Hollis blew out a breath. "There's no way Francis is going to allow you to put up a live tree in one of the resident's rooms. Trust me, I asked about putting one in Pop's room. How can a lifelong tree farmer possibly have a room without a Christmas tree during the holidays?"

A thin sheen of tears formed in Mallory's eyes. "I just have this feeling it'll help her. Is there anything you can do?"

"Aside from smuggling it into Nan's room?" He rubbed a hand along his short beard, letting the sensation distract him from soaking in Mallory's eyes. The shine of her hair. The little freckle at the far edge of her right cheek.

"If you can bring a dog into Memory Oaks, I'm guessing you can find a way to bring a tree." She leaned toward him, her hands folding in front of her in a pleading gesture.

Did Mallory Blue know that he would do just about anything for her? He cleared his throat. "Meet me at the tree farm tomorrow. I'll be out there all day. We'll walk around and find a Memory Tree–size blue fir. Not too small, not too big."

Mallory's face lit up. "What about Francis?"

"Fran owes me a favor. I do my best not to collect on favors, but in this case, I think it's appropriate."

Mallory's gaze searched his. "Why does Francis owe you a favor?"

He shrugged a shoulder. "I may have built a wheelchair ramp overnight when her husband had his accident last spring. I donated my time and even the lumber. That's why I did it instead of Matt's crew. Love Matt, but pro bono isn't his thing."

"No, but it is yours." Mallory gave him a knowing look. "You're still trying to make up for things long forgiven and forgotten."

Hollis leaned over his knees and clasped his hands. "Maybe. For the record, good deeds don't make a good man."

"Well, that's exactly what you are. Thank you, Hol."

"Don't thank me yet."

Mallory's hands stopped wringing, and her shoulders hung relaxed at her side.

Hollis had noticed she'd been tense lately, as if carrying the world on her shoulders, which was typical for the Mallory Blue he knew. Lately it had concerned him though. Sometimes a person's world got too heavy, even for the strongest person to bear. That's why Nan had called him into her office last year as well, and just like Mallory tonight, Nan had asked for a favor that he couldn't deny. "I want you to know I'm here for whatever you need. With Nan or the play. You have a lot on your plate."

When Nan had met with Hollis last Christmas, she'd warned Hollis that Mallory would shy away from confiding in anyone about how overwhelmed she was. Nan had said Mallory would also hesitate to ask for help.

Mallory looked down for a moment, avoiding his gaze. "It's not that much. The play pretty much runs itself at this point. I'm just a warm body who can open the theater doors and make sure everyone has their lines and costumes. At least that's what I'm hoping."

"People underestimate how big an ask it is just to show up sometimes," Hollis said quietly.

"Well, my sister certainly does." She exhaled and held up a hand. "She's the one with a lot on her plate. Me? I'm fine."

Her words didn't match the tension rolling off her.

"Thank you so much, Hollis." Standing, she turned and headed toward the door.

Hollis followed her onto the porch. "I'm glad you know you could ask me for whatever you need."

Mallory looked at him. "Sometimes you're too nice for your own good. People could take advantage of that."

"Not you," he said quietly. "I could count on one hand how many times you've asked me for anything."

"Maybe I'm setting myself up for disappointment, but some part of me hopes that creating this Memory Tree will help Nan remember. This afternoon, I learned something about her I didn't know. I'm excited to see what else I'll discover. But also kind of scared."

"Even the best of us have skeletons in our closets." And he of all people was in no position to judge. Nan had shared a few of her secrets when he was at his lowest points just to show that change was possible and no one was beyond reform. Mallory seemed to have her grandmother on a pedestal. He didn't think that would change, but she was in store for a few surprises.

Mallory tilted her head as she looked at him, her eyes subtly narrowing. "I'm sorry. I burst right in and didn't even ask how you're doing. Everything okay?"

"Yeah. I'm good. Just tired." He'd been working extra hard on the construction crew these last couple of weeks knowing that he would be running Pop's Christmas Tree Farm after Thanksgiving. Matt always worked Hollis harder right before the holidays. Hollis suspected it was payback for him helping Pop at the farm. If not for Hollis, Pop would probably have had to sell a long time ago. As he'd gotten older, he couldn't do the heavy lifting, and every year he'd relied more heavily on Hollis.

"You're tired, and here I am bothering you with yet another thing to add to your to-do list." Mallory flashed a guilty grin.

"You're not bothering me. In fact, now I have something to look forward to." Maybe that comment was a little too strong. Yeah, he'd always had a crush on Mallory that he tried to keep in check. He knew nothing was ever going to happen between them and didn't want to make things weird. "I love the thrill of the hunt for the perfect tree."

"Who would've thought the reformed bad boy of Bloom would turn into a regular Saint Nick? Certainly not me," she said honestly. "If you remember, you were *supposed* to play Mr. Claus when we were fifteen."

"Oh, I remember," Hollis said with a frown. "I've been regretting fumbling that opportunity most of my life."

Mallory gave him an unreadable look. "I can find you a role in this year's play if you want."

"Nah. I'm good staying behind the scenes."

"Okay. Well, thank you again, Hollis. I guess I'm one of those people who owe you now. If there's any way to repay you."

"Not necessary." Pop's voice played in his head. Hollis cleared his throat. "Actually, maybe there is a way you can repay me. Any chance you'll be attending the dance at Memory Oaks next Friday?"

Her smile faltered. "I was considering it. Are-are you going too?"

Why was he so nervous right now? Sweaty palms and everything. "Pop asked me to go."

She watched him, her eyes sliding back and forth across his face, as if reading him like a book. "You mentioned me repaying your favor?" she asked.

"Yeah. Uh, Pop seems to think I should, uh, discuss dog poop with someone."

Mallory burst into quiet laughter. "You want to talk about dog poop at the dance?"

"It's kind of a metaphor. And it would make Pop happy, which makes me happy." He shoved his hands into his pockets and looked away because looking at Mallory was making his words jumble. "So, if you were to go to the dance next Friday, maybe we could show the older generation how to bust a move."

Mallory laughed again, giving him the kind of confidence that only came from making a woman laugh. "Bust a move and discuss dog poop. Wow, I'm not sure I want your help with the tree anymore," she teased, heading down the porch steps. "Just kidding. See you tomorrow, Hol. Have a good night."

"Night." He watched her get into her car. Then he walked back inside, where his Hot Pocket was waiting for him. And Buster was on the other side of the glass back door, watching Hollis with large brown eyes. His tail wagged at the sight of Hollis, which Hollis took as progress. A couple of laughs from Mallory and tail wags from Buster. He must be doing something right these days.

Chapter Five

I regard the theatre as the greatest of all art forms, the most immediate way in which a human being can share with another the sense of what it is to be a human being.

—Oscar Wilde

If Mallory could bottle up the smell of a Christmas tree farm, she would. And maybe she'd sell it and not have to worry about affording Nan's healthcare or selling off the theater.

"Hey, you," Hollis said as he approached the gate to Popadine's Tree Farm.

Mallory felt her insides light up like the festive bulbs around the business's welcome sign. "Do I look tree-farm-ready?" She laughed lightly, angling her body from side to side. Proper attire was jeans, boots, and flannel, preferably in a bright red or green check print.

Hollis dutifully ran his gaze from her face to her boots. "You're the poster child for a tree farm customer."

Mallory glanced around as she walked beside Hollis. She'd worked a nursing shift early this morning at six until early afternoon. Then she'd gone home, taken a quick shower, and changed. "I hope all the good trees haven't been taken."

"Good ones?" Hollis slid her a look. "Don't let the trees hear you say that. You might hurt their feelings."

"Oh." She lowered her voice. "I'm sorry."

He started chuckling. "I'm joking."

"Oh." She laughed nervously. "Well, I've heard some say that the trees respond to us."

"They do," Hollis confirmed. "I convinced Pop when I first started helping out here on the farm. We began playing cheerful holiday music, and I swear the trees were brighter and more vibrant."

"That's fascinating."

"Yeah?"

"Mm-hm. I like to play calm, soothing music for my pediatric patients on my floor at the hospital. Music is a powerful tool."

"When I'm able to take more foster dogs, I'm going to use music to regulate their nervous systems."

"Wow. I love that," Mallory said, genuinely interested as they approached rows and rows of trees. She bounced softly on the balls of her feet. Her excitement turned to a fluttery, dancing feeling in her chest. "There's something about a tree farm that still makes me feel like a little girl."

"That's a nice change. All I've seen of Mallory Blue lately is the grown-up version with too much responsibility on her shoulders. I like this side of you. Childlike Mallory is nice." He stepped closer and nudged her gently with his shoulder. "It's good to see you smiling and laughing."

They were walking casually down the lines of trees, looking from side to side and inspecting each one as they chatted.

"In general, being at a hospital with sick or injured patients doesn't lend itself to smiling and laughing. Neither does watching my grandmother struggle with dementia." The childlike feeling slowly faded as her day-to-day worries returned to the forefront of her mind. So much for trying not to think about all the things on her plate and having one carefree hour. Her chest suddenly felt tight. "I don't want to be the person in the room who is all work and no play. I want to be the laughing, smiling Mallory of old. I do."

"Hey." He laid a hand on her shoulder. "I'm not criticizing you. I'm looking out for you."

"Do I strike you as a woman who needs looking after?" She felt her hackles rising, which was more about herself than Hollis, and she knew it. She prided herself on being self-sufficient, and over the last month, she was hanging on by a thread. Could he see that?

Her gaze dropped to his hand on her shoulder, and he immediately drew it back. "You remind me of your grandmother. No one could ever accuse her of being anything less than self-sufficient. But she allowed me to have an ego boost every now and then by letting me offer up a helping hand."

"Nan is good that way. She did that for me too." Mallory hated talking about Nan in the past tense. Nan was still alive, for goodness' sake. She wasn't as present as she once was though, and it stung like the cold on Mallory's cheeks right now.

Taking another step forward, Mallory's gaze caught on one of the trees. "That's the one!" she said, practically jumping up and down.

Hollis turned to observe the tree that had caught her eye. "Really?"

Mallory could tell by his tone that he didn't agree. "You don't think it's amazing?"

His expression told her he didn't. "If you're just tired, I can carry you through this farm. I don't mind." His tone was teasing.

"No, I'm serious. Look at this tree." She flung one arm forward, gesturing at the beautiful blue fir. "It's perfect." It was almost as if the tree had an aura around it, making it glow without a single string of lights. "This is the tree. I love it."

Hollis gave his head a subtle shake. "I've been working this farm with Pop for the past decade. It never ceases to amaze me what folks end up picking. A tree says a lot about a person's personality."

Mallory narrowed her eyes. "Okay. What does this tree say about me?"

Hollis studied her. "You're simple, yet classy. You don't need the biggest tree or the one with the deepest or brightest color. Imperfection is actually what you find endearing…"

Mallory felt exposed as she listened.

"That means there's hope for a guy like me," he said, his words coming out jokingly.

"Hope for what?"

He looked away and didn't answer the question. "Anyway, doesn't matter what I think. All that matters is that you like this tree." Bending, he reached into his pocket, grabbed a tag, and used a zip tie to attach it to the tree's base. "There we go. I'll wrap it up and deliver it to Memory Oaks."

"Now?" Mallory had thought he would need to take his time to pack it up and deliver it.

"No time like the present, right?" He nodded his head in the direction of the parking area. "Want to come along?"

Mallory usually braced herself to see Nan these days. There was a process for getting into the right headspace for greeting her grandmother, who might, or might not, remember her. "Um…" She looked up at Hollis, into his hopeful brown eyes. He was a hard man to say no to. "Sure. I think I should be there when the tree arrives, just in case Nan gets upset. She's not a fan of change these days."

"These days?" Hollis led her toward their vehicles. "Nan has always followed a calendar. Some things never change." He glanced over. "There's comfort to be found in that."

She hugged her arms around herself as a cold breeze blew through.

"You go ahead and get in your car. I need to grab the utility vehicle to get the tree and drive it back up. Then I'll wrap it, toss it on the truck's bed, and we can head over to Memory Oaks."

"Since I have my car, I think I'll just go ahead of you and visit with Nan first. You can let me know when you get there."

"Sure. Good plan." He gave her a wink, which was something he'd do for anyone. She'd seen him wink at others. Just like Pop did. Hollis had adopted the gesture from the man he looked up to, which Mallory found adorable.

Heading to her car, she got in out of the cold and turned on the heater, soaking it in for a moment. Then she set off for Memory Oaks. A few miles later, the familiar building loomed ahead, its brick adorned with festive wreaths.

Francis, the ever-present receptionist, offered a small wave as Mallory walked inside the building. "Mallory! I wasn't expecting you today."

Mallory shrugged. "I've had early shifts at the hospital lately. I'm not a fan of waking before the crack of dawn, but it's nice getting out early enough to spend my afternoons doing fun things. Like going to Pop's Tree Farm and picking out a tree for Nan's room."

Francis's cheerful expression faltered a touch. Mallory knew that Hollis had had to pull some big strings to get permission for the tree to begin with.

"My grandmother loves a Christmas tree, and I have some special ornaments I want to hang up for her. I'm hoping maybe they'll refresh her memories. Hollis is packing the tree up now and then bringing it over."

Francis was grimacing now. Mallory hoped that Francis wasn't about to go back on her agreement to allow this to happen. "Oh. Well, there's a small issue. I'm afraid today might not be the best time to put up the tree."

"Why is that?" Mallory asked, concern mounting.

Francis held out her hands. "Don't worry too much. Nan is safe and comfortable. She's just having a bit of a rough day. All this talk of next week's holiday dance is throwing her for a whirl."

"The dance. Right." Mallory remembered Hollis asking her about it last night. He'd acted strange. He hadn't asked her to attend with him, but he'd been nervous all the same. She could see it in his eyes.

"You can certainly try to put up the tree in your grandmother's room today though," Francis offered.

Mallory knew better than most that the "bad days" for Nan were difficult to turn around. She hesitated as she weighed what was the right thing to do. She was so eager to get Nan's Memory Tree started, hoping it would help Nan remember something. "Well, I have some time to visit with my grandma before Hollis gets here. I'll see if I can get her in the Christmas spirit."

"That sounds like a good plan," Francis said. "You visit with Nan and see if you can't work your magic."

Magic? That was laughable. Mallory wasn't one of Nan's favorite people these days, which weighed heavily on her. In the past, Mallory could go to Nan whenever she needed, even if it was in the middle of the night. Nan's door and heart were always open.

Making her way to Nan's room, Mallory paused outside her door and took a deep breath to compose herself before knocking gently and stepping in. "Nan? It's Mallory. Can I…visit with you?"

The room was dimly lit with only a small bedside lamp casting a soft glow. Nan was lying in bed with a thin blanket pulled over her. She turned her head to look at Mallory, her eyes cloudy with confusion.

"Mallory?" she asked, her voice trembling slightly.

"Hi, Nan. It's me. I came to visit."

For a moment, Nan stared at Mallory. Then, slowly, she seemed to relax. "Mallory. I'm so glad you're here."

Mallory's heart lifted. Maybe Nan was feeling better today. "I'm glad I am too." Mallory stepped closer, eager to give Nan a kiss on the temple.

"I've been waiting for an hour, at least," Nan said, her tone turning grumpy. "I'm glad someone finally came to help me to the bathroom."

Mallory's steps slowed. Evidently, Nan thought she was one of the medical aides.

"Oh. Yes, I'm happy to help you." Mallory took off her scarf and the bag she'd carried in, laying them in the chair beside Nan's bed. Then she helped Nan scoot to the edge of the bed and stand behind her walker. Mallory kept a hand on Nan's low back and guided her to the restroom inside the spacious room. Once she had Nan standing with her back to the toilet, she helped Nan lower to a seated position and turned away.

Nan was a very private woman. She never wanted to "misplace" her dignity. That's what Nan used to say. *Once you misplace your dignity, that's when you start leaving your house in your slippers and bathrobe.*

Mallory could hear Nan's voice in her head with its soft Southern lilt. Nan said all kinds of unusual things that were strangely poetic. None of them told Mallory much about her grandmother though. It was hard to think that, even though Mallory had known Nan all her life, there were parts of Nan's life Mallory knew nothing about.

"Is this the kind of job you always wanted?" Nan asked, the sound of her peeing echoing off the walls in the bathroom.

"What do you mean?" Mallory was anxious for Nan to finish so that she could show her the ornaments she'd brought. Maybe Nan would have another memory.

"Helping folks like me use the bathroom. It doesn't sound thrilling if you ask me. Certainly not fulfilling."

Mallory wasn't the nursing aide here, but she was a nurse and she did help a lot of patients get to the bathroom at the hospital. "It's not so bad. I enjoy helping others."

"Mm. When I was younger, I wanted to be a star." Nan finished peeing but continued to sit on the toilet. "I just loved the spotlight. I loved to pull on a character like it was a piece of clothing and wear it. Then when my role was over, I'd slip it off before I laid my head on the pillow that night."

Mallory turned to face Nan. "You remember?"

"It's all I ever wanted until I met him." Nan reached for Mallory's arm as Mallory helped her stand. Then Mallory helped her pull her pants back up around her waist. There was a clear look in Nan's blue eyes as Mallory waited for more.

"Until you met who, Grandma? Who?"

Nan blinked. "What did you call me?"

Mallory shook her head. "Until you met who, Nan?" she pressed.

Nan's brow line lowered, and the blue shade of her eyes darkened to a stormy gray. She started pushing her walker forward, nearly knocking Mallory over as she worked to get out of the small enclosed area.

Oh no. Mallory had seen this happen to Nan many times before. The smallest things agitated her.

"You were talking about wanting to be a movie star," Mallory went on, trying to bring Nan back to the version of herself she'd been just moments before.

"Not a movie star!" Nan snapped. "You don't know me. If you knew me, you'd know I didn't want to be in the movies. I wanted to be onstage. On Broadway." She lifted her walker and banged it on the floor as she turned and backed up to the edge of her bed. "I want you to leave," she said quietly.

"Nan." Mallory felt like the air had been knocked out of her. "Nan, I'd like to stay a while longer. I brought something to show you." Mallory started to reach for the bag with the two Christmas ornaments inside.

"Leave!" Nan demanded with more force. "Leave! Leave! Leavvvvve!" she screamed angrily.

One of the nurses stepped inside Nan's room and looked between Nan and Mallory. "Everything all right?"

"No!" Nan yelled. "I want this woman out of my room. Now!"

The nurse looked at Mallory apologetically. "I'm sorry but…"

Mallory stood and nodded, collecting her scarf and bag but leaving the bag of ornaments. "I understand. I'm going." She looked at Nan, desperately wanting to bend and kiss her temple. But, in recent days, Nan had been known to swat a person who got in her space. "I'm going."

Mallory held back her tears as she slipped out of Nan's room, taking slow, deep breaths and reminding herself that Nan, her Nan, didn't mean any of those things. Her Nan would never speak to her that way.

"Everything okay?" Francis asked as Mallory passed the front desk, her expression revealing that she already knew the answer.

Mallory nodded quietly, fearing that allowing herself to speak would open the floodgates of her tears.

"We can wait for the tree trimming until tomorrow," Francis reassured her.

"Okay." Mallory turned and headed out of the building. Once she was standing on the pavement, she sucked in the air around her as if it were life. Part of her wanted to continue past her car and go for a nice, long walk to clear her thoughts. She had things to do though. Rehearsals started tonight.

As if on cue with that thought, her cell phone pinged with an incoming text. Mallory welcomed the distraction until she opened the messages and read.

It was from Adam Barclay, the long-running actor who played Santa for the community theater's production.

Adam: Sorry, Mal. I really am. But I can't play Santa this year.

Mallory's already aching heart felt like an earthquake had hit, cracking it right down the middle. She clutched the phone, hand shaking.

Adam: Times are tough and I need a second job that pays. I know Nan would understand. I hope you do as well.

Mallory's first instinct was to say, "No, she didn't understand." Here she was, working her full-time job and extra shifts but still planning to direct this entire production. That was because Nan was her family though. Adam did not owe Nan anything—not the way Mallory did.

On a sigh, she tapped out a text as tears welled and blurred her vision.

Mallory: Of course, I understand, Adam. Let me know if there's anything I can do to help.

Nan was ever understanding. The play rehearsals began tonight though. Santa was the most important character, and the understudy for the role had moved in the past year. "What on earth am I going to do?" Mallory said out loud, standing in the middle of the parking lot.

"About what?"

Mallory whirled at the sound of Hollis's voice as he exited his truck with the little tree tied to the back. Judging by his expression, she guessed she looked as bad as she felt. "I can't do this."

He walked in her direction until he was only a couple of feet away. "Can't do what?"

"Any of it. All of it." She gestured to the tree in his cab. "What's the point of celebrating the season when you don't have anyone to celebrate with?"

Hollis lifted a brow. "You still have Nan. You have Maddie. Savannah." He held her gaze. "And me, although I admit I'm no consolation prize."

Mallory shook her head. "Can I just skip Christmas this year? Forget the tree, the presents, the play. Forget it all… Nan isn't in the mood for the tree today. I guess I'm not either now. It's just disappointing, you know." She pulled in a steadying breath. "I caught the slightest glimpse of holiday excitement when we were on the farm earlier. The smell of pine brought me back to this place in my heart where Christmas was still magical. Then Nan threw me out of her room, and to top it off, Adam just quit the leading role of the play. There's no play without Santa."

Hollis nodded as he seemed to process her long list of complaints. "Santas are a dime a dozen. We'll find one. And you'll catch that Christmas spirit again."

"How?"

"When you join me at the dance Friday night. You're not backing out on me, are you?"

"Did I ever really agree to go in the first place?" She tilted her head to one side, feeling unfamiliarly playful and…flirty?

Hollis stroked his fingers along his beard. She didn't even like guys with beards. Except right now, she kind of did. "Do you promise going to this dance will help me find my holiday spirit?"

He looked at her for a long moment before exhaling softly and lowering his hand. "No. No, I don't make promises I can't keep. Not these days, at least. But"—he held up a finger—"I do promise that you'll be like Stella."

"Stella?" Mallory shook her head. She didn't know any Stellas.

Hollis did a slow-motion dip and shake of his hips. Then he bit his lower lip. "Stella got her groove back."

Mallory burst into laughter. Once she caught her breath, she said, "You're going to help me get my groove back? That assumes I ever had a groove to begin with."

"You did." He gave her a knowing look. "You might not have known it, but I did. We are going to rock that dance floor on Friday night. That's a promise I can make."

Releasing a sigh, Mallory wondered if she was about to make a big mistake. Her plate was already full. More than full. "Okay, okay. I'll go to the dance with you."

He lifted his brows.

Her heart tumbled. Maybe she'd assumed he'd been asking her to go with him. Was he just asking her to go, but not with him? Why did he look surprised? "I mean I'll see you there," she corrected. "I'm going for Nan."

"But you're saving a dance for me," Hollis said with a slow-growing grin. Then he rubbed his hands together. "Mallory got her groove back. And her Christmas spirit." He offered that wink she knew he gave everyone. Somehow this one felt different though. Somehow everything between them shifted and felt…different. In a good way.

The Wildflower Ornament

Look inside the box and pick up the envelope with a number 2 written on the front. Inside you'll find a small square of pressed wildflowers with a hole punched at the top and a violet-colored ribbon looped through it. Hang this keepsake on the first branch down from the top where the Santa Hat sits.

Here's the story behind the Wildflower Ornament.

Our little high school play ran for five shows that year with Ralph playing Santa for all of them. Each kiss onstage was hotter than the last. Wow, that man could kiss.

After the last night of the show, he came up to me with a bouquet of wildflowers, saying something about tradition. No one else brought me flowers. Just him. He didn't ask me out though. Mickey, however, the original Santa, did, and I said yes. Part of me agreed just to get back at Ralph for waiting too long. Maybe I read the signs incorrectly. Maybe Ralph wasn't interested in me and it was all just acting.

On the night of my date with Mickey, I put on my best dress and curled my hair. Mickey drove me to the nicest restaurant in Bloom. I think he wanted to impress me and flaunt his family's money. I admit, I was impressed. As we sat down, I admired the establishment and guess who walked in? This wasn't the kind of place Ralph could afford, yet he strolled through the double doors wearing his Sunday best and that darn Santa hat. He didn't look my way. Instead, he simply took his seat a few tables in front of mine and ate his meal alone.

It was impossible to focus on my date with him there!

I wanted to get up and go tell Ralph to leave. But I also wanted to sit down with him instead.

"If you were jealous, that's your own fault," I halfway yelled at him the next Monday, making quite the scene. "You had your chance to ask me out, Ralph. You had your chance to—"

"Go out with me," he interrupted, his voice so gentle. Then he shook his head, as if he'd messed up. "That's not the way I wanted to do it. I wanted to do it the right way…" He took a breath. "Nan, I was at that restaurant because I didn't want you to be the girl—"

"Woman," I corrected stubbornly.

"Woman," he repeated. "Nan, I just wanted to make sure Mickey was a gentleman. If he were to hurt you, in any way, it'd be my fault because I was too much of a coward to ask you out."

I stared at him, weighing whether I was supposed to be angry or appreciative. "You're lucky I didn't have a good time on my date with Mickey anyway." I looked at Ralph stubbornly, folding my arms over my chest. "Probably because you were there, and I would have rather been eating with you than listening to Mickey drone on about how wonderful he and his family are."

"Is that a yes?" Ralph asked, a subtle lilt to his tone of voice.

The hope in Ralph's eyes was adorable. I remember looking at him and thinking, *I'm in trouble. I'm halfway to falling for this guy and we haven't even gone on a real date yet.* I also felt this thread of fear zip from my head to my toes. Falling for Ralph could ruin my Broadway dreams.

It might sound foolish, but I felt like my future hinged on my answer to Ralph's question. Isn't that how life is?

One moment, one decision, can change the course of everything.

"One condition." I pointed my finger at him. "We're just having fun. Nothing more."

"Just having fun." He nodded.

"You have to promise, Ralph."

I knew he was a man of his word. "I promise to be a stand-up guy who will treat you the way you deserve. And I'll never force you to feel any way about me that you're not comfortable with. And...I'll keep the way I feel about you to myself."

It wasn't the promise I was looking for, but it was enough for me. "Okay, then. Yes, I'll go out with you."

Chapter Six

Ever tried. Ever failed. No matter. Try again. Fail again.
Fail better.

—Samuel Beckett

Buster eyed Hollis suspiciously. The older dog was beginning to show signs that he understood that if he did what Hollis wanted him to, he would get a treat. So far, Hollis had worked with Buster on walking on a leash just around the path of the Christmas tree farm. When some of the employees came around after hours, Hollis encouraged Buster to look at him. It was important for a dog not to fixate on other people or dogs. Or a stray cat. Hollis was the alpha in his little pack, and that was the primary lesson Buster needed to learn.

Over the last few evenings, Hollis had been working on teaching Buster to sit and stay.

"Sit," Hollis said with a steady tone, pleased when Buster immediately lowered onto his back legs. Then Hollis held up a treat with one hand.

Buster started to return to all fours, but Hollis redirected him. "Sit!"

Buster returned to his seat position, his eyes trained.

"Good boy," Hollis said with a hopeful heart. He held up the treat again and then lifted his opposite hand back to show his open palm. "Wait," he commanded.

Buster licked his lips but didn't budge this time. The first few nights of trying this simple command, Buster had turned himself in circles and whimpered. He had wanted that treat so badly. Hollis guessed that Buster had rarely been given a treat, and the anticipation of devouring it was just enough to keep Buster from running into a corner to hide.

Hollis allowed about thirty seconds to pass before changing his tone of voice from calm and quiet to a higher pitch full of praise. He knelt and offered the treat. "Good boy."

Buster's brown eyes grew impossibly wider.

"Here you go." Hollis crouched down, making himself smaller as he continued to hold his palm out patiently. Patience was key, especially with a dog who'd been abused. After another thirty seconds, Buster slowly crept forward, eyes pinned on Hollis, and lapped his tongue across Hollis's palm and then nabbed the treat between his teeth.

"You're a good boy," Hollis said, lifting a slow hand to pet Buster's head. "You are a good dog," he said again, his eyes burning as he remembered how much he'd wanted someone to say that to him when he was a foster kid. No one ever called him "a good boy." And when Hollis didn't get the positive attention he craved, he sought attention in the only other way he could get it. By acting out, running his mouth, destroying property, and even pocketing things that didn't belong to him. Back then, he wasn't even aware of the reasons behind his actions. All he knew was that he had a crater-size void in his heart that couldn't be filled no matter how hard he tried. He missed the father he never had. He missed the mother who was never going to nurture and love him the way he needed to be.

Returning to a standing position, Hollis decided this was enough training for one night. He still needed to attend to Duke and take him for their nightly walk along the rows of Christmas trees. One day, Buster would feel confident enough to join them, but not yet. All things worth achieving took time, and Buster was worth it. A little time and a little love could fix just about any dog. Hollis wholly believed that, and he couldn't wait to open his training facility to prove it.

The next day, Hollis breathed in the clean scent of lemon and bleach as he strode down the familiar hallway of Memory Oaks.

Pop's eyes lit up with recognition as Hollis entered the room. "Hollis, my boy!" Pop's weathered face broke into a wide grin. "Come in, come in!"

Hollis walked over and then dipped to hug his grandfather, feeling the familiar mix of joy and sadness that always accompanied these visits. Pop's memory was fading in the way that seasons faded, steady with momentary swings in either direction. But Pop's love for Hollis remained as strong as ever. At least to this point.

Hollis settled into the chair beside the bed. "How are you, Pop?"

Pop waved his hand dismissively. "Oh, I'm fine, fine. Tell me about my trees. Is the farm getting good business?"

"The trees are perfect, Pop. We have our usual seasonal staff, and I'm overseeing a few kids from the boys home too."

Pop patted Hollis's hand. "I knew the farm would be in good hands with you managing it. You've always had a way with those trees, just like your father."

Hollis felt a lump form in his throat. Pop had started treating Hollis like his own flesh and blood from the first day Hollis went to stay with Matt and Sandy. Because of Hollis's age, Matt and Sandy never legally adopted him, but legality had never mattered to Hollis. Families were built on love and proven over time.

"Thanks, Pop," he managed to say, his voice thick with emotion. "Learned from the best."

As they chatted about the farm and Christmases past, a commotion erupted in the hallway. Hollis tuned in to the familiar voice full of distress.

"No! I don't want it! Take it away!" Nan yelled from her room down the hall.

Hollis's heart took a steep dive into the pit of his stomach. Hollis knew the staff had planned to bring the Christmas tree to Nan's room today. They had promised to give Nan plenty of warning, but considering how early it was in the day, Hollis didn't think that had happened.

"What's all that about?" Pop said, squinting, as if that would make him hear any better.

"Not sure, but I'll go check. Be right back." Hollis squeezed his grandfather's hand before getting up and hurrying into the hallway.

The scene that greeted him made his chest tighten. Nan was backed against the wall, trembling with wide eyes as two staff members tried to maneuver a small Christmas tree into her room.

"Hey, guys. What's going on?" Hollis asked, keeping his voice calm as he approached.

One of the staff members turned to him with flushed cheeks and pursed lips. "We're just trying to set up Mrs. Nan's Christmas tree, like we were told."

Hollis positioned himself between Nan and the tree. "Nan," he said softly, "it's okay. You don't have to have the tree in your room if you don't want it."

As he turned to look at her, Nan's eyes focused on him, and a flicker of recognition crossed her expression. "Hollis?"

He offered a reassuring smile. "It's me. Everything's okay."

Turning to the staff, he said, "Could you please take the tree away? Nan doesn't want it in her room."

The staff members exchanged glances.

"But we were instructed—"

"I'll talk to Francis. It's okay," he said. "Take the tree to Pop's room instead. He'll love it."

After a moment of hesitation, the staff wheeled the tree away. Then Hollis gently guided Nan back to her recliner in the corner of her room. He pulled up a stool to sit in front of her. "Not a fan of trees these days, huh?"

Nan wrung her weathered hands in her lap. "I've never liked a tree. They belong outside, don't they?"

Hollis looked down momentarily. Nan had loved a Christmas tree. She'd forgotten that, but yet, she'd looked at him a moment ago and remembered his name. She was still here, just a little harder to reach at times. "It's almost Christmastime. It's kind of a tradition to put up trees and decorate them."

She studied his face thoughtfully. "Oh. Is that what those people were doing?" She suddenly looked worried. "Were they doing something nice for me?"

Hollis laid a hand on her lap. "It's okay. Now they're doing something nice for Pop."

As Nan settled back into her favorite chair, an idea began to form in Hollis's mind. If Nan couldn't have a tree in her room, why not create a communal tree that all the residents could enjoy? Sure, there was a tiny artificial tree in the lobby but it wasn't placed where residents could enjoy it daily or even add their own ornaments.

"Nan, what would you think about having a big Christmas tree in the community room? One that everyone could decorate together?"

Nan's eyes lit up. "Like the one in the town square?"

Hollis grinned at another memory from Nan. "Exactly like that."

"That sounds lovely."

Hollis nodded. "It does. And I think I'll make it happen. Don't you worry."

He didn't want Mallory to worry either. He wanted to make this new plan happen before Mallory was privy to any of this morning's events.

After making sure Nan was comfortable, Hollis headed back to Pop's room, his mind racing with plans. He'd bring the biggest, most beautiful tree from the farm and set it up in the community room. He knew Mallory had a box of Nan's special ornaments, each one telling a story of Nan's life. If the tree was big enough though, each resident at Memory Oaks could hang their own memory ornaments, creating a shared celebration of life.

As he explained the plan to Pop, his grandfather nodded enthusiastically. "Why didn't we think of this a long time ago? The biggest tree should come here to serve as the biggest field of memories." Pop gave a thoughtful look. "Was that a movie title?"

"*Field of Dreams*," Hollis said with a low chuckle. "Close enough. So, I have your blessing to donate a tree?"

Pop frowned. "What kind of question is that? Of course you do. You're running the tree farm now. I trust your decisions." Pop leaned forward and patted a hand on Hollis's shoulder. "I trust you," he said with his signature wink. It was the same wink that Hollis had been imitating for the past decade.

Hollis said goodbye to Pop and headed back to the farm, debating whether to call Mallory. She didn't need the extra stress, he decided, remembering his conversation with Nan last Christmas.

"*Look out for her? Be there for her, even if she insists that she's okay.*"

Mallory didn't know about this conversation, of course, and Hollis intended to keep it that way.

As Hollis headed out, he stopped by the front desk to talk to Francis.

"Did Nan's tree go up okay?" she asked.

"Not really. We put it in Pop's room instead." He leaned against the counter and cleared his throat. "I, uh, have another request."

Francis raised her brows. "Well, I do owe you for all of your help over the years. What do you need?"

"I want to put up a tree in the community room. I want to put up the biggest tree on Pop's lot."

"That would take so much effort," Francis said. "It would need to be trimmed. Decorated. Cared for. There's a lot of upkeep with live trees. That's why we always stick to artificial."

"I'll handle it all. Mallory wants to put up some of Nan's ornaments. They're special to her." He rubbed his beard absently. "But, seeing that we're going to put up the biggest tree on the lot, I was thinking we might invite everyone here to add their own ornaments."

Francis smiled quietly. "Typically, I would need to check with the fire marshal first, but it just so happens he gave me permission the other day when he was here. His great aunt is a resident and had inquired about a live tree. I think it's a great idea."

Hollis had hoped she'd think so. "Perfect. Then I'll go back to the farm and return with the biggest tree I can find."

"You're a regular Santa Claus," Francis teased, to which Hollis belted a *ho-ho-ho* on his way out of Memory Oaks, stepping into the biting cold of early December. As he drove, he called the farm and instructed the small team of employees to select and deliver the perfect tree to Memory Oaks.

Hopefully, Mallory would approve and see his actions as supportive rather than overstepping.

By the time evening fell, the massive tree stood proudly in the Memory Oaks community room. Hollis had personally overseen its installation. The staff had rallied around the idea, gathering lights and garlands, and the recreational therapist, Linda, had already planned a day for the residents to create their own memory ornaments to place on the tree.

As Hollis stood back, admiring the tree, a sense of accomplishment washed over him. He glanced at the clock. Mallory should be off-shift and arriving soon. Hollis would love to stick around and see her, but he needed to get home to his dogs. Whenever he had a new dog, especially one who'd been through trauma, he tried not to leave them alone too long. Building a bond was important if he wanted to turn Buster's life around.

Plus some part of him didn't want to be here when Mallory arrived. This tree was big, and his efforts were even bigger. This was a grand gesture on his part that Mallory might misinterpret—or actually, a gesture she might interpret correctly. He'd gone above and beyond, and not just because they were friends and she'd asked him to get Nan a tree. This was the action of a friend who thought of her as more.

That's why Hollis had asked Francis to leave his name out of the situation. Technically, Pop had provided the community room tree, not Hollis—and that might somehow be more palatable because Nan was right when she'd called Mallory stubborn. Mal prided herself on being self-reliant. Independent. Maybe that was why he'd always been drawn to her. One reason, at least.

Chapter Seven

*The theatre was created to tell the truth about life and a
social situation.*

—Stella Adler

Mallory's breath caught as she stepped into the community room
of Memory Oaks and saw the large Christmas tree filling up the far
corner, nearly reaching the ceiling. "Wow," she said under her breath.

Francis stepped up beside Mallory. "I told you it was nice."

"It's stunning," Mallory agreed, turning back to Francis. "Thank
you again for doing this."

"Well, Pop donated the tree. All I did was say yes to a very per-
suasive Hollis. I'm so glad he was here to help with Nan this morning. Usually, once she's upset, it's hard to press reset on the day. But
he de-escalated the situation quickly enough that Nan was able to
recover."

Mallory turned toward Francis curiously. "Hollis was here earlier?" Hollis hadn't mentioned anything to her when he'd called to
invite her to trim the tree with him this evening.

Francis's expression turned sheepish. Mallory was a good read of
people, and it looked like there was something Francis wasn't saying.

"He's coming again tonight," Mallory said. "We're going to trim the tree and add all the lights your staff was able to come up with." Then Mallory planned to add the first of Nan's Memory Tree ornaments. "I love Linda's idea of having the other residents make their own memory ornaments. That's so perfect."

Francis was quiet again.

Mallory gave her an assessing look. "It wasn't Linda's idea, was it? Was it Hollis's?"

Francis tugged her lower lip between her teeth. "Oh, I'm awful at keeping secrets."

Why on earth would Hollis not want Mallory to know this was his genius?

"I guess he thought it'd be better if you thought this whole idea came from someone else."

Mallory wondered why he would think that. "Well, whoever's idea it was, it's great. Over the last couple of years, my grandmother has started putting up a Memory Tree with each ornament telling a story. How perfect to bring the tradition to Memory Oaks."

Mallory had hoped the tree would be in Nan's room, but she could still bring the memory journal and read the stories behind each ornament to Nan as they hung the ornaments on the tree. Mallory could learn a side of Nan that she'd never known while reminding her grandmother of the life she was slowly forgetting. Even if Nan couldn't remember, the journal did.

"Sorry I'm late," Hollis said, stepping up beside Mallory. "The farm was a bit busy, and I wanted to make sure the seasonal employees had things under control before I left. But I'm here now. Let the wild rumpus begin." He looked over and offered Mallory a wink.

She lifted a brow. "Have you been hanging around Eleanor today?"

Eleanor was Savannah's great-aunt who loved to speak in book quotes.

Hollis chuckled. "Actually, yes. She and your grandpa Charlie were at the farm today, picking out their own Christmas tree."

Mallory was so happy that her paternal grandfather had found love again after losing his first wife. He liked to tell people that lightning had struck twice for him when it came to love… Whereas it hadn't even struck once for Mallory.

Hollis rubbed his hands together as he redirected his attention to the tree. "Wow. That's a beauty, huh?" He said it as if he'd never seen the tree before, but Mallory was on to him. "Shall we get trimming?"

Mallory ignored the fluttery feeling inside her chest as he made eye contact. "Yes. Let's get started."

"How about I make you both some hot cider while you work?" Francis offered. "It's the least I can do."

"I won't say no to apple cider," Hollis said. He turned to Mallory. "What about you?"

"I'd love a cup as well." As Francis disappeared, leaving them alone, Mallory reached for some clippers. "I'll take the bottom and you take the top, seeing that you're much taller than I am."

"Seeing that you're much shorter," he shot back, giving her another wink.

Her chest fluttered again. He needed to stop with all that winking. In her mind, she knew he wasn't flirting but her heart missed the memo. "So, have you found a Santa for me yet?"

"I'm working on it. Today was a bit busy," he said casually, grabbing his own pair of cutters.

Mallory chewed at her lower lip, wondering how he'd respond to what she'd been thinking about all day. "Well, you can stop looking. Because I think I've found the perfect Santa."

He looked up from the tree branch he was working on. "Yeah? Who?"

"You. You should be Santa this year."

Hollis's brown eyes narrowed as he straightened back into an upright position. "What?"

"I know you're constantly being asked for favors and you always say yes, no matter what. I also know you're busy, so I hate to add more to your plate. But you're Santa, Hollis." He was big and jolly, and he was so generous with his time and energy. "You can say no, of course. But I really hope you'll say yes. For Nan."

"Nan? You and I both know this is the opposite of what Nan would want."

Mallory folded her arms over her chest. "No. You and I both know that Nan loves you and she would trust you with anything. She'd trust you with her life. She'd definitely trust you to play the lead in her play." Mallory pressed her hands together. "Please," she said, her voice growing small. She'd never liked asking for help, but Nan's play couldn't run without a Santa. "You're perfect for the role. You were made for it. Be Nan's Santa this year."

"Nan isn't the director. You are," he said, his eyes glinting in the dim light.

Mallory felt another unwanted flutter. "Right... Then be my Santa."

Mallory's body felt restless later that night as she tried to fall asleep. She had too much weighing on her mind. Between the play and her excitement over decorating the tree for Memory Oaks, her brain was still buzzing. Also, she could still smell Hollis's cologne. It wasn't as if they'd even touched, but his scent was on her skin, making it impossible to get him off her mind.

She'd always found Hollis to be a handsome guy, but she wondered if her preoccupation with him tonight was more because she was lonely. Usually after getting off a shift at the hospital and visiting Nan, she was so tired once she got home that she fell asleep on the couch some nights. And when she awoke, she went through her rushed morning routine that led her back to the hospital, Memory Oaks, and home. Her days were on autopilot.

Rolling onto her side, Mallory exhaled softly and tried to get comfortable but only ended up shifting and squirming until she sat up and turned on her nightstand lamp, illuminating Nan's journal on the table. Mallory pulled it to her lap and opened it. She had read only two entries so far. *The Santa Hat Tree Topper* and *The Wildflower Ornament*. She'd hoped to read that second entry to Nan, but Nan couldn't control her good days any more than Mallory could. Maybe Nan's recollection of the *Santa Hat Tree Topper* was just a fluke. Maybe the rest of the ornaments wouldn't refresh Nan's memory.

Mallory blinked the sleep out of her eyes as she settled in to read the next entry. She was tempted to devour Nan's entire journal in one sitting, but Nan had specifically requested that Mallory read only one entry at a time and hang one ornament at a time as she created the Memory Tree.

"Getting to know someone doesn't happen overnight. It's a journey," Nan had said last Christmas.

"I already know you, Grandma." Mallory placed a hand over Nan's at the time.

"You know Nan, the grandmother." Nan gave her a steady look. *"A person, like an actor, plays a lot of roles in their life. I want you to remember me, all of me, even when I can't."*

Mallory nervously turned to the page she'd left off on. There must be a reason why Nan had kept some details of her life hidden. There was always a reason for keeping secrets, and from Mallory's experience, none of them were good. Using her pointer finger, she kept her place as she read the story behind the next ornament.

The Butterfly Barrette Ornament

Locate the small box wrapped in silver paper adorned with sapphire blue ribbon. The tag will have the number 3 written on it. Inside you'll find the Butterfly Barrette Ornament. I use the term *ornament* loosely because you'll easily see that it's really a hair barrette with a beautiful silver-and-white braided rope fastened into the metal clip. Hang it with care, the third keepsake on your tree. Hang it on a branch that best catches the light in the room.

Here's the story behind it.

After that Christmas, Ralph and I were inseparable. We went everywhere together and everyone in town knew we were in love. I was a mere seventeen years old, dreaming of heading to try my hand at Broadway. Ralph and I never discussed it. I knew he had no intention of ever leaving Bloom, but Ralph always said he wouldn't hold me back. For Valentine's, he gave me a beautiful jeweled butterfly barrette, almost too gorgeous to wear in my hair. The colors were mesmerizing.

"I love the gift." We were sitting in his car and I recall worrying because he seemed suddenly serious.

Then he turned and looked at me. "The barrette isn't the gift. The gift is the message." He was quiet for a long time, which wasn't like him at all. "Nan, when it's time, don't say good-bye. Don't feel guilty, don't second-guess yourself, and don't look back. Just spread your wings and go. Fly like you were born to do."

Tears flowed down my cheeks because it was a gift. I didn't want to be the villain by breaking his heart. I didn't want to leave and maybe I wouldn't have been able to if he hadn't given me this beautiful gift. He released me to follow my dream.

So that's what I did.

The morning after graduation, I got up and packed my car. My eyes were so blurred with tears that I'm surprised I even made it to New York. I missed Ralph so much, but I kept myself busy, working as a waitress and going to every audition I could. It didn't even take long to land a part. My first big break. It seemed like fate. The total elation that I always envisioned would consume me, however, never came. All I felt was an immense pressure. The spirit of competitiveness was strong, and I'm pretty sure my understudy hated me.

I also felt sick. It was more than nervous butterflies. Between scenes, I'd run to the bathroom and throw up.

I thought it was just a stomach virus. Or the old take-out food I'd eaten for breakfast. Then I started to wonder if this sickness that wouldn't go away was something more life-altering. My clothes felt snug. The costumes I was fitted for would no longer fasten and I had to use a rubber band looped through the button-hole to attach to the button. Desperate times, desperate measures.

Deep down, I knew the truth. Standing at a crossroads, I had a secret that I was carrying alone. I had a decision to make that would determine the rest of my life—and less than seven months to make it.

Chapter Eight

If you ask me what I came into this life to do, I, an artist,
will answer you: I am here to live out loud.

—Émile Zola

Hollis opened the crate door and squatted to greet Buster. "Hey, buddy. How're you doing?"

Buster gave a soft wag, his eyes bright and calm.

After attaching the leash, Hollis led Buster through the back door and trudged through the snow-dusted Christmas tree farm. As Hollis had taught Buster over the past weeks, the dog trotted obediently by his side. The crisp winter air nipped at Hollis's cheeks, but he hardly noticed, his attention laser-focused on the dog beside him. Hollis had been working on walking with Buster on a leash in the yard and on the farm, but today, Hollis paused in a small clearing. It was time.

Bending, Hollis unclipped Buster's leash, his heart racing with a mixture of excitement and apprehension. What if Buster darted off and didn't return? Hopefully the time they'd spent training was enough for the dog to see him as alpha.

Hollis straightened back to a standing position.

For a moment, Buster just stood there, looking up at Hollis for direction.

"Go on, boy," Hollis encouraged softly, gesturing slowly. "You're free."

Then, as if a switch had been flipped, Buster took off, bounding through the trees with unbridled joy.

Hollis's heart dropped momentarily as Buster disappeared among the trees. Hollis resisted the need to call him back or run after him. He inhaled deeply and stayed rooted for a few minutes. Hollis let out a laugh as Buster reappeared, darting among the trees, disappearing and reappearing like a furry phantom.

Hollis's mind drifted back to his own youth. He remembered sneaking onto this very farm as a troubled teenager, long before Matt and Sandy had taken him in. The farm had been his sanctuary, a place where he could escape the chaos of his various foster homes.

He'd come here to smoke cigarettes pilfered from foster parents' packs or to sip beers stolen from forgotten corners of refrigerators. But more than that, he'd come for the peace. The scent of pine, the whisper of wind through the branches, the solid presence of the trees themselves—it had all worked to calm his restless spirit.

Hollis recalled the times Pop had caught him trespassing. But instead of calling the authorities, the old man had welcomed him, offering hot chocolate and a listening ear. It was Pop who had eventually introduced him to Matt and Sandy, setting in motion the events that would change Hollis's life forever.

Hollis couldn't help but laugh at Buster's infectious enthusiasm. Then he lifted two fingers to his lips and whistled.

Buster had slipped out of view, and Hollis no longer saw him. Uh-oh.

"Buster!" he called, his voice echoing through the trees. No response.

Hollis whistled again, the sound piercing the winter stillness. He held his breath, straining to hear any sign of the dog. Seconds ticked by, each one increasing Hollis's worry. Had he misjudged their bond? Had Buster seized the opportunity for freedom and run away?

Just as panic began to set in, Hollis heard it—the faint sound of paws pounding against packed snow as Buster came barreling into view. The dog's ears were flying behind him, his mouth open in what could only be described as a canine grin of pure joy.

Kneeling to greet the returning dog, Hollis opened his arms wide. Buster skidded to a stop in front of him, panting happily. For a moment, they just looked at each other, man and dog, a newfound understanding passing between them.

Then Buster leaned forward and licked Hollis's hand. The gesture was so unexpected, so filled with trust, that Hollis felt his throat tighten with emotion.

Eyes burning, Hollis reached out to scratch behind Buster's ears.

"Good boy. Good boy. You are such a good boy," Hollis said, his throat tight.

As they sat there amid the Christmas trees, Hollis marveled at how far they'd both come. He thought about the angry, distrustful teenager he'd once been, and how this farm—and the people connected to it—had changed his life. Now, years later, he was helping another wanderlust soul find its way.

The parallels weren't lost on Hollis. Just as Pop, Matt, and Sandy had seen past his rough exterior to the good heart beneath, Hollis had overlooked Buster's initial presentation to see the loyal, loving dog waiting to emerge. It was a powerful reminder of how patience, understanding, and love could change any circumstance.

"Come on, Buster," he said, reclipping the leash and returning to a standing position. "Let's head home."

They walked side by side through the rows of trees, their breaths creating small clouds in the cold air. Here, surrounded by the trees that had always been Hollis's comfort, with a dog who had learned to trust him against all odds, Hollis felt truly at home.

As they reached the edge of the farm, Hollis paused to look back at the sea of green behind them—the farm that he'd been helping Pop with for years. The farm that he wanted to continue running for Pop. It was the most peaceful place on earth, in Hollis's opinion.

Buster let out a happy bark. Apparently, he thought so too.

"Merry Christmas, Buster." He dipped and gave the dog a final pat before heading inside. He had somewhere to be tonight, and part of him was excited. The other part, nervous as he'd been the first time he'd ever laid eyes on Mallory.

It was just a dance at Memory Oaks. No big deal. Pretty similar to a middle school dance, he guessed, although he'd never been to one.

An hour later, Hollis pulled up to Mallory's house and climbed her porch with a skip in his step.

"Hi." She opened her front door, dressed festively in a red sweater dress that hugged her curves with her dark hair cascading around her shoulders.

For a moment, Hollis struggled to make words. She was just as mesmerizing as anything he'd admired in nature on his walk with Buster tonight.

Mallory didn't seem to notice what a goof he was. Instead, she locked up behind her and headed down the steps, veering toward the passenger side of his truck. She opened the passenger door before he could do it first.

"I would have gotten that for you."

Mallory slid into the passenger seat and looked up at him. "This isn't a date, remember?"

Hollis pushed down a twinge of disappointment. "Of course not," he replied, keeping his tone light. "We're friends." Wouldn't want to mess that up, like he tended to do with any romantic relationships. Heading back around to the driver's side of his truck, he slid behind the steering wheel and breathed in.

Big mistake. The air smelled like the garden in Eleanor's backyard. Floral and heavenly. He should stop breathing. He held his breath as his mind whirred.

"Earth to Hollis." Mallory poked his shoulder. "Are you going to drive?"

Hollis released a breath and looked over. "Drive. Right." He chuckled and got another whiff of her perfume. He put his truck into drive and remembered to breathe, even though he just wanted to lean closer to Mallory.

"I can't believe we're going to a dance at a dementia care facility," she said on a small nervous-sounding laugh as he drove. "It feels like we're in middle school, heading to a dance."

Hollis glanced over. He'd had that very same thought earlier tonight. "I never went to one of those."

"What?" She smacked the side of his arm playfully. "You never went to a school dance?"

"I'll make up for it tonight. I can't promise I'm a great dancer though. I hope I don't embarrass you." He stole a glance in her direction.

"We'll see."

As they parked, entered Memory Oaks, and headed into the community room, Hollis felt a surge of pride at the sight of the large Christmas tree that he and Mallory had trimmed and decorated last week. The facility was beautifully decorated with twinkling lights and festive garlands adorning every surface. The lighting was dim but not too dark, accommodating the needs of the older residents.

"Hey, you two," Nancy said, stepping over to them. "Welcome to our dance!"

Hollis and Mallory glanced around the room. It was festive and merry, but the dance floor was empty. Most of the residents were seated around the edges of the room, looking bored.

Nancy's smile wobbled as she seemed to read their minds. "Maybe we should have stuck to bingo. I'm not sure most of these folks want to throw their hips out shaking a leg tonight."

"Nonsense," Hollis said with a grin. Then he looked at Mallory. "Let's show 'em how it's done."

Mallory offered a suspicious look. "I thought you said you weren't sure you could dance."

He shrugged. "I have faith you'll make me look good out there. Be right back." He winked as he headed toward the corner where a DJ was set up behind a table with a black cloth draped over it.

"Hey, man," Hollis said, getting the DJ's attention. "You taking requests?"

The DJ was younger than Hollis, with his hat flipped backward on his head. "Of course. What do you want?"

Hollis thought for a moment. The first song that came to mind felt appropriate. "Do you have 'I'll Be Home for Christmas'?"

"A slow dance." The DJ nodded. "Sure. Let's do it."

Hollis made his way to Mallory as the opening notes of "I'll Be Home for Christmas" filled the air. He extended his hand in her direction. "Dance with me?"

Mallory hesitated. Then she placed her hand in his and allowed him to lead her onto the center of the community room's dance floor.

"Not a date," he whispered under his breath.

"I'm sorry?" she asked, looking at him intently.

"Sorry. Just talking to myself," he said with a slow grin. He had promised Nan he'd take care of Mal. But holding her close, breathing in the soft scent of her perfume, it was hard to remember why this couldn't be more than fulfilling that request.

At first, Mallory was rigid in his arms, but as the song progressed,

Hollis felt her relax and lean into him. He thought he even heard her sigh softly as they swayed.

"Nancy is dancing with Mr. Alps," Mallory said, tipping her face up to look at Hollis.

Her lips were dangerously close to his in the moment, and his focus was there to read what they were saying over the music. He looked over her shoulder. "Ms. Lester is dancing with Charlie."

"Charlie?" Mallory asked. "My grandpa Charlie?"

Hollis nodded. "I invited him and Eleanor when they were at the tree farm the other day."

Mallory turned and waved, turning back to Hollis excitedly. Once again, her face was close.

Linda had put on a great party, but she'd forgotten one detail that Hollis wished he had right now—mistletoe. An excuse to kiss the woman in front of him was all he needed.

Someone tapped on his shoulder. "Mind if I cut in, young man?"

Hollis turned to see Nan standing there holding onto a rolling walker. Her eyes were twinkling as she met his gaze.

"Of course not, Nan," he said, surprised to see her.

"Grandma!" Mallory released her hold on Hollis and cautiously gave Nan a hug. "Hi." She pulled back and looked at Nan.

Hollis worried for a moment that Nan might get frustrated if she didn't recognize Mallory.

"Excuse me, dear." Nan smiled brightly. "I hope you don't mind if I steal your date for a dance?"

Mallory shared a glance with Hollis. "Oh. Of course not." She gave Hollis a nod. "In fact, I think I'm going to go find Pop to dance with."

As Hollis began to dance with Nan, he waited to see what she would say.

"I went to a dance once," she finally said, looking up at him. "I think." Her brow wrinkled.

"Yeah?" he asked.

"Mm." She looked younger as she swayed, lost somewhere between her past and the present moment. "I don't remember his name, but I recall how he made me feel."

"How's that?" Hollis asked, encouraging her to keep talking.

Nan held on to him firmly as the festive music played. "Love feels like falling. Terrifying and futile to try and stop." She closed her eyes for a moment.

Hollis wondered if she was thinking of Mickey. Of course, she was. That was her late husband. As they swayed, her eyes closed, her wrinkles seemed to soften, and an expression of peace washed over her.

"I'm floating," she said quietly.

Hollis suspected she was lost in a memory when usually she was lost without them. He didn't let go when the song ended, and neither did she. Not until she looked at him again, a thin sheen of tears in her eyes. "Nan? You okay?"

She looked confused and upset, and Hollis's stomach knotted in dread.

"Nan," a man's voice said from somewhere behind Hollis.

Hollis turned toward his grandfather, who'd tapped his shoulder. "Pop."

"May I have this dance?" Pop asked.

For a moment, Hollis thought his grandfather wanted to dance with him. But then Pop reached for Nan's hand, and Hollis stepped away.

Nan's confusion shifted subtly as she looked at her new dance partner, her eyes becoming clearer. Nan and Pop had always known each other. They'd both grown up in Bloom. Even so, most were strangers to Nan these days, and Hollis hesitated to leave Pop to possibly upset Nan.

"Don't you have someone else to go find?" Pop glanced over his shoulder and winked at Hollis. "I think I saw her at the punch bowl."

Hollis turned to look in that direction, and sure enough, Mallory was there, preparing a cup of bright red punch. He looked at Pop again, but his grandfather and Nan were fine. Laughing even.

"Thank you for the dance, young man," Nan said, and Hollis got the message. He wasn't needed, not here. Instead, he was needed more at the refreshments table. Or, rather, what *he* needed was there.

The rest of the evening passed in a whirl of music and laughter. Hollis found himself dancing with resident after resident, each one eager to share their splintered memories of Christmases past. He even danced with Eleanor as Mallory danced with her grandpa Charlie.

"You need to come visit me sometime soon. We'll have a cup of tea, and I'll loan you a book," Eleanor said, holding on to him tightly. She'd fractured her pelvis a couple of years back, and Hollis knew she was still a little unsteady on her feet.

"Not sure I'll have much time for reading in the future," he said honestly.

Eleanor beamed brightly. "Ah. Love does take quite a lot of time." She glanced over at Mallory. "A woman is like a book that you never stop reading."

Hollis took a moment to process that thought. Eleanor was always talking in book quotes. "Which book is that from?"

Eleanor patted a hand on his chest. "Those are my words, and it's the truth. When you find the right woman, think of her as a book that doesn't end. You always have to keep turning the pages and discovering her."

"Why are you giving me love advice, Eleanor?"

Eleanor laughed. "Love is contagious, I suppose. Once you're in it, you want everyone else to be in it too."

Hollis loved that Eleanor and Charlie had found love late in life. It was inspiring to watch the two of them together.

Charlie returned and interrupted their dance. "Don't even think about stealing my lovely bride."

Hollis lifted his hands, palms out. "I wouldn't dream of it."

Eleanor visibly blushed as Charlie pulled her back in. Then Hollis looked around for Mallory, spotting her on the other side of the dance floor.

He watched her twirl an elderly gentleman around the floor, her face beaming. Mission achieved. That's all he'd wanted for tonight. To see everyone here have fun, but especially Mallory.

As the night wound down and residents slowly began to return to their rooms, Hollis walked over to the punch bowl. Pop sidled up next to him, a knowing glint in his eye.

"That Mallory," Pop said, nodding toward where she was chatting animatedly with a group of residents, "she's something special."

Hollis nodded, unable to take his eyes off her. He'd had a hard time taking his eyes off her all night. "She really is."

Pop clapped a hand on his shoulder. "You know, son, sometimes the best things in life are worth taking a risk for."

Before Hollis could respond, Mallory was making her way over to them, her cheeks flushed and her eyes bright with excitement.

"Hollis, I'm so glad you made me come." Impulsively, she threw her arms around him in a quick hug.

Hollis savored the brief contact, wishing he could hold on longer. "Practically kicking and screaming," he teased as she pulled away. "You seemed like you needed a little Christmas cheer. And I guess I did too."

"You?" She lifted a brow. "You're Santa Claus in the flesh."

Pop chuckled. "Don't let this big lug fool you. It's all show. Sometimes the biggest smiles hide the loneliest hearts. I knew that the first time I caught him trespassing on my farm."

Hollis was amazed by how many memories Pop still had, even though so many had vanished to wherever memories go when they were lost.

"I'll remember that." She nudged him slightly. "Word in the room is that they're kicking us out in five minutes. Dance is over at eight."

"Oh, man." Pop swung his arm with exaggerated disappointment. "I was just working up my nerve to ask Nancy to dance with me."

"The recreational therapist?" Mallory glanced around the room. "Don't worry, Pop. I'll find her and ask her for you. I think there's still time for one more dance."

Pop gave her a wink. "Then you and Hollis here can have one last dance too."

As they said their goodbyes and headed out to Hollis's truck, he couldn't help but feel a sense of accomplishment. He'd seen a glimpse of the carefree, joyful Mallory she could be when she wasn't lugging around the worries and responsibilities that weren't solely hers.

Driving home, with Mallory humming softly to the Christmas carols on the radio, Hollis wished the night didn't have to end. As he pulled up in front of her house, he turned to her. "I won't try to walk you to your door. I got the memo loud and clear that tonight was not a date."

Mallory's soft brown eyes were warm. "Wow, all that dancing really wore me out and I, um, have an early shift at the hospital."

"Really? Haven't you worked three twelve-hour shifts already this week?"

She glanced up. "Are you keeping tabs on me?"

He shook his head, even though, yeah, he kind of was.

"I'm covering for one of the other nurses so she can attend some family stuff for the holidays. The extra shifts help with Nan's care."

Hollis nodded. "Nursing. Visiting Nan. Putting on a play. Don't burn the candle at both ends. You'll burn yourself out."

She breathed a laugh. "I may have been close to doing just that, but tonight was good for me. It was fun."

"Laughter is good medicine," Hollis said. "Just let me know when you need more. I'm at the ready if it means keeping you from burning out."

The air between them felt charged—at least to him. Even knowing that tonight wasn't supposed to have any romantic implications, he found himself leaning in, drawn by some invisible force—a string that had always pulled him toward Mallory. As he leaned, however, Mallory blinked, breaking the spell.

"Thank you, Hollis," she said, her voice barely above a whisper. Then she gathered her bag, avoiding looking at him directly. "Good night."

He watched as she slipped out of the truck and walked up her driveway to her front porch. Then he expelled a long breath as she disappeared inside the home. "Night, Mal."

Driving home, Hollis wondered if it was his imagination or if something had shifted between them tonight. It might not have been a date, but it felt like more than friendship.

The Rustic Nail Ornament

You'll find the Rustic Nail Ornament in a bright red velvet box labeled with the number 4. Open the lid and prepare to be...well, underwhelmed. The rusted and bent nail looks as if it's seen better days, and it has. This nail came from the Old Bloom Mill House. During its transformation, as I walked the property, I nearly stepped on this nail, which might have altered the whole story I'm about to tell. Instead, I spotted the nail, like a copper penny on the ground, picked it up, and slid it in my pocket like a good luck charm. How desperate I must have been to think a rusty, old nail would serve such a purpose... This rusted nail should be hung fourth down on your tree. I've tied a gold ribbon around its head.

Here's the story behind it.

The day I drove home from New York on my way back to Bloom, it rained the entire trip. Looking back, I can't decide if it was actually raining or if it was just my tears blurring my vision that gray afternoon because the windshield wipers couldn't seem to make anything more clear. Truthfully, I'm shocked I made it back to the house where I grew up. But I did.

I was home. That's how I felt when I passed the WEL-COME TO BLOOM sign. Some part of me also felt like I was returning with my tail between my legs and a secret baby in my belly.

I didn't want anyone to know about the pregnancy at first. Least of all Ralph. I'd left him with no good-bye, just like he told me to. And I was terrified he might not take me back. I wouldn't if I were in his shoes. My worst fear was that he wouldn't want our baby.

It was ours, of course. I'd never been with any man before Ralph. He was my one and my only.

All I knew as I drove those miles back to North Carolina was that I did want the baby. Whether it was a him or a her. Or one of each. Twins run in the family, you know. I hadn't even been to a doctor yet to confirm the pregnancy, but I didn't need to. A woman knows these things even if she's never experienced them before.

My first stop when I returned to Bloom was my parents' house. I parked inside their garage, went inside the house, and closed myself off in my childhood bedroom. I didn't show my face for three days. On the third day, my mother knocked on my bedroom door and came in without waiting for me to respond.

"How far along are you?" she asked with a knowing look.

The tears exploded out of me. Uncontrollable sobs. Holding in a secret is so lonely, but I didn't know how to tell them. I knew they'd be so disappointed in me and, after a lifetime of trying to be the good girl, the one my parents could brag about to their friends, I felt like a failure. I couldn't face her. Instead, I turned my gaze out the window that overlooked my mother's beautiful flower garden in the backyard. "I-I don't know." My voice was barely more than a whisper, and my body was trembling. My cheeks were wet with the tears streaming down.

My mother stepped over and kneeled at my bedside. She laid a gentle hand on my forearm. "Does Ralph know?"

I shook my head quickly, nearly choking on my sobs. "I haven't spoken to him since I left town. I made him promise that we wouldn't...he couldn't..." I could barely get the words out, and I didn't want to explain. Explaining made me feel like a bad person. There were all these ideas in my head about how things were supposed to look and feel and be. Having a baby was supposed to feel joyful, and that wasn't at all how I felt. I was scared. Lonely. Heartbroken. I'd even heard that Ralph had been seen around town with an old classmate of mine. "Does Daddy know?"

When my mother didn't answer, I finally looked in her direction.

What I saw was so unexpected. There was no disappointment in my mother's eyes. Instead, I saw warmth. "Mom?" I asked again.

She squeezed my forearm, a tiny hug and show of support. "Men aren't as intuitive when it comes to these things. And your father is more clueless than most." She laughed quietly. Then her expression grew serious. "Is this something you can live with? Leaving your dreams of Broadway behind to raise a child? It isn't easy. In fact, motherhood is the hardest thing you'll ever do."

I'd been asking myself the same question since the moment I knew. "Broadway wasn't what I thought it'd be." I took a steadying breath. In Bloom, I had been the best. I don't say that in an egotistical way. A person knows when they're good at something, and I knew I was good. Every time I stepped onstage, my entire body had this electric feeling, buzzing from my head to my toes. That's how I felt onstage in Bloom, at least. But in New York, there were hundreds of young women just like me, all competing for the same role. It was a wake-up call. I was no longer buzzing. No longer happy. After dozens of auditions, I got the smallest of roles—smaller than anything I'd ever played before. "I've always thought the-ater was like playing dress-up, but that's not how it felt when I was there," I told her.

My mother looked at me as if she were reading me like a book. I'm not sure how long that moment lasted, but when she was finished, she took a quick breath and expelled it quietly. "Nannie, this is what we're going to do." She was in full mom-mode, even though she'd been great about giving me my independence once I was eigh-teen. "I've saved quite a bit of money. When I married your father, my mama told me to put away a couple of dollars here and a couple there. In case a time ever came when I needed to get out of a situation."

"With Daddy?" I asked, surprised.

She waved her hand as if to erase whatever thoughts were rushing into my mind. "I realized long ago that wouldn't be an issue. Your father isn't perfect, but he tries. And he loves me. I've never for a moment ques-tioned that."

It struck me that Mama didn't say she loved him too.

"The mill is for sale," she finally said decisively. "We're going to buy it."

I honestly had no idea what my mother was talking about. "A mill?" Did she think I had come home preg-nant, dejected, and desperate enough to run a mill? I had no training or knowledge of what even happened in a mill.

"We'll buy it and turn it into a theater. All these years, watching you onstage in the school cafeterias or random buildings, I always thought that Bloom should have a proper stage. A community theater."

Pride was reflected in her eyes. When I'd wondered

how she'd react when I finally told her my secret, I'd never imagined her offering to buy an old mill and turn it into a theater.

"Mom, that will cost a small fortune," I whispered, too afraid to hope that her idea had any merit. And what kind of community theater could possibly be built inside a building that was halfway falling apart?

"Good. Because I listened to my mother."

At that time, my grandmother was suffering early-onset dementia. The grandmother I knew wasn't the wise woman who my mama loved to tell me about. Leaning in, as if telling me something very important, only for my ears, my mother said, "Because a small fortune is exactly what I've stored up all these years. And now I'm giving it to you."

The thing about nails is that they may be small, but they're strong. They weather the storm, even if they come out a bit rusty. Nails have teeth and they can do a lot of damage with one misstep. Have you ever stepped on one? Oh, but in the right conditions, a nail can build homes, cities…a theater. A nail can even build a dream.

Chapter Nine

Every now and then, when you're onstage, you hear the best sound a player can hear.... It is the sound of a wonderful, deep silence that means you've hit them where they live.

—Shelley Winters

Mallory's chest ached as she finished reading an entry in Nan's journal and looked up at her grandmother.

Nan held up the ornament, rolling the piece of metal between her fingertips and inspecting it as if she'd never seen a nail before. "What did you call this again?"

"The Rustic Nail Ornament," Mallory said, hoping with every fiber of her being that Nan would remember.

Nan shook her head on a deep chuckle that almost sounded like the old Nan. "The Rustic Nail Ornament," she repeated. "Who ever heard of such a thing?"

Mallory took hold of the ornament and allowed the nail to sway from its ribbon looped over the edge of her fingertips. "I'm going to hang it on the Christmas tree in the community room. Would you like to come with me?"

Nan blinked. "Yes, I would. We'll need a ladder. It needs to hang near the top. Fourth from the top," she said automatically.

Mallory resisted the surge of hope that sprung up inside her. "Oh? Why do you say that?"

"Because that's where it belongs, dear," she answered, sounding like the Nan that Mallory had known until about twelve months ago.

That was all Mallory needed. Just that little nugget to keep her going.

"Well, let's go hang the Rustic Nail Ornament, shall we? I'll make sure I find a stepladder so that I can hang it, fourth from the top."

Nan looked pleased, her eyes sparkling.

Mallory helped her sit on the edge of her bed and then transferred her to a wheelchair. Nan could walk, but she was unstable at long distances, and Mallory preferred for Nan to spend her energy visiting rather than getting exercise. "Did you enjoy the dance the other night?" she asked as she pushed Nan's chair.

"Oh, yes. I danced with the nicest man," she said.

Mallory wondered if she was talking about Hollis. As far as Mallory had seen, Hollis was the only man Nan had danced with. After that, she'd seemed worn-out. Exhausted from either being on her feet or from her emotions.

"A nice man, huh?" Mallory grinned at the description. *Nice* was an understatement. She rolled Nan's chair to the tree and stopped when they were just a few feet away.

"It's so big!" Nan said, as if she'd never seen it.

"The largest from Pop's Tree Farm." Mallory's mind slid back to her trip to the farm with Hollis when they'd picked out a much smaller tree. Things worked out for a reason though, because if that little tree had gone up in her grandmother's room, this huge one in front of them probably wouldn't be here, already full of so many ornaments and memories that belonged to the other residents.

That day at the tree farm was when things had started to change between Mallory and Hollis. There'd been a shift, and Mallory had started to see Hollis differently, as more than a friend.

Nan brought her hands together at her chest and cleared her throat, drawing Mallory's attention. "Are you thinking about a special someone?"

"Hmm?" Mallory asked, blinking away the memory of the tree farm and refocusing on Nan.

"You're glowing. Like the tree." She pointed to the blue fir in front of them.

Mallory shook her head. "No. No, I'm just thinking about, well, a good friend."

Nan ignored Mallory's claim. "I had a special person once too, you know?"

Mallory pulled up a chair from a nearby table and sat it beside Nan's wheelchair. "Who was he?" Even though the journals mentioned a man named Ralph, Mallory didn't know who that was. Nan had never spoken about this person who'd been so important to her. Were the journal writings a false memory that Nan had penned during the initial moments of her Alzheimer's?

Nan seemed to think, her demeanor shifting from light to heavy as she shook her head.

Mallory reached for her grandmother's wrinkled hand. "It's okay." She knew how upset Nan got during these moments where she struggled and failed to recall her past. Instead of pressing, Mallory diverted Nan's attention by holding up the Rustic Nail Ornament again. "Fourth from the top, right?" she asked with a cheery tone, hoping Nan would relax.

"Yes. Fourth from the top."

"Okay." There was a stepladder against the wall that Mallory had used to string the lights. "I need to hang the first three first," Mallory went on. They were in the bag as well. "The Santa Hat Tree Topper. The Butterfly Barrette Ornament. The Wildflower Ornament.

Then the Rustic Nail Ornament." Mallory stood, grabbed the ladder, and set it up in front of the tree. One by one, she carried each keepsake to the top as Nan watched.

When Mallory was done, she looked at Nan. "I'll hang some more with you tomorrow. But tonight, I need to get to the theater for the play."

"Play?" Nan's face lit up. "Oh, I've always loved the theater."

"Oh?" Mallory asked, as if she didn't know. "If you want, I'll take you to the play on opening night. Would you like that?"

Nan looked uncertain. "My home is here now. I don't want to leave."

And that's why Mallory needed to do whatever it took to keep Nan here at Memory Oaks. Whether it meant working extra shifts at the hospital or listening to Maddie justify why they should sell the theater after this final show.

Nan had cared for Mallory and Maddie when they were children, and Mallory needed to return the favor and take the best care of Nan that she could. Reaching down, she squeezed Nan's hand. "Let's get you back to your room, Gr—" She stopped herself, remembering how upset Nan had gotten last time she'd said the *grandma* word, and continued wheeling Nan to her room where she helped her back into her recliner. "Okay, off to the theater I go," she said on her way out. "See you tomorrow."

"Break a leg!" Nan called behind her, giving Mallory pause. And hope. Nan was still here, though hard to find.

A noise coming from the attic of the theater got Mallory's attention. The theater was old, and it creaked when the wind blew. Still, she looked up in the direction of the attic as she listened attentively. Then she screamed as the front entrance door to the theater burst open.

"Ho, ho, ho!" Hollis stopped in his tracks and stood on the indoor mat, his brows crinkling as she relaxed back into her natural posture. "You all right?"

Heat crawled up her cheeks. "You scared me."

"Me?" Hollis dug a finger into his chest.

"You ever heard of knocking?" she teased.

He grinned in response. "The sign on the door says COME ON IN. Want me to leave?"

"Of course not. You're the first to arrive for play practice. That bodes well for you as our lead actor. Punctuality is a plus. That's what Nan always said." Mallory tilted her head. "Speaking of Nan, she told me about that dance you two shared. I think she has a soft spot for you."

Hollis stood a little taller and puffed out his chest. "Must be my handsome good looks."

Mallory knew he was only teasing, but she couldn't argue. He had a rugged look about him that she'd never really been attracted to. In the past, she'd dated guys who worked at the hospital, polished and prone to tucked-in polos and fancy cologne. Not Hollis. He was different, in a good way. "I appreciate how good you are to Nan."

Hollis gave Mallory a long look. "She means a lot to me too, you know. Your grandmother stood by me at my worst. Can't say that about too many people. I'm a loyal guy."

"Is that why you still work on Matt's construction crew?" Mallory wasn't sure where the question came from, but she could see that it visibly hit a nerve with Hollis. His gaze dropped, and he shifted uncomfortably.

Hollis pinched the bridge of his nose. "Matt is the dad I never had. And the crew is like the brothers I've always wanted. We're one big extended family. That's hard to walk away from."

Mallory understood that perfectly. "I always felt that way here in this theater. The cast was like my family. I'd come home from school, and they'd help me with my homework."

Hollis grinned. "Same. I loved coming here as a kid."

Mallory looked around the old, run-down theater. "If these walls could talk."

"They'd say a whole lot," he agreed, his voice low, making Mallory lean in. "These walls might tell on me."

Mallory shook her head. "What do you mean?"

He looked off to the side and then back to her. "I didn't go after school for Nan's milk and cookies. Or for the help with my homework."

Mallory crinkled her brow. "You certainly weren't here for the plays. You begrudgingly took that role Nan gave you when we were fifteen."

Hollis stared at her.

"Why did you come here every day?" she asked, suspecting she knew the answer.

Hollis opened his mouth, but before he could respond, the theater door opened again and three more cast members filed in noisily.

She greeted them, and when she looked at Hollis again, his back was to her and he was walking over to the table against the wall where she'd set up supplies for the night.

"Okay, everyone," Mallory said. "I have scripts printed for all of you. Hollis will hand them to you." She pointed. "Grab yourself a copy and start reacquainting yourself with your lines. It's been a year since some of you have read them, and some of you are completely new. We'll do a table reading once everyone has arrived. There is coffee in the pot on the table as well. And cookies. Help yourselves."

Most of the actors were the original cast of *Santa, Baby*, but some folks had moved. A couple had passed away. And a few were unable to reclaim their roles due to personal situations. That's why Hollis was there to play Santa.

She knew he never wanted to act in another play. Not after the way he royally messed things up that one year as a teenager. He didn't trust himself. Mallory trusted him though.

She stood there and watched Hollis as he prepared a plate of cookies and chatted with her Grandpa Charlie and Eleanor. Charlie had been in the play for the past decade, but not his new wife. In fact, until last year, Eleanor hadn't gotten out of her house very much at all. She and Charlie were good for each other.

Savannah was here too, standing near the coffeepot, showing off her diamond ring to Maria Linley.

I wish Nan was here.

The thought sent Mallory's mood into a nosedive. Nan wasn't gone-gone. Mallory couldn't grieve in a traditional sense because she still had Nan in her life, and Mallory was thankful for that. But Nan wasn't the same woman who'd nurtured and raised Mallory anymore. She was different. The memories that made her who she used to be were gone.

More folks filed into the theater lobby until there were fourteen actors and two understudies for the larger roles. Once everyone had arrived, Mallory led them all to the Reading Room, which was one large open space with a long rectangular table where everyone sat and read through the entire script aloud. As the director, Mallory sat at the table's head, where Nan usually sat.

The meeting essentially ran itself. Everyone here knew what to do, and Mallory was pleased that all the actors seemed to take their roles seriously, already delivering their lines with an appropriate level of emotion. When it came time for Hollis to say his lines, he ducked his head, seeming to hide behind the hand he had raised to his forehead.

"Ho, ho, ho!" he belted.

Giggles broke out around the room.

"Now, Hollis, don't go spoiling this play like you did that one time," a middle-aged woman, Esther Woods, said with obvious disdain.

All the actors around the table froze, their eyes wide as they glanced at Hollis. He'd done his best to redeem himself, but it was difficult to live down anything in a small town.

Clearing his throat, he looked up and said, "I don't intend to spoil anything. I read my line, didn't I?"

"If you're embarrassed to play the part, tell us now so we can find a new Santa," Esther went on, ignoring him.

Mallory wondered if she should step in, but Hollis put on his usual charm.

"No need for that," he assured the woman.

Esther turned to Mallory. "As the director, I'm sure you understand that it's your job to ensure this play runs smoothly, the way Nan would have wanted it."

Mallory's lips parted. If she remembered correctly, Hollis had pranked Esther a few times in his rebellious youth, which probably played a role in her distaste for him. "I think Nan would approve of Hollis filling the role of Santa. She was a big believer in second chances."

"Not as much as she believed in this theater."

The actor seated next to Esther laid a hand on the woman's arm and leaned to whisper something in her ear.

"Fine," Esther finally huffed before fluttering a hand in the air. "Let's move on with this reading."

To Mallory's relief, the actors continued to read. As they did, Mallory kept a close eye on Hollis. He wasn't an easy man to read, but Mallory thought he looked upset as he sat through the rest of the reading. When it was over, he pushed back from the table and stood up quickly. Mallory wanted to talk to him, but on her way, she was stopped by several of the actors wanting to know how Nan was doing and what the plan for the rest of the rehearsals would be. By the time Mallory was finally free, she looked around, and Hollis was gone.

The Skeleton Key Ornament

The Skeleton Key Ornament is tagged with the number 5. Tear off the green paper. Inside the box, you'll find a skeleton key. The original doors to the theater required one. Of course, years later, we installed new doors and this key was no longer needed. Not functionally at least. So here it is, a symbol of so many things, but mostly it represented second chances.

Here's the story.

The day my mother gave me her rainy day fund and we purchased the old mill to turn into the Bloom Community Theater was the day I realized that my great grandmother was right. Sometimes dreams can come true even if they don't happen the way you always envisioned they would.

Running the Bloom Community Theater became my dream, and after opening the doors, I never regretted not "making it" on Broadway. In fact, as my stomach grew, still too small for town folk to suspect, I knew I'd made the best decision for my little family. It would just be baby girl and me, two souls against the world—even if I secretly pined for Ralph. Another secret. Hadn't I learned my lesson the first time?

In a small town, I couldn't help but run into Ralph almost daily. My foolish heart would leap every time I saw his face, and then my heart would stumble and fall when I saw the hurt flash in his eyes. I knew I was the culprit. I put the hurt there. I left him for something that could never make me happy. I walked away, telling myself that it was fine because he gave me permission at the start. He was the one who told me to leave and not even tell him good-bye. I wanted to cling to that and put the blame on him, but I knew it was all mine. Our breakup was my fault.

The Bloom Community Theater was my second chance. Our baby together was my second chance. It would be foolish to hope that I'd have a second chance with Ralph as well. I have never been that lucky—and as someone who firmly believed in fate, shouldn't love be the one place where fate is real? If Ralph and I were meant to be, I never would have left for New York. I would have stayed in my small hometown. Ralph and I would have worked out the first time around.

I was starting to second-guess that thought when I saw him one day in town, holding hands with someone. I watched from a distance, my heart falling into my stomach, sharing space with the baby. He made her laugh and then he leaned in. Everything inside me screamed. No. No, no, no. He was mine.

Their kiss broke me. I'd lost him. No. I gave him away. This was my fault—no one else's.

Laying a hand on my belly, I tried to catch my breath. I meant to turn away before they saw me, but I was frozen. I didn't budge even as Ralph caught me watching and headed in my direction, holding her hand.

"Hi, Nan," he said.

The woman echoed the same greeting.

It was painful as I put on a smile and stepped into the role of the woman who'd moved on. Who wasn't bothered. Wasn't still in love. In love?

This moment was brief, but monumental no less. I could have fought for him. I could have stopped the train and begged him to get off. Instead, I remained frozen and gave the greatest performance of my life—before my theater had even opened the doors.

Hang the old skeleton key ornament fifth down from the top of the Memory Tree, below the rustic nail, the pressed wildflowers, the butterfly barrette, and the Santa hat at the tip-top of the tree.

Chapter Ten

Art, especially the stage, is a place where it is impossible to walk without stumbling.

—Anton Chekhov

The winter temperatures were mild tonight, even for North Carolina. It didn't feel like Christmas if Hollis could sit on his back deck without so much as a jacket. On a sigh, he relaxed into his deck chair and closed his eyes just for a moment. He was still wound up from tonight's play rehearsal.

He shouldn't let Esther Woods's comments get to him, but she'd said those things in front of the entire cast, and no one had stood up for him. Not one person.

Maybe he should back out. He didn't want to bring any negativity into this play. Nan would never have stood for Esther's behavior tonight, but this was Mallory's first time serving as the director. Things needed to run as smoothly as possible.

Hollis opened his eyes when something pressed against his lower leg. "Hey, Duke." He patted his dog's head. "Are you sensing that I'm in a mood tonight? It's okay. I'll be okay."

Duke leaned more heavily into his calf muscle, his brown eyes wide and sad.

Dogs were incredible animals. They had to be the most empathetic. That's one thing that drew Hollis to them. He'd seen how much they could help.

Maybe instead of playing Santa in this play, he should be focusing on the plans for expanding Popadine's Tree Farm. He'd love for things to progress while Pop was still around to see it.

Hollis's phone buzzed from the patio table beside him. He glanced over and saw Mallory's name. It was a text.

Mallory: You disappeared tonight before I could catch you. You okay?

Hollis picked up his phone and tapped his finger along the screen.

Hollis: You know me. Things just slide right off my back. It was a good rehearsal. Nan would be proud of you.

Dots began bouncing along the screen.

Mallory: She'd be proud of you too, Hol. And she would have put Esther in her place if she'd been there.

Hollis: You think so?

Mallory: I know. I'm not letting you back out of the play. You're the kind of guy who sticks to his word. I'm holding you to that.

Hollis was honored that she would think that highly of him. He tapped out another text.

Hollis: Ho, ho, ho.

Mallory: That's better. See you tomorrow night.

Hollis: I'll be there. Hey? I have a question.

He'd heard something from Mallory's brother-in-law, Sam, who sometimes helped out with the deliveries on the farm. He hoped it was a false rumor, but considering the source was Mallory's own sister, he doubted it.

Hollis: Are you really considering selling the theater?

There was a delay in Mallory's response, and Hollis realized he was holding his breath. Was she really considering such a drastic change?

Mallory: I can't work extra shifts indefinitely to keep Nan at Memory Oaks. And I'm a nurse, not a theater director. Maddie thinks it might be best.

Hollis's heart broke at the thought, but he understood. His main concern was what was best for Mallory. What would make her happiest?

Hollis: If that's what you decide, I'll help you in any way I can.

Mallory: You really are a lifesaver this holiday.

Hollis woke early the next morning to put in some extra training time with Buster before heading over to one of the current construction sites. December was usually an off month, but one of the guys had called out sick yesterday, leaving Matt and the crew scrambling to make their deadline. In Hollis's experience, deadlines were like dominoes. Once you missed one, all the next scheduled jobs fell behind as well.

Hollis took a walk through the rows of trees with Buster off-leash. Buster had proven that Hollis could trust him not to go anywhere without his verbal okay. On the first couple walks, Hollis had rewarded Buster frequently and immediately, and he only made Buster walk a few minutes before allowing him to have freedom. Hollis was working on Buster's self-control though. He could see in Buster's alert eyes that he was eager to take off, chasing the wind. But he showed restraint, waiting for permission. "Good dog," Hollis said, his words coming out with a puff of white air.

Hollis stopped walking and faced Buster. "Sit."

Buster folded his body onto his hind legs, his gaze fixed on Hollis.

"Good boy," Hollis said again. He didn't need treats anymore.

Buster would still get them, of course, but they weren't required for Buster's obedience. "Stay." Hollis held up a hand before walking away from Buster, leaving the dog right where he was. When Buster started to return to all fours, Hollis gave another firm command. "Stay."

Hollis waited a moment longer, wondering what was going through his foster dog's mind. *I'm not leaving you, buddy. Not anytime soon, at least.*

"Come!" Hollis finally commanded, patting his hand to his thigh.

Buster took off toward him, practically flying into Hollis's open arms as Hollis squatted to meet him.

"Good boy, good boy." Hollis laughed at the dog's attention. This time he reached inside his pocket and pulled out a treat. Straightening again, he nodded at Buster. "Run free!"

With a happy bark, Buster ran circles around Hollis before racing off to weave through the trees.

Hollis did one more training session with the dog before going inside the house to shower and get dressed for work. He added an extra layer of clothing because the weather had finally gotten the memo that it was December and the temperature had plunged accordingly.

Growing up the way he did, Christmastime had tended to be when Hollis acted out the most. In hindsight, he understood why. It was the season of hope, and the one thing he'd wanted most back then—a family—had seemed hopeless. He wished he could give the little boy he'd been a great big hug and tell that kid that things would work out. It would take until he was seventeen and nearly out of the system altogether, but the family he'd hoped and dreamed of every Christmas would finally welcome him in. Matt was the father figure he'd always dreamed of.

After locking up the house, Hollis climbed into his truck and sipped his coffee, noting the subtle layer of dread he felt facing a day of construction ahead. He didn't love the work anymore. He was supposed to be done. It was going to be a difficult transition for

Matt, but Hollis hoped that Matt would adjust and support him the way he always had.

Ten minutes later, gravel crunched under Hollis's tires as he pulled up to the Maynard property. He parked beside a towering oak under an umbrella of branches, and then he pushed open his door and stepped out.

"It's cold out here," Matt said, walking toward Hollis, wearing a heavy jacket.

Something about the way Matt looked this morning gave Hollis pause. He was pale, amplifying dark bags under his eyes. He worked harder during the holidays. Everybody seemed to.

"Sure is," Hollis said. "How're you today?"

"Good." Matt rubbed his gloved hands together. "Just wishing I was inside my own house by the fireplace and drinking coffee instead of out here, to tell you the truth."

"Sounds nice." But the words also sent off alarm bells in Hollis's gut. Matt usually got his adrenaline from the jobs, not a coffee mug. Hollis glanced around. "Where are the others?"

"On their way. I asked you to meet me earlier than the rest of 'em." Matt gave Hollis a meaningful look.

"You wanted to discuss something?" Hollis asked, feeling his body stiffen and his mind become more alert as it prepared.

"Yeah." Matt gave a quick nod. "You're at the top of my list for taking over the company when I retire," he said, jumping straight to business. "I don't need to tell you that you're the son I never had. Not biologically, at least. In every other way, I think of you as my son. So does Sandy."

Hollis's throat tightened.

Matt patted a hand on Hollis's back. "And I'm proud of the man you've become, Hol." He took a long breath as he turned his attention to the Maynard Farm and beyond. "Construction is hard work, and I'm not sure I can handle the physical part of it much longer." Matt glanced over.

Hollis smiled at him, but inside, he was frowning. He'd already told Matt many times about his plans going forward. Hollis had saved the money, made the contacts, and his mind had been set. Now he felt like he'd been hit over the head with this opportunity with Matt's construction crew. Anyone in his shoes would be grateful for it. "Wow." Hollis searched for the right words that wouldn't offend Matt but also wouldn't commit to what Matt was offering. "I feel honored that you'd think of me."

"Of course you're the first person I think of. You've earned this. There's no one else I would even feel comfortable leaving the construction crew in the hands of. It's only because of you that I can even consider stepping back."

A sense of panic grew inside of Hollis like an unruly weed springing out of nowhere. He pulled a breath into his lungs, but he only felt more suffocated.

Another truck crunched along the gravel, grabbing both of their attention.

"There's Rodney." Matt made a show of glancing at his watch. "I asked Rod to get here an hour ago to help me unload the supplies."

It occurred to Hollis now that Matt didn't usually ask Hollis to get to a site early because he knew Hollis worked with his dogs during the morning hours. He always had one or two fosters that he trained in the early morning, just like he had Buster this morning. Matt had always worked with Hollis to support Hollis's dog training "hobby." That was the word Matt always used, and now it felt like a slap in the face.

"Better late than never," Hollis said quietly, talking about Rodney.

Matt scoffed. "Since when did you become Mr. Positivity? Must be the Santa role that Mallory Blue somehow managed to get you to play." Matt's brow lifted subtly. "I don't even need to ask how she got you to agree to put on a red velvet suit. My main question is how you got her to give you the role."

That question kind of felt like a slap in the face as well. If Hollis was a stand-up guy enough for Matt to offer his entire construction crew, why wouldn't Mallory offer him the lead in Nan's play? "Trust me, it was her idea. Not mine," Hollis joked, feeling anything but jovial.

"Hmm. Maybe that crush you've had on her all these years is finally being reciprocated, huh?" Matt chuckled.

Hollis cleared his throat and decided not to respond. He didn't let things ruffle his feathers as much as they used to. But he still had to bite his tongue some days and work at not letting the Hollis of old, the one who acted before thinking, out.

Matt started to walk toward Rodney but stopped and turned back to Hollis. "Hey, I'm meeting with the Anderson family this evening to discuss a project they have for us early next year. Want to come with me?" Matt asked.

Hollis kicked the dirt at his feet as he tried to find the best response for the moment, until he could think about what Matt had said. Matt already knew that Hollis didn't have plans to return to working construction full-time.

"Don't tell me you're still planning on opening that dog place." Matt chuckled, leaving Hollis breathless. He didn't wait for Hollis to respond. Instead, Matt headed toward Rodney, tossing out comments about Rodney's tardiness.

Hollis stood there frozen, despite his hat and heavy flannel jacket. Matt had always supported him in every way that counted, except in this one. Why didn't Matt understand Hollis's passion for training dogs?

"Come on, son. Let's get this show on the road!" Matt called to Hollis over his shoulder as he walked toward his parked truck, which was closer to the site. The supplies needed to complete today's job were loaded in the back and needed to be pulled off in preparation for the work. And, in Hollis's mind, this was his last official construction project, whether Matt liked it or not.

Chapter Eleven

Drama is life, with the dull bits cut out.

—Alfred Hitchcock

Mallory stared at Nan, who had been sleeping for the past forty-five minutes since Mallory had arrived. She had the journal in her lap and a bag with a couple of ornaments to hang on the tree.

The door opened, and Sheila, one of the nursing aides, walked in. Her gaze bounced from Mallory to Nan.

"Arguing with the night crew wore your grandmother out." She laughed quietly under her breath.

"Oh, I didn't know she had a rough night."

"Oh, yes, she sure did. She was carrying on about your grandfather," Sheila said casually, as if it were no big deal. "I'm not sure I've ever heard Nan speak about him before."

Mallory found this tidbit interesting. Memories were good, yes, but not if they were going to torment her grandmother.

Sheila faced Mallory and glanced down at Mallory's bag. "She mentioned that you were reading her a story."

Mallory's heart leaped. "She mentioned me? By name?"

"Well, she called you a nice woman." Sheila offered an apologetic expression. "I know it's hard. I see family members day in and day out. Being forgotten by your loved one is…"

"Crushing," Mallory supplied.

Sheila reached for Mallory's hand for a quick squeeze and release. "She likes the story. Whatever it is that you're reading to her. What is it?"

Mallory hesitated. "Her journal. My grandmother has a box of ornaments for something she called the Memory Tree. There's a story behind each ornament. Her life story." Mallory shrugged, and she looked down at her hands. She needed a moment to take a deep breath. "A love story too," she said, looking back up.

Sheila's brows lifted. "Well, who doesn't love a good romance?"

Nan stirred in her bed and opened her eyes, focusing on Mallory. "Mallory? Is that you?"

Mallory sat up straighter, tears immediately pricking at her eyes. She knew this moment would probably be fleeting. "Hi, Nan. It's me." There was so much she wanted to tell Nan before she disappeared. "We're rehearsing for the play. Just like you asked me to do."

Nan's eyes lit up. "*Santa, Baby*," she repeated. "I wrote that one, I think."

"You did. You did." Mallory kept her tone of voice even, worried she might accidentally pull Nan out of her fragile, clear-minded state.

"I always knew you'd take over the theater. In my heart,"—Nan placed a hand on the left side of her chest—"I always knew you'd run it once I was gone."

Guilt crashed over Mallory like an unexpected ocean wave. She didn't have the heart to tell Nan that she and Maddie were considering selling the theater. It wasn't just a consideration. It was pretty much the plan because otherwise they wouldn't be able to keep Nan here. Mallory loved the theater, but she couldn't just give up her nursing job. That wasn't practical—even if Mallory thought it sounded like a lovely life. Nan had led a lovely life. She'd always known it, but the ornaments were giving Mallory a different viewpoint. It wasn't all roses, but hardships made the journey worth it. She'd heard Nan say that more than once. "We're using the original cast. Mostly."

"Mm. Good. I only chose those who I knew would follow through. An actor needs to be as reliable as he or she is talented," Nan said, pounding a fist in the air, her passion bubbling up.

Hollis came to mind. Nan had felt like she'd misplaced her trust in him that year when they'd been teens. Mallory remembered the rant Nan had gone on with Grandpa Mickey that night when she thought Mallory and Maddie were asleep. "I'm not mad because I put my play in jeopardy. I'm mad because I thought he was ready. This could set him back," Mallory remembered hearing Nan say, her voice thick with tears.

Mallory had been baffled as she pulled her knees to her chest, sitting on the floor right next to her bedroom door. Why was Nan worried about Hollis when he was the one who'd ruined opening night?

"I thought a shining moment would be good for him, but what if it spins him back down that old self-destructive path? All because I pushed him before he was ready."

The rest of the conversation had been muffled by Grandpa Mickey's soft voice and Mallory's own tears. She'd been embarrassed that night. She'd depended on Hollis, and he'd let her down. Broken her heart. Listening to Nan crying in the kitchen, she'd been hit with a deep shame. Hollis's life wasn't easy. She knew that. But neither was hers. Why should he get a free pass for bad behavior?

"Actors are puzzle pieces. Every piece matters," Nan said now, her voice slowly losing its strength. Nan's gaze fell back to the journal in Mallory's hands. "You found it. Good. That's good. I always wanted to tell you that story."

"The story of the Christmas ornaments?" Mallory asked, leaning in.

"Mm. I wasn't always old, you know."

Mallory reached for Nan's hand. "You've always been young at heart, in my opinion. I've been reading the story to you. Do you remember?"

Nan's blue eyes became unfocused as she seemed to think. "I don't remember. You've been reading to me?"

Mallory felt a jolt of panic as the conversation suddenly felt like walking on eggshells. She shook her head quickly, desperate to keep Nan with her but instinctively knowing Nan's memories were slipping like sand in an hourglass. "Stay with me, Grandma."

"Grandma?" Nan pulled her hand away and looked at Mallory as if they were strangers.

"I-I'm sorry. It's just, you remind me of my grandmother," Mallory said quickly. "My own grandmother had loved it when I read from this journal. Do you mind if I read it to you?"

Nan's gaze lowered to the book in Mallory's hands. "I suppose so. If you would like."

"I would. I'd like to very much."

Mallory opened the book where she'd left off and took a breath before reading aloud, flicking her gaze up to Nan to gauge her reaction. "This one is titled 'The Wooden Heart Ornament.'"

Nan chuckled quietly. "Strange name for an ornament."

"I think so too." Mallory used her pointer finger to hold her place as she continued. "The Wooden Heart Ornament hangs sixth from the top of your tree. Here's the story behind it."

Nan shifted restlessly.

"You okay, Nan?"

Nan blinked, coming back from some distant place in her mind. "I'm fine." She frowned and fluttered a hand in the air. "All right, then. Let's just go hang that ugly thing in your lap, if it'll make you happy."

Mallory's mouth fell open. "I don't think it's ugly."

"Well, you need to get your eyes checked," Nan snapped. "It looks like something made from scrap wood." A trace of a smile returned to her lips. "I need to get out of this room. Will you take me?"

"Of course." Mallory closed the journal and dropped it back into her bag, even though she'd barely read a couple of sentences. Then she stood and helped Nan transfer to her wheelchair.

"This play. Will you perform it here when you're ready?" Nan asked as Mallory pushed the chair down the long, brightly lit hallway.

Mallory was surprised that Nan even remembered the play Mallory had mentioned fifteen minutes ago. "That's not a bad idea."

"Well, of course not. I don't have bad ideas." Nan's voice held an amused tone. "That's what I used to say."

Mallory stopped pushing the wheelchair momentarily. "Do you like the theater?"

"Oh, I'd say so. I went to New York when I was younger, you know. I wanted to be on Broadway."

"You don't say." Mallory wheeled Nan's wheelchair through the double entry doors to the community room. "What happened when you went to New York?"

"Well, I guess I'd say it wasn't what I expected. Like a lot of things in life."

"Any regrets?" Mallory asked.

"If I do, I don't recall 'em." Nan shrugged. "I think though, I would have regretted never going. I'm glad I went and glad I left." She looked over at Mallory. "I feel in love after that. Or maybe before." Her gaze wandered to the tree. "Oh, how I love a Christmas tree. That one is so big. It's going to be beautiful when it's finished."

Mallory held up the Wooden Heart Ornament. "This one goes sixth from the top." She hadn't read the rest of the ornament's story yet, but she was intrigued.

Nan stared at the ornament as it dangled on Mallory's index finger. "The building we purchased was a money pit," she said quietly, almost under her breath. "It took Mama's every last cent to buy the place, which was maybe more than it was worth."

Nan must not have been remembering correctly. "The community theater is lovely. It's always been a huge staple in Bloom."

"Oh, I know. But only because the man I loved rebuilt every square inch by hand."

As rehearsal came to a close later that evening, Mallory couldn't help but notice that Hollis had seemed less talkative tonight. He wasn't smiling and seemed to be keeping to himself. Had the comment from Esther Woods the night prior gotten to him?

Mallory headed in his direction as the actors and actresses, most of whom she considered friends, slowly made their way out the theater's door. "You okay?"

He blinked himself out of deep thought the way Nan had earlier. "Yeah. Yeah, I'm okay. Just been a long day, that's all."

She pushed her hands into the low-slung pockets of her bulky cardigan sweater. "Yeah. For me too. So, how do you think tonight went?"

"Good. It's amazing how much everyone remembers their lines from year to year."

"Memory is a strange thing. Sometimes you remember something completely random and forget the important stuff. Like the people you love." Mallory had been emotional since visiting Nan earlier. She hadn't expected this all to be so hard. Some part of her thought she should be grateful. She still had time with Nan. It wasn't like Nan was snatched in a moment. It would be a long good-bye versus the kind of exit that didn't give loved ones a chance for real closure.

This wasn't easy though. It was maybe the hardest thing Mallory had ever gone through. "How's the new foster dog?"

"He's coming along. Learning to trust me."

Mallory tilted her head, letting her hair brush along her shoulder. "I'm guessing maybe you're the first owner to treat him well."

Hollis expelled an audible breath. "Except I'm not his owner. I'm temporary."

Mallory shrugged. "You don't have to be."

"A dog trainer who takes in rescues needs to have boundaries. Can't keep 'em all." A light shone in Hollis's eyes when he talked about his dogs. Mallory admired his passion. A passion that visibly lit up a person was rare. Nursing used to be that for her, but admittedly she was in the thick of burnout. Nursing colleagues had warned her of caregiver burnout for years, and she'd always said it wouldn't happen to her. She'd considered herself invincible.

Surprise. She wasn't.

Working long hours and feeling like there were invisible chains strapped to her, preventing her from caring for her patients the way she wanted to, had taken their toll. "How's the plan for the new business going? I know you said you were planning to purchase a building and open full-time next year."

The light in his eyes dimmed just slightly. "Working on it. But, well, Matt needs help with the crew. I hate to leave him high and dry."

"High and dry? You've given ample warning, and there are lots of people around here eager to work."

"Maybe so."

"You'd still work Pop's Farm though, right?"

Hollis shrugged. "As long as Pop has a say. If it were up to Matt, the tree farm would have been sold off by now though. He hasn't said it in so many words, but he's annoyed that I'm keeping it going for Pop. He'd rather take the property to expand his construction business. We need a warehouse and a place for more equipment and trucks."

The injustice of selling someone's life work angered Mallory. "Bloom needs Pop's tree farm."

He narrowed his eyes. "Just like Bloom needs Nan's community theater."

Mallory's argument caught in her throat. He was right. She was considering the same thing that Matt was. "Why does growing up have to involve so much change and compromise?"

Hollis massaged a hand on his forehead. "The other night, Matt invited me to a consultation on a project scheduled for next year. As if I haven't told him a half-dozen times that I'm starting my business in the new year. He actually laughed when I reminded him about my plans."

That didn't sound like the Matt that Mallory knew. Matt was a great guy.

"Guess he thought I was kidding. Or maybe it was genuinely funny to him. He's always harped on how proud he is of building his business from the ground up. He did it. Pop did it. They're man enough to make it happen, but I'm not."

Mallory placed a hand on his shoulder. "Yes, you are. Make him understand that you're serious. Sit him down and make him listen."

Hollis met her eyes. Between the touch and shared gaze, she forgot to breathe for a moment. "That was my plan this week," he said. "I even rehearsed what I was going to say."

"And?"

"And Matt sprung the news on me that he plans to retire in the spring." Hollis's expression was pained. "And he wants to leave the construction business to me. The whole company to me, a kid that no one ever really believed would amount to anything, a foster care kid from juvenile detention that everyone assumed would end up in prison as an adult." He laughed, even though they both knew it wasn't funny.

"Not everyone." She removed her hand from his shoulder. "He, um, must trust you if he's planning to leave you his business."

Hollis nodded. "I've never earned someone's trust like that. The idea of breaking it..." He released a long, pent-up breath. "I don't want to do that. I won't."

"But you deserve to do what makes you happy. You deserve to live your own life and have your own dream."

Hollis cleared his throat. "Do I? Esther Woods doesn't even think I deserve a part in Nan's play."

Mallory gritted her teeth. She had half a mind to take Esther's role away from her. Esther didn't deserve a spot if she was so ready to treat others the way she had Hollis the other night. "Anything wrong you've done in your past was just the actions of a wounded kid who deserved a family."

"A family that I finally got when Matt and Sandy welcomed me into their home. Which is why I'm going to work construction for the rest of my life. Dogs are a hobby. Anyways..." Hollis headed toward the door to leave. "I need to get back to Duke and Buster." He glanced over his shoulder. "You going home too?"

"In a bit."

"You okay here by yourself?" He flicked his gaze around the room and then at the ceiling. "You're not scared of the theater's ghost?"

Mallory let out an unexpected laugh. "I don't believe in ghosts. I do believe in the living though. To include you."

"And I believe in Mallory Blue. In fact, the girl I remember used to love this theater. She's half the reason I came here every day after school."

"Really?" Mallory asked.

Hollis shook his head. "No."

The moment of silence was just long enough to make Mallory feel foolish for thinking he was being real.

"She's the entire reason I spent every afternoon here." He stepped out and closed the door before Mallory could respond. She wasn't sure she could say anything anyway. She was speechless.

Then, as if maybe there was a ghost in the theater after all, her bag beside her fell over and Nan's journal slid out. Instead of packing as planned, Mallory sat in the dark and opened the book to where she'd left off. Her focus was fragmented though, split between the journal's pages, her mixed emotions about Hollis, and the possibility that there might be a ghost in the attic.

The Wooden Heart Ornament

The Wooden Heart ornament is in a small pine box with brass hinges. This ornament is to be hung sixth from the top of your tree.

Here's the story behind it.

It wasn't until after my mother used most of her savings to her name to purchase the old mill to be my theater that we realized it was a hazard. Even standing on the porch of the building meant risking your life because the place was all one breath from crumbling. My mother cried and so did I. Here I was, pregnant and single. Unemployed and the reason that my mother's life savings was gone. When I thought things were finally looking up, they got worse by a landslide.

I'm not sure who told Ralph about the theater, but there are no secrets in Bloom—not for long at least. Ralph was still being weird around me, not that I could blame him.

"I'll rebuild the entire building myself," he told my mother. "Just tell me what you want and I'll do it."

"I can't pay…" she said.

"I wouldn't let you anyway." He didn't hesitate. Somewhere between the time I'd been gone, he'd grown from an almost-man to a full-blown man. A good one too. Someone else's man. "I'll do it free of charge."

"You're trying to win my daughter back?" my mother asked, suspicious as ever.

"There are no conditions to me helping you and Nan. Nan and I may be over, but I still care about her. Let me help."

My mother agreed, and she made sure I knew I didn't owe Ralph anything. I didn't even owe it to him to tell him he was the father of my baby. I didn't want him to feel stuck with me. I knew that if he found out I was carrying our child, he would come back to me. I also knew that I had hurt him. It was a mess of my own making. A wrecking ball of my own choosing.

The following week, Ralph and a few of his friends showed up at the old mill and tore it down. They made a party of it, a bunch of young men taking out their worries and stress by pulling a place apart bit by bit. But then they built something new. Something greater. It took three months of them all working after hours when they weren't at their paying jobs. They worked hard and for free until my very own theater was complete. The Bloom Community Theater. By the time it was done, I was wearing baggy clothing. I'm sure people were talking.

As I looked out on the building that had grown along with my belly, my eye caught a smooth wood piece. Smooth as stone. Perfectly carved. My mind immediately went to earlier that day, around noon, when Ralph had sat on the bottom step, whittling a piece of scrap wood. He always had a pocketknife handy. It wasn't easy to bend over, not these days, but I lowered myself to sit on that same step, and I reached for the wood piece in the shape of a heart. Before I knew it, I was smiling, my thumb running over the trinket that Ralph had left in the dirt. It felt like a treasure.

Picking it up, I studied it. The size. The weight.

"Looks like you found it."

I looked up, surprised to find Ralph standing there, watching me. "Oh. Yeah." Without thinking, I lifted the wooden heart carving toward him.

He pushed it back in my direction. "You keep it."

This is a moment I've often looked back on.

"Thank you for this." Tears flooded my eyes, and the flood of emotion brought with it a wave of nausea. I covered my mouth with one hand. I probably looked green because the next thing I knew, Ralph was holding out a mint.

"Want one?" he asked.

"No. No, no, no." I squeezed my eyes shut and turned away, feeling the bitter taste of bile in my mouth. You would have thought he'd dangled something vile in front of me.

When I opened my eyes, I saw his concern.

"Sorry. I remember how Jillian was when she was pregnant," he said quietly.

Jillian was Ralph's sister who'd had her first baby the year before.

The moment was awkward as we stood there staring at each other. I realized Ralph was comparing me to his pregnant sister.

The bile retreated to make way for my rush of adrenaline. "You know?" I asked.

He offered a brisk nod, avoiding eye contact. "I've known a while. I didn't want to say anything until you were ready to talk about it."

I placed a hand on my belly, feeling a host of emotions. Embarrassment. Shame. Anxiety. Hope. "I wanted to tell you."

"I'm happy for you, Nan. I am." His voice was quiet as he glanced around to make sure no one was overhearing.

"Really?" He didn't look happy. Instead, he looked hollowed out and broken.

"Is the baby why you didn't stay in New York?" he asked.

I rubbed my belly, trying to soothe my nerves. "I guess I would have stayed longer if I wasn't pregnant, but it would have only been to prove myself. I would have stayed because I was too proud to admit how miserable I was there. This baby is such a gift because it forced me to come home. Which is exactly where I wanted to be just as soon as I made it to the big city."

I searched his face for any sign that he wanted us. That he was happy to realize he was going to be a father. My heart fell, taking jerky notches on a downward elevator whose wires were snapping one by one.

"Does the—does the father know?" Ralph finally asked.

At first, I couldn't process the question. Then I realized that no, the father didn't know. In Ralph's mind, I had found someone to replace him as soon as I'd gone to New York. Did he think I'd had a one-night stand?

The realization felt like a slap in the face. He knew me. He was the only man I'd ever been with, and it had taken months of dating for our first time together to even happen. Did he think I had changed that much?

"You could have told me," he said. "I'm guessing it's hard keeping a secret."

"I wanted to." There was still more to tell. My mother had told me I didn't owe him the truth, but I did. I owed it to him and our child. "I…well, I…"

He cleared his throat and looked off into the distance. "I know how it must look to you. Me dating a friend of yours so soon after…us." He looked at me again. As he met my gaze, I saw something in his expression. It wasn't something I was used to seeing in Ralph. "The guys told me the quickest way to get over a broken heart is to jump back into the pond." A laugh tumbled off his lips, but it seemed more sad than humorous. "Anyway, her father offered me a job, and I guess I got carried away. We're getting married next month."

The wooden heart fell out of my hand, hitting the dirt at my feet.

"You've moved on," he said, looking down at my midsection and then away. I watched him swallow slowly and then return to look at me again. "I want you to know that I'm not mad at you. I don't hold whatever happened up there against you." His eyes softened. "And if I hadn't promised myself to someone else, I'd probably try to step in and play the part."

Play the part. As if this were one big stage.

He clearly knew I was pregnant and clearly thought the baby was someone else's. It stung. Not that there was anything wrong if that was the truth, but I hadn't jumped into another pond to get over him. I wasn't over him.

"I don't need a pity dad for my baby," I found myself saying, rising to my feet.

Ralph took a step backward. "Is the father going to help?"

This was the moment. I'm not sure what came over me, but the lie rolled out, fully formed. "He's an actor. Very talented. He doesn't want to be involved, and I'm fine with that. Like I said, I don't want or need a pity daddy."

Ralph seemed at a loss for words. Then he nodded, as if everything I said had made perfect sense. "Well, I'm here. No matter what. Whatever you need, I'll always be here."

It took every ounce of energy I had to hold back the sobs that wanted to rip out of me. They could wait until later when I was alone in my room.

Crouching, he bent and picked up the wood carving and unfolded my fingers to place it in my palm. "You'll always have a special place in my heart, Nan."

Chapter Twelve

Theater is, of course, a reflection of life. Maybe we have to improve life before we can improve theater.

—W. R. Inge

Hollis's phone buzzed on the kitchen counter, the name of the head of the local boys home flashing on the screen. He picked up the phone and answered excitedly. "Hey, Steve. How's it going?"

"Hey, Hollis. Doing all right. Hope you are too." Steve's familiar voice crackled through the speaker. "Listen, I've got three boys here at the home who could really use some work this holiday season. You think Pop's Farm might have a need for a little help?"

Hollis leaned against the counter, memories of his own time at the boys home flooding back. "Absolutely," he said without hesitation. "We could definitely use the extra hands, especially with me tied up with the Christmas play rehearsals."

He knew Steve had already guessed his answer would be yes. Boys from the system had come out to help over the last few years under Hollis's direction. "That's great, Hollis. These kids remind me so much of us at that age. They need a fighting chance, you know?"

"I agree," Hollis said softly. "They can tag trees, wrap them up, load them onto cars. It'll be good for them."

"You're a lifesaver, man," Steve said.

"Happy to help. You know, we should catch up sometime. How've you been doing?"

There was a brief pause before Steve answered. "Taking it one day at a time, you know? But having this job at the home, being able to help these kids, it's good for me."

"Glad to hear it," Hollis said sincerely. He knew Steve had struggled over the years, battling his own demons. "Hey, how's Bart? That beagle still keeping you on your toes?"

Steve laughed. "Man, that dog is the best thing that's ever happened to me. Man's best friend is right. I can't thank you enough for training him."

Hollis felt a warmth spread through his chest. "Dogs have a way of healing us, don't they?"

"They sure do. Healing us and tearing up our best shoes," Steve agreed with a laugh. "Hey, speaking of dogs, I heard you're finally going to open that rescue and training business of yours in the new year. That true?"

"Yeah, it is," Hollis confirmed, excitement bubbling up inside him at the thought. "I've found a great property, just working out the details now."

"That's awesome, man. You know, I was thinking, maybe you could take some of the boys from the home, teach them how to train dogs like you used to do. It could be really good for them, you know?"

The idea had never occurred to him, but now that Steve mentioned it, it seemed perfect. "I'd love to do that. It would give the kids a skill, something to be proud of."

"Exactly," Steve said. "And who knows? Maybe you'll inspire some future dog trainers."

They chatted for a few more minutes, ironing out the details for the boys who would be working at the tree farm. As they wrapped up the call, Hollis felt a renewed sense of purpose. "Thanks for calling, Steve. It's always good to hear from you."

"You too, man. Take care of yourself, all right?"

After hanging up, Hollis stood in his kitchen for a moment, lost in thought. The conversation with Steve had stirred up a lot of memories—some good, some painful. But it had also reinforced his commitment to giving back to the community that had given him so much.

Glancing at the clock, he realized it was time to head to the theater for another rehearsal. His eyes fell on the Santa hat sitting on his dresser. With a grin, he picked it up and placed it on his head. Maybe wearing it would help him get into character.

As he drove to the theater, Hollis's mind wandered from the boys home to Mallory, who'd been on his mind a lot lately. Maybe too much. Every thought he had led back to her and how she would see certain things. What she would say. He'd always valued her opinions, but now he craved them. Talking to her satisfied a need for deep connection.

When he pulled into the theater parking lot, Hollis caught sight of his reflection in the rearview mirror. The Santa hat sat slightly askew on his head, and he couldn't help but grin. Who'd have thought that the troubled kid from the boys home would end up playing Santa in the town's beloved Christmas play?

With a spring in his step and the red Santa hat on his head, Hollis stepped out of his truck and headed into the theater, ready to embrace his role as Santa, both onstage and offstage. After all, wasn't that what the spirit of Christmas was all about? Bringing joy, offering second chances, and believing in the magic of new beginnings.

Christmas music spilled out as he pushed open the theater doors, followed by heated voices coming from the auditorium. Hollis paused for a moment, his gaze jumping around to assess the situation. Esther Woods was wagging a finger in the air while raising her voice at Mallory.

"Your grandmother would be ashamed. Absolutely ashamed."

Hollis zeroed in on Mallory's flushed cheeks. Even from a distance, he could see the shine in her eyes.

"Well, I'm sorry you feel that way," Mallory said in a shaky voice. "If you would like to remove yourself from the performance, I will not stand in your way." She looked at the entire group. "In fact, if any of you are having second thoughts, tell me now so that arrangements can be made to fill the roles. This play is in honor of my grandmother."

"But then you're going to just throw away her life's work," Esther shot back. The older woman turned to face the group. "Mallory isn't telling us the whole story, but at least her sister is honest. They're going to sell this theater right after the holiday. They've already spoken to a real estate agent."

By the look on Mallory's face, that was news to her.

Hollis's feet started walking with a quick, determined pace. "Easy to run your mouth, but how many of you have helped Mallory keep this theater afloat? If you are so concerned, why aren't you donating to the cause? Why is Mallory spending all her money on this project? And, another thing. If you all love Nan so much, why aren't you visiting her at Memory Oaks? I'm there a couple of times a week, and from what I'm told, Mallory and I are the only guests Nan sees." To include Mallory's sister, Maddie.

Esther's mouth gaped open.

"I'll answer that question. It's because you're a hypocrite," Hollis said, focusing on Esther. "And one thing Nan always despised was a person who would say one thing and do another."

"Who are you to talk?" Esther said, wagging that finger of hers again.

"At least I don't pretend to be perfect and judge others for being human." He looked around at everyone except Mallory because he was worried she might be upset with him right now. "So? Who's staying? This is the point-of-no-return moment. You're either in or out, but decide now, because we have a play that the entire town is depending on."

Esther shook her head with disgust. "I'm out. This is a disgrace." She looked at the others. "Who's with me?"

The members of the cast looked at each other, no one moving or speaking. There was a long silence finally punctuated by Esther's exasperated sigh.

"Whatever." She threw her arms up in the air and then grabbed her coat to storm out.

Hollis lowered his voice as he sidled up beside Mallory. "Sorry if I overstepped."

She looked up at him, the shine still in her eyes. "No, you're not."

He grimaced because she was right. "Well, I'm sorry if I upset you."

"You didn't." She didn't look exactly happy though. Raising her voice, she addressed the group. "Does the fact that the rest of you are still here mean you're in this for the long haul?"

The cast members nodded.

"We know you're doing your absolute best and your best is no less than your grandmother's. We're not just here to support Nan. We support you too," Marvin Long, the town's former mayor, said.

"Thank you." Mallory took a deep breath and then clapped her hands together. "Well, then let's do this. Let's run the play from beginning to end without our scripts. We better start now or we'll be here all night."

Hollis admired the way Mallory stayed strong when he knew she probably felt like crumbling. He'd come to see that most people were doing the same. Barely convincing the world around them that they had their act together. Maybe that's why Esther had just behaved so rudely.

They ran through the script, and when Esther's lines came up,

Hollis took the initiative to say them. They rolled through the motions without skipping a beat. When the curtain closed, everyone talked among themselves as they collected their belongings and said good-bye to one another. Hollis stayed, like he'd been doing since the first night of rehearsals.

Mallory finally looked at him. "Thank you for tonight. Now I just need to find a real actress to fill Esther's role. With three weeks until opening night."

Hollis held out his arms. "No, you don't. I'll do it." When Mallory gave him a strange look, he held out a palm. "Granted, it's a female role. Just change the part of the mother to a father and I'm your guy."

Mallory gave him a strange look. "You're already playing Santa."

"In a costume, covered from head to toe. None of the Santa scenes are shared with Esther's part. I'll be Father Christmas and the part of Little Ella's Father. No problem."

Mallory's eyes searched his, as if she didn't believe he was being serious at first. "I've lost count of how many favors you've given me in the last month."

"I just want you to be happy." Truly, regardless of his promise to Nan. That was why he was here. And why he'd showed up to this very theater every day after school as a kid.

Mallory released a soft laugh.

"Why is that funny?"

She shook her head. "I don't know. Happiness feels like such a childish concept. Is there any such thing as real happiness or is it some make-believe thing. Like Santa Claus." She gestured to the Santa hat on his head.

"Wait. You're telling me Santa isn't real?" He didn't take her smile at face value because she'd just told him that she didn't believe in true happiness anymore.

"Are you sure you can handle taking on a whole other role? This one has a lot of lines to learn."

Apparently, she hadn't realized that he'd been reading his lines tonight without a script. He puffed up his chest and began to recite the new lines, one by one, as Mallory's lips parted and her eyes subtly widened.

"How did you do that?"

"I know all the lines. I've been attending this play every year since I was a kid. If every single cast member decides to quit, I've got you covered. I'll be like Tyler Perry in all those Madea movies. Or Eddie Murphy in *The Nutty Professor*."

Mallory tilted her head. "You'd even take the roles of the ladies in ball gowns? I'm not sure I have a gown that will fit you."

Hollis loved the teasing glint in her eyes, a spark of life, even though the burden on her shoulders was heavy lately. "How about we just keep the actresses in the fancy gowns happy so that they don't quit."

"Probably a good idea."

"Yeah." Nervousness bubbled up inside him. "I have another good idea."

She lifted a brow. "Do tell."

"Hot chocolate," he said.

"Now?" She looked taken aback.

"Why not now? I'm always in the mood for hot chocolate in the winter. Plus we have a lot to celebrate."

"Celebrate?" she repeated, looking unconvinced. "What are we celebrating?"

"You. The way you've been such a rock star in organizing this play. Your grandmother would be so proud of you. You're making plans to take care of her, and you're basically just kicking butt being you."

Mallory crossed her arms over her chest. "First off, the play is a mess. I've already had two people drop out, one because they don't believe in my ability to pull this off. And the only way to take care of Nan is to sell the place she loved the most in the whole world, which my sister, Maddie, is in favor of. We're selling our grandmother's legacy."

"Well, in my mind, you're a rock star," Hollis said. "And rock stars deserve hot cocoa. So what do you say?"

Mallory glanced around the empty theater and looked at him again. "Only if I can pay. I owe you so much at this point. Not only for me, but for connecting Maddie with your friend. She's texted me a few pictures this past week. She's cycling again. And she's talking about rock climbing." Mallory released a laugh. "I can't tell you how happy that makes me. Nervous, but in a good way."

"There's a difference between being excited for others and doing things for yourself, to fulfill yourself."

She narrowed her eyes. "What do you mean?"

"What makes you happy? That's what I'm interested in."

Chapter Thirteen

Life is a play that does not allow testing. So, sing, cry, dance, laugh, and live intensely, before the curtain closes and the piece ends with no applause.

—Charlie Chaplin

While sitting up in bed, Mallory lowered Nan's journal to her lap and leaned her head back against the wall. There was so much she never knew about Nan's life. How amazing that she was meeting the younger version of her grandmother as the older version was slowly disappearing inside herself.

Closing the journal, Mallory placed it on the nightstand beside her. She was forcing herself to read just one entry at a time, no more. She wanted to savor these stories. She was about to turn the bedside lamp off and go to sleep when her cell phone vibrated against the table's glass surface. Mallory flicked her gaze at the clock. Ten p.m. She reached for her phone and glanced at the screen.

Hollis: Good night. Thanks for having cocoa with me earlier.

Their outing had been brief on purpose. Otherwise, Hollis might have considered it a date. Nan had warned Mallory against falling for him when they were younger, before the thought had even crossed Mallory's mind.

"I love Hollis. I do," Nan told Mallory with a small frown. "But he's had a hard life. Hollis has been hurt far more than we even know. And the thing that life has taught me is that hurt people hurt others. It's just the way of life. That boy has never had love so he'll never know what to do with it when some foolish woman hands him her heart."

Foolish woman.

Mallory remembered being shocked by the phrase. From Mallory's experience, Nan wasn't a judgmental person. Now that Mallory had started reading Nan's story, however, Mallory wondered if Nan had been thinking of herself when she'd said those words: hurt people hurt people. Nan had been hurt in her life, and Mallory was only beginning to learn the depths of that pain. Nan had never hurt anyone though. Or Mallory wouldn't have thought her grandmother would have.

Even though Mallory had ignored her attraction for Hollis, when she was around him, her heart still kicked a little harder. She'd enjoyed having hot cocoa with him tonight. He'd flirted with her, but he hadn't done anything out of line. Hollis was a complete gentleman.

Maybe Nan wasn't right about everything. Maybe Hollis had been hurt in his childhood, but Matt and Sandy had been good to him. Mallory believed that people changed. She believed that loved conquered all. She had also believed that, if her heart was in the right place, everything would turn out okay, and look where that Pollyanna-mindset had gotten her.

Picking up her phone, Mallory tapped out a reply to Hollis.

Mallory: I enjoyed it as well.

Hollis: Maybe we should do it again sometime.

Mallory: Hot cocoa?

Hollis: Not necessarily. I was thinking more about joining me for a shopping date.

Mallory's brain stumbled on that unusual request. If Savannah invited her to go shopping, that would be different.

Hollis: I typically go shopping for the boys home and buy some things on the kids' holiday wish list. Shopping isn't exactly my favorite thing, but with you...

Mallory's heart melted in a puddle of goo. He'd said "shopping date" though, which made her hesitate. The *d*-word was daunting. Was he asking for help or for something different?

Mallory: Maybe so.

Hollis: How about this weekend?

Her hand shook as she clutched the cell phone in her hand. Before responding, she clicked out of her chat with Hollis and opened her ongoing text thread with Savannah.

Mallory: S.O.S.!

Mallory saw the little gray dots begin to bounce on her screen, letting her know that Savannah was responding.

Savannah: What's up? Everything okay?

Mallory: No. Maybe. I think Hollis just asked me out.

Savannah: What?!?!?! Finally! You said yes, right?

Mallory: No. Not yet. I'm not sure I'm going to. I'm not even sure if it would be a date... I can't date Hollis.

Savannah: Why not?

Mallory considered her reasons. Because she was busy. Tired. Stressed. Because Nan needed her. And dating seemed like one more job. Because this was Hollis. He was her friend, and they had too much history. Another text came in from Savannah.

Savannah: Psst... Hollis is texting Evan right now. He's freaking because he asked you out and now you're ghosting him.

Mallory let out a squeal. She was taking too long trying to decide what to do.

Savannah: Just say yes. What's the worst that could happen?

It was supposed to be a comforting thought when people asked that question, but for Mallory, all the worst-case scenarios flooded her mind. The absolute worst-case would be losing Hollis as a friend. She valued having him in her life so much. What if they were awkward? What if the chemistry wasn't there? What if things happened between them and they crossed the uncrossable line? There'd be no going back.

Savannah sent another text.

Savannah: You're torturing Hollis. Say yes and put that poor man out of his misery. Say yes, Mal. You need this—a reason to smile.

Wow. Had her life become that serious? She knew the answer was yes, and she knew that Hollis was the main reason she found herself smiling lately.

Mallory: Okay, fine. I'll go out with him. But you have to rescue me if it's a disaster.

Savannah: You're my best friend. I'll always rescue you. But this is Hollis. If it's awkward, you just tell him. Then he'll come home, whine to Evan, and I'll tell you every word.

Savannah followed that text up with a laughing face emoji.

Savannah: How perfect that both of you have best friends to spy on the other. This will be so much fun.

Mallory fidgeted with the hem of her sweater as she stood in front of her bedroom mirror. Her heart raced as she glanced at the clock for what felt like the hundredth time in the past hour. Hollis would be here any minute to pick her up for their shopping date. She couldn't deny the butterflies in her stomach or the warmth that spread through her chest at the thought of him.

No. They were friends. Feeling this way about him was already crossing a line.

As she applied a final touch of lip gloss, Nan's warnings about Hollis echoed in her mind.

Nan had been one of Hollis's biggest supporters, and yet she hadn't wanted Mallory to be more than friends with Hollis just because he'd come from a rocky past. Her past hadn't been all that smooth either. She'd been raised by her grandparents. If not for Nan and Grandpa Mickey, she'd have been in the foster care system too.

She took a deep breath, smoothing down her hair one last time. Then she turned as the doorbell's chime sent a jolt through her body. Her hands trembled slightly as she grabbed her purse and made her way to the front door. With one final steadying breath, she turned the handle and pulled it open.

Hollis stood on her porch, looking uncharacteristically nervous and holding a beautiful bouquet of white daisies. "Hey," Hollis said, his voice a touch softer than usual. "Uh, these are for you." He extended the bouquet in his hand.

Mallory's fingers brushed against his as she took the flowers. "Wow. Thank you. These are…beautiful." And completely unexpected.

Hollis rubbed a hand along the back of his neck. "I've never brought a woman flowers before. Maybe that's what I've been doing wrong all these years. Maybe that's why I'm still single."

Her heart skipped a beat. "If you've never brought anyone else flowers, why start now?"

The intensity of his eyes as they searched hers made her knees want to buckle. "I guess no other woman has inspired me to get flowers until now."

She buried her nose in the daisies, inhaling their sweet scent while trying to hide her expression, which would probably give away too much. She could feel the heat in her cheeks. And yeah, Savannah was right. She was smiling—hard. "Daisies are my favorite flower."

"I know."

Mallory waited for him to look at her again.

A shadow of something—maybe regret—passed over his expression. "You told me back when we were teens. That year we had leading roles. I mean, you could have changed your mind. Women have every right to do that."

Mallory laughed.

"You can change your mind now too. If you want. I wouldn't blame you."

She lowered the flowers, suddenly confused. Was he trying to back down from this date?

"I actually bought you a bouquet of daisies that night. Opening night. When we were teens."

Mallory shook her head. "What are you talking about?"

"But then my old insecurities got the best of me." He trailed off, looking ashamed. "I broke into my foster dad's liquor cabinet, maybe for liquid courage or maybe because I never felt worthy of Nan's trust. Or yours."

"So you got drunk, walked into the audience, and booed me?" she asked, feeling the hurt from that night rise inside her as she remembered seeing Hollis stumble into the back of the auditorium.

"I bought you a bouquet of daisies that day." Hollis's voice was strained.

Why was he telling her this right now? Before they'd even left for their first date.

"Obviously, I chickened out that night, so here you go." He gestured at the flowers. "Long overdue."

Mallory stood there, stunned. The flowers in her hands suddenly held so much more meaning—an apology, a plea for forgiveness, and perhaps something more. He was laying everything on the table and giving her an opportunity to change her mind about stepping off this porch with him. "Hollis, I..."

"I just wanted you to know that I remember everything, and I'm sorry. I've been trying to make up for that night ever since."

"That's why you asked me out and brought me flowers tonight?" she asked.

He looked down momentarily. "Not entirely. The main reason is the same one I needed liquid courage for that first opening night. I liked you. I still like you. I just didn't like myself back then." A grin kicked up on his lips. "I like myself now. And I still like you. A lot, actually."

Chapter Fourteen

Don't wait for the perfect moment. Take the moment and make it perfect!

—Aryn Kyle

The bustling department store was a riot of Christmas colors and tinkling carols as Hollis and Mallory navigated the aisles, their shopping cart gradually filling with items for the local boys home. Hollis couldn't help but steal glances at Mallory, still hardly believing that this was their first official date.

"Okay, next on the list is…warm socks." Hollis consulted the crumpled paper in his hand as Mallory steered them toward the appropriate aisle.

"Socks are always a good gift," she mused.

Hollis chuckled, a hint of melancholy in his voice. "You'd think so, wouldn't you? But one Christmas at the boys home, all I got was a pack of new socks and a Lakers hat. The socks weren't even my size."

Mallory's eyes widened. "I'm sorry."

He shrugged it off. "I gave the socks to another kid who could use them. But, man, I'd been hoping for a Green Bay Packers hat. Guess beggars can't be choosers, right?"

Mallory reached out and squeezed his arm gently. "You weren't a beggar. You were a child who deserved so much more than you got."

Her touch sent a warmth through him, and Hollis found himself opening up further about a topic he rarely talked about with anyone. "It's funny how those memories stick with you, you know? But hey, it made me appreciate what I have now."

As they continued shopping, picking up toiletries, school supplies, and warm clothing, Hollis found himself having a better time than he'd had in ages. Their hands brushed as they reached for gifts, and each accidental touch sent a jolt of electricity through him.

"How 'bout you?" Hollis asked as they debated between two different board games to put in the shopping cart. "What were your Christmases like growing up?"

Mallory's expression turned wistful. "Oh, the holidays were nice. Nan and Grandpa Mickey always tried their best. But…I was always afraid to ask for too much. I didn't want to be a burden, you know?"

Hollis nodded. "I understand that."

"I usually asked for things I knew Maddie wanted," she said. "That way, she'd get more presents."

"Sounds like you and I have more in common than I would have thought," he said softly.

Mallory's eyes twinkled as she looked up at him. "You think?"

Hollis offered a playful smirk. "The difference is, your hardships made you the 'good girl' while mine made me the 'bad boy.'"

She laughed, the sound warming Hollis from the inside out. "Oh, please." She nudged him with her elbow. "I'll have you know, I had my share of rebellion… And you're not the bad boy anymore, Hol. You're just…a really nice one."

Her words hit him with an unexpected blow. He had to look away momentarily to compose himself. When he turned back, Mallory was studying the boys home wish list intently.

"Looks like we've got everything." She ran her finger down the items. "Check. Check. Check... Oh, wait, no. There's one more item we need."

"What's that?"

Mallory steered their cart toward the men's clothing department. He followed, wondering what on earth they'd forgotten. He'd been tracking the list as they'd walked through the large department store.

He watched Mallory scan the racks with purpose, finally zeroing in on a display of sports merchandise.

"Aha!" She plucked a Green Bay Packers hat from the shelf and held it out to him. "We're getting this."

His throat was tight as he stared at the hat that had been on his teenage Christmas wish. "Mal, that's not on the list..."

"Maybe not this list." She tapped the paper. "But it was on a list at one point. I'm buying this for you as an early Christmas gift, and I'm not taking no for an answer."

Hollis's fingers brushed against hers as he took the familiar green-and-gold ball cap. He cleared his throat, some part of him wishing he hadn't told Mallory the story about this hat he'd wanted because now he felt vulnerable and was fighting back tears.

Stepping closer, she placed the hat on his head. "There." She adjusted the cap slightly. "It's not a Santa hat, but it looks good on you."

"Thank you. This means more than you know."

Mallory's smile was soft and understanding. "We have a lot in common, remember? I think I have an idea."

They stood there for a moment, lost in each other's eyes, the bustling store fading away in the background. That's when he knew. It wasn't the hat that was on his wish list this year. It was the woman in front of him.

"Come on," Mallory said finally, breaking the spell. "Let's pay for all this stuff and get it to the boys home. I bet they're excited for their Christmas surprises."

After paying at the checkout, they loaded the gifts into Hollis's truck as the winter sun was setting, casting a golden glow over the parking lot. Hollis turned to Mallory, taking in her flushed cheeks and bright eyes.

"That was so much fun," she gushed.

"Yeah. Thanks for coming with me today. And for the hat." He tapped the brim of the cap.

"I've always loved shopping, but buying things for kids was extra fun," she said once she was seated beside him in his truck.

Hollis shopped for the boys home every year, but he'd never enjoyed it as much as this afternoon. "Well, let's keep the fun going."

She gave him a curious look. "What do you have in mind?"

"It's a surprise." He cast her a sideward glance and put his truck in motion. "You'll love it. Trust me." They'd had to drive outside of town to go shopping, so the ride back to Bloom was lengthy, which Hollis didn't mind. Twenty minutes later, he pulled into the parking lot for the Bloom Café.

"Mm. I think I like this surprise," Mallory said with a growing grin. "More hot cocoa? Are we planning to sit inside?"

He shook his head and leaned forward to glance up at the sky through his windshield. "No way. It'll be dark soon."

Mallory paused before pushing open the passenger door. "You're a secret werewolf? I knew it."

He opened the door to the Bloom Café for her as they walked in. "Not a werewolf. Just a secret lover of Christmas lights. And I know where all the best ones are. Shh. Don't tell anyone."

She pretended to zip her lips. "Secret's safe with me."

Mallory sighed as Hollis drove slowly around some of the older neighborhoods in Bloom thirty minutes later. "I love Christmas lights." The houses were massive with large open yards lit up with elaborate decorations and festive scenes.

"There was this foster family who took me to look at lights one year," Hollis shared. "The Dusters. They liked to pile in their minivan and drive painstakingly slow around neighborhoods like these to admire the lights. I remember thinking, *What's the big deal? It's just lights.*" He pulled up to a stop sign and stopped, even though there were no other cars around. "But as I watched this family and their real kids ohhing and ahhing, I kind of slipped into the excitement of it all. At first, I was trying to fit in. I was always trying to fit in." Pressing the gas, he let his truck continue rolling forward.

"But you like the lights now?" she asked.

He stole the hundredth glance at her tonight. "Oh, yeah. They're not boring anymore."

"Definitely not boring. Magical. My grandpa Charlie used to take Maddie and me to see the lights."

"Magical with you for sure." He shook his head and laughed quietly at himself. "I'm definitely cheesy tonight."

"I think you're being sweet."

"Good. That's what I'm going for." Hollis rolled into a vacant parking area in front of Bloom Lake and turned off the engine. From across the lake, a million more bright and colorful lights could be seen from the houses on the other side.

"Why didn't you stay with that family? The one who drove around looking at lights? They sound nice."

"They were. So nice that I messed up their vibe." He sighed. "Not their fault. It's just who I was back then. I was angry and rebellious. I pushed buttons on purpose."

"Because you wanted them to send you away?" she asked.

"Because I wanted them to prove that they weren't going to send me away. I know. It was a messed-up plan."

She reached for his hand. The feel of her soft skin covering his sent shivers down his spine. He looked over at Mallory and noticed the tears in her eyes.

"Hey, what's wrong?" Because making his date cry was not on his bingo card for tonight.

"I just wish I would've been one of those people who proved that you were worth the extra effort. Instead of being one of those—"

"Instead of being one of those who discarded me," he supplied. "Mal, you were one of the first people to prove I was worth more." Shifting in the seat, he angled his body toward her. "Actually, let me rephrase. You were one of the first people to make me want to be more than I was."

She looked away for a millisecond. "I'm not any good at this."

"At what?" he asked.

She looked at him again. "I don't really go on many dates. It's hard for me to relax, and I certainly don't know how to respond when someone is showering me with compliments and telling me how I've changed their life. I just... I don't know what to say. Or what to do."

His hand covered hers. "You're doing a fairly good job right now... If it helps you feel better, I'm not any good at this stuff either. All I know is—" He shook his head.

"What?" she asked.

He weighed whether to tell her. "I want to kiss you right now, maybe more than I've ever wanted to kiss anyone in my entire life. But I don't want to ever do anything you're not comfortable with."

Mallory's eyes sparkled with the lights reflecting off the water into the front windshield. Then she leaned in his direction. "Maybe I want you to kiss me too."

His heart felt like a fish that had flopped right out of that lake in front of them, landing on the banks, gasping for breath that could only be found on her lips. "Maybe?"

"Definitely."

"You don't have to ask me twice," he said, his voice dipping low as he leaned in the rest of the way, hoping he didn't screw this moment up because this would be their first kiss, but he sure as heck didn't want it to be their last.

The End Ornament

The End. It's the two most precious words a writer can type. Find this ornament in the box numbered with a 7. It should fall right around the middle of your tree on the branches. The middle of a play is always the intermission, but here's a secret. The intermission is for the audience. The characters in the story usually feel like that moment is The End.

Here's the story.

After Ralph and the crew finished up the theater, my mother paid them to build a tiny home for me and the baby to live in right there in the back of the property. It wasn't much bigger than a living room, but in that space, I had a bedroom, a bathroom, and a small kitchen. A laundry room too!

While the tiny home was being built, I wrote my first play. I wanted it to be the theater's first production and, appropriately, I titled it *Santa, Baby* because Christmas was coming and so was this ball of joy growing inside me. I'd come to terms with my first love marrying another woman. I won't say it didn't hurt watching them exchange their vows. My mother begged me not to attend. I think she worried I might stand up and object to the union. I didn't. I stayed quiet, fancying myself a martyr because Ralph would surely pick the baby and me if he knew the truth. Was that what he wanted?

In hindsight, I know that's all rubbish. I was young and foolish though.

"Thought you wanted to be a star," Mickey Whatley said one night, taking a seat beside me on a little love-seat in the theater dressing room. Mickey had helped with the construction of the theater and the house. He'd taken to lingering after the work, not in a bad way. His company was nice.

"I am the star," I said, this silly grin on my face. "I feel like the main character in this play as I'm writing it. I can see everything in my mind. My mind is, well, it's the stage, I guess."

"So, if you're the star in your head in that play of yours, who's the leading man?" he asked.

Ralph. I couldn't say that, of course. Ralph was a married man now.

"Listen, Nan," Mickey said, "I know I'm not some handsome actor. I know I'm just some small-town guy. I can't give you the world…"

The serious note in his voice caught me by surprise. I remember thinking he was so cocky on that date we'd gone on, but now I saw something different. Had I mistaken his efforts to impress me?

"A baby needs a father figure. A mother needs support."

"I'm fine," I said.

"I know. You're a strong woman, Nan. That's what I admire about you. You're strong and smart. Maybe you don't fancy me that way."

"What way?" I asked.

"The way I fancy you."

The air was thick. Here I was, pregnant. My feet were swollen. I had reflux. And I was starving. Insatiable. "What are you trying to say, Mickey?"

He looked nervous. Adorably so.

"We've been on one date," I told him. And I'd had my eye on someone else for half of that night. "I may be mistaken, but you are talking nonsense."

"One date, but I've known you our entire lives. Nan, I've always liked you."

"What are you saying?"

I expected him to rise to his feet to look at me, but instead, he dropped to one knee and fumbled for something in his pocket.

"Mickey? What—what are you doing? For heaven's sake, get up."

Then he raised a small velvet box toward me. "You and your baby should have a man to provide and protect." He shook his head. "I know you can do it alone, Nan, but you are a star. I don't want you to burn out. I want to help you shine."

My jaw must have been on the floor. "I won't marry for money."

"Then marry for love. The possibility of it." He rose to his feet now, standing a foot taller than me. He was so close, and I felt a flutter. A tiny flutter with the possibility of becoming more.

"You want to marry a swollen pregnant woman?"

"Only if she's you," he said, his voice dipping low. This was a very different Mickey than who I'd always assumed him to be.

"You'll be souring your good name, marrying someone who's pregnant with another man's child. I know what people are saying about me. They're talking."

Mickey shrugged. "Let's change the narrative. Give 'em something else to discuss."

"Like?" I asked, that fluttering feeling growing stronger.

"Like a wedding."

Time sped up from there. Suddenly, it was our wedding day, and the baby kicked wildly as I stepped into my rose-colored wedding dress. My mother wouldn't hear of me wearing white when it was plain as day that I hadn't saved myself for my wedding night. She was old-fashioned that way, and said if I did wear white, all everyone would be talking about was that I wore a color that represented purity.

The gazebo was special. Everyone who'd ever married there was still together. Marriages in Bloom Gardens under that gazebo lasted forever. "Here Comes the Bride" played and my father walked me down the aisle, which was a series of stepping-stones into the garden. I held Mickey's hands, and my heart was full. Under that gazebo, in front of our friends and family, including Ralph, we made vows and shared our first kiss as man and wife. Then we danced. We ate. We celebrated. And after all was said and done, we retreated to the honeymoon cottage. It was expensive, but Mickey's family had money. They had clout. And I knew that he would trade all of it for me and my child.

We made love that night, and it was, well, awkward. I was pregnant after all. It was also special. I initiated because Mickey was a gentleman. He was so many things I'd never realized. Afterward, lying in bed exhausted from it all, he laid a hand on my belly, and I closed my eyes. Soon, he moved his face to my stomach, and he began to whisper to our baby.

Tears streamed down my cheeks as I listened. He was going to be an amazing father to our child.

"You haven't even done anything yet," I heard him say. "But even so, you are loved. You are cherished. You are enough, no matter what this life brings."

I laid my hand on my stomach too, wanting to

connect with my baby. Our baby. In that moment, Mickey became the father, biological or not. As he fell asleep, I reached for my little pad of paper and my pen and finished my first stage play. It was the messy story of Santa and Mrs. Claus. A love story that wasn't perfect. And as much as I wished I felt differently, the hero in the play that took place in my mind was still Ralph.

I couldn't help my feelings, amplified by my baby hormones. But I also had feelings for Mickey, slow-growing but real. Love wasn't what I thought it was. That narrative of there only being one—The One… Maybe there were two. Or there could be.

My hand shook as I wrote these two words. The End. Looking back at my husband, I returned to bed for a new beginning.

Chapter Fifteen

The theater is a tragic place, full of endings and partings and heartbreak.

—Iris Murdoch

Mallory tried to read a page in Nan's journal, but the words blurred in front of her tired eyes. She'd spent most of the night before gazing up into the darkness, replaying her date with Hollis. She chewed her bottom lip as she sat in the office chair at the theater with Nan's journal in her lap.

Mallory had come to the theater early this morning to meet with a property inspector. It was a precursor to selling the theater. Her phone buzzed from the desk where she'd placed it. She set Nan's journal down and reached for it, reading a text from her sister.

Maddie: Is the inspector there yet?

Mallory: Still waiting. How's your morning hike with Renee?

Mallory couldn't fault Maddie for ditching her for the great outdoors. It was Maddie's passion. The fact that she was rediscovering it made Mallory's heart full.

Maddie: You won't believe what Renee wants to do. She's trying to open a whole adaptive sports business. For Bloom and surrounding towns.

Mallory grinned as she watched a series of emojis fill her phone screen.

Mallory: Sounds cool.

Maddie: Very! Not just for people in wheelchairs. Renee wants to welcome all abilities. Even yours.

That text was followed by a winking emoji that made Mallory laugh.

A knock on the front entrance door got Mallory's attention.

Mallory: The inspector's here. Gotta go. Be safe!

Mallory headed toward the main entrance and opened the door to a large man in a pale blue uniform shirt tucked into a pair of dark rinse jeans.

"Hello, ma'am. I'm Jimmy Benson with the county inspection department."

Mallory put out her hand for the man to shake. "Hi, I'm Mallory Blue." She gestured behind her. "Please, come inside."

Mallory suddenly felt nervous, even though she didn't think she had any reason to be. "Um, how long will this take?" Because there were rehearsals this evening. The rumor mill was already active in Bloom, but Mallory didn't want to feed it.

"Not too long. Unless of course there's something wrong," Jimmy said. "More than an hour is never a good sign."

"Oh. Okay." Mallory nodded. "Well, don't let me bother you. If you need something, let me know."

"You're selling this place, huh?" Jimmy's gaze ping-ponged around the front entrance area. "That's a shame. I used to come to the theater with my nanny when I was a kid. She loved theater. Used to sing Broadway songs to me as I was falling asleep."

Mallory smiled politely. "That's nice."

"Yeah." Jimmy hooked his thumbs in the pockets of his jeans. "All right. Well, I'll find you when I'm done."

"Great." Mallory pointed at the office. "I'll be right in there."

"Sure thing."

As Jimmy went forward with his work, Mallory returned to Nan's office, where there were several boxes of stuff packed up and sealed with masking tape. On the top of the boxes, in black Sharpie marker, she'd written STUFF TO KEEP. So far, there was more to keep than give away. She couldn't keep it all though. In fact, at some point, she'd have to open those sealed boxes and get rid of at least half. Maddie already said she didn't want it. Maddie liked to say that she lived in the moment and holding on to sentimental things kept a person in the past.

Maybe there was truth to that.

Plopping into Nan's leather chair, Mallory released a soft sigh. Then she startled at the sound of a tap on the office door.

"Knock, knock," a woman's voice said.

Mallory turned toward the voice. "Savannah. How did you get in?"

Savannah crinkled her brow in response. "The door, just like anyone else."

Savannah didn't need permission to come inside, of course. She was welcome anytime.

"I didn't know I'd be seeing you today."

"Well, I was just out and about and thought I'd see if you needed a hand." Savannah glanced around the small office space. "What can I do?"

"Sit and keep me company. And convince me that I don't need to keep all of Nan's belongings." Because Nan had never been a hoarder. If she'd kept these things, it meant they were important to her. But Mallory didn't recognize half of them.

"I can definitely keep you company." Savannah sat right down on the floor and picked up a small frame made from Popsicle sticks. "Keep, trash, or giveaway?" Savannah asked, holding it up. Without waiting for Mallory's response, she decided, "I vote keep. It's sentimental."

"That's the problem. Everything is sentimental." Mallory tipped her head at the frame. "Toss." She swiped the Popsicle frame from

Savannah's hand and dropped it in the trash pile. Then Mallory reached for a homemade card that she had made for Nan when she was in second or third grade. "This whole drawer is full of things that Maddie or I made for Nan."

"Aw. That's sweet." Savannah tilted her head to one side. "It shows how much she loved you."

"I know. My grandparents must have loved us to put up with some of the things we put them through." Mostly Maddie, who had been the wilder, more irresponsible of the two. The ying to Mallory's yang.

"We can't just trash all these treasures. They're memories," Savannah said wistfully.

Mallory stared at the discard pile. The things there were physical representations of the memories that Nan was losing. Savannah was right. Trashing them wasn't the right thing to do. Mallory wasn't sure what was, which was becoming a theme in her life these days.

"Subject change," Savannah said, visibly perking up. "I need the deets on what's going on with you and Hollis. Are you two official yet?"

Mallory rolled her eyes, even as she felt a small smile lift the corners of her lips. "We've had one date, Sav." Mallory held up a finger for emphasis. "One."

"And? Are you going out again?" Savannah leaned in as Mallory narrowed her eyes.

"I'm on to you. You didn't come to help. You came over to interrogate me."

Savannah laughed. "Isn't that what friends do? Interrogation. Aka, best friend talk."

Mallory sighed. "I have too much going on in my life right now. Too much uncertainty. Hollis and I are just having fun. That's all."

"Fun?" Disappointment flashed in her expression. "Does he know that?"

"Of course. His life is the same as mine."

Savannah looked confused. "What are you talking about? Hollis has had the same job since he was a teenager. He's as steady as they come these days. Or do you know something I don't?"

Mallory tossed another card in the bin. "See? More interrogation. Why don't you tell me about what's going on with you and Evan?" Mallory effectively flipped the conversation to Savannah and partly listened as she cleared out the bottom drawer of the desk and her thoughts splintered into a million directions, one of which was Hollis and the date they'd had this past weekend.

Before she knew it, an hour had passed and Jimmy knocked on the office door, looking less friendly than he had earlier.

"Hi, Jimmy. Everything okay?" Mallory asked, her heart dropping as she took in his demeanor. Instead of smiling, he wore a deep frown that made him look ten years older.

"Afraid not."

"What is it?" She really couldn't take any more bad news, but from the look on Jimmy's face, that's exactly what she was about to receive.

Jimmy glanced at Savannah and back to Mallory. "Maybe we should discuss this privately?"

Savannah shook her head and reached for Mallory's hand. "I know you like to handle things on your own, but I'm not allowing it. I'm staying."

Mallory was relieved by Sav's insistence. It was getting harder to carry life's burdens on her own. "Thank you," she whispered before turning to Jimmy. "Bad news before the good. Give me the bad news first."

His frown deepened. "I'm sorry to say there is no good news."

Once Jimmy had left, Mallory paced back and forth in the empty theater, her heels echoing off the worn wooden stage. Her hands shook as she ran them through her hair, her mind racing with panic.

"What am I going to do, Sav? You heard Jimmy. The theater isn't safe for the production. There are leaks in the pipes, and some of the wood under the flooring is wet. There's mold in the air. We can't perform here. All this work, all Nan's hopes…it's all falling apart."

"Just stop for a second," Savannah said. "Stop pacing and look at me."

Mallory gulped a breath and faced her best friend.

"We'll figure something out, okay?" Savannah said. "It's not the end of the world."

No. Just the end of a world that Nan had created. A world that Mallory had grown up in and had adored.

"I've been killing myself trying to make this work. Every night, I'm up worrying about money, about Nan, about this damn play. And now…now it's all for nothing!" They probably wouldn't even be able to sell the theater, which meant no money to keep Nan at Memory Oaks. This was the worst possible news.

"It's not for nothing," Savannah said firmly, getting up and stepping closer to her friend. "You've been doing an amazing job. We'll put our brains together and figure it out. Maybe Maddie has an idea. I'm sure she'd want to know what's going on."

Mallory nibbled on her fingernail. "Maddie won't be sad that we'll have to cancel. Trust me."

"Cancel? Aren't you getting ahead of yourself?" Savannah asked.

Mallory didn't think so. If the theater was shut down, then so was *Santa, Baby*. The actors would be so disappointed. Everyone would.

Savannah pulled her into a tight hug, rubbing soothing circles on her back. "You don't have to do everything alone. Lean on the people who love you. Let us help you figure things out."

For a moment, Mallory allowed herself to sink into the embrace. Then she pulled back and wiped her eyes. "Not right now. I need to go for a drive. That's how I clear my head. I just… I need to be alone for a little while."

Savannah's face creased with worry. "I don't think you should be alone right now. Not when you're so upset. Let me call Hollis."

"No. No, I just need some time." Mallory was already heading toward the front door, grabbing her purse on the nearby hook along with her keys. "I'll be fine. I just need some air and some space to think," she called behind her.

"Mallory!"

Mallory didn't stop to respond. Instead, she pushed through the theater doors, welcomed by the cool air against her hot cheeks. She fumbled with her keys, her hands shaking as she unlocked the car door.

Part of her knew Savannah was right. She should call Hollis, or Maddie, or anyone. She shouldn't be alone right now.

But the larger part of her, the part that had been taking care of everyone else for so long, couldn't bear the thought of being vulnerable or admitting she couldn't handle it all.

With a shaky breath, she slid into the driver's seat and turned the ignition. She needed to drive, to feel the road beneath her tires, to lose herself in the familiar rhythm of the town she loved so much. She needed to figure out her next move, but there wasn't one.

She was so tired of being strong, of being the one everyone else leaned on. Just once, she wanted to be the one who could fall apart, who could ask for help without feeling like a failure.

But old habits die hard.

The sun began to set as she drove aimlessly through the streets of Bloom, finally pulling her car into Eleanor Collins's driveway. Savannah's great-aunt Eleanor had a Little Free Library in the backyard for the community to enjoy, buried in the center of a lush garden. It had always brought Mallory peace, so if there was any peace to be found today, maybe she'd find it here.

Mallory parked, grabbed her purse with Nan's journal inside, and walked along the stepping-stone path. Her phone buzzed inside her purse, but she ignored it. She wanted to ignore everything in her current life and instead go back in time. Way back. She wanted to disappear into Nan's story and leave her own behind—at least for the moment.

Chapter Sixteen

Works of art make rules; rules do not make works of art.
—Claude Debussy

Hollis stared at his phone's screen for a long moment, reading and rereading the text from Mallory.

Mallory: Theater rehearsal is canceled for tonight.

It was in a group chat for all the cast of *Santa, Baby*. The last time he'd spoken to Mal, rehearsal was still on. In fact, there was no room for cancellations. Not with the shortened schedule. What was going on?

One of the hired employees for the tree farm slapped a hand across Hollis's shoulder as he stepped up beside him. "Hey, bro. Why the long face? Another dog out there that you want to take in?"

Hollis glanced over at Damian, who'd been a seasonal worker for Pop's farm for the last two years. "There's always another dog. But no, that's not what I'm looking at." He shook the phone in his hand. "Rehearsal is canceled for tonight."

"Shouldn't you be cheering?" Damian would never sign up to take a part in a play. He'd spent a few years at the local boys home before turning eighteen. He was still taking the hard knocks that life had handed him and turning them into lessons that would eventually mold him into a central part of this community.

"It's not like Mal to cancel. Something must be wrong." Was it Nan? Was Nan sick? "I need to call her," Hollis told Damian. "You got this?" he asked, referring to the farm. The lot wasn't busy right now, and the boys knew how to tag and carry the trees up to the front for transportation.

"Yeah. Sure. Between the five of us, we'll be okay without you, big guy." Damian grinned. "Go call your girl."

Hollis would have normally found a teenager talking to him like that amusing, but right now he was too worried. Hollis had been accused of having a "sky-is-falling" mentality. The next shoe was always about to drop with him because of the way he'd grown up. His gut didn't lie though, and his gut was signaling hard.

He pulled up Mallory's contact in his phone and tapped to place the call. "Come on, Mal. Pick up, pick up, pick up." When the call went straight to voicemail, he tapped the screen again. And again. After the third unsuccessful attempt at reaching her, he called Memory Oaks.

"Hey, Francis. Just checking on Nan today. Is she okay?"

"Oh, yes. She's doing great, Hollis. She just loves sitting in front of that tree in the community room. All the residents love it. The lights are so calming."

Hollis was relieved that Nan was well, but that didn't explain where Mallory was and why she'd canceled rehearsal. "Have you seen Mallory there by chance?"

"Today? No, not yet. Should I be expecting her?" Francis asked. "I think she's having rehearsals at the theater tonight, isn't she?"

"That's unclear. I'm actually trying to get a hold of her." Actually, he hadn't seen or spoken to Mallory since their date last night.

Their amazing date.

Shopping. Driving through the older neighborhoods in Bloom and admiring the lights and decorations. Kissing. It was the best date of his entire life. Simple as it was, the air had been thick with endorphins.

Was that what this was about? He'd thought the date had gone well, but maybe that opinion was one-sided. Maybe Mallory hadn't gone home and lain in bed restless and unable to quiet her mind because of how wonderful the night had been.

No. Mallory was a mature adult. Surely, she wouldn't cancel rehearsal just to avoid him.

"If I see her, I'll tell her you're looking for her," Francis promised.

"Thanks." After disconnecting the call with Francis, Hollis scanned the lot, studying the trees and listening to the birds while his mind pondered what to do.

Savannah. She'll know what's going on.

Tapping on Savannah's contact, he fidgeted impatiently as the phone rang in his ear. When she didn't respond, he called Evan.

"Hey, buddy," Evan answered.

"Where's Sav?" Hollis asked, skipping pleasantries.

Evan cleared his throat on the other line. "I, uh…"

"I know you know something. If you don't tell me, I'm heading to your house."

Evan was quiet for a moment.

Then Savannah took hold of Evan's phone. "She's okay, Hollis. She told me she just wants to be alone right now, and I'm respecting that."

Hollis's stomach dropped into the pit of his stomach. "Why does she need to be alone?"

Savannah didn't respond.

"Savannah, please?" Hollis asked a bit more forcefully, feeling a funnel of panic in his chest. "Did something happen? I just need to know she's okay." He'd made a promise to Nan last Christmas, but more than that, he cared about Mallory. He cared more than he ever wanted to admit.

"It's not my place to tell you what's going on, Hollis. I'm her friend."

"I'm her friend too," he snapped back. He pinched the bridge of his nose. "I'm just… I'm just concerned."

She exhaled audibly into the receiver. "Fine. The property inspector came to the theater today and delivered some pretty bad news. From the sound of it, the theater is in not-so-great condition. It didn't pass inspection. The theater is not fit to hold an audience for the holiday play," Savannah said. "And it's definitely not in condition to sell."

Hollis shook his head. He'd been inside the theater recently. He hadn't seen any signs that anything was amiss with the building. Granted, his attention was usually on Mallory when he was in the theater, but he would have noticed if conditions were so bad that it couldn't pass inspection. "That's not possible."

"Well, that's what happened. I was there."

Hollis felt like someone had reached into his chest and grabbed hold of his windpipe. "She didn't tell me. She hasn't responded to my messages all day." He'd peppered a few texts in Mallory's direction from the farm today between talking to customers, teaching the boys about the job, and working with the dogs, telling her that he hoped she was having a good day. That he was thinking of her. That he couldn't wait to see her this evening.

"She's pretty devastated. She can't afford the repairs," Savannah said. "I mean, that's the main reason she's working so many extra shifts at the hospital. She can barely afford to keep Nan at Memory Oaks."

Hollis didn't speak for so long that Savannah finally said his name. "Hollis? Are you still there?"

"I'm here. Where do you think she'd go to be alone?"

"The point of being alone is to go where others can't find you."

"When people say they want to be alone, that's usually because they don't trust others with their emotions. Mallory can trust me. Where is she, Savannah? Please."

He heard her soft exhale on the other line. "If I had to guess, she'd be somewhere in her car driving."

"Driving?" Hollis asked.

"That's what she does when she's upset. She drives."

How the heck was he going to find Mallory if she was driving all over Bloom? "Any other tips?"

"She likes to eat cheesy fries when she's upset. Or she did when we were younger."

"Cheesy fries? From Daryl's Diner?" Hollis asked. He somehow doubted Mallory still enjoyed grease and ketchup, but he was willing to flip the entire town upside down to find her...and hold her.

"Okay. Thanks for the tip. Let's hope she's there."

"You're going to look for her?" Savannah asked. "Let me know if you find her. I want to make sure she's okay too. As okay as someone can be when they're losing a family member to dementia and struggling to keep that person safe. And also balancing the expectations of the town and their obsession with this play on her shoulders... Wow, Mallory really is under a lot of pressure."

Just like Nan had predicted last Christmas. "I'll find her," he said. Even if it took him all night.

An hour later, Hollis had driven from one end of the county to the other and back. He'd gone to Daryl's Diner three times, driving around the lot and looking for Mallory's car. And in the process, he'd had a lot of time to think. Men were fixers. Isn't that what everyone said? And he was even more of a fixer than the average guy, thanks to Matt.

If the play couldn't happen at the theater, there was nothing saying it couldn't happen somewhere else.

Think, Hollis, think.

A text came through, and Hollis immediately snatched his phone, expecting it would be a message from Mallory. Instead, it was from Damian about the tree farm, giving updates on sales and goings-on. The kid was a godsend this season.

Damian: Closing up now. Just giving you an update, boss.

The tree farm's hours were different during the week, based on the day. From Monday through Thursday, five thirty was most cost-effective because most sales happened on the weekend, between Friday and Sunday.

Hollis: Great. Thanks, bud.

As Hollis started to put his cell phone away, an idea clicked into place like a missing puzzle piece. *Of course.* The play could happen on Popadine's Tree Farm—if Pop agreed. The property was more than big enough, with generous parking space. All it would really take was for Hollis and the construction crew to build a modest platform as a stage inside of Pop's large, empty barn. In just a couple of hours' work, they could bring the props over from the community theater.

Veering toward Memory Oaks, Hollis went to speak to Pop directly. Fifteen minutes later, he had Pop's blessing. Hollis had even gotten a friend to donate all the seating inside the barn—the same chairs that had been used for Maddie's wedding to Sam last summer. Matt owned outdoor heaters for the construction crew when they worked in the most frigid temperatures. With a few texts and phone calls, Hollis felt confident he'd solved most of Mallory's dilemma.

This was one of many things he loved about Bloom. When there was a need in the community, folks showed up. All that was left was figuring out what the issues were with the theater, and fixing those as well. He was committed to keeping his promise to Nan to take care of Mallory.

Everything would be okay. Now he just needed to locate Mallory and make her believe it.

The Rattle Ornament

The Rattle Ornament is in the box numbered with an 8. It's a simple yellow and white plastic rattle with a shiny golden bow tied in the middle. Hang it eighth down from the top, just south of the middle of the tree.

Here's the story.

I didn't feel any movement from the baby for the remainder of our honeymoon. At one point, I even called my mother to ask her what I should do.

"Babies go quiet in there sometimes. I'm sure the little guy is just giving you and Mickey some privacy. It's fine, dear. Focus on your new husband and your happy future."

I allowed myself to believe her too—for a couple of hours. Then I called my doctor.

"Are you bleeding?" he asked.

"N-no." The only thing I had to report was that the movement had stopped.

"You're a nervous mother," the doctor said. "That's normal for first timers. I just examined you last week, Nan, and everything was A-OK. Relax and make an appointment when you get back from your honeymoon."

"Okay." With shaky hands, I hung up the phone and turned to Mickey.

"See? Everything is perfect. Life is perfect," he whispered.

I hadn't realized that he'd walked up behind me and overheard. He waved me over to come sit with him on the bed.

I did. I curled up into the crook of his arm, my safe place, but no one had relieved my fear. Deep down, I knew something was off. The next morning, I quietly slipped out of bed and headed to my doctor's office anyway. Nervous mom or not, I needed confirmation. I needed more than words. I wanted to hear my baby's heartbeat. I wanted proof.

The examination room was cold as I sat there in a paper gown, all alone. Wasn't the purpose of marriage that you never had to go through the hard things alone anymore?

Doctor Weston humored me by seeing me first thing. The amusement in his eyes slowly faded like falling stars, and my heart dropped into the pit of my stomach.

I wasn't a nervous new mom. My instinct was right. After hearing the news, I returned to my new husband and, as an actor, I put on the biggest performance of my life. Part of me liked the denial. When I was playing the part, I didn't have to accept reality. I preferred the fantasy world, the lie over the truth.

The following day, when the honeymoon was over, I pretended to sleep for the entire drive back to the tiny house behind the theater. Then, as soon as we got home, I burst into sobs. While we were away, Mickey had arranged for our friends and family to create a small nursery for our baby. The one we'd lost.

The one I'd lost.

The grief process is so strange. It evolves at the same time that it lessens. Or, truly, it never becomes smaller, it just goes into hibernation, ready to wake up at the least-expected, least-opportune time.

We were a new couple, and I hadn't learned to lean on Mickey as a husband yet. I hadn't learned that life and grief were so much easier when shared. While my parents and I had a great relationship, it wasn't one where I divulged all the details of my life. My mother being there for me when I came home from New York pregnant was really the first and only time that had ever happened.

So I did what felt natural to me. I pushed Mickey away. I told him that I'd lost our baby and that we should file an annulment. I'd assumed that's what he would want, given the situation, and I wouldn't hear any different.

I didn't tell Mickey that I still needed to go through the painful delivery. It was horrible enough that I would have to experience this. Mickey shouldn't be haunted by this moment as well.

I was so foolish. As I lay in the hospital bed, ready to have what's called a still birth delivery, fear consumed me. I was so alone, and I didn't know what to do. Should I call my mother? I'd lied and told her the delivery was scheduled for the next day because I knew she'd be there for me, but I somehow thought it would be better to do this on my own. I remember sweating and crying, trembling and wishing I was anywhere but there.

Then the door to my hospital room opened and Mickey walked in. I wondered if I was hallucinating. If so, I didn't care. I just wanted him by my side.

"Shh-shh." He climbed into the bed beside me and curled his arm about my shoulders, pressing his lips to my temple. Then he grabbed my hand. "Squeeze it. I've got you, Nannie."

He didn't tell me everything would be okay, because it wouldn't. Not for a while. He didn't say much at all. Instead he cried with me. He was strong and allowed me to be weak. He absorbed at least half the pain because it suddenly got easier as I pushed a baby into the world.

The day after I was discharged from the hospital, we

held a service, just for myself, Mickey, and my parents. Then we buried him.

"Let's go home," Mickey said once the burial was complete.

"My home is with my parents," I told him, pushing him away. Or trying to.

He held my hand, refusing to let go. "We've done this already, Nannie. And, if I'm being honest, I'm sick of you pushing me away. I made a promise to you and I meant it. If you didn't mean it, if you want to take it back, tell me now. Otherwise, let's go home."

Tears washed my cheeks. As I hugged my arms around myself, I realized I was tired of holding my own self. Being my own support system. My instinct was to continue pushing him away, but I was tired. And Mickey made me feel…something.

He gestured to the small grave behind me.

I didn't follow his gaze. I couldn't. I just wanted to walk away and find a quiet place to dissolve. Disappear.

"If you leave, it's your choice. I'm not going to block your path. What I will do this time, however, is tell you that I want you to stay. I'm not going to throw you over my shoulder and demand that you come home with me. That's not who I am, and I'll never be that guy."

We stared at one another, a battle of wills between two grieving people who were sad and confused.

I knew my parents were watching and all the ghosts, if ghosts exist, in that graveyard.

I stomped my foot and growled, feeling like a wounded animal. Then I collapsed, but he didn't let me hit the ground.

"Stubborn woman. You're determined to make me a

liar, aren't you?" he whispered, sweeping me up into his arms. "I said I wouldn't throw you over my shoulder, but here I am, practically doing just that."

Looking up into his face, I laughed quietly, which felt like some sort of madness. No one laughs at their child's funeral. Or in the midst of a potential breakup.

"Happy?" he asked, carrying me back to his truck and placing me in the passenger seat as I continued to clutch the plastic rattle, even though my hope was gone. Now instead of hope, it felt like all I had left to prove was that my baby was real. He had existed, and he was mine.

"Where do you want me to take you?" he asked once he was behind the steering wheel. I heard the tremor in his voice. He was worried that I'd leave.

I laid the rattle in the middle console and reached for Mickey's hand. "Take me home. Our home."

Chapter Seventeen

I am confused by life, and I feel safe within the confines of theatre.

—Helen Hayes

Mallory swiped tears from her cheeks as she clutched Nan's journal and read aloud, whispering the words. She doubted anyone else could hear her, but she didn't want to be found right now. She wanted to stay hidden, tucked away in the Finders Keepers Library. After driving around Bloom and trying to figure out what to do, she'd found herself here of all places, surrounded by books, even though the only book she wanted to read right now was her grandmother's journal.

"I slept in the bed and Mickey slept on the couch for the first week after Michael's funeral," Nan wrote. *"Then, slowly, we grew back into what we were. It was a process and it didn't happen overnight."*

Mallory's eyes blurred, and she took a moment to close them and attempt to settle her emotions. Then a text pinged from her phone lying next to her on the floor of the little library. Mallory didn't even want to look at her screen, but she did, almost reflexively.

Hollis: Meet me at 212 Blue Cedar Road. 6:30.

Mallory quickly blinked past her blur of tears and reread the message. That was the address of the barn on Popadine's Tree Farm. *What's going on?* The very last thing she felt like doing tonight was seeing Hollis. Yes, last night's date had been lovely, but she was in no mood for romance right now. All she wanted to do was crawl under her covers and disappear.

Hollis: You owe me, remember?

He'd picked some time to collect on debts. With a sigh, she closed Nan's journal and dropped it back into her bag—the revelations of Nan's last entry reverberating through her. Why had her grandmother never mentioned Michael? This whole time, Mallory had assumed the baby Nan was carrying in these entries was Mallory's mother, Daisy. But that wasn't the case.

Mallory's phone pinged again. Looking down, she felt a fluttery feeling in her chest at the sight of Hollis's name.

Hollis: We'll have heaters, but wear something warm just in case.

"What is he doing?" Getting up quickly, Mallory dusted off the bottom of her pants. She just wanted to be alone. But because of Hollis busting into her business, she couldn't. On a heavy sigh, she stepped out of the library.

"Would you like a cup of hot tea, dear?" Eleanor asked as Mallory came closer.

Mallory hadn't even seen her there. The older woman was sitting on the back porch with a colorful blanket wrapped around her and an open book in her lap. "I would love a cup, but I actually have somewhere I need to be right now. Next time."

"Of course." Eleanor closed the book she'd been reading. "Savannah was looking for you earlier. From what I hear, everyone has been looking for you, dear. Except your grandpa Charlie. He's the one who told me you were here."

Mallory wasn't surprised. She'd always had the most special bond with Charlie. Maybe that was why she'd been avoiding him lately. He could always look at her and see through her pretense of being fine.

She loved her grandfather, but she didn't want to worry him. Just like her sister, Maddie, Grandpa Charlie was leading his own life with his new spouse.

This was Mallory's problem to solve. No one else's, and certainly not Hollis's.

Mallory glanced around. "Did you tell them where to find me?" Because no one else was here—just she and Eleanor.

"I told everyone who asked that a woman who wants to be alone should be... Are you feeling better?"

Mallory's shoulders felt tight as she shrugged and let them fall by her side. "Not exactly." As soon as her honest answer came out, she forced a smile. "But it's okay. I'm fine."

"I doubt that." Eleanor looked at her knowingly. "Come back anytime. For tea. Books. A listening ear."

"Thank you." Mallory waved and took the path around Eleanor's house, walking toward her car. Once she was seated behind the wheel, she cranked the engine and directed her car to the address that Hollis had texted.

She didn't doubt his intention, but she wasn't up for facing anyone tonight. There was too much raw emotion swirling around her chest, making it tight and uncomfortable. Ten minutes later, she pulled onto a gravel path that led to Popadine's Tree Farm.

Why did Hollis invite her to meet here at a tree farm of all places?

Mallory followed the dirt path and parked behind Hollis's truck, near a large open barn. She blew out a breath as she pushed open her driver's-side door, grabbed her coat, and stepped out. The cold air nipped her cheeks and the tip of her nose.

She followed the sound of voices, stepping into the large candy-apple-red barn and stopping to scan the cast members gathered inside, all chatting and prepping to run lines. What was this? She'd canceled tonight's rehearsal. Why was everyone here?

Mallory scanned the interior of the barn. She didn't think she'd ever even been inside before. It wasn't part of the tree farm business, and Pop had only recently had it built prior to his health decline. The space was large and open. It was also surprisingly warm, despite the dropping temperatures outside.

No one seemed to notice her at first as she stood there, assessing the situation. Then Hollis looked over, seemingly midconversation with Evan, who was an understudy. She couldn't decide if she was angry with him for taking over as the director or grateful for the fact that he cared enough to try to help.

He patted Evan's shoulder and headed toward Mallory, his gaze unwavering.

She shifted uncomfortably, averting her gaze and trying hard to rein in her feelings. And her attraction. It wasn't easy to do, with monarch-size butterflies flapping around inside her stomach.

"What's going on?" she asked when he was only a couple of feet away.

Hollis gestured, holding his arms out to his sides. "We're having play rehearsal. There's no time to waste, given that we're less than two weeks from opening night."

"I'm the director. I canceled," she said as he stood in front of her, folding her arms tightly over her chest, feeling the beat of her heart against her forearms. Hard and rapid.

Hollis's voice was soft in response to her raised one. "I had no right to take over the schedule, and I'm probably way out of line," he admitted. "It wouldn't be the first time."

She inhaled through her nose, realizing that people around them were watching. "You heard about the inspection?" she asked in a near whisper. Of course he had. "So you know how bad it is?"

Hollis gave a one-off nod. "Sounds worse than I'm guessing it actually is. I can take a look if you want." A small glimmer of a smile lifted the corners of his lips. "This play is important. To your family. To the community… To you." He ran his tongue along his bottom lip.

If she had a Christmas wish list, the top item would be that she didn't melt at the sight of his tongue on his lip. Or the little scar on his temple. He had several scars, reminding her of his younger, wilder days. *Dear Santa, all I want for Christmas is for you to numb my heart to this man in front of me.* Because she wanted to be mad at him right now. Angry, even.

"And because this play matters to you, it also matters to me," he continued. "Canceling the production is rash."

"I didn't cancel the play. I canceled rehearsal. One rehearsal."

He lifted a brow. "And you disappeared all afternoon. Are you telling me you weren't going to throw in the towel on the whole thing?"

She heaved a breath. "No stage, no play. What choice do I have?"

He stepped in closer. "Well, if you would have answered my calls, we could have gone over your choices." He leaned farther in, making her heart swell and lift into the base of her throat. "Emphasis on *your* choice. You are the director, after all."

She flung her arms out to her sides and shook her head simultaneously, on the brink of tears. No crying. Nope. Not happening, especially with all the cast here, pretending not to watch her interaction with Hollis right now. "This inspector is the final nail in the theater's coffin. I have no hope of keeping my promise to put on this play this Christmas. Much less future Christmases." Mallory pressed her lips together. This is exactly why she hadn't wanted to meet with anyone tonight. Her emotional state was paper thin.

Hollis lowered his head, dipping closer so that only she could hear what he had to say. So close that she could feel his breath on her skin. "Nan is the one who once told me this. When you have no hope left inside you, that's when you borrow a little from the person beside you."

That did it. Mallory began to tremble as she tried with all her might to hold her tears at bay. Nan had never said that to her. Mallory felt like she was losing her grandmother but gaining her at the same time. How was this even possible? She was losing control of her world. It was spinning out of orbit, but then, here was Hollis, offering his big, calloused hand for her to take. A lifeline.

He offered his hand.

She understood the question. If she took it, she was in on whatever options he had up his sleeve. If she didn't, her answer was no, and she was giving up. She'd never been one to give up easily. "Okay," she said, placing her hand in his, feeling the warmth of his fingers wrap around hers.

"I wasn't always the guy with the most hope, but I've stored some away in my old age. More than enough to offer you this Christmas."

"You've already done so much over the last couple of weeks." Her gaze slipped past him, bouncing among cast members, new and old.

"Honestly, I'm not offering a whole lot. My proposal is that we have the play here, in Pop's barn." Hollis rubbed the back of his head. "When I mentioned that Nan's granddaughter needed help finding a place for the Christmas play this year, you should've seen his face light up like a Christmas tree. First time I've seen him that happy in weeks."

Mallory searched Hollis's expression, trying to decipher if he was joking, but she didn't think so. "You want to hold my grandmother's play in a barn? No offense, but …?"

"Use your imagination, Mal. Obviously, the theater is where everybody would prefer to gather. But outdoor productions are popular, you know. And we have space heaters in every corner to make sure everyone is warm and cozy." He pointed them out. "This is where you use that imagination again. Visualize chairs and a makeshift stage. The crew and I can make that in half a day's work."

Mallory was surprised that she caught his vision, a little glimmer of light in the darkness. "It could work," she finally said.

Hollis's grin came in full force. "That's what I'm talking about."

"With the space heaters, we wouldn't be cold. And we could have hot cider."

"And cocoa." His eyes twinkled as his voice dipped. Hot cocoa was their thing. They'd only been on one official date, and already they had a thing. "This would only be for this year, of course. Next year Bloom Community Theatre will be back in working order. I'll see to it myself."

Mallory wasn't so sure of that. Somehow she felt like nothing would ever be normal again. Staring up at Hollis though, maybe change wasn't always a bad thing.

"The repairs won't happen right away because the crew is booked through the end of December, but Matt's already volunteered the work pro bono. It's not just me. We all want to do this for you. For Nan. All you have to do is say yes."

He made it sound as if he were asking for a favor. "I appreciate your offer to help with the repairs," she said, "but once they're finished…we're planning to sell. I don't see any way around it."

Hollis stood straight. "I was kind of hoping you would change your mind on that."

She hadn't made the decision lightly. In fact, it felt heavy on her shoulders. At least she could give Nan this last production. "All right. If we're going to do this, have the play in Pop's barn, I don't want to make a disaster out of Nan's play. The final production of *Santa, Baby* needs to be fitting of my grandmother's legacy."

"I've made a mess out of a lot of things in my life," Hollis told her, "but I would never do anything to make a mess out of Nan's life, or yours."

She gave him the side-eye. "Except for that one time you booed me off the stage in my first leading role? Except for that time?" She was only teasing him, of course. She gave him another pointed look. "Thanks for the help. And the hope. You're a good f-friend, Hollis."

His eyes narrowed. They both knew they were well past friends, regardless of the number of dates they'd been on.

Two hours later, Mallory released the crew to go home. Rehearsals had gone off without a hitch, in a barn of all places. Mallory wasn't sure if Nan would be amazed or horrified.

Nan was always so meticulous. Her theater was a nice environment. Most of the people in the audience dressed up when they went to the theater. Attending a Bloom Community Performance was considered a special occasion. Having Nan's play performed inside a barn would be a whole new experience.

"Well?" Hollis stepped up beside Mallory, looking quite proud of himself. "What are you thinking?"

"I'm thinking that I can't wait to visit Nan tomorrow and tell her that we rehearsed her play in a barn." Mallory was only being half-way serious. Discussing anything from Nan's past was a risk. The struggle to remember was a trigger sometimes. It was as if Nan was wavering somewhere between her fantasy world and the real one, and she couldn't figure out where she belonged.

"The Nan I know these days," Hollis said, "would think this turn of events is amazing. In fact, I think she'll want to be front and center for opening night."

Mallory didn't think that was likely, but she didn't want to get into that discussion tonight. "Thank you again," she said, feeling a warmth spread from the top of her head down to the tips of her toes. She thought she hated accepting help, but right now it felt kind of good. Hollis's kindness felt like receiving a Christmas gift, and she'd never minded those. Hollis himself felt like a gift this year, bringing humor and joy to her whenever he was around. She found herself longing to see him more and more lately.

Oh no. No, no, no.

There was no way she was going to allow herself to fall in love right now. Nan was depending on her. Maddie was depending on her. The entire town of Bloom too. "No!" Mallory whispered, taking a backward step.

Hollis gave her a strange look as his mouth slid into a thin frown. "Second thoughts about the barn theater?"

"No." She laughed nervously. "Just talking to myself."

Hollis lifted a brow.

She waved a dismissive hand. "Nothing to worry you about.

You've done enough. Truly." Mallory's eyes began to burn. *Really? More tears?* She wasn't normally a crier. She wasn't typically someone who got rattled by a handsome, bighearted guy either. Big heart. Big shoulders. Wide chest that she felt the sudden need to bury herself into. How would it feel to have him wrap his arms around her, making her feel safe and warm?

No, she thought, keeping the word to herself this time. *Snap out of it, Mal.*

"Okay, well, I'll see you tomorrow night," she said, eager to run, as fast as her feet would carry her, back to her car. Maybe she needed another hour or two in the Finders Keepers Library to clear her mind.

"Same time, same place," he said with a wave.

She turned back to him as she walked away, giving him a teasing glance. "I'm still the director, right?"

"Of course. You're the boss."

Boss. Friend… Nothing more, she repeated to herself all the way home. Once she was there, she washed her face and changed into her pj's. Afterward, she pulled Nan's journal out of her purse and brought it to bed with her, settling in to learn more about her grandmother's secret life.

In a way, Mallory was learning about herself too. Maybe there were reasons Mallory acted the way she did. Maybe she got all her insecurities and strengths honestly.

Opening the journal to the page where she'd left off, she pulled in a breath and started to read, anxious and terrified at the same time. Her entire life these days was a roller coaster of emotions, similar to the holidays of her childhood, when she knew joy was supposed to be the predominant feeling, except she masked a lot of sadness and loneliness too. But she'd never shared any of those raw, deeper hurts with anyone.

Was that how Nan had been? Was that why she'd turned her stories, her feelings, into these memory snapshots inside this journal? Into the ornaments for her Memory Tree?

The Glove Ornament

The Glove Ornament can be found in the box with the number 9 on the tag. Lift off the lid, and yes, that is a boxing glove. Anything can be turned into an ornament with a little string of ribbon, which I've added. The Glove Ornament should be hung ninth down on the tree.

Here's the story behind it.

The first draft is never the final one. All writers know that. The first draft of *Santa, Baby* was actually very different. It was merry and exactly what you'd expect from a holiday play. It didn't feel like the truth anymore though. As I healed and leaned into being a new wife, the seed of an idea in my mind formed. What if Santa and Mrs. Claus weren't always the jolly couple? They must have had their early years, right? The ones that determined if they, as a couple, would stick or fall apart. No couple is exempt from those times.

The edits poured out of me like honey onto the pages, and many of the pages of that original notebook have watermarks from my tears. In every bad situation, there's a blessing if you look for it. I felt like Sylvester Stallone writing my own script the way he did for *Rocky*—thus the boxing glove. I think Sylvester wrote *Rocky* in a week. It took me more like two and a half weeks to completely transform my original play. And when the script was done, I stood from my desk and walked through the house. It was late at night, so Mickey was sleeping. I tapped his shoulder, stirring him awake.

"I'm done."

His eyes widened as he woke up faster than I'd ever seen. I guess he thought I was leaving again.

"No." Shaking my head, I put my hand on his arm. "I'm done writing that story. I'm ready for a new one. I'm ready to fight."

That got his attention. "What's wrong?"

I remember laughing at him. "Nothing's wrong. I want to fight for my life. To get back to living. To be your wife again."

"You never stopped being my wife," he said.

"I want to have a baby with you," I told him, my eyes welling. I'd wanted it so badly that it hurt like nothing I'd ever experienced. I wasn't going to allow myself to roll around in my sorrow or self-pity though. "We will. We'll try for a baby together," I said with determination. "Not now, of course. Dr. Webber said it'll be a while before my body is ready to hold another baby." I assumed it wasn't even possible. "But we can practice."

He looked at me, and I can only wonder what was going through his sweet mind. "Now?"

That's not exactly what I meant, but I wanted to feel his arms around me, wrapping me in love and making me feel safe. "Or we can put on the boxing gloves," I suggested, "and fight for real."

"I do have a pair," he admitted, leaning toward me. "But I'm more of a lover than a fighter."

During my life, I've been equal parts lover and fighter. You have to fight, especially when you've been knocked down. If you lose the will to fight, then you also lose the will to love. That's what Santa and Mrs. Claus taught me in the rewrites.

So, darling granddaughters, put your gloves on. Channel your best Rocky. Live. Love. And fight for what matters.

Chapter Eighteen

Those who say it can't be done are usually interrupted by others doing it.

—James Baldwin

As Hollis finished cleaning and closing up the barn, he headed outside, where Savannah was still waiting for Evan, who'd stayed around to help Hollis with a few things.

"You made my best friend happy this afternoon, and for that, I owe you," Savannah called out from where she was seated on Hollis's tailgate.

As he grew closer, Hollis noticed Savannah's slightly pink cheeks. After finding out about Savannah's autoimmune disease last year, he wondered if she was in another lupus flare. Stress could induce one, and the holidays were nothing if not stressful.

She seemed happy though, and he knew Evan would take good care of her if that were the case. Savannah and Mallory were best friends but complete opposites from his point of view. Savannah had kept her lupus diagnosis hidden when she'd first returned to Bloom, but she hadn't shunned help. In fact, allowing Evan to help her with her aunt Eleanor's library after a summer storm was what had brought them together. Opposites often attracted when it came to friends and lovers.

Stop right there, Hollis Franklin. His mind was already feeding him the ways that he and Mallory were different. Good girl, bad boy—at least once upon a time.

Savannah narrowed her eyes as she seemed to be reading his mind. Leaning in, she said, "You can deny it if you want, but I can tell when a man has a crush on a woman."

"Any man with two eyes, or even one, would have a crush on Mallory." He held up a finger and clarified. "Any man that's not already married, of course. And any nonmarried man with a single working brain cell. Because it's not about her looks. Although she's gorgeous." He cleared his throat. "But she's smart too. She's great."

Savannah grinned, her blue eyes sparkling in a knowing way. "If you're trying to convince me that you don't have a thing for my best friend, you're failing."

Hollis looked away momentarily.

"So, Evan and I are considering getting a puppy," Savannah offered, changing the subject. "Did he tell you that?"

"No. He didn't." Hollis was surprised, because Evan had just gotten a new puppy last year for his teen daughter, June. "Another dog?"

Savannah shrugged. "Well, maybe it's more me than Evan. I'm trying to convince him that Monday needs a friend." Monday was the name of Evan's daughter's puppy—a nod to the dog in the *Anne of Green Gables* series.

Savannah folded her arms in front of her. "It would also be a service dog for me. Not that I really require a service dog at this point, but I might one day. I've read that dogs can be helpful with different health issues, such as mine. And my husband tells me you're the best dog trainer in town. In fact, anytime that anyone mentions a dog in this town, the very next words out of their mouths are Hollis Franklin. Maybe I can be one of your first clients at the new business."

Hollis hesitated, which told him just as much as it told Savannah. Was this going to be another year where he put his dream on the back burner? He knew exactly where he was going to set up his business. He had a list of potential clients already on his waiting list, and he had enough money in his bank saved up to cushion him as he let his new business take root.

Some part of him still doubted his ability to make it happen though. It was the part that listened to the voices from the past. The voices of former teachers, former coaches, and foster parents. Even former parole officers who'd followed him after being put in juvie for trespassing and getting into a few fights that he never started but always ended.

"Yeah," he finally said, realizing that Savannah was still waiting for an answer. "I think so." His lips curved upward as he let himself speak his dream into existence. For most of his childhood, he had ignored dreams. Wants. Even needs. "I'd love to help with training a service dog for you." And that was still the dream, even if it was suddenly on shaky ground. He didn't want to hurt Matt or insult him by turning down his offer to take over the construction company.

That was a worry for another night though. Hollis wanted to stay in this warm feeling he was coated in after helping Mallory with her predicament. He wasn't a knight in shining armor, and he didn't think Mal needed one. She needed a friend though, and maybe more one day.

The next day, Hollis sensed a different vibe in the air as he visited Pop at Memory Oaks.

"Hol, I know Matt doesn't want to take over the tree business. Now that I'm in here," he said, "the tree business is going to go to some other guy. To the competition." The skin between Pop's brows pinched softly, and there was a nervous twitch to the muscles in his hollowed-out cheeks.

Hollis wasn't sure how to respond. Since Hollis wasn't a blood relative, he was only a foster son and grandson, he had never felt like it was his place to take over anything that belonged to Pop or Matt. He would be glad to care of the tree farm every Christmas for the rest of his life, but the farm didn't belong to him. It was Pop's, and after Pop passed away, it would legally belong to Matt.

Hollis knew good and well that Matt didn't want the Popadine Tree Farm. He'd made that clear so many times. In fact, Hollis had heard Matt ramble on about how they should cut down all the trees, at some point, and expand the construction company. Hollis didn't have the heart to tell that to Pop, even though he suspected Pop knew.

"The sales good?" Pop looked at Hollis, hanging on every detail that Hollis could give him about the farm.

"I'd say it's been one of our best seasons in recent years," Hollis said.

Pop's eyes were bright and clear. "That's great, son."

"Yes, it is. Do you remember how I asked you if Nan's play could take place in the barn at the farm?" Hollis asked.

Pop's forehead wrinkled as he seemed to search his thoughts. Then he chuckled softly. "I can't believe Nan would allow one of her plays to be performed in a barn."

"Actually, her granddaughter, Mallory, is the one directing the play this year. And, considering that the theater didn't pass inspection, the family is grateful to have a place for the production."

"Right. Right. The show must go on," Pop said dramatically, sounding like Nan herself. "I know Nan is a little...forgetful these days, but I think she'd be happy about the way things are turning out this year."

Hollis eased back into the chair, sprawling his long legs out in front of him and getting comfortable. He was in no hurry to leave. Instead, he stayed for a good thirty minutes, chatting with Pop before straightening back into an upright position and preparing to leave.

"How's the grand ideas and plans for the farm going?" In contrast to Matt, when Pop asked Hollis about his aspirations, he looked excited. Not that Matt hadn't supported Hollis throughout his adult life. Hollis certainly owed a lot to the man he thought of as a foster dad. "I'm, uh, not sure." Hollis ran a hand through his hair. "Matt's not thrilled, of course."

"You've always taken great care of my farm, Hollis." Pop leaned toward him. "I don't want my farm to go to the competition. I don't want my farm turned into something it's not. I wasn't humoring you when I listened to your suggestions for Popadine Farms. I like your vision. I want you to take over for me," Pop said. "I know you have a heart for the land and for the trees. You'll do a good job."

It was possible that this was Pop's dementia speaking, but Hollis didn't think so.

"I appreciate the offer but I don't think Matt would be too thrilled if I accepted the farm." Hollis exhaled a long breath. "In fact, Matt told me that he wants to retire and leave the construction company to me."

Pop's thin lips dropped into a deep frown. He pointed a finger in Hollis's direction. "You hate construction. I could always tell. You were just happy to have a job and food to eat. It was about survival, but you're not hand-to-mouth anymore. It's time for you to thrive."

Hollis wanted to grab hold of this idea. This offer. It felt like a gift, whereas Matt's offer had felt like a death sentence. Turning down Matt's offer would be spitting in the face of the only person who had ever helped him though. And taking Pop's farm would only add insult to injury. Matt was the one who should inherit Pop's property.

Pop seemed to understand the ethical dilemma and sighed miserably. "My brain isn't so far gone that I can't see every thought playing through your mind."

"Then you know I can't accept."

Pop exhaled quietly. "I think of you the way I would a grandson. Heck, I think of you the way I think of Matt." Pop seemed to think quietly. "What if I talk to Matt? I can explain my reasons."

Hollis shook his head. Matt was a reasonable guy, but Hollis could predict exactly how that conversation would go.

"It's okay, Pop. I'm honored just to work this Christmas season at the farm for you. Although I sure do wish you were there with me. It's a lot more fun with you."

Pop laughed, the sound rolling on the way it always did, like a truck with brakes that didn't quite work. Pop had a laugh that seemed to stretch out longer than most. It was something unique about him and something Hollis was already missing, even though Pop was still very much alive and kicking.

"I just want to see you happy… I saw you talking to Nan's granddaughter the other day." Pop raised his brows. "She's a pretty young woman. If I was your age, I'd have my eye on her for myself. I might even try to marry her before some other chump swept her off her feet."

"Marry, huh? You can look at a woman and tell if she's the marrying kind just with one look?"

"Of course," Pop said. "The kind of woman you marry is more than beautiful. She carries herself well. With confidence and a smile that shows up in her eyes. Her focus is on others. She's kind. Considerate. There's a quietness about her. A subtleness that keeps most heads from turning because, if you blink, you'll miss her."

"Sounds like you're speaking from experience, Pop."

The older man in front of him chuckled. "Every man experiences that woman once in their lifetime, but only a few are smart enough to know it when they do. The other chumps marry the wrong woman. The one who turns heads and then demands the world, and when you're young, you think you can give her that." Pop nodded more to himself than to Hollis. "When you get older, wiser, the young man who thought he was invincible realizes he's only human and he doesn't have the world to give. Just his beat-up, broken-down heart. That's not really enough for the wrong woman. For the right woman, though, it's everything." Pop blew out a breath and chuckled some more. "You never realized your old grandpa here was so deep and romantic, huh?"

Hollis grinned. "Any guy who builds his life around a Christmas tree farm can't be anything less than deep and romantic." Pop had been married for nearly two decades before his late wife passed away a couple of years back. "Alice was a lucky woman to have a romantic for a husband."

Pop looked out the window in his room where there was a birdfeeder set up. "I was the lucky one. Alice gave me our son, Matt. I could have been a better husband. She deserved more."

Hollis found this interesting. "What more could she have possibly wanted?"

Pop looked at him, sadness reflecting in his eyes. "My whole heart. I gave my heart to someone else before I met Matt's mother."

Hollis didn't think Pop was confused. Pop's eyes were clear. "Who was she?"

Pop pulled in a deep breath. "I'm afraid some things should be kept quiet. For Matt's sake, if nothing else. I loved his mother very much, but the woman I was *in love* with was another woman. It's not something I'm proud of nor something I could help. Once you give your heart to someone, it's hard to get it back."

Chapter Nineteen

Creativity is allowing yourself to make mistakes. Art is knowing which ones to keep.

—Scott Adams

Mallory could barely believe her eyes as she blinked away tears and scanned the barn.

It had taken all of twenty-four hours, and it now looked as if it had been made for theater. It was like a scene out of a Hallmark movie. On the outside, the barn was already painted a bright apple red, as if it were made for the holidays. It was rustic and festive at the same time, surround by trees and twinkling lights. On the inside, it was warm and cozy with plenty of seating. Hollis and the crew had built an amazing stage, and all the backdrops from the Bloom Community Theater had been transported to the barn.

It's absolutely perfect.

Maybe it wasn't the theater that Nan had created, but her productions couldn't be matched or recreated, and if that was true, putting on the play at the barn was an awesome second choice.

Mallory breathed a sigh of relief. With the help of Hollis and his construction crew, she felt like she could breathe again for the first time in months.

"Ho, ho, ho," Hollis belted, coming up behind her and making a grand entrance.

Turning, she felt something warm like honey oozing through her as she met Hollis's deep brown eyes. "This is perfect. All the cast knows their lines. Everyone has their costumes. The set is ready. You truly are Santa Claus. You literally saved Christmas."

"See? Told you everything would work out. You should've trusted me."

"I *did* trust you. Eventually." She tore her gaze from his for a moment. Otherwise, she felt a little breathless. Now she could focus on other things that were less about survival and more about wants than needs. Like romance.

Her phone buzzed inside her pocket, and she reached for it automatically, taking a glance and not expecting that her relaxed, good mood would crumble in the blink of an eye. But it did. "Oh, no."

"What's wrong?" Hollis's jolly tone turned suddenly serious. "What's going on?"

Mallory reread the text, and then she read it again, hoping she was misunderstanding. But nope. For the third time this season, a cast member had bailed. "Miss Carson just texted. She can no longer play Mrs. Claus." Mallory looked up at Hollis. "Mrs. Claus has half the lines. She's one of the main characters. Aside from Santa, you, she *is* the main character." The relaxed feeling she'd had moments before suddenly disappeared, her muscles stiffening like newly poured concrete. "This ruins everything."

Hollis held up both hands. "Hold on, hold on. Take a breath. We can fix this," he said. "We just need to step back for a moment and figure out how."

Mallory shook her head. "Miss Carson has played Mrs. Claus for the past ten years."

They were both quiet for a moment. The solution was obvious, but Mallory didn't want to be an actor in the play. She didn't want to perform onstage.

"You know this is an easy fix, don't you?" Hollis said, rubbing his fingertips over his beard.

Mallory prepared to argue against what he was about to say.

"I'll be Mrs. Claus," Hollis said before she could protest.

Mallory burst into laughter. "You're kidding, right?"

"Yeah." His grin stretched wide, and she felt her heart squeeze. "You can be Mrs. Claus." He poked a gentle finger into the side of her arm.

"No." Mallory shook her head. "I don't act anymore."

"Come on. It's like riding a bike. And, from what I remember, you used to love being onstage."

A bubble of panic grew inside Mallory's chest, becoming larger and threatening to burst. "Maybe when I was a kid." In fact, at one point, she'd wanted to go to school for theater. It was in her blood, growing up with Nan and the theater life in the background. "I'm a nurse."

Hollis glanced upward in a teasing eye roll. "And I'm a construction worker, tree farmer, and dog trainer. Your point?"

She looked away. Being onstage made her feel vulnerable. She'd love to blame the feeling on the time that Hollis had booed her, but they both knew that wasn't the reason she didn't want to act.

The truth had more to do with her mother. Acting had also run in Daisy's veins—so much so that she'd chosen that life over her own children. The older Mallory had gotten, the more she'd resented the thing that had stolen her childhood and, even more, the thing that had robbed Maddie of hers. Being onstage flooded her body with adrenaline like a drug, and it was addictive.

Mallory had spent her life trying to walk this narrow path that had become a tightrope in the air. One misstep and her family would crumble.

She needed to be an easy child for Nan and Grandpa Mickey so that they'd keep her and Maddie.

She needed to fill all the roles in Maddie's life so that their mother's void would be smaller.

As a nurse, she needed to fix her patients' ailments. Over time, Mallory's logic had become that following her heart, for any reason, was selfish… But saying no to playing Mrs. Claus on Friday would be selfish too.

"I don't know the lines."

"Yeah, you do. Miss Carson was beginning to forget the lines, and I've been watching. You know every line of the entire play. Just like me." He narrowed his eyes, his gaze fixed entirely on her. "You told me once that being onstage felt like flying. The truest feeling of freedom that a person can hope for. That's how you got me to agree to play Santa that year when we were fifteen." He cleared his throat. "I'd been in and out of foster homes and juvie, and freedom sounded unattainable for me."

"It did feel like flying," Mallory said quietly.

Hollis reached for her hands. "Okay, then. Fly with me, Mal. You won't embarrass yourself, and if you do, I solemnly promise to fall on my face on that stage and make everyone laugh at me instead."

She cracked a smile. "Why is that somehow appealing to me?"

He stared at her, waiting for her to say yes.

Mallory didn't have time to weigh this decision. Not this close to opening night. Everything hinged on what she did next. The play was part of the town's holiday festivities, and the community's joy hinged on her decision. "I don't have much choice, do I?"

Hollis squeezed her hands in his, making her look at him again. "You always have a choice. If you say no, I'll play Mrs. Claus too. I meant what I said. I'm not afraid to make a fool of myself… But I'd rather you be Mrs. Claus to my Mr."

Mallory relaxed as she met his hot cocoa-colored eyes. He was dressed in a Santa costume, and she felt a spark in her chest while she was standing right there in front of him. Being forced into the lead role felt scary, but playing the romantic counterpart to Hollis's character sounded fun. Like flying. "Okay," she said, nodding to herself. "I'll have a mic in my ear, and someone can feed me lines if I forget. You're right, I know the play inside out. Yes," she said for the second time, and this time it was real. "The show must go on, right?"

"Right. We got this."

She liked how he said "we." She wasn't alone. "We got this," she echoed.

The thick velvet costume of Mrs. Claus was heavy and hot. Even so, there was a lightness in Mallory's heart and in her step. She'd forgotten just how much she enjoyed putting on, not just a costume, but also a role.

She'd always enjoyed stepping into a character, as if she were putting on a new pair of shoes. She loved absorbing the character and reflecting it out to the world, as if she were somebody completely different. It was like playing when she was a kid, only better.

Mallory had yearned for the theater back then. Bloom Community Theater ran six plays a year, and Mallory had taken roles in all of them. Maddie, on the other hand, usually went kicking and screaming and preferred to do the backstage work when she was forced to be involved. She'd started off with small roles at first, but then, as the years went on, Mallory got to play bigger roles with more lines and more responsibility. When Nan had given Mallory her first leading role in the theater, Mallory was beside herself.

Mallory hadn't changed her mind about theater life until her mom, Daisy, showed up out of the blue for one of her rare, unplanned visits.

"A theater major?" her mom had said. "Wow. Just wow. My girl is following in my footsteps. You're just like me at your age." It was supposed to be a compliment, but the words had stuck to Mallory's heart like burrs.

"I mean, you don't want to stay here and run a little nowhere theater, right?" her mom had asked. "Your grandmother barely makes ends meet here in this little unknown town. You wouldn't even be able to support yourself. You'll need to move to a big city to make anything of yourself. Maybe you can room with me. We can go to auditions together," she said excitedly.

Mallory realized then that she hadn't thought out her life path clearly. She just knew she loved acting and everything theater. But no way was she going to abandon her sister. Or Nan. It was true that Nan had struggled financially after Grandpa Mickey had died. The meager earnings of the bimonthly plays barely covered expenses. Looking at her mother that day, she realized too that she didn't want to be like Daisy.

Daisy who had left her daughters to chase her own dreams.

Mallory didn't want to struggle financially either. She wanted to repay Nan by making her life easier. Mallory's grades had always been good, and there were scholarships available to her because of her hours of volunteer work and the fact that she was adopted, even if her adoption was by blood relatives.

After that visit from Daisy, nursing was her future. Acting was her past.

Mallory pulled off the gray wig of Mrs. Claus with a sigh of relief, still reflecting on her youth and the theater. On Daisy and Nan. Now that Mallory was reading Nan's story, she understood the woman behind her grandmother so much more. She wished she'd known earlier all the things Nan had been through, so she could've spoken to Nan about them. She wished she could've asked questions, because there was so much more she wanted to know. Details that only Nan could fill in and maybe never would.

"So, how's it feel to play Mrs. Claus?" Savannah stepped into the dressing room. She leaned against the wall and folded her arms across her chest.

Mallory looked at Savannah through the mirror. "Amazing."

Savannah waggled her brows. "Is it playing Mrs. Claus that's amazing or playing the other half to Hollis Franklin?"

If Mallory were honest, it was both. Okay, maybe one was more fun than the other, but she was still nervous about ever allowing herself to fully fall for Hollis.

Savannah rolled her eyes. "Whatever. Don't tell me. I'm only your best friend who you're supposed to share every detail of your life with." Her expression turned serious. "The fact that you're holding your feelings closer to your chest tells me everything I need to know."

Mallory began to pull off the heavy red velvet dress, transforming herself back into herself. A single, almost thirty-year-old woman who was well on her way to becoming a burnt-out nurse.

"I like him," she told Savannah, turning to face her friend.

"Well, duh," Savannah said with a small laugh. "Is that all the tea you're going to spill?" She lifted her brows high on her forehead.

Mallory had been keeping the kiss she'd shared with Hollis to herself. She was savoring it and protecting the moment from outside opinion. Looking at Savannah now, though, she suddenly wanted to talk about it. "We've only kissed once," she finally said.

Savannah squealed softly. "Now we're talking!" She pointed a finger in Mallory's direction. "And, for the record, he doesn't kiss and tell because Evan knows nothing." Her friend rubbed her hands together. "Is he a good kisser?" Savannah asked.

Mallory pretended to zip her lips, but heat burned her cheeks. "I don't kiss and tell either," she said, hesitating before saying more. "But yes, he is."

The Friendship Ornament

The Friendship Ornament is in the box labeled number 10. It'll be a tiny red box. Inside, you'll find a safety pin with sparkling, eye-catching beads threaded through the pin. It was probably made as a friendship item. I remember when that was a popular trend. When I found the beaded safety pin on the ground outside my doctor's office, I needed a friend more than anything. I picked it up and put it in my pocket, drawing comfort from it somehow as I walked inside the building. Now, the lost and found item is part of this Memory Tree. A crucial part.

Here's the story behind it.

The cast of *Santa, Baby* had been rehearsing three times a week for over a month, and everything to that point had been running so smoothly. The actors were fantastic, the set was coming together beautifully, and Mickey...oh, Mickey. He was the perfect Santa to my Mrs. Claus. After Michael's stillbirth a couple of months earlier, I had worried it might create a distance between us. But if anything, we were more in love than ever.

Then one morning, I woke with a start, my stomach lurching. I barely made it to the toilet before the contents of my stomach came rushing up. Was this the flu? No, no, nooooo.

I headed down the stairs, but the smell of coffee only made my nausea worse. Mickey was at the kitchen table with a newspaper laid out in front of him. When he looked up, I remember how his ready smile dropped.

"Nan? You okay, sweetheart? You look a little green."

I didn't want to worry him. "I'm fine, just a little queasy. Probably something I ate."

He immediately got up and poured me a glass of water, leading me to the chair that he had been sitting in.

"I can't be sick. I can't direct this play if I'm laid up in bed. And I certainly can't play Mrs. Claus if I feel..." I couldn't even finish my sentence before I sprung up out of the chair and raced down the hall toward the bathroom.

I was sick. Oh no. "What if I've infected the entire cast?" I cried to Mickey with my head over the toilet. It wasn't like me to cry in front of him. "If we all come down with the flu, the play will be ruined."

"It's okay, Nannie. If you're sick, it's probably just a twenty-four-hour thing. The play is a week away. It'll work out... But to be safe, I think you should see Dr. Webber today." Mickey placed a hand on my back. "I'll call and see if they can fit you in this morning."

An hour later, I parked in the lot in front of my doctor's office and walked across the pavement as a light sprinkle began to fall. Something caught my eye just before stepping under the awning. A little safety pin strung with colorful beads that made a lovely rainbow design. I don't know why I picked it up, but I put it in my pocket and continued into the office. It wasn't until I was sitting on the exam table in Dr. Webber's office, my legs swinging nervously, that I pulled it out again, admiring it. All my senses were heightened in the moment. The paper crinkled beneath me as I shifted my weight, waiting for the doctor to return and tell me it was nothing. I was fine.

"Well, Nan," he said, finally walking in, "I know what's going on with you. You're not sick." Dr. Webber cleared his throat. "You're pregnant."

The words hit me like a physical force. "Pregnant?

But-but… How? Well, I know how, of course. Mickey and I have been…well." I looked away. "But after the stillbirth, I thought…"

A whirlwind of emotions swept through me. Terror was the first. After losing our first baby, the thought of going through that again was almost unbearable. What if something goes wrong? What if my body can't handle it?

But right on the heels of that fear was a glimmer of excitement. A baby. My rainbow baby. My eyes dropped to the beaded safety pin in my hand and then the tears broke out.

"Nan?" Dr. Webber's voice broke through my thoughts. "Are you okay?"

"Yes?" My voice shook as I sniffled, closing my fingers around the safety pin. "I-I'm just surprised."

Dr. Webber sat on a stool in front of me. "I know this must be overwhelming, especially after what happened before. But, Nan, this pregnancy looks good. Strong. We'll monitor you closely, of course, but there's every reason to be hopeful."

Hopeful. The word echoed in my mind as I left the doctor's office. Hopeful. I placed a hand on my still-flat stomach, trying to wrap my mind around the fact that there was a new life growing inside me.

As I drove home my thoughts grew louder. The worries, fear, everything grew louder. How was I going to tell Mickey? How would this pregnancy affect the play?

As I pulled into our driveway, though, a sense of calm settled over me. Yes, I was scared. Yes, this was unexpected but it was also wonderful.

Mickey was in the backyard, stringing lights on the

big pine tree out back. His face lit up. As he walked toward me, he held out his arms. "Nannie! You okay? How did it go at the doctor's? Let's get you to bed. You need to rest."

"Mickey, I... I'm not sick. I'm pregnant," I blurted out, the words tumbling from my lips.

The string of lights slipped out of Mickey's hands. Uncertainty flashed in his eyes, as if maybe he thought I was joking or he'd heard me wrong. But then his face broke into the most beautiful smile I'd ever seen.

"We're...we're having a baby?"

"We're having a baby." I nodded, laughing and crying at the same time.

In an instant, Mickey swept me up into his arms. Then he set me down gently, as if I might break. "A baby," he said again, his voice full of awe. Narrowing his eyes, he looked at me. "I'm not afraid, Nannie. Scratch that. I'm terrified, but I'm not going to give in to the fear. I'm going to lean into the joy, and whatever happens, from here until the end of time, I'm going to stand with you."

I pulled back and looked up at him. "The play."

"It'll go on, Nannie. Even if you use a barf bag between scenes." He laughed, running a hand through his hair. "You know the show will always go on, and I support that. I'll make sure that always happens because whatever is important to you is important to me." His gaze seemed to drop to the rainbow-colored safety pin that I had attached to my jacket. Lifting a finger, he traced the beads. "What's that?"

"A sign, I think. A good sign." I nodded to myself. "The show will go on and this baby will join the cast."

Chapter Twenty

You are enough. You are so enough. It's unbelievable how enough you are.

—Sierra Boggess

There was a growing restlessness in Hollis's chest.

Whenever things felt too good to be true, he typically found himself worried that he'd suddenly wake one day and realize it was just a dream. It didn't take a psychologist to understand why.

When something good happened, he was wired to think that he'd get double the disappointment as his penance for the momentary joy. Sometimes triple. He'd tried to work through this belief system. If he worked hard, he was rewarded with success.

Even though Hollis had turned down Pop's offer, he'd been chewing on the prospect in the back of his mind. He wanted nothing more than to continue maintaining the trees and running Pop's business during Christmases to come. During the off seasons, he could foster and train dogs. There was so much he could do with a property of this magnitude. Pop's offer was everything he could possibly hope for, and more.

Well, there was one more thing that would make his life next to perfect. Mallory. He'd always assumed she was out of his league, but here they were, and the attraction was mutual. They liked the same things, got along well, and could talk for hours and never run out of things to discuss. Every time he saw her, she got prettier in his eyes. Even at the end of rehearsal, when she had her hair pulled back into a messy ponytail. Actually, that was when she was the prettiest.

When Hollis had imagined what love would be and feel like, this was exactly what he'd envisioned. His thoughts stumbled over themselves, coming to a sudden stop. *Love?*

Hollis scratched the back of his head, feeling that restless energy grow inside him again. The problem with allowing yourself to have feelings like love was that the more you cared about someone, the harder it hit when they decided they no longer cared.

Hollis's very first memory was of watching the taillights of his father's truck drive away, leaving Hollis at the boys home when he was six years old. The taillights were bright at first, and then they dimmed and burned out. Hollis remembered seeing a firefly flash in the distance. In a split second, his heart lifted with the tiniest glimmer of hope, because he thought his father had changed his mind and was coming back for him. For that moment, he thought his father had decided that Hollis was, in fact, a good boy, worthy of his love.

The fireflies lit up and went out, lit up and went out, and Hollis had the painful realization that it was just his imagination playing cruel tricks. His heart doing the same.

Hollis didn't want to be the guy who was too afraid to have dreams and chase the happy ending. Some of the boys he'd been in foster care with had ended up in jail over the years. Some of them were divorced several times over.

And a few actually got it through their thick skulls that they were never at fault. They had never done anything wrong. They weren't bad boys. Just boys who had desperately needed love.

There was that *L*-word again. Hollis was one of the lucky ones, who'd found a family with Matt and Sandy. And Pop.

"I don't care about what you've done," Matt had said when Hollis was seventeen and fresh out of juvenile lockup for the fifth time. "I really don't. All I care about," Matt had told Hollis, "is what you're going to do now. You have a choice."

Matt waited for a long beat as Hollis wordlessly debated what Matt meant. What choice did he have? Did he have a choice about staying with Matt and Sandy or going to live somewhere else? Did he have a choice about doing something else and getting tossed back in juvenile detention? He was nearly eighteen. Getting locked up again probably meant prison.

Matt nodded to himself, as if Hollis had asked the questions out loud. "You have a choice about what kind of man you're going to be. In four months, you'll be a legal adult. The boy that you were and have been will be gone. You'll be a man, and as a man, there are different paths you can take. Actually," Matt corrected himself, "there are only two paths. You can go down the straight and narrow path or you can choose the path that leads to trouble. Misery. You can choose to hang out with the wrong crowd, the kind that gets you in trouble. The kind that pulls you down. Or you can choose to be a real man, something your birth father wasn't."

Those were fighting words. Hollis remembered this ball of fury gathering inside his chest like a small hurricane. Every muscle in his body tensed. The muscles in his jaw bunched and his teeth gritted as he held back all kinds of things that he wanted to spew at his new foster parent. He held back though, because he was scared and had nowhere else to go.

"I didn't know your dad personally, of course," Matt told Hollis. "But a man doesn't leave his child. A man makes mistakes but not by choice. There's a difference, you see," Matt said. "Everyone makes mistakes, but when you know better, you do better. And if you don't, that's a choice. Hollis, I'm not just offering you a chance to live with me and Sandy until you're eighteen. I'm offering you a seat at our dinner table. A job with the crew. A second chance." Matt shook his head. "I don't give free rides though. A man works for the roof over his head. He works for the food on his plate. A man works, and he works hard."

Hollis was still quiet. His anger had fizzled out, and he was just confused. Lost.

"Take your time," Matt told him that day. "The offer isn't going anywhere tonight. Just know you have a choice. Life isn't about what was done to you; it's about what you make of it."

The truth and wisdom in those words seeped in over the following week, and he realized the gift that he was being handed. Since that time, all those years ago, Hollis had been working on Matt's construction crew. He worked hard, like Matt said, and earned his own place. He supported himself and worked on himself.

Once again, Hollis was at a fork in the road, facing two paths. How had the right one when he was almost eighteen suddenly become the wrong one at almost thirty?

"Deep thoughts there, buddy?" Evan asked, making his presence known as he approached.

Hollis glanced over his shoulder. "Yeah."

"Usually you're the guy that no one can sneak up on." Evan stepped up right beside him. "Mr. Hypervigilance."

Hollis shoved his hands into his coat pockets. "Matt's retiring, and he wants me to run the construction company, starting early next year."

Evan didn't pat Hollis's back. That's because Evan understood the dilemma. "Okay."

"There's more." Hollis blew out a heavy breath. "And Pop offered to hand over the tree farm to me."

This time, there was a response from Evan. His eyes widened and his jaw went slack. "Whoa! What do you mean by that?"

Hollis faced his friend. "Pop offered me the farm. Not just to run it during the holidays or to stay in his house. He offered to sign over the land to run the tree farm and use the land as I see fit. I could take in more rescue dogs. I could train them and run events through the barn."

"That's amazing!" Evan looked around, admiring the landscape. "I don't get it, bud. Why aren't you jumping up and down right now? Why the long face?"

"As much as I'd love to, this land isn't mine. After all Matt has done for me, I can't just take his birthright."

The joy slowly faded from Evan's expression.

There. There was the too-good-to-be-true moment being realized.

"I see," Evan finally said, turning his attention to the trees as the cool air blew around them, rustling leaves and branches. "Matt doesn't want to run this farm though."

"Right. Matt wants to level the land and, in his retirement, he wants me to expand the construction company." Hollis blew out a breath. "I can't choose one family business over the other. It's not even my family."

"Wrong. You're their family. And Pop offered the farm to you because he knows you'll value what's he built. You'll protect it. Pop trusts you."

"Matt trusts me too." The stress of the situation made Hollis want to pull his hair out. "You're my best friend. That's why I called you. I need you to talk some sense into me."

"Here I thought we were going to discuss your love life," Evan said.

Hollis chuckled, even though there was nothing funny about any of this. "What would you do?"

Evan pushed his hands in his pockets and rocked back and forth on his heels. "It was hard when June came to live with me after her mom passed. June wanted to live with her grandma on the West

Coast. Her grandma wanted her to live there too. Some part of me wondered if a good man would let his daughter go where her heart wanted to be. If I was a bad man for keeping her with me. Another part told me that a good man would care for his daughter."

"Of course," Hollis said.

"What I realized is there is no black and white. It's all gray. A good man weighs his choices and does what he thinks is best, hurting as few people as possible in the process."

Hollis shook his head. "People are hurt either way." He kicked the dirt at his feet. "I guess the path forward is the one that hurts me and not them."

"Being the martyr is never the answer." Evan patted his back. "Leveling the tree farm is absurd. You love the farm the same way Pop does. And it'll allow you to take in the dogs. Matt will understand. Just sit down and talk it out."

Hollis shrugged. Talking to Matt was definitely the right thing to do, but disappointing or upsetting Matt was the last thing he ever wanted. "You thought we were going to discuss Mal and me, huh?"

"Mr. and Mrs. Claus. That's cute, buddy," Evan said in a teasing tone. "Real cute."

"It is, isn't it?" Hollis's bad mood lifted a touch just thinking about Mallory.

"See?" Evan pointed in his direction. "There's always a bright side, right? And I'm sure there's a solution to this other situation. I mean, you have two men wanting to leave their life's work to you. That's a good problem to have."

It didn't feel good though. "Yeah." He glanced over. "You haven't gotten your tree yet. Don't tell me you're buying from the competition. Or worse, using an artificial tree."

"Never. I wouldn't dare pick out the tree without Savannah though. Picking out a tree is one of the most romantic dates a guy can plan with his other half."

"Other half? Wow." Hollis rubbed a hand along his cheek. "I'm still adjusting to the fact that my best friend says things like that. It's a bit cheesy, if you ask me."

Evan elbowed him. "Just wait. You'll be speaking the same language this time next year."

"What language is that?"

"The language of the happy and in love. If I was a betting man…"

Hollis humored him. "I think you are. What're we betting?"

Evan looked at him thoughtfully. "If I win, you have to read one of the classic novels that my senior students read."

Hollis's best friend was a high school English teacher, but it wasn't a shared interest. "All right." Hollis nodded. "If I win, you have to adopt one of my rescue dogs next year."

Evan side-eyed him. "I have a new puppy at home you know. Or my daughter does. Adding another dog to the mix is a big ask."

Hollis shrugged. "And I only read thrillers and have the attention span of a gnat when it comes to books. Reading Dickens is a bigger ask."

Evan stuck out his hand. "You'll be whispering cheesy sweet nothings next year, so I'll win this bet. Nothing for me to worry about."

During Wednesday night's dress rehearsal, Hollis stepped onstage in full Santa costume and faced Mallory. She was radiating a brightness he wished he could take credit for. He suspected a large part of her shift in mood was from running the theater. Directing. Even acting.

"It's not up to you to make the whole world full of children happy, Santa," Mallory said, reciting a line that Nan had written fifty years ago. She looked at him expectantly, making him realize that he had a line to deliver.

"I know," he finally said, realizing that this role was made for him right now. He felt just like Santa, trying to satisfy everyone's wish lists and neglecting himself. "Making others happy is what makes me happy."

Mallory stepped closer and laid her hand on his shoulder. It was part of the stage directions. "All year long, you take care of everyone else. It's my job as Mrs. Claus to take care of you."

He looked at her, all dressed up in her costume, but all he saw was the girl he'd grown up with and the woman he had grown to love. "And then, if I'm caring for the children of the world and you're caring for me...who's caring for you, Mrs. Claus?"

He watched Mallory's role slip for just a moment and wondered if she'd just felt the same way he did. These lines were hitting close to home. Stepping toward her, he touched her cheek. It was also part of the stage directions, but she was looking at him differently. "There's so much on our shoulders. I just want to make sure that the most important thing to me isn't forgotten behind all the ribbons and bows."

Mallory's eyes filled with tears. Either she was a good actress, which he knew she was, or these words were resonating in her personal life. "I can take care of myself."

He tipped his head toward her. That wasn't a line Nan had written. Not even close. She was supposed to say she didn't worry about being behind the scenes because Santa would always return home after his long trip around the world. "I know," Hollis said, responding to Mallory's unscripted line. "But I'm an expert in gift-giving, and sometimes the greatest gift you can give someone is allowing them to care for you. That's what I want this Christmas." He cleared his throat and got back on the script. "And after flying around the world, just know I'll be back to do exactly that because you're my greatest gift, Mrs. Claus."

Applause rang out from the small audience for the dress rehearsal made up of stagehands and understudies. Hollis doubted they'd even caught that change in lines.

Thirty minutes later, they were back in their normal attire and locking up the barn.

"What are you doing now?" Hollis asked, fishing for some extra time with Mallory.

She tilted her head. "I'm heading home...unless you have an offer I can't refuse."

"I was wondering... Do you want to head over to the theater and see what the crew and I did today? We're nowhere near finished, but we checked off a few of the line items."

Mallory's eyes lit up. "Really?"

Hollis could see the wheels turning in her mind. He held up his hands. "There's no possible way to finish and have the play at the theater this year."

"I'm not sure I'd want to switch back anyway. It's perfect the way it is this year. But maybe next. I mean..." She trailed off.

"Mallory Blue, don't hold back with me. Don't you know I can read your mind at this point?"

She grinned up at him. "I sure hope not."

There was something flirty in her tone.

"It's true. In fact, I know exactly what you're thinking right this second."

She blinked and visibly swallowed. Why did she look so nervous?

Hollis wobbled his head side to side. "Or I could be self-projecting that you're thinking about kissing me again." He nodded and looked away. "Yeah, that's probably the case."

Surprising him, she reached for his hand. "Actually, you're right on the mark."

Hollis's heart thumped against his ribs. "This is such a bummer." He didn't let her have time to take insult. "Because I made a bet with Evan that I wouldn't turn into some cheesy love-stricken guy. If I do, he wins, and I'm stuck reading a Charlie Dickens classic along with his senior class next year."

The corners of her lips curled. "That is a bummer," she agreed before leaning in closer.

He mirrored her movement. Then he lifted his hand to touch her cheek, just like he had in his Santa suit onstage not even an hour earlier. He wasn't acting anymore though.

His gaze dropped to her lips, which she parted as she watched him, flicking her eyes to his mouth as well. He'd been thinking about kissing her again since that shopping trip more than a week ago. He'd been unsure if that's what she wanted, and in fear of losing her as a friend, he'd kept things platonic, pretending that it hadn't happened. Now, however, he found himself leaning in. It was too late to change his mind. The pull was too strong.

"Hollis," she whispered.

He froze, his heart sinking to the Santa boots that he was still wearing.

"Here." She pushed a sprig of mistletoe in his direction. "If you hold this over our heads, we can pretend like we had no choice. If things don't work out, we can always blame it on the mistletoe."

He glanced down and took the sprig but didn't hold it over their heads. "If you need to, you can blame me."

Chapter Twenty-One

You just have to be open and ready, and let it all happen.
—Angela Lansbury

Electricity zipped from Mallory's lips all the way to her toes. A million thoughts raced through her mind. As the kiss evolved, her hands acted separately from her mind and reached up to frame Hollis's bearded cheeks, her fingers sinking into the softness. Their first kiss had been...nice. This time, however, had Mallory feeling weak in the knees. She felt like the ground was falling away. Like she was flying.

As if sensing that she needed grounding, Hollis slipped a hand around the small of her back, holding her in place.

It was confirmed. Hollis Franklin was indeed a very good kisser.

Pulling away, she looked up at him in a dizzy haze. She should probably say something, but at the moment, she couldn't find any words.

"I've heard that actors and actresses tend to fall for their costars," Hollis said, still standing very close to her. "Just so you know, that's not what this is. Not for me, at least. I've always had feelings for you, Mal."

She was struck by his sudden seriousness. Hollis was one to tease and make light of things. But he wasn't laughing or joking right now; he was being real.

"So," she said, finding her voice again, "you want to take me back to the theater and show me some of the repairs you've done?"

What a ridiculous first thing to say after being kissed like that. No wonder she didn't go on many second dates.

Hollis didn't answer immediately. Instead, he continued looking at her in a way that made her feel vulnerable and seen. "There are a lot of things I want, Mal. I want to take you back to the theater. I want to take you to a fine restaurant and have a nice dinner. I want to go on a hayride and hold your hand. Maybe I even want to play a game of basketball with you."

She burst into laughter. "Basketball?"

He pulled his hand from around her back and shrugged, one corner of his lips hiking up. "It's just, I want to do everything with you. Even the things I don't like to do, I want to do them with you, because maybe I'd like them with you." He ran that same hand through his hair, creating a disheveled look that was unreasonably adorable. And sexy. "I don't like reading one bit, but I want to read a classic novel with you too. I think I'd enjoy almost anything, as long as you were beside me."

Her lips parted. This was a side of Hollis she'd never known. She was beginning to realize that everyone in her life had these hidden sides, like facets on a diamond waiting to shine once the light hit them.

Nan. Hollis. Even Mallory was discovering the same was true for herself.

"Sorry." Hollis took a step back. "Did I say too much? I'm sure the last thing you need is some big lug like me trying to take more of your time."

"No. No, I think a big lug to spend time and laugh with is actually exactly what I need." She was usually so good at shoving down her feelings, except right now she couldn't seem to keep them at bay. First tears, and then laughter.

"What's funny?" A little divot formed between his eyes.

"It's just, I remember telling Savannah that a good man was hard to find. I know that's so cliché." She waved a hand in the air. "So cliché and so judgmental and so wrong. Because look." She gestured toward him. "You are a good man, and here you are, standing right in front of me. I found you."

Hollis stepped toward her again. "Actually," he pointed a finger into his chest. "I think I'm the one who found you. Yep, I'm pretty sure it was me. You needed help, and I forced my way into your life this Christmas. I pretty much made sure that you couldn't say no to me." The corners of his lips dropped just slightly.

"Something wrong?" she asked. The longer he took to respond, the more worried she became.

"Mal, before we go any further, I need to tell you something," Hollis said grimly.

Her guard walls immediately rose. "Okay." The way he hesitated worried her. Mallory didn't trust easily, but Hollis had gotten to her. It was the kiss. Kisses—plural. The endorphins had gone to her head and caused temporary insanity. As she waited for him to say whatever was weighing on him, her hand moved to her chest.

Hollis reached for it and pulled it into his own hand. There went her body separating from her mind again. His skin was warm, and she longed to step into his full embrace, but her mind was spinning out a million scenarios, all of which pointed to the conclusion she'd come to as a young teenager—letting people in meant allowing yourself to be hurt.

"Just say it," she said.

He nodded. Then he tugged her forward, leading her toward the tree farm. "Last fall, I got a call from Nan. She said she needed to talk to me."

Nan had called Mallory to the theater last Christmas as well. "What-what did she say?"

"When I got there, Nan sat me down, and she asked me to do something for her." Hollis kept his gaze forward. "I kind of suspected she knew something was going on with her health. I mean, even I had started noticing little things here and there. She said she was worried about you and Maddie. But primarily you because Maddie has Sam now. Even before Sam, Maddie took care of herself. Nan knew that you took care of everyone else before yourself." Hollis glanced over. "She asked me to make sure you had someone in your corner. She asked me to be that person."

Mallory wasn't understanding. "I mean, yes, Maddie has Sam, but I have people in my life too. Savannah is my best friend."

Hollis nodded, as if he'd expected that answer. "Savannah has Evan and June. She also has Eleanor to look after and a chronic health condition. Nan knew that you were more likely to be the one checking on Savannah and refusing to acknowledge that you needed anything."

Mallory could see Nan worrying about this. Nan had told her as much in the months leading up to Nan's quick decline. "What did she say?" Mallory asked, almost scared to know.

"That you're stubborn. You don't accept help. You push people away when you need them the most." Hollis blew out a frosty breath. "Nothing I didn't already know."

"So that's why you're with me this Christmas?"

Hollis squeezed her hand as she tried to pull away from him. "No," he said quickly. "No, that's not it at all. I hesitated to even tell you this, but I don't like hiding things, and I wanted you to know that I was more than happy to step in and help. If Nan hadn't made me promise to, though, I might have hesitated and taken you at your word that you didn't need anything." Hollis stopped walking and turned to her again. "I would have told myself that I have nothing to offer."

"Well, that would have been a lie," she said quietly.

"Nan wouldn't let me leave her office until I agreed that, no matter what you said, I would keep coming back and making sure you were all right. She didn't ask me to be a nuisance, but she wanted me to keep an eye on you. Nan said she knew I was a man of my word. When I make a promise to do something, I follow through," he said, looking at her seriously.

"So, you promised my grandmother to do whatever I needed? To be my own personal Santa. That's why you did the repairs on the theater?"

"No," he said firmly. "Even if I hadn't made that promise to Nan, I would have done the theater repairs, Mal. I have always been the guy who would've done anything for you." He stopped walking and turned to face her. "I just always felt like you deserved better."

She folded her arms over her chest. "I didn't know Nan asked you to watch over me. You could've said no."

He offered a humorless laugh. "Have you met Nan? She doesn't take no for an answer. And you're missing the point of this confession. I didn't want to say no." Stepping toward her, Hollis tugged gently on the hands he was still holding and lowered his face to hers.

Her gaze stayed fixed, and she could see the question in his eyes. Was she going to cling to an excuse to push him away or was she going to take him at his word?

He'd earned the latter. And so had she.

"You still have that mistletoe in your pocket?" she asked, her body melting against him.

"I sure do. And I'm not afraid to use it."

Going up on her toes, she kissed him for the second time that night. "You don't have to."

As soon as Mallory got home, she changed into her pajamas, but she was too worked up to sleep.

They'd shared a second kiss. This one had been so much more than the first. Longer, deeper, more magical.

She couldn't wait to share every detail with Savannah. Pulling out her cell phone, she pulled up Savannah's contact and tapped the screen.

"Oh, hey, friend," Savannah said as she answered. She lowered her voice to a whisper. "Evan is on the phone with Hollis, and he's jumping up and down hollering right now. I was growing jealous of the fact that you hadn't told me whatever Hollis is sharing with my husband."

Mallory giggled like a silly schoolgirl, which was so unlike her. "We kissed," Mallory said, squealing softly. "Twice. And it was... amazing." All the details of the night spilled out of her at a dizzying rate. She told Savannah all about how Nan had called Hollis into her office last Christmas and made him promise to look after Mallory. She told Savannah everything, including the fact that she thought she was falling head over heels for him. In fact, she was sure of it.

"Of course you are," Savannah said with a laugh. "Everybody in the cast can already see it. You're not acting on that stage. The chemistry between you two is real. Mr. and Mrs. Claus are official," Savannah said with a laugh that mirrored Mallory's. "I am so happy for you. This is amazing."

Mallory could hear Evan in the background talking.

"Tell Mal that Hollis needs to pull up the senior reading list for next school year," Evan called out in the distance, "because my buddy has officially lost our bet, and he is now committed to reading a literary classic just like my students."

"I have no clue what he's talking about," Savannah said.

"I do." And Mallory loved that she knew exactly what Evan was talking about because Hollis had already told her. He hadn't had to tell her about his promise to Nan, either, but he had, which only made her trust him more.

When Mallory disconnected with Savannah, she wanted to tell somebody else. She wanted to shout her good news to the world. Most of all, she wanted to call up Maddie. Ever since Maddie had started dating and then married Sam, Mallory had slowly felt out of touch with her younger sister. She'd pulled back from their frequent contact, giving the newlyweds time and space to enjoy each other. But Mallory missed her sisterly chats.

Mallory decided that, even though she might be interrupting Maddie and Sam's time together, she had something to share, and it was time they caught up with each other's lives.

Tapping on Maddie's contact, Mallory held the phone tightly to her ear and waited with anticipation.

"Hello," Maddie said, breaking into a long yawn.

"Yawning at this time of night?" Mallory teased. "Where is my sister and what have you done with her?"

Maddie laughed on the other line, sounding genuinely happy. "Mallory," she said, "I didn't even glance at the caller ID before answering. Everything okay? You don't normally call at this hour. At least not these days."

A thread of guilt weaved through Mallory. "Well, you've been a little bit busy with Sam, and all of your exciting adventures with your new friend, Renee. I just haven't wanted to interrupt," Mallory said, keeping her teasing tone. "Nothing wrong, but I did want to catch up. How are you, Mad?" Mallory asked, making initial conversation. She couldn't just start gushing over Hollis immediately. That would be rude.

"I'm good," Maddie said. "Better than good. We need to have lunch one day so I can tell you everything, but Renee and I are discussing becoming business partners. Sam is all for helping me."

"Of course he is," Mallory said.

"I'm just… For a while, I thought my life was over, and now, it feels like it's just beginning."

In a way, Mallory felt the same.

"Anyway, enough about me. How's the play going?"

"Good. Surprisingly, very good," Mallory said.

"Awesome. I was shocked to hear that you agreed to have Nan's play at Popadine's Tree Farm."

Maddie's tone hit a sour note with Mallory.

"Why's that?"

"Well, you know Nan and how she always wanted things to be just so. At least when it came to her theater. I could hardly stand to be there when we were young. No running. No eating. No this, no that. It felt like a prison."

Mallory didn't share that opinion, but Maddie had always resented boundaries and rules.

"Believe me, I know Nan was very particular about her theater, and rightfully so. But I think she'd be happy about how things are going. This year's play is not the same, but all the important elements are." Mallory was about to add that some of the actors had changed and that she and Hollis were playing Mr. and Mrs. Claus. She didn't think Maddie had heard about that yet.

Before she could continue, however, Maddie interrupted. "I just think that one of the silver linings of Nan's declining memory is that she can't see what's happening to her precious theater."

Mallory's whole mood dropped like a bag of cement in her gut. Instead of responding, she let her sister continue.

"I mean, I saw the inspection report. The theater is falling apart at the seams. I hope it can be salvaged but certainly not by opening night. And did I hear correctly that Hollis is playing multiple parts? I almost wonder if Nan would've canceled altogether instead of lowering her standards to having the performance in a barn, of all places." Maddie laughed into the receiver. "I mean, I guess Jesus was born in a barn," she joked.

Mallory didn't find anything funny. "Jesus was born in a stable," she corrected.

"Right. Aren't a barn and a stable the same thing though?"

Mallory suddenly felt numb, and she wasn't at all in a sharing mood. "Not really."

"Well, I'm sure we can sell, even if it's an as-is kind of situation. I know this is harder on you than me, Mal. I was never a theater nerd like you were."

Were. Past tense. But Mallory's love for the theater had only been in hibernation, waiting to come alive at just the right time. This Christmas. She had no desire to do theater full-time, but it was fun, and it made her feel a sense of long-lost joy.

"I love Nan, and I know you do too, but that doesn't mean we should make our lives harder just to keep up something that she can't really appreciate."

"Nan is here," Mallory said quietly. Maddie rarely visited Nan. She didn't get to see their grandmother's moments of clarity. And Maddie wasn't reading Nan's journal or putting up her Memory Tree, learning a history she'd never known.

"I do feel bad that you got stuck doing all the work for this play. You're probably miserable doing it all by yourself."

Mallory clutched her cell phone, debating whether to toss it across the room in frustration at her sister's tone-deaf, one-sided conversation. Instead, Mallory focused on her breathing and remained silent.

"Did I say something wrong?" Maddie asked.

"No." Mallory worked to keep her tone of voice light. "You're right. It has been a lot of work to juggle alongside my hospital job." This wasn't the sisterly chat she was hoping for. "But it's been a rewarding experience. Will you and Sam be there tomorrow for opening night?"

"Oh. That's why you're calling," Maddie said, her voice full of relief.

"Of course it is," Mallory said, even though the thought hadn't even crossed her mind until now. She'd just assumed her sister and brother-in-law would go.

"Is the barn even wheelchair accessible?" Maddie asked.

Good question. "We can make sure you're able to get inside the barn."

In the background, Mallory heard Sam adding to the conversation.

"I'll carry you over the threshold of the barn if I have to," he said sweetly while Maddie giggled.

"Hollis and Matt's crew have a ready-made ramp they could easily set up before the show. We'll figure it out," Mallory promised. "You should be there." And the fact that Maddie even had to think about attending was making Mallory irrationally mad right now. It was the least her younger sister could do after all that Mallory had done for her over the years.

Everyone in this town would bend over backward to make sure Maddie had access to the barn tomorrow night. Maddie just didn't want to attend.

"Please come." Mallory was proud of the production. It meant a lot to her, and she rarely asked Maddie for anything, but she was asking for this.

Maddie made another audible yawn. "We'll see."

Mallory resisted the tears pressing behind her eyes. She bit her tongue and some of the pent-up things she wanted to unload. "Sounds good. Have a good night." She didn't wait for Maddie to reciprocate. Instead, she disconnected the call, feeling deflated and disappointed.

The whole reason for the call was to tell Maddie about all the positives in her life. She'd wanted to tell Maddie about her relationship with Hollis. And the kiss.

But now all she wanted to do was put on her pj's and climb into bed alone. Actually, she didn't want to be alone anymore. She'd discovered something better than turning inward when she was upset—and that was turning outward, to Hollis.

The Number 11 Ornament

As you know, I don't believe in coincidences. Everything is ordered. Nothing is by chance. Open the small silk sack, and inside you'll find a little metal tag with the Popadine Tree Farm logo and the number 11. It's a tag from a live tree that your grandfather and I purchased our first year of marriage, the day after Thanksgiving. Mickey had insisted the tree be live, and there was only one place to get it. I would have shied away if I could, but that would have raised brows. So I went, hoping I wouldn't return again until the following year. Boy, was I wrong.

Here's the story.

Opening night of a play is like preparing for a wedding. As the director, screenwriter, and lead actress, I felt the pressure. Not to mention the additional pressure that my now full-size baby was putting on my bladder. TMI? We're family. If you can't tell your dear granddaughters about things like this, then what is family for?

So, on opening day of *Santa, Baby*, I was in a bit of a panic. The excited, good kind. We were just hours before the curtains opened, and then…disaster struck. When I stepped into the front area of the theater and felt something wet on my feet, I thought I'd wet my pants. Or that my water had broken.

It wasn't me though. As I scanned my surroundings, with our first live Christmas tree in the corner, I realized the entire room was flooded. My heart slowly dropped as Mickey stepped up behind me. I heard him gasp, and I knew I wasn't overdramatizing what a disaster this was.

"What are we going to?" I turned toward him, my eyes glistening with tears.

For a moment, Mickey looked speechless. His lips parted, and his eyes were dazed and confused.

"Mickey," I said again. "Do we cancel the show?" My heart was pounding, and my knees felt weak under the weight of our baby, who suddenly felt far heavier. The thought of canceling was soul crushing. We needed to sell tickets to pay the overhead. If the first production didn't even happen, then there was a good chance the theater itself might not even survive.

"No," he said quietly, his eyes becoming clear as he looked at the tree in the corner of the room too. Then he turned to me. "The show must go on."

I guess people around town think that's my tagline. I was always saying the phrase in any circumstance. But the truth is, your grandfather said it first. "You wrote the whole script. We rehearsed. We have the actors, the props. We have everything except the stage." He stood there thoughtfully. I could practically see the wheels turning in his head. "I'm going to talk to Ralph."

"Ralph?" I looked at my husband. Over the last couple of years, Ralph had made a name for himself as the owner of the Popadine Tree Farm. In Mickey's eyes, Ralph was old news. I'd dated him in high school before going off to New York, but that was all. Ralph had moved on and gotten married. According to everyone else, we were history. My secret was mine, and mine alone. "Why him?"

I could see that Mickey was swept up in his thought process. "I've heard talk of him building a huge barn on the tree farm property. I think he had big plans for it, but he ran out of funds. Or something along those lines." Mickey shrugged.

"I'm not following what you're trying to say," I said,

preoccupied with Ralph's name in the same conversation as my play. Hearing his name still flustered me more than I liked to admit.

"The barn, Nan. Ralph is a great guy. I'm positive he'll let us hold your play there if we ask."

"You're suggesting that we put on the production in a barn?" I asked, equal parts intrigued and appalled. Theater was meant to be carried out like teatime in high society. People dressed up. They arrived early because, once the doors were closed, they didn't reopen until intermission. Barns were...well, barns were for animals.

Mickey's eyes lit up as he spoke, suddenly alive with passion. "The Popadine family is into construction. I'll hire them to build a stage. The tree farm has a huge parking lot to accommodate attendees. It's perfect." Mickey looked at his watch and gave a small nod. Then he leaned in and kissed my temple. "I'll make the calls right now," he said before walking out of the theater and leaving me there, still flustered, confused, pregnant, and standing in several inches of water on the floor.

What other options did I have? And, I had to admit, it wasn't an awful idea. It was perhaps even...genius. Everyone loved to visit Popadine's Tree Farm during the holidays, especially now that Ralph had taken over, with a healthy dose of change and his undeniable charm.

My only hesitation was the obvious. I was a married woman now. Pregnant too. I wanted to be a good wife to Mickey, but my heart betrayed me at the very thought of my first love. In a small town, you can't escape your first love. You just can't. But you could do your very best to avoid that love, which was why Mickey's idea seemed like a disaster waiting to happen.

Chapter Twenty-Two

The most important thing about acting is honesty. If you can fake that, you've got it made.

—George Burns

Hollis's stomach felt like a pit of acid.

Earlier this afternoon, he'd called up Sandy and invited himself to dinner tonight, which wasn't out of the norm. They tried to have a family meal at least once a month. More often if possible. But things had been busy lately with the construction crew and Christmas season upon them.

Tonight's visit wasn't just a casual catchup, however. Hollis had an ulterior motive, which made him feel guiltier than the time he'd graffitied his old principal's vehicle—and that was saying a lot, because that '57 Corvette meant a lot to the former administer of Bloom High, and everyone in town knew it.

Pulling on a nice polo shirt, Hollis glanced at his reflection in the mirror. His beard was a little overgrown, which was fitting for a guy who worked at a Christmas tree farm. He kind of felt like a lumberjack.

On a shaky breath, Hollis turned from the mirror and headed toward the front of the house. Grabbing his car keys, he left to have a meal with Matt and Sandy—and the talk Hollis was dreading. Both Evan and Mallory had convinced Hollis that it wouldn't hurt to at least broach the subject of not being the one to take over the construction crew for Matt. It wasn't that Hollis was ungrateful. Or that he wasn't honored that Matt thought so much of him. It wasn't that he didn't think highly of the business that Matt had spent the last three decades building. Matt had achieved so much, just like Pop had in opening Bloom's first tree farm.

Driving slowly down the dirt path from his home, Hollis rehearsed what he was going to say. Hollis wanted to follow his heart, but doing so felt like he was infringing on Matt's birthright—even if Matt didn't care about maintaining what Pop had built.

Hollis let his gaze roam over the lot of trees as he approached the end of the dirt road where the large wooden sign for Popadine's Christmas Tree Farm was posted in the ground. Evan had insisted that Matt would understand. After all, Matt had been a young, ambitious guy at one time, and Matt hadn't wanted to follow in his father's footsteps. Instead, he'd stepped out and followed his own dream. The old saying that a person should follow their heart was all well and good until it conflicted with the next person's heart.

"Your heart will never lead you wrong," Mallory had told Hollis just this morning. He wondered if she knew his heart was tugging him toward her as well.

Just the thought of Mal sent his blood coursing through his veins. *Don't get your hopes up, Hol.* Yes, they'd kissed, more than once, and yes, those kisses had short-circuited and then rewired his entire nervous system. He liked what was happening between them, but he wasn't a fool. She had the potential to break his heart. He'd already explored that possibility in his mind and decided that, whatever happened, it'd be worth it.

It was the alternate what-ifs that scared him most. What if Mallory didn't break his heart? What if she stuck around? What if she actually liked him for who he was as much as he liked her? He'd attended enough therapy and group sessions while he was in juvenile detention to know that he was the ultimate self-saboteur. What if *he* was the heartbreaker in this situation? Not because he didn't want to be with Mallory. No, if he ended things, it would be because he let his fear and insecurities spur him to do something idiotic—which wasn't too far-fetched.

As Hollis turned his truck into Matt and Sandy's neighborhood, he lifted his foot off the gas pedal and slowed.

Worst-case scenario tonight: Matt got angry and asked Hollis to leave. Matt could be a hothead, but he always cooled down eventually. Matt was a rational man. A good man. And Hollis wasn't trying to steal Matt's inheritance. The proposition that Hollis was coming in with was that the land would remain legally Matt's one day. Hollis just wanted to strike a deal where he ran Pop's tree farm and also upstarted his own dog-training business on the property.

Best-case scenario tonight: Matt immediately saw the good in the situation and gave him his blessing.

The evening sun blinded him momentarily as he cut the truck's engine and stepped out in Matt and Sandy's driveway.

"Hollis!" Sandy called, opening her arms wide to give him a hug as soon as he climbed the porch steps. Sandy was a small-framed woman, barely five feet tall, and yet, when he had been a rebellious seventeen-year-old, she could put the fear of God in him when she was angry. These days, Hollis didn't give her much reason to get that heated. Instead, she was more of the grandmotherly type. Since she and Matt didn't have any biological children, they had recently started to nudge Hollis about settling down and giving them some grandchildren.

"Come on in." Sandy closed the door behind him and walked past, talking as she led him toward the kitchen, where he could smell something delicious cooking.

"Where's Matt?" he asked, glancing around.

"Oh, you know him. Always working late, especially during the holidays when you're at the tree farm." Her tone was a little pointed. "He says he's going to retire next year, but I'll believe it when I see it." She shook her head and laughed quietly. "But he'll be here soon. He promised. He just wanted to wrap up whatever he was doing at the new site and then drop by to see Pop on the way home."

Matt didn't visit his dad nearly as much as Hollis. Matt had a lot on his plate. He always had. "That's great." Hollis rubbed his hands together as he breathed in the yummy aroma in the air. "I'm sure Pop will appreciate the visit."

Sandy nodded knowingly. "I need to get over there and see him myself." There was a slight hint of guilt playing in her facial expression as she glanced over her shoulder at Hollis. "He loves my chocolate chip cookies. Maybe I'll whip up a batch and carry them over this weekend."

"I'm sure he'd like that."

Hollis heard the front door open.

"Oh, that must be Matt now," Sandy said excitedly. She patted Hollis's shoulder as she hurried out of the kitchen to greet her husband.

Hollis remained in the kitchen, stepping over to the stove to see what she was creating that had such a delicious aroma. Sandy was an amazing cook, and her meals didn't disappoint. He'd grown up eating fast-food and packaged junk. Home-cooked meals were rare until Matt and Sandy had taken him in.

Guilt flared in the pit of his stomach, suppressing his appetite. He wasn't looking forward to tonight's conversation. Matt is a reasonable man though, he reminded himself.

"There you are!"

Hollis turned toward Matt's raised voice. His angry voice. At first, he thought Matt was playing, because Matt rarely showed his temper. When Hollis saw Matt's flushed cheeks, however, he knew this was serious.

"Matt," Sandy said, her expression dropping along with her jaw in surprise, "what's going on?"

Matt pointed in Hollis's direction, his finger shaking. "He knows."

Hollis was at a loss, his brain on overdrive as it worked to put the pieces of the puzzle in place. Matt had stopped at Memory Oaks tonight.

Oh no.

Pop must have told Matt about the offer. Hollis hadn't accepted, although he'd been strongly considering doing so. But Pop didn't know that.

Hollis lifted both hands with his open palms turned out in surrender. "Let me explain."

Sandy continued to look between them, her brow line softly pinching. She stomped and put her hands on her hips. "Somebody tell me what's going on right this minute."

Matt glanced over at his wife, and then looked at Hollis. "Go on. Tell her. Tell my wife the reason why I'm so upset."

Hollis opened his mouth but no words came out. He took several shallow breaths, feeling like a fish out of water. "This isn't the way I wanted to tell you." He kept his voice quiet. Wasn't Matt the one who'd taught him that a calm tone was the easiest way to turn away wrath? "You have the wrong idea about the situation. I'd like to sit down and calmly discuss things." Hollis gestured at Matt and Sandy's dining room table. "Please."

Matt emitted a noise from deep in his throat that sounded like a low growl—the kind of warning that dogs gave before they attacked. "Get out of my house," he said, his voice equally quiet, but in an unsettling way. "Get out before I throw you out."

The setting sun cast long shadows across the peeling paint of the front door as Hollis trudged up the porch steps of the house where he'd been living for the better part of a year. Matt's words still rang in his ears, a bitter blend of disappointment and rejection.

"No son of mine would ever do this to me. No real son… Get out and don't come back."

Fumbling with his keys, Hollis's hands shook as he tried to fit them into the door's lock. He'd always believed in second chances, in the power of change. It was what had gotten him through his years in the foster system, bouncing from home to home. It was what had driven him to take in Duke, the scraggly mutt no one else wanted and, more recently, to foster Buster, a lab mix with a history of aggression.

As the front door finally swung open, Hollis just wanted to go inside and take a long, hot shower, rinsing off the filth of the day he'd just had. He was hit with a heaviness as he entered the front door, however. Something heavier than he was already feeling.

His eyes scanned the dimly lit room, looking for something. He wasn't exactly sure what, but there was a tension in the air wrapped in the faint smell of blood.

And then Hollis heard a tiny whimper.

"Duke?… Buster?"

Another low whimper answered him, coming from the mud room near the back door where he kept the two dog crates. Hollis rushed in that direction, his breath catching as he took in the scene. Duke lay on his side, just in front of his crate, his golden fur matted with dark blood.

"Duke!" Hollis's knees buckled in front of his dog. In response to Hollis's gentle stroke on his forehead, Duke's tail gave a weak thump against the tiled floor.

What had happened here tonight? Hollis looked in the direction of Buster's crate—it was empty. He scanned the room, but Buster was nowhere in sight.

He was positive he'd left both dogs crated. The crate doors were open, however. Hollis's gaze jumped to the doggie door that led to the fenced area in the backyard. Bloody paw prints made a path from the doggie door to the spot where Duke was lying. Hollis looked at Duke again. "Did you two get out somehow?" He quickly got up, hesitant to leave Duke's side, but what if Buster was injured as well? Stepping onto the back porch, Hollis looked around. "Buster!" he called. "Buster, come!" He waited for a long beat, but there was no sign of the lab mix. The gate was closed, but it was possible that Buster might have gotten on the roof of the outdoor kennel and jumped the fence.

"Buster!" he called again. He couldn't search right now. Duke's condition seemed serious. He'd been Hollis's constant over the past five years, his anchor in a world that always seemed ready to cast him adrift—just like it'd done tonight.

"Come on, buddy." With gentle hands, he scooped Duke into his arms, wincing at the dog's painful yelp. "It's okay, boy," he murmured, blinking away the sting of tears. "I'm gonna get you help."

He cast one last look at the doggie door, hoping Buster would bust through. He hated to leave, knowing that Buster was out there. Was he injured too? Or was he responsible for Duke's condition?

"I'm sorry, Duke," Hollis whispered. There was too much blood matted on the dog's fur to see if the injuries were punctures or gashes. What was the extent of his injuries?

The drive to the emergency vet was a blur of red lights and frantic prayers while Duke whimpered and panted softly in the passenger seat. Hollis's mind raced, replaying the events of the day in an endless, torturous loop. Matt's rejection, Duke's injuries, Buster missing—it all swirled together into a maelstrom of pain and doubt. He'd had that familiar feeling of everything being too good to be true a lot this season. He should have known that life would backhand him and knock him to the ground.

"Hollis," Dr. Lynch said ten minutes later when Hollis walked into the veterinarian's office. "Follow me." She led him to an examining room and motioned for Hollis to lay Duke on the metal table.

Stepping back, Hollis watched, feeling helpless as the doctor gave Duke a sedative to calm him. Then she took her time cleaning and assessing every wound.

"No sugarcoating. Just say it," Hollis said after ten minutes of holding his breath and floating up prayers.

"His condition is serious," she said gently. "I think he's stable for now, but I'll need to keep him here. I need to sew up some of the deeper gashes, and with all these wounds, there's a risk of infection."

Hollis nodded numbly.

"He was definitely attacked by something," Dr. Lynch continued. "Where's..." She hesitated.

"Buster didn't do this," Hollis said, even though the thought had crossed his mind. He was ready to insist that Buster was a good dog. Buster hadn't shown any aggressive tendencies since coming home with Hollis.

"I'm not saying he did," Dr. Lynch said. "I'm still assessing the nature of the injuries. I've got this though, Hollis. Duke is in good hands with me. You know that."

He nodded. "I do know that."

She forced him to meet her eyes. "You need to go find Buster right now. Because something happened while you were gone. If Buster isn't responsible for Duke's condition, he could be injured too. Or..." She trailed off again.

Or worse. Yeah.

Hollis nodded. "Right. I need to find him." He didn't move though. Not until Dr. Lynch reached out and laid a hand on his shoulder.

"I'll call you as soon as I have more information on Duke. Trust me."

He did trust Dr. Lynch. He'd been working with her for years through the rescue and with his dog training clients. "Thank you," he said quietly. Then he turned and forced himself to leave the vet's office when all he really wanted was to stay by Duke's side.

The Star Ornament

The Star Ornament is in the box labeled with a 12. Inside, yes, you'll see a sparkly, glittery star. Usually, the star goes on top of a tree, but not this one. This one is hung twelfth down. It was a gift from the Bloom mayor, if you can believe it. An honor and a treasure, and the reason my play became a Bloom holiday staple.

Here's the story.

That first year of motherhood with my baby girl, I felt like I was stumbling through a thick fog, never quite sure if I was doing anything right. Every cry, every sleepless night, every moment of uncertainty chipped away at my confidence.

I remember standing in the nursery one night, my daughter wailing in my arms, and feeling completely overwhelmed. The theater, my pride and joy, felt like a distant memory. My dreams of Broadway stardom seemed laughable now. In that dark moment, I considered running away from it all—my husband, my child, the theater. Everything.

That feeling lingered for days until my mother, bless her heart, took me aside. She must have sensed the exhaustion and seen the doubt in my eyes. "Nannette," she said, using my full name, like she always did when she was being serious, "good mothers always feel like they're doing things wrong. It's a sign that you care and that you want the best for your baby girl."

Those words were like a lifeline. They didn't magically make everything easier, but they gave me the strength to keep going.

Mickey, my dear sweet husband, was a rock through it

all. He'd get up in the middle of the night to tend to the baby, insisting that I needed my rest. "You've got a theater to run, darling," he'd say with a wink. "And you're doing it with a baby on your hip, literally carrying the load all day. Let me handle the midnight feedings."

Not all women are as lucky to have a spouse who understands how hard it is. I'd direct rehearsals while bouncing Daisy in my arm and rewriting scripts one-handed while she napped on my chest. The actors and crew were wonderfully understanding, cooing over her between scenes and offering to watch her when I needed a moment.

It certainly wasn't the life I'd envisioned when I'd set off for New York with stars in my eyes and Broadway dreams in my heart. But as the months went by, I realized it was so much more. The theater became not just my passion, but also a second home for my little family. My daughter's first steps were on that stage, her giggles echoing in the wings as she watched rehearsals from her playpen.

Being a mother changed me in ways I never could have foreseen. It softened my edges, making me more patient, more understanding. It gave me a new perspective on the stories we told onstage, a deeper appreciation for the complexities of human emotion.

That first year flew by in a blur of sleepless nights, baby giggles, and theater productions. Before I knew it, my little girl was toddling around, babbling her first words—many of which, I'm proud to say, were theater terms she'd picked up from all the time spent there. As the next Christmas approached, and the one after that, the town folk asked about our annual production of *Santa, Baby*. They didn't just ask—they practically demanded it. The mayor came to me personally because *Santa, Baby* had been the topic of a town meeting. The town wanted the play to continue. As if I might say no, the mayor brought me a gift. A beautiful brass star to represent what he said I was to Bloom—a shining star.

Who needed Broadway when they had the entire town of Bloom as their fan base?

I think it was more the play that had struck a chord than me, actually. Santa and Mrs. Claus having a "real" marriage? The kind that all married couples knew. The well-kept secret that kept hopeless romantics believing the fairy tales they'd grown up believing. My debut play had become such a beloved tradition in such a short time that it drew people from neighboring towns every year, more and more as word of mouth spread.

The rest, as they say, is history. Bloom history. *Santa, Baby* became an annual tradition, one that would shape our little town for years to come. It was more than a play; it was a piece of who we were, a testament to the power of family, community, and the magic of theater.

Looking back now, I wouldn't change a thing. My daughter grew up in that theater that was our wonderland. And then my granddaughters too—but that's a different story. More plays came along, some that stuck and some that didn't. But *Santa, Baby* continued. The magic captured in that script was what got me through the darkest moments. That magical feeling spoke to the town as well.

It brought the community together for a shared experience each year, to laugh and cry and catch that glimmer of hope that shimmers brightest during the holidays.

And, if you ask me, that's the real magic, the kind that lasts long after the curtain falls.

Truthfully, I think the reason that play resonated was because of the leading man—the one in my head when I'd written the story. It was this imaginary story of me and my first love. The only place we ever got to exist after that whirlwind romance in high school.

Chapter Twenty-Three

To be an actor you have to be a child.

—Paul Newman

Mallory's fingers drummed against the steering wheel as she navigated the winding road to Memory Oaks Nursing Care, her conversation with Maddie echoing in her mind. It wasn't like Mallory to let her emotions get the better of her, but Maddie's insistence and vastly differing opinion about something so sentimental stung.

But Maddie did have a point. Selling was the only answer to being able to afford Nan's continued long-term care. She was wrong about Mallory not wanting to deal with the theater though—even with the now-necessary repairs.

Mallory pulled into the parking lot of Memory Oaks and took a deep breath, trying to push aside her discombobulated feelings. Nan was sensitive to everything around her. Mallory didn't want to set Nan off, especially tonight, with the holiday celebration happening in the community room.

As Mallory entered the facility's lobby, she took in the festive decorations, garlands draped along the reception desk, and the small

Christmas tree twinkling in the lobby's corner. Mallory checked in with Francis at the front desk.

"Is Hollis here yet?" she asked.

Francis shook her head. "Not yet, but he told me earlier that he was coming."

He'd told Mallory the same. And if he said it, he meant it.

"Nan is already in the community room," Francis told her. "I'm sure she'll be happy to see you."

Mallory knew Francis meant well, but they both knew that wasn't always the case. "We'll see. Thanks, Francis." Mallory followed the noise down the hall to the open double doors of the community room, where residents and staff were milling about. Christmas music played softly in the background. The large, beautifully decorated tree from Pop's tree farm dominated one corner, its branches laden with an eclectic mix of ornaments in addition to Nan's for the Memory Tree.

Mallory looked around until she saw Nan sitting at a table near the tree. A half-eaten cookie with red and green sprinkles was on the plate in front of her. Her silver hair was neatly combed, and she was wearing a red sweater that Mallory recognized as one of Nan's favorites from years past. Nan had always loved crazy Christmas sweaters, which contradicted the rest of her simple, yet classy wardrobe.

Nan's eyes brightened with a spark of recognition when she saw Mallory approaching. "Hello there, dear." Nan's voice was warm but slightly uncertain. "Are you here for the party?"

Mallory managed a smile as she sat down next to her grandmother. "I'm actually here to see you, Nan. It's me, Mallory."

Confusion deepened the soft wrinkles on her face. "Mallory, you say? My, that's a lovely name." Nan averted her gaze and scanned the room. Her brow crinkled the way it used to when she was focused on outlining a script or rearranging stage directions during the rehearsals of a play. Then she turned back to Mallory. "Do you like the theater?"

Nan hadn't talked about the theater in months. "I l-love the theater," Mallory finally managed, surprising herself because her answer was sincere. "I practically grew up in one."

Nan's face lit up. "Oh, that sounds nice! I used to run a theater, you know."

Mallory nodded. "That sounds nice too."

"It was…" Nan said, hesitating as if reaching for the exactly right words. "It was the most magical place in the world."

Mallory blinked back tears. "I bet it was magical."

As they talked, Mallory found herself slipping into the rhythm of conversation with this new version of her grandmother. Nan might not remember their shared history, but her love for the theater shone through in every anecdote, every enthusiastic gesture, as she described her favorite plays.

Alzheimer's was such a complicated illness that Mallory still didn't understand, even though she'd exhausted Google researching it. Even though she was a nurse. Deep down, Mallory knew that Nan probably wouldn't hold on to this sudden knowledge of theater. Tomorrow, she might not remember the theater at all.

After a while, a staff member announced that it was time for residents to hang their memory ornaments on the community tree.

Mallory reached into her bag and pulled out the next ornament in Nan's story. "I brought you something special." She held up a pink baby bootie. "Look how cute this is."

Nan turned her gaze and took in the ornament. "A sock?" she whispered quietly. "That's an ornament?"

"Unusual, isn't it?"

Nan stared at it intently. "I think… I think that meant something to me."

Mallory's heart nearly stopped. When Nan had a good day, she really did have one.

Slowly, Nan reached out and touched the ornament, her finger tapping it and causing it to sway gently like the pendulum of a clock. "Did you know that I had a daughter? Her name was…Daisy." Nan narrowed her eyes. "She looked like you. Are you—are you my Daisy?" Nan's eyes filled with tears. "Oh. Oh, my. You are, aren't you?"

The hope in Nan's eyes broke Mallory's heart. She wanted to tell her yes, but she didn't want to lie. She'd never lied to Nan, and she wasn't about to start now. "No, Nan. My name is Mallory."

"Oh." The light in Nan's eyes was like a star burning out as it fell from the sky. Nan looked down at her lap.

Mallory gently placed the ornament in Nan's age-spotted hands. "Here. Let's hang the bootie ornament on the tree."

Nan held the ornament, but she didn't move. "I'm not as sprightly as I once was. I don't think I can hang it on my own."

Mallory stood and took control of Nan's wheelchair, steering her toward the front of the room. "That's why I'm here. I'll help you."

"Such a sweet girl."

Once they were standing in front of the tree, Mallory locked the chair's brakes and guided her grandmother to stand.

Nan's hands shook as she reached out to hang the ornament, but her face was serene, almost reverent. "Daisy grew up in the theater just like you," Nan said, talking to herself as much as to Mallory.

Mallory was encouraged that Nan was still engaging in the same conversation that they'd started five minutes earlier. "Daisy must have been such a happy child."

"Of course. Even an adult can feel like a child again in the theater," Nan quipped. "I always did, at least."

Mallory had too. And she'd felt freer lately than she had in a long time.

As Mallory helped Nan settle back into her chair, they admired the tree with all its ornaments and lights, tinsel and garland. Then Mallory turned to take Nan back to her spot at the table but noticed Pop sitting at the opposite corner of the room. Hollis's grandfather looked small and somewhat lost in an oversize armchair. He was a newer resident here, and she imagined he didn't quite feel at home yet.

Mallory glanced at the large clock on the wall above Pop. *Where is Hollis?* It wasn't like him to be late, especially not for something involving Pop.

"Hey, Nan, would you like to say hello to Pop?" Mallory gestured toward the elderly man.

Nan's gaze followed the direction of Mallory's pointer. "That man's name isn't Pop."

Mallory frowned, afraid that Nan's moments of clarity were gone. "It is. He's a good friend of mine."

"Oh, he's a friend of mine too. Or used to be." Nan craned her neck to look at Mallory behind her pushing the wheelchair. "His name is Ralph."

Mallory stopped in her tracks, her breath catching as she looked at Nan and then Pop, sitting by the window. No. No, this was just Nan's memories blurring. Mallory wasn't sure who the man in Nan's journal entries was, but surely he wasn't Hollis's grandfather. "Well, he looks like he could use some company. Let's go say hello?"

As they crossed the room, Mallory pulled her phone from her pocket and quickly typed out a text to Hollis:

Mallory: Everything okay? We're at Memory Oaks for the tree decorating. Pop's here, but no sign of you yet.

Pop's weathered face broke into a small grin as he saw Mallory and Nan approach. "Well, hello there, Nan," he said, his voice rough but warm. "Come to join a brooding man in the corner?"

Nan laughed, the sound light and carefree. "Now, now," she chided. "No brooding allowed at Christmas. Have you hung your ornament yet?"

"My grandson is supposed to bring me one," he said, making a show of looking around. "Hollis must be caught up in something more important than an old man like me. Maybe he's found himself a date. I gave him a few pointers the other day," Pop added, smiling at Mallory and offering a wink.

Mallory laughed quietly and listened as Nan engaged Pop in more conversation. They talked like old friends, which warmed Mallory's heart. This was a wonderful place for Nan. Safe and joyful despite the pain and frustration that the patients' ailments brought. The joy on Nan's face right now was priceless. Except it did have a price. One that Mallory was having a difficult time affording.

Mallory's phone buzzed. That must be Hollis. Mallory reached inside her pocket for her phone, disappointed when she realized the message was from Savannah.

Savannah: How's Nan? Tell her hello for me.

Mallory was always happy to hear from her best friend, but growing concern niggled in her gut. Hollis had been attending events like these at Memory Oaks long before his grandfather moved in. Hollis brought his therapy dog and his charming personality. What was keeping him tonight?

"Oh, look." Pop pointed across the room as the staff gathered along the wall wearing red Santa hats. Then they broke out in song. "Carolers."

Nan hummed along, occasionally using her full voice for a line or two that she seemed to remember.

Watching and listening, Mallory felt a fierce protectiveness well up inside her. She had an impossible choice to make, but there really was no choice. Keeping Nan at this facility was the most important thing. Mallory could only work so many extra shifts at the hospital before she burned out completely.

Nan touched Mallory's arm, her eyes clear and bright. "Having you here means more than you know."

"I wouldn't be anywhere else, Nan." Mallory's gaze jumped to Pop. Hollis wouldn't be anywhere else either. Not if he could help it.

The niggling concern hit a discordant note in the otherwise harmonious evening.

Where is he?

Chapter Twenty-Four

No matter what they tell you, words and ideas can change the world.

—Robin Williams

"Buster!" Hollis had searched the inside of his house, calling Buster's name until his voice was hoarse.

Buster was nowhere to be seen.

Hollis had followed the trail of Duke's blood through the kitchen and onto Pop's back porch. He'd searched the entire backyard and beyond. Now he climbed the back porch steps and sat on one of the metal chairs. Leaning over his knees, he lowered his face into his palms, sending up the millionth silent plea to the Big Guy upstairs. Almost immediately, his phone buzzed in his pocket. No way God was on the line, answering his prayers. Hollis guessed he'd surpassed the limit of answered prayers. Instead of pulling his phone out of his pocket, he left it there to vibrate. He wasn't in a conversing mood, and there was no one he wanted to speak to right now.

Not Sandy and surely not Matt. He knew Mallory was concerned, but he didn't want to talk to her either. Ever since his earlier conversation, Hollis had been wondering if Matt was right. Maybe

Hollis had fooled everyone, including himself. The last thing Mallory needed was a romantic partner who would let her down. The kind of guy that Matt had painted Hollis to be. Nan was wrong. Mallory didn't need him. She would be better off without him.

His phone buzzed again. On a sigh, he pulled it out and read the screen.

Mallory: Why didn't you show up tonight?

Hollis reread the message. *Show up?* He was stumped for a moment, and then it hit him. The event at Memory Oaks. With all the stress of tonight, it'd completely slipped his mind. He got up and headed around to the front of the house in the direction of the tree farm.

His phone buzzed from within his pocket again. Instinctively, he knew who it was. "Sorry, Mal," he whispered before inhaling deeply. He breathed in the familiar pine scent that felt like a balm to the ache inside his chest.

Pop had found Hollis when Hollis was eighteen on a kind of night similar to this one. Hollis was already living with Matt and Sandy, so he wasn't exactly trespassing. He'd just driven his old pickup here, needing a place to think. He'd wanted to be alone, but Pop had come alongside him as he roamed these same rows.

That night, Pop began talking to Hollis's nonreceptive ears. His weathered hands demonstrated how to check the trees for freshness, how to trim the branches just so, how to care for each tree as if it were destined for the grandest living room in the world. For the White House.

"This farm, Hollis," Pop had said, his eyes twinkling with pride, "it's more than just trees. It's tradition, it's family, it's…magic." He'd clapped a hand along Hollis's shoulder blade then, his grip firm and reassuring. "And someday, son, it'll be yours."

Hollis hadn't believed Pop. Not by a long shot. Promises were meant to be broken. But now, as Hollis ran his hand along the prickly branches of a Douglas fir, it wasn't the promise that crept in around his heart like a winter chill. Broken promises weren't the worst thing that could happen.

Hollis knew the strain the farm put on Matt when Hollis left the construction crew for the holiday season. He also knew maintaining the tree farm was more than an eight-week job. It was yearlong, and there were a hundred variables to track, including weather and pests. Pop had meant well in offering this land to Hollis, but maybe... maybe it was time for Pop to let go.

Hollis walked to the far end of the lot and stared out at the dark fields beyond. "Buster! Come! Buster!" He waited, listening for an answering bark or the sound of paws padding across the frozen ground. The only sound he heard, though, was the loud voice in his mind.

He felt like he had a choice to make, but honestly, there was no choice. Matt had now made it clear how he felt and Hollis would not do anything to hurt Matt more.

As he turned to head back, another thought struck him with the force of a physical blow. He'd watched Mallory come alive this holiday season, shifting from an overworked, overwhelmed nurse to a woman renewed. Restored. She'd always been beautiful to him, but never more than these past few weeks. Staring at her, memorizing every detail of her face, every expression...it was contagious. Addictive.

He loved that she was feeling freer and more relaxed these days, but everything he touched eventually fell apart. Some part of him wanted to argue that he was being dramatic, but just look at his life. One dog was possibly dying. The other was missing. He'd hurt the only family he'd ever known, and now, not only was he out of work in construction—because no way was Matt keeping him on the crew—but he would also be losing his job at the farm along with all the plans he'd made.

"Buster!" he called again, walking up and down the rows of trees. "Buster! Come on, boy!"

In his heart of hearts, he didn't believe that Buster had hurt

Duke. Maybe Buster had run because he was scared. Running felt like the natural thing to do when you were hurt or scared. That was exactly how Hollis felt right now. And perhaps Hollis leaving would be best for everyone.

By the time Hollis reached the front porch again, his mind was set. He'd make it clear to Pop that he couldn't accept the generous offer of taking over the tree farm. Then he'd apologize to Matt and offer his official resignation. Considering all things, he'd also plan on moving out of Pop's house.

He was unemployed, homeless, and dog-less. All in a day's time.

His phone buzzed again. No doubt it was Mallory calling, but he didn't have it in him to connect. He'd already let her down tonight by not showing up. He was also letting Nan down by breaking last year's promise to her.

Nan hadn't told him to kiss Mallory though. And now that Matt had called Hollis's character into question, he wondered if he'd unintentionally taken advantage of her vulnerability. Pulling in a deep breath, he suddenly reflected on himself from a different point of view than the one he'd come to see himself from. Maybe he wasn't the good guy he'd worked so hard to become. Was it possible that he was still that rebellious troublemaker of the past?

Hollis tipped his face toward the sky, feeling the cold sting of a snowflake landing on his cheek. Protect Mallory from herself. That was Nan's request. But maybe, by doing so, he also needed to protect her from him. Mallory was soaring these last couple of weeks, and he didn't want to weigh her down. All his life, he'd told himself that real men didn't leave the way his father had done, but perhaps, in some situations, if it meant everyone around them was better off, they did.

Pulling out his phone, he opened the latest text thread with Evan and tapped his fingertip along the screen.

Hollis: I need you to take my place in the play tomorrow. Someone can feed you the lines in your ear mic.

Evan: You're kidding, right?

Hollis: Sorry. I'm finally cashing in on all the favors.

Evan: You okay?

Hollis stared at his phone's screen. No, he wasn't okay. Not even a little.

Hollis: I'm good, buddy. Thanks for the help.

Turning off his phone, he went inside Pop's house, changed his clothing, and climbed into bed. And in the darkness of the room, he did something else he'd always thought a real man didn't do—he cried.

The Pink Bootie Ornament

The Pink Bootie Ornament is number 13. When you open the box, you'll see the impossibly tiny little baby sock. The little foot that wore it grew too big. The baby learned to walk and boy, did she go far. But before her little feet walked, I held them. I tickled them and adored every toe, all ten. You may think you know whose feet I'm talking about, but I think you'll be surprised.

Here's the story behind The Pink Bootie Ornament.

My daughter, your mother, Daisy, was a spitfire. You should have seen her, barely tall enough to peek over the edge of the stage, eyes wide with wonder as she watched the actors rehearse. She'd toddle around backstage, trailing ribbons and sparkles in her wake, a tiny whirlwind of creativity and joy.

As years went on, things changed, though, as they tend to do. Daisy grew older, and that spark I'd seen in her eyes began to dim. Gradual at first. So subtle that I didn't see it happening. But then, one day, I turned around and found a stranger standing where my little girl used to be.

I tried to help her, to bridge that growing chasm between us. I'd ask about her day, try to engage her in conversations about the things she liked. But it was like trying to catch smoke with my bare hands. The more I reached out, the further I felt her slipping away.

We just didn't have much in common anymore. Where I saw magic in the swish of a curtain or the hush of an anticipating audience, Daisy longed to be on a screen—small or big. It didn't matter. She didn't see the point of theater, which was captured in the moment but gone after the last bow. She begged me to drive her to the closest auditions, which were hours away. My schedule didn't allow for that.

"I'll live with Aunt Mauve then," Daisy had said. As you know, Mauve is my sister, at the time, a single woman who lived in Boston. "Aunt Mauve has already said I could."

That fact felt like a betrayal.

"I'm your mother."

"Then let me be happy."

I said no, of course. Over and over. Then one day, I came home, and Daisy was gone. I was frantic, imagining all sorts of terrible scenarios. But Daisy came back after a day, sullen and not at all apologetic. After that, it became a pattern. She'd disappear for a day or two and then return as if nothing had happened.

Then came the Christmas when she was sixteen years old. It was the night of the big show, *Santa, Baby*. I was backstage, fussing over costumes and last-minute changes when Mickey told me Daisy was gone. Not just gone to a friend's house or the mall. Really gone.

For the first time in Bloom's history, that year the Christmas play didn't go on. Not that night, at least. I canceled the show, much to everyone's disappointment. But how could I stand on that stage, spouting lines about joy and family when my own child was out there somewhere, alone?

We found her a week later, holed up in a run-down motel two towns over. She'd been hitching rides, trying to get to Mauve's home in Boston. Daisy was cold, hungry, and more angry than I'd ever seen her. When I told her about the canceled play, she flew into a rage.

"See?" she screamed. "Your precious show is more

important than me! You only came looking because you had to cancel it!"

"That's not true, Daisy. I canceled the play because I love you more. You mean more to me than the entire world. And without you, the show doesn't go on. It can't."

"If you love me, let me live with Aunt Mauve. Let me chase my dream. Don't punish me because you never lived yours."

It felt like a slap in my face.

"I'm not going back with you," Daisy said.

"You'd rather be here? Cold and hungry?"

Daisy lifted her chin, her eyes flashing a million feelings. In a way, I saw myself in her. The me that had gone off to New York, chasing things that I thought were bigger and brighter. And better. I never would have found my true happiness had I not gone off and realized it was all a lie. The grass was not greener on the other side. "Yes. And if you force me to go back with you, I'll just leave again the first chance I get."

I knew she was telling the truth. She'd leave. This cycle would continue. I had to let her go and pray she'd return the way I did to my family.

"Okay. I'll drive you to Mauve's." At least Daisy wouldn't be living on the streets or at the mercy of whoever gave her a ride.

So I took her to my sister's, making sure Daisy knew my door would always be open to her. Then I returned to Bloom, and the Christmas play went on the following week. The town was understanding, rallying around us with a spirit of unity I'll never forget. Christmas wasn't the same without my daughter though. My joy was gone. My heart was broken.

The new year came and went, and I prayed for my Daisy all day every day. Bring her home. Bring my Daisy home. Then one day, a year later, my prayer was answered. Standing on my porch like a vision, looking older, tired...and carrying a bundle in her arms. For a moment, I thought I was dreaming. But then the pink bundle moved, and I heard the unmistakable cry of a baby.

A warmth spread through my chest.

My granddaughter. Oh, she was the tiniest, most perfect thing I'd ever seen, dressed in a little onesie with the teeniest booties on her tiny feet. In that moment, looking at Daisy's uncertain face and that precious baby, I knew that everything was going to be all right.

"Aunt Mauve didn't know," she said, almost as if hearing my unspoken question. "She doesn't really pay attention to me."

This didn't surprise me. Mauve was a workaholic. She'd agreed to have Daisy stay with her, but I was under no illusion that she was filling the role of Daisy's mother.

"I haven't asked, but... Well, I don't think Aunt Mauve will let us both stay." Daisy was sheepish.

"You both can stay here. Of course, you can," I told her, my heart bursting at the idea of having my daughter back.

"That's not what I'm asking," Daisy said, lowering her gaze. "I want to go back."

"Oh." Time slowed as my mind raced.

"Please," Daisy whispered.

She was asking us to take her daughter so that she could return to chasing foolish dreams. She'd always accused me of loving the theater more than her, but here she was, loving the idea of being a famous actress more than the one of a loving mother.

I opened my arms and took the tiny human, holding her against my chest. Tears slid over my cheeks as I looked down at her.

"Her name is Mallory," Daisy said quietly. Then she turned and walked away without looking back.

Life is a lot like theater. Full of unexpected plot twists, moments of high drama, and the occasional intermission. And, if it's a good play, there'll be a happy ending.

Mallory, you grew out of those little pink booties, but they are so precious to me. So much so that I made one into an ornament for my Memory Tree. When I see the tiny sock, my mind immediately goes to the first moment I met you. I knew life after that day would never be the same.

Chapter Twenty-Five

The theater is a weapon, and it is the people who should wield it.

—Augusto Boal

Mallory unlocked her front door, tired from the night's festivities but also worried. She checked her phone again—still no response from Hollis. It wasn't like him to go silent, especially when he'd promised to be at the event.

She kicked off her shoes and left them beside the door. Then she pulled up Savannah's contact and paced the living room as the phone rang in her ear.

"Hey, Mal," Savannah finally answered. "I just heard what happened. How's Hollis?"

Mallory pulled the ponytail tie from her hair, letting her locks fall free along her shoulders. "What do you mean? I haven't heard from him all night. He was supposed to be at the Memory Oaks event but never showed. Is he okay?" It was amazing how many worst-case scenarios could fill her mind in the time it took to ask the question and wait on Savannah's answer.

"You didn't know? Evan just spoke to Dr. Lynch. That's the only way he knew."

"Dr. Lynch," Mallory repeated, pausing her pacing to stand still and try to process this information. "The veterinarian?"

"Yeah. Hollis rushed Duke to the emergency vet tonight. She said Hollis was upset, and she called Evan to check on him. She told Evan that Hollis was going to be searching for Buster."

Mallory combed her fingers through the front of her hair. "Why? Is Buster missing?"

"You know as much as me now," Savannah said. "Evan tried to call Hollis too, but he's not responding."

Mallory's heart sank. "Duke means everything to Hollis."

"I know," Savannah said softly.

Mallory glanced at the clock—nearly midnight. As much as she wanted to rush to Hollis's side, she doubted she'd be able to find him anyway. She knew from experience that when a person wanted to be alone, they'd find a way to disappear, just like she'd done in Eleanor's Little Free Library. "Thanks for filling me in."

"I kind of just assumed you already knew," Savannah said. "Worrisome that he's not answering you or Evan."

Yeah. Mallory was even more worried, now that she knew it wasn't just her that Hollis was avoiding. "I'll drive by his house and check on him first thing tomorrow before my hospital shift."

"I'm glad you're being sensible and not trying to go over there now. There's the most responsible friend I know," Savannah teased.

Responsible. That was her.

After disconnecting, Mallory sat on her couch and debated throwing responsibility out the window and going out in the dark woods to look for Buster herself. It was a recipe for disaster though. The North Carolina woods had black bears and coyotes, and she had no clue where Buster's last known location was to even decide where to begin looking. Feeling helpless, she fired off one more text:

Mallory: Just heard about Duke. I'm here if you need anything.

As she prepared for bed, Mallory set her alarm earlier than usual. Whatever news the morning brought, she was determined to be there for Hollis, just like he'd been there for her this past month. His loyalty had been unwavering, and she'd done something she rarely allowed herself to do—she'd leaned in when someone offered their support.

Now she wanted to return the favor.

Mallory's alarm yanked her from a fitful sleep. Fumbling for her phone, her heart sank when she saw that there were no new messages from Hollis.

She got it. He was upset. Probably devastated. This past month, he had become her fiercest protector, and she imagined he didn't want to burden her with the things that were going on in his life right now. *That's probably why he hasn't called or texted.* He was wrong though. She wanted to be there for him. She just had to find him.

Worry gnawed at her as she hurriedly dressed and grabbed her keys, determined to do just that before her hospital shift.

As she drove, her mind picked through all the possibilities of what might be going on in Hollis's head. She didn't have much information to go on. Just that Duke was in bad shape and Buster was missing.

Poor Hollis.

When she finally pulled onto the dirt road that led past Popadine's Tree Farm to the little house where Hollis was staying, her stomach dropped. His truck was gone, and the house sat dark and silent.

She parked anyway and got out, approaching the front door to see if she could find a clue to where he'd gone. As she poked around, another vehicle pulled in behind hers, and Sandy stepped out.

"Mallory? What are you doing here so early?" Sandy asked, heading in her direction.

"I was worried about Hollis. He missed last night's event at Memory Oaks, and he's not answering my texts. Have you heard from him?"

Sandy's face scrunched with concern as she nodded. "He texted early to ask if I could help you with the Christmas play tonight. He said he wouldn't be able to fulfill his commitments."

Mallory felt like she'd been doused with ice water. "What? But... but he can't just not show up for the play. He has two major roles. He was the one who insisted that I didn't give up when others dropped out. He volunteered for those parts, and I only agreed to keep going because I trusted him."

Sandy wrung her hands in front of her. "He told me to let you know that Evan would take his place. He's already made the arrangements. He said that Evan would be a better Santa than him."

"What? No." Mallory pressed a hand to her chest as panic swept over her. "This is opening night!" she said, her voice strained as she struggled to breathe.

Sandy reached out and placed a gentle hand on Mallory's arm. "I'm sorry, dear. I don't know why Matt spoke to him the way he did."

Mallory narrowed her eyes. "Matt? Did something happen at dinner yesterday?" She knew that Hollis was supposed to eat with Matt and Sandy before the Memory Oaks event.

"I thought you knew."

"I only knew about Duke and Buster."

Now Sandy looked confused. Apparently, there was so much more to what was going on with Hollis than Mallory even knew.

"All I know is that Hollis rushed Duke to the emergency vet last night, and Buster is missing."

Sandy drew both hands up to cover her mouth. "I had no idea. Poor Hollis."

Mallory's anger deflated slightly.

"I hope he's not gone-gone," Sandy said quietly, glancing around the front porch.

Mallory didn't like the sound of that. "What does that mean?"

Sandy's expression seemed to wilt. "When Hollis first came to live with us, he'd sometimes, I don't know...he'd run away when things got too overwhelming. He hasn't done it in years, of course. He's a grown man. But..."

"Sandy, what did you mean about something happening with Matt last night?" Mallory asked, concern mounting.

Sandy sighed. "Matt can be so irrational when he's angry. It was awful," she said, voice tight. "He came in with a raised voice, pointing his finger at Hollis as if he'd done something horrible. Accusing Hollis of trying to steal the farm." She pressed a hand to her chest. "I know Hollis would never steal from us, but whatever Pop told Matt, well, it got him fired up. Hollis just shut down and left. And now with Duke being sick..." She looked at Mallory with pain reflecting in her eyes. "I'm afraid it may have been too much."

Mallory's mind whirled as she tried to process everything. "So Hollis is just...gone? And he's abandoning the play? Abandoning..." *Me*, she thought but couldn't bring herself to say it. How could she be angry when Hollis had had a day like that one?

Sandy grimaced subtly. "Christmas has always been a little shaky for Hollis. Shaky for a lot of people, to be honest... I think he just needs some time."

"Time?" Mallory didn't have time to offer. The show must go on! That was the rule. Set your personal issues aside, just like Nan had. Nan had continued after the loss of a child and through a pregnancy with another. She'd continued when Mallory's mom had run away and then when Daisy had returned with a newborn baby.

Mallory leaned against Hollis's porch railing, suddenly feeling exhausted. "I wish he would let me help instead of freezing me out.

All month he's preached to me about leaning on others and accepting help. Now he's doing exactly what he told me not to."

Sandy reached up and gave Mallory's shoulder a squeeze. "Oh, honey. You know Hollis as well as I do. He's first to offer a helping hand, but sometimes he'll dig himself in a bigger hole rather than reach up and allow someone to pull him up. He's always struggled with feeling worthy of the good things in his life. And, I hate to say it, but Matt may have set Hollis back with any progress he's ever made toward self-worth. Believe you me, I gave my husband a piece of my mind after he ran Hollis off." She breathed a heavy sigh. "Mallory, you're one of the best things that's happened to him in a long time."

"If that's true, he wouldn't be ghosting me," she muttered, knowing she had no right to take this personally. She knew it in her mind, but her heart felt broken. She thought that she and Hollis were close. She'd begun to lean on him. Why couldn't he do the same and trust her as well?

"I think maybe you're looking at it from the wrong perspective. I suspect Hollis has himself convinced that he's protecting you by pulling away."

"That I'd be better off without him," Mallory whispered, realizing that what Sandy was saying was right. That sounded exactly like something Hollis might do.

Mallory nodded slowly, the pieces of the puzzle slowly falling into place. "What do we do now?"

"You know the answer to that. As your grandmother would say..." Sandy said, trailing off.

Mallory nodded, understanding completely. "Okay. Let's figure out how to have the play without our leading man." And she'd just have to hope that Hollis was okay, wherever he was.

The Compass Ornament

The Compass Ornament is in the box labeled number 14. Inside, you'll find Mickey's treasured compass with the face cracked right through the middle. When you hang it, you'll note that the little arrow points wherever it wants. There is no north or south, west or east—and I think there's a message to be learned there, up for interpretation.

Here's the story.

Deep down, I knew that Daisy did the right thing by leaving. And, some part of me was proud of her for choosing Mallory's well-being over her own desire to cling to her. Even so, I waited for Daisy to return. Every day brought new hope that this would be the one when she appeared on my doorstep, the prodigal daughter, renewed. I told myself that she would find herself wherever she was and then she would come home again.

As those days passed, Mallory grew more beautiful, more vibrant. She had Daisy's eyes and what Mickey liked to call my stubborn chin. Her laughter filled our home in a way it hadn't in years, chasing away the loneliness that had settled in after Daisy left.

I found myself staying up late, rocking Mallory to sleep and whispering stories of the stage into her tiny ears. Unlike Daisy, who had grown to resent the theater, Mallory seemed entranced by it. Her eyes would light up at the sight of the heavy velvet curtains, and she'd clap her chubby hands in delight at the sound of applause.

As her third birthday approached, I realized something had changed in me. I no longer prayed for Daisy's return. Instead, I found myself hoping, guiltily, selfishly, that my own daughter would stay away. That Mallory would remain with Mickey and me forever.

"We have a second chance," I confided to Mickey one night after we'd put Mallory to bed. "A chance to do it right this time."

Mickey seemed to agree with me, although he didn't say a word. He'd been there through it all—the fights with Daisy, the sleepless nights wondering where she was, the pain of her absence. He must have seen new hope in Mallory too.

Two years later, though, it happened again. Daisy showed up, and I knew, with just one look, she wasn't in a place to be a mother. Not to Mallory and not to Madison, the second baby she handed off for me and Mickey to take care of.

"I raised you better than this," I said that time, resentment building, even though I wouldn't trade my granddaughters for the world. Yes, maybe it was the wrong reaction, but we all say things we wish we could take back. Even as we say them, we know we should stop because the regret is inevitable. Inescapable.

"Are you sure about that?" Daisy retorted. She didn't even stay long enough for dinner. She just placed the second baby in my arms. "Her name is Madison. Maddie. Her birthday is April eighteenth." Then she turned and left.

Mickey wanted to chase after her, but I grabbed his arm.

"She's not ready. She can only cause more harm for Mallory." And truthfully, for me too.

That was the last time for a while that Daisy showed

up at my door. Years went by. Christmases passed. By the time Mallory was five, she knew every nook and cranny of our little theater. She'd sit in the wings during rehearsals, her eyes wide with wonder.

Both Mallory and Maddie had been involved in the theater, but Mallory had it in her blood. She also had Daisy's beauty but none of her restlessness. Where Daisy had been like a storm, Mallory was more of a gentle breeze. She brought joy wherever she went, and the theater became as much her home as it had ever been mine.

Madison, on the other hand, found her passion in the great outdoors. Sometimes she would wander and I'd have to search for her. In those moments, I'd wonder if my youngest granddaughter was going to follow in her mom's footsteps. She never ran away though. She always came home from her outdoor adventures.

It was on one such Christmas Eve, Mallory's twelfth, that everything changed again. We'd just settled in for our usual tradition. Mallory, despite being too old for such things, as she'd started claiming, was curled up on the couch, her eyes bright with anticipation as Mickey began to read.

Suddenly, there was a knock at the door.

Maddie's head lifted, her eyes wide. "Do you think it's Santa?" she whispered, a hint of her childhood excitement creeping into her voice.

Mickey and I exchanged amused glances. "Why don't you go see?" I suggested with a chuckle.

Maddie shot up, knocking an ornament from our tree as she bounded to the door. I reached for the ornament, a frown settling on my face.

"What's the matter?" he asked.

"The compass. It's broken."

I remember that he'd placed the compass on the tree a few days earlier. It wasn't a traditional ornament, and I remember finding it odd that he'd looped an old compass with a piece of ribbon and hung it, as if it was the most natural thing to do. I'd been meaning to ask about his reasoning.

"The face is cracked," I told him as I handed it to him. "Looks like the arrow doesn't know which way to go."

Mickey didn't seem bothered. "It was already broken when my father gave it to me."

Before I could reply I heard a squeal from the front of my house that sent me racing in that direction.

There, illuminated by the porch light and dusted with snow, was Daisy.

Time stood still. Daisy was older, of course, but her eyes were clearer than I'd seen them in years. There was a hesitance in her stance, a vulnerability I'd never associated with my headstrong daughter.

"Mom?" Her voice was barely above a whisper. "Dad? I... I'm h-home."

I couldn't speak. Couldn't move. I was Daisy's mother. I was supposed to welcome her with open arms, heart bursting with joy. But I also saw myself as Mallory and Madison's mother now. And some part of me saw Daisy as the enemy. A person who could possibly steal away these two treasures in my life.

Mickey eventually broke the silence. "Welcome home, sweetheart." His voice was thick with emotion as he hesitated, looking unsure about whether he should stay put or give his prodigal daughter a hug.

"Mom!" Mallory burst onto the porch, more excitement

in her eyes than if it actually had been Santa at the door. "You're here. You came back for us."

The hope in my oldest granddaughter's voice just about broke me. As I watched Daisy tentatively return Mallory's embrace, her eyes met mine. There would be explanations needed, wounds to heal, trust to rebuild. And I wasn't going to make it easy for her. No way. I loved my daughter, I did. And I respected her leaving if that's what she felt was best for Mallory and Maddie. I needed to trust that whatever was happening now was still best for them, and I didn't.

Mickey stepped up beside me, the broken compass in his palm. He slipped it in my hand and whispered in my ear. "Read the inscription." Then he moved forward to hug Daisy.

Squinting my eyes, I angled the compass trying to let the inscription catch the light.

WHEN YOUR COMPASS IS BROKEN, FOLLOW YOUR HEART.

Looking up at Mickey with Daisy in his arms and our grandchildren gathered around, I couldn't help but hope that's what this was. Daisy's long-broken compass had led her away, but now, here she was, hopefully home to stay. I didn't want to think about what it would do to Mallory and Maddie otherwise.

Chapter Twenty-Six

Art is the only way to run away without leaving home.
—Twyla Tharp

Hollis stood in the living room of Pop's house, his few belongings packed into a duffel bag by the door. The weight of disappointment and failure pressed down on him, making even the familiar surroundings feel alien and unwelcoming. He'd let everyone down—his foster family, Mallory, and even Duke. The thought of facing them all seemed impossible.

Outside, he could hear the seasonal employees moving about the Christmas tree farm. The once-bustling lot was now quiet, most people having already selected their trees for the season. It was a stark reminder of how quickly things could change, how easily the warmth and excitement of the holidays could fade into loneliness and regret.

His phone buzzed with a message from Sandy, confirming she'd passed along his message to Mallory about the play. Hollis's stomach twisted with guilt. He could picture the hurt and confusion in Mallory's eyes. He'd disappointed her, just like he'd disappointed everyone else.

The shrill ring of his phone cut through his thoughts. Dr. Lynch's name flashed on the screen, and Hollis's stomach dropped. This was it—news about Duke. Hollis had stayed up last night bargaining with God, knowing that didn't work. As a kid, he'd made a lot of bargains with the Big Guy upstairs and usually his prayers weren't answered, but even if they were, Hollis never upheld his end of the deal.

Hollis would do whatever it took for Duke to get better though. If there was a deal to be struck, he'd make it.

Last night, Hollis had promised God he'd do better. He'd even offered to give up his dream of opening his dog-training business if that's what was needed. Taking that out of the equation took Pop's offer out as well—kind of. Family mattered most, and that was the biggest ask Hollis had ever made from the man upstairs. All he'd ever wanted was a family and he'd got one in Matt and Sandy. And Pop. He didn't want to lose them. He'd get back on track, but *please God. Let Duke be okay.*

Hollis's hand shook as he tapped his phone's screen and connected the call.

"Hollis!" Dr. Lynch's voice was urgent. "I found Buster."

"What? What do you mean you found Buster?" He'd expected news on Duke.

"Well, I didn't," Dr. Lynch clarified. "Mr. Gordan from Holly Springs brought him in. Mr. Gordan was hunting in the north woods and happened upon Buster."

Hollis paced the room as he listened to the veterinarian explain. "Is he…?"

"He's fine. A bit thirsty and hungry, and there's one defensive wound on his left shoulder, but he's okay."

"A defensive wound?" Hollis repeated, trying to make sense of what had happened.

"It's large, but not too deep. My best guess is a bear," Dr. Lynch said. "Mr. Gordan said there's been a black bear coming around. It went after one of his hunting dogs the other week. My hunch is that it was the bear that got to Duke, since Duke took a good bit of the injuries."

Hollis stopped walking as he played out that scenario in his mind. "And Buster came to Duke's rescue."

"That's a real possibility. Buster has a bark on him." Dr. Lynch laughed to herself. "If I were a bear and a dog like Buster came at me, well, I'd leave too."

Hollis knew exactly what she meant. At Thanksgiving, when Buster had come after him with that forceful bark, it had caused Hollis to trip over his own feet trying to run away. "What about Duke?"

"More good news. Duke seems to have perked up, now that Buster is here with him. I think these two are destined to be lifelong friends. And I think Duke's life is going to be long and happy. His injuries are healing faster than expected. I stopped the IV antibiotics this morning."

Relief washed over Hollis. The worst-case scenario hadn't happened. If anything, this was better news than he'd allowed himself to imagine.

"Duke needs to stay another night, but you're free to come get Buster."

"Be right there." Hollis grabbed his keys on the way out of the house and climbed into his truck. He'd been so certain he was going to lose at least one dog, but now, by some Christmas miracle, he might get to keep both.

The drive to the vet's office was a blur of racing thoughts and emotions. Hope. Guilt. Shame. Disappointment in himself. He'd been too quick to give up on Buster. Too quick to shut down.

Running a hand over his face, Hollis parked and half-walked, half-jogged toward the clinic door. On the other side of the glass, Buster was waiting on a leash in Dr. Lynch's hand. He propped his front paws on the door and seemed to smile at the sight of Hollis. His tail wagged.

Dr. Lynch pushed the door open. "Here's the hero of the hour," she said, talking about the scraggly lab-mix.

Hollis knelt to pet Buster's head. "Hero indeed. You ready to go home?" His throat tightened at the word and the meaning behind it. Every boy in the boys home had wanted to hear those words, and he imagined every dog did too.

With a thump of his tail, Buster let out a high-pitched bark.

"That sounded an awful lot like a yes to me," Dr. Lynch said cheerfully. The vet's tone quickly turned serious. "It's going to be a tough road ahead for Duke, but I think it's safe to say, he'll be home for Christmas too. Having you and Buster there—that's going to make a world of difference for him. We all need to know we have others in our corner, rooting for us."

Hollis's thoughts drifted to Mallory. Instead of turning to her, he'd reverted to his old ways and pushed her away. This whole time, he'd been working hard to convince Mallory to accept help from others. To let him help her. Then he'd done the very opposite when times had gotten tough for him. "Can I—can I see him?"

"Of course." Dr. Lynch led him to Duke's kennel in the back room.

The sight of his longtime best friend, battered and hooked up to an IV, nearly broke Hollis. But as he approached, Duke's tail gave a weak thump against the bottom of the crate.

"Hey there, bud." Hollis reached out to gently stroke the top of Duke's head. "I'm here. We're both here," he said, allowing Buster to prop up on Hollis's thigh, turning his head to sniff the air around Duke. "And we're not going anywhere."

He'd done things all wrong yesterday, and there were a lot of things to make right. No, it wasn't his fault that Matt had stormed in and yelled at him, but Hollis had walked away too easily. He should have made sure Matt understood what was going on instead of letting his fight-or-flight response send him storming out as well. He should have called Mallory and told her what was happening instead of turning inward and letting his thoughts spiral.

Pulling his phone from his pocket, Hollis tapped on Mallory's number.

As the phone rang in his ear, Hollis looked at his two dogs—one injured but fighting, one loyal and misunderstood—a lot like Hollis in his youth.

Mallory's voicemail message came on. He tapped the screen and tried again but realized she either wasn't available or she was ignoring him.

He wouldn't blame her. Yes, it was only one night, but a lot of damage could happen in a short amount of time. Sometimes enough damage that it could never be fixed.

When the tone sounded, he left his message. "Mallory, it's me again. Please call me back when you get this. I need to explain... I'm s-sorry." Disconnecting the call, he took a moment to consider next steps.

Mallory might not want him back in her life. Or in the play for opening night. But he owed it to her to put himself out there and try. He'd already gotten two prayers answered with Duke and Buster. Maybe it was too much to hope for one more Christmas miracle. But it was the season of hope, after all. He had to try.

Savannah. He quickly scrolled through his contacts and tapped her name.

"Hollis?" Savannah answered on the second ring. "Is everything okay?"

"Not really. I mean, yes. Everything's good. Better than good, but I'm trying to reach Mallory. I messed up."

"Yeah, I know," she huffed. There was a pause on the other end of the line. "She worried herself sick last night, Hol. You let her spend a sleepless night before going to a long nursing shift. You froze her out, so if she's doing the same to you, well, I'm sorry to say, it's well-deserved."

Hollis winced. "I totally agree. That's why I need to talk to her."

Savannah audibly sighed into the receiver. "I think she needs space. To process everything. She'll reach out when she's ready."

He wanted to argue, to insist on fixing things right now, but Savannah was Mallory's best friend. If this was what Mal needed, he needed to respect that. He'd promised Nan last year that he'd protect Mal. He just didn't realize he'd be protecting her from himself. "Yeah. Okay. Will you...will you tell her I called?"

"Of course. Just...be patient, okay?"

After hanging up, Hollis glanced around the waiting room, feeling lost. He felt the urge to run again, to escape the mess he'd made, but he pushed it down. That was his instinct, but it wasn't the answer. There was someone else he needed to make amends with. He called Matt and Sandy's home number.

"Hollis?" Sandy answered. "I've been worried. Are you okay?"

"I'm... I'm fine," he said, but quickly decided to tell the truth. "Actually, I've been better. Is Matt there? I need to talk to him."

"He's home. Come on," she said without hesitation.

Fifteen minutes later, Hollis stood on the porch of his foster parents' home, his heart pounding. The door opened before he could knock, revealing Sandy's worried face. Hollis was inclined to step in and hug her but stopped when Matt walked up behind her.

Everything inside him froze. He didn't want to argue. Part of him wanted to turn around and get right back in his truck. What he wished most was that he could go back in time and undo what felt like irreparable damage.

"Come in," Sandy said, ushering him inside.

Hollis cautiously stepped forward, hearing the front door close behind him. He kept his hands clasped, and his head tipped low. He was ready for whatever Matt wanted to say to him. He'd take every word.

"Have a seat," Sandy urged, gesturing to the sofa.

They settled in the living room, an uncomfortable silence stretching between them.

Hollis took a deep breath and steeled himself. When Matt didn't immediately start yelling at him, he led the conversation himself. "Listen. I'm sorry," he began, his voice shaky.

To his surprise, Matt leaned forward and placed a hand on Hollis's knee. "I don't accept your apology."

Every muscle in Hollis's body tensed.

"No, Hollis. You have nothing to be sorry for. I'm the one who needs to apologize. My behavior last night was…inexcusable. I don't even recognize the man who walked into this house last night. That wasn't me."

Hollis blinked as he looked up to meet Matt's gaze.

Matt's words rushed out. "Jealousy turns a man into a boy, Hollis. I guess I was jealous of your relationship with Pop, of the way he wants to hand over the tree farm to you."

"You told me that you never wanted the farm," Hollis said quietly.

"I don't. But selfishly, I still felt entitled to the land, which just makes me, well, it makes me a jerk. Instead of being proud of and supporting you, I lashed out. I asked you to leave, and I'm so ashamed." Matt's voice broke.

"Matt," Hollis said, but Matt held up a hand.

"Lemme finish. I let my insecurities cloud what Pop tried to do for you, and I'm sorry. You were nearly grown when you came to live with us, but you are our son, Hollis. In every way that matters. And I know Pop thinks of you as his grandson. You deserve the farm."

A lump formed in Hollis's throat. He'd spent so long feeling like an outsider, never quite believing he truly belonged. To hear Matt say these words…

Sandy reached out and took Hollis's hand. "We love you, sweetie. We always have, and we always will. There is nothing you can ever do or say to change that. Ever. We are your forever family."

Hollis tried to speak, but his throat was too tight. He took a breath and nodded, managing a quiet "Thank you."

Matt cleared his throat, obviously trying to regain his composure. "Now, about the farm. If you want it, I encourage you to accept the offer."

Hollis felt his eyes widen. "Really?"

Matt nodded. "Really. The construction crew won't be the same without you, but it'll survive. Hollis," Matt said, "you're fired."

Hollis sat upright.

Matt broke into a wide grin. "You need to follow your heart. Pop is giving you the land, and I'm offering the crew's help to build whatever you need for those plans of yours. We'll set up kennels, fix the barn, build a little store. Whatever you want."

Hollis was overwhelmed, and humbled. After days of feeling like his world was falling apart, everything seemed to be falling into place. Well, almost everything.

"I don't know what to say." Hollis thought of Duke, fighting for his life at the vet's office. Of Buster, who had saved his friend despite everyone's initial assumptions. He thought of the tree farm, of the dogs he could help, of the family surrounding him now.

And Mallory. Savannah had advised him to give Mallory time, but he didn't want her to spend that time thinking he didn't want her in his life. That he wasn't going to fight for her and try to make things right.

That he didn't love her.

"I appreciate everything," he finally said, his voice steady and sure. "I appreciate your support and welcoming me into your home. Your family." He leaned forward and gave them both a hug that lasted at least a minute. Then he pulled back and looked at them. "I'm sorry, but I have to go. I need to find someone."

"Mallory," Sandy said, knowingly. "I know exactly where she is."

The Fathers Ornament

The Fathers Ornament is in the box labeled 15. Inside you'll find a clear ball-shaped ornament with a handful of items inside. Hang it on the lower part of the tree, fifteen down from the Santa Hat Tree Topper.

Here's the story behind it.

Daisy stayed just long enough for us all to believe that things had shifted, and she was finding her roots. She seemed comfortable and happy. The restlessness she'd always shown seemingly had gone.

Daisy even got a job at the local diner and read bedtime stories to Maddie at night, revealing her upbringing in the theater as she read in varied voices and used animated gestures. She attended Mallory's school events too. At first, Mallory was guarded, always waiting for her mom to leave. But then her walls slowly slipped away. If I had any inkling that Mallory's heart would be broken, I would have stepped in. I would have made sure she was protected. I didn't though. I was just as wrapped up in this new life and the promise of that broken compass.

Things started to derail about five months later. It was early summer, following that Christmas reunion. I found myself standing in the doorway of Mallory's bedroom one night, watching Daisy braid Mallory's long, dark hair. They giggled like schoolgirls. I recall thinking they looked more like sisters than mother and daughter. Inwardly, I scolded myself and told myself I was being jealous. I had been raising Mallory and Maddie as my own.

The two didn't see me, so it felt like I was spying.

Daisy leaned in and whispered something in Mallory's ear the way I'd seen Mallory do to Maddie many times, and they laughed harder. Hysterically, even.

Daisy snorted at whatever Mallory had told her. "Don't let Mom hear you say that," she warned.

Mallory's brow wrinkled softly.

"My mom," Daisy corrected, gesturing at herself. "Your grandma."

It was an awkward moment made worse when they realized I was standing there watching.

"Are you spying on us?" Daisy hissed, jumping to her feet.

"Spying?" I repeated. "The door was open and..." I looked between them. "What are you doing?"

Mallory looked pale. She sat up straighter, looking as if she'd just been caught in a crime.

"We're hanging out, Mom. And you aren't invited." With that, Daisy slammed the door in my face, leaving me with my mouth gaping and my heart aching.

"You know that you're her mother," I told Daisy the next day.

Daisy seemed taken aback. "What's that supposed to mean?"

"You two were acting like schoolgirls yesterday. I'm guessing Mallory told you about a boy and that's why you were giggling and whispering."

Daisy's expression transformed from carefree to defensive. "So?"

"Did Mallory tell you that I've told her to stay away from that exact boy? Hollis Franklin, right? He's not good for her, Daisy. But instead of acting like a parent, you encouraged your teenage daughter to sneak out."

"It's no biggie. I snuck off with boys at her age," Daisy said with a shrug of her shoulder.

"And you think Mallory should follow in your shoes?" I asked, working to keep my tone as gentle as I could muster.

Fury lit inside her eyes, and I felt myself wanting to shrink away. "Hollis has a troubled past. He's a good boy, but he has healing to do, Daisy. He's nowhere near ready to handle Mallory's heart. And Mallory has healing to do too."

Daisy shot up from the bar stool she was seated on, nearly knocking it down. "Healing because of me? Because of her crappy mom, right? You're judging this boy in the same way you've always judged me!"

Zero to one-eighty right before my eyes. Proof that Daisy wasn't ready either. She was acting irrationally. Irresponsibly.

"Being a parent means sometimes you can't be your child's friend." I was no longer talking to Daisy about how she interacted with Mallory. I was also talking about myself and how I had interacted with my child. I wasn't a perfect parent. I could have been there for Daisy more. Could have been softer. Stricter. A better mix of both. I didn't think any of her shortcomings were her fault. No, I knew for a fact that they were mine. More than anything, I wanted to help her, but at the moment, I needed to protect my grandchildren.

Hollis Franklin wasn't the biggest threat in Mallory's life. Not by a landslide.

Daisy's eyes burned with tears. Her bottom lip trembled. "Okay, maybe I shouldn't have told her to sneak out."

"Mallory has never snuck out before. She's never broken a rule as far as I can tell," I said quietly. "She came home with her jacket smelling of cigarette smoke and beer." I held up my hand. "I don't think she was smoking or drinking, but she will if she continues hanging out with the wrong crowd and heading down the wrong path."

"Like me," Daisy said, the defensiveness gone. She looked more defeated than anything.

"Are you sober?" I'd been reluctant to ask before, but I needed to know. Daisy was an addict. She got hooked on anything that made her feel a tiny bit better in her own skin. Drugs and alcohol. Men.

"No." She didn't meet my gaze.

I swallowed hard. If I allowed myself to cry, I might not be strong enough to hold my ground. There were times when parents had to be the villain in order to be the hero. "Then you understand what I have to do."

"Yeah." Sniffling, she said, "They won't understand why I'm doing this to them again. But…I do. I get it. And you're right." She rolled her eyes. "Wow. Never thought I'd utter those words." She looked down at her hand, weaving her fingers together. "Mallory will take this the hardest."

"She's strong. Like you." I was so proud of Daisy in that moment. She was putting her children first. And maybe that meant one day she'd be ready to be a full-time mother.

"I'm not so sure." Reaching into her pocket, Daisy pulled out a handful of items and laid them on the table. A piece of gum, a business card, a picture of herself with some guy I didn't recognize, and a ring. "This is all I have of their fathers. They'll ask and I wish I could tell them more. Mallory's father was an actor." Her gaze flicked to meet mine. "We had feelings. He gave me the ring."

I noticed now that it was an engagement ring.

"Anyway, he had an accident and, well..."

The pain that struck my heart was immediate. All in a second, I understood that Daisy had fallen in love with a man. She'd been pregnant and she'd faced the same path that I had so long ago.

Picking up the ring, Daisy seemed to admire it one last time. "I said yes, and I was ready to give everything up for him. It didn't even feel like I was giving up anything. It felt like I was taking on the role of a lifetime." She looked up at me, my sweet baby girl. "Tell Mallory, one day when she asks, that I loved her father and he was destined to be a star. Tell her that her father was kind and creative. That he was a good man." She placed the ring in my palm. "And give her this. It's all I have of his. She should have it."

I gave her a moment, waiting because there were more items on the table.

"Maddie's dad was a stagehand. He was witty and strong. I never told him about her. Something told me he was the type of guy who'd do the "honorable thing." I didn't want to fall in love. I'd already been there, done that, had the broken heart to show for it. This is his business card, should she ever want to find him."

"The gum?" I asked.

Daisy surprised me with a smile. "Leo traded me a stick of gum for a kiss." The way her eyes sparkled, I didn't need to ask which of the two men was Leo. The look of love is unmistakable.

"The penny?" I asked.

"Maddie's father. Heads we have sushi. Tails we go back to his place." Daisy shrugged and stood. "Tails it was. Maddie came nine months later."

"Better than sushi."

"I wish I had more to give them."

I reached out and held Daisy's hand, finding her skin cold and clammy. "You have given them everything you can. The best thing you can do for them is to take care of yourself." I dipped my head to meet her eyes and hold her gaze. "I am your mother first. I'll always be here, and if you should want help getting sober, I will find the best professional help that you need."

Daisy was right. Mallory took it the hardest. She was inconsolable for months after Daisy left. I was at a loss for what to do, and then an idea struck me. *Santa, Baby* was coming up on its nineteenth run, backed by the community's insistence for an encore year after year. As the screenwriter and director, I decided to write a new role into the story. What if Santa and Mrs. Claus adopted a young girl? I tailor-wrote the role for Mallory.

When I told her about it, she shied away until I revealed I'd also written a part in for Hollis, who I knew she had a crush on. Suddenly, Mallory was fifteen again, straddling the line between childhood and adulthood. There was a skip in her step again.

I knew Hollis was troubled. I knew that "hurt people hurt people." Especially when they're young. I knew that Hollis Franklin was still a threat to Mallory's fragile heart, but he was the only solution to her sadness. A temporary solution. And, in hindsight, a big mistake.

But that is a different story. And a different ornament.

Chapter Twenty-Seven

Memory is not an instrument of exploring the past, but its theater.

—Walter Benjamin

Mallory closed Nan's journal and looked out at the bustling energy of the cast and crew as she sat on a bale of hay. Tonight wouldn't be the first time Nan's play had been performed in the Popadine barn. That was a detail Mallory never would have known if not for her grandmother's journal. There were so many facts that might have been lost along with Nan's memories if they hadn't been written down inside this book.

Placing the journal back inside her bag, Mallory glanced at her watch and felt a twinge of anxiety. In just a few hours, the curtain would rise on *Santa, Baby*—the play that she wasn't just directing but had somehow also found herself starring in, thanks to Hollis.

Hollis. Her heart ached, and a sudden rush of emotion threatened to overtake her. There was no time for that right now though. She had a play to put on. Pushing thoughts of Hollis aside, she placed Nan's journal back in her bag and focused on her lines and cues. The show must go on. With or without him.

As the rest of the cast arrived, Mallory slipped out momentarily and headed to Memory Oaks. Even though Nan might not understand what Mallory was doing for her tonight, she wanted to visit and let Nan know that she'd kept her promise. She also hoped to draw strength and inspiration from her grandmother's presence.

The familiar halls of Memory Oaks greeted her as she walked along, admiring the festive decorations adorning every surface. When Mallory didn't find Nan in her bedroom, she changed direction and spotted her in the common room, sitting by the window, a blank expression on her face.

"Hi, Nan," Mallory said softly, settling into the chair beside her. "It's me, Mallory."

She instantly regretted that greeting, knowing Nan would have no idea who she was.

Nan turned to her with unfocused, confused eyes. "Hello, dear... Are you new here?"

Mallory tried not to take it personally. As a nurse, she knew the lucid moments were unpredictable and fleeting. "No. Just visiting. I actually came to tell you a story, if that's okay?"

"Really?" Nan looked delighted. "I do love stories."

"Me too." Taking a deep breath, Mallory pulled out Nan's journal and turned to the page for next entry. "It's a love story, actually. About my grandmother and her husband, Mickey."

As Mallory spoke, she realized it was a love story, but not necessarily the romantic kind. It was a story quilted together, square by square, ornament by ornament, about the kind of love that existed in families, and among friends too.

She began to read, taking her time and looking up every now and then to analyze Nan's expression. Or lack thereof. There was no spark of recognition, no hint that Nan realized the story was about her own life. But there did seem to be genuine interest.

Mallory's eyes stung as she described, through Nan's lens, the last time Daisy ran away from home, leaving Mallory and Maddie behind once more, and how Mallory stoically mothered her younger sister. Then she read about being cast alongside Hollis and how Nan had regretted that decision.

As if sensing Mallory's pain, Nan reached out and patted her hand.

"She sounds like a strong young lady," Nan commented.

Mallory blinked back tears. "Why is it that people consider all the pain we endure a sign of strength? Why is it spoken of like it's a good thing to be taken advantage of, lied to, to have our hearts broken?" She felt the tears slip onto her cheeks. "I don't think that's very fair."

Nan watched her, still holding her hand. Then she offered a gentle squeeze as her eyes cleared for just a moment. "Because we need to think there's some good to come out of all the bad things we go through. If thinking the pain makes us stronger is what helps us heal, then so be it."

There. There was the wisdom of the grandmother Mallory needed so much right now.

She choked back a sob and leaned forward to hug Nan, knowing it might break the moment of clarity, but she didn't care. She needed Nan so much it hurt.

Nan's arms enclosed around her, soaking in the hug that was all too brief.

When Mallory finally pulled back, Nan's gaze lowered to the book in Mallory's lap.

"Whose story is that?" Nan asked.

Mallory had thought it was Nan's but she realized now it was so much more. It was also her mother's story. And Maddie's. And hers. "It's my family's story."

"Well, I hope it has a happy ending. I never did like those tragic stories. Shakespeare was the worst," Nan said distastefully.

Mallory found herself bursting into unexpected laughter.

"Agreed… I hope it has a happy ending too. Speaking of which, I need to go. I'm directing a play tonight. And starring in it too."

Nan clapped her hands together in front of her chest. "How exciting. Oh, I'm so happy for you. There's something I should say." She looked down, as if searching for a lost earring, and then finally back up at Mallory. "Break a leg." Her lips immediately dropped into a frown. "I'm so sorry. I'm not sure why I said that."

Mallory laid a hand on Nan's shoulder. "It's theater talk. It means good luck."

"It does?"

Mallory wished she could lean in and kiss her temple, but that was a risk she best not take tonight. "Thank you for visiting with me."

Nan grinned. "Come back and see me, and tell me all about how tonight goes."

"I will."

After she left Memory Oaks, she climbed into her car, realizing she hadn't taken her cell phone into the facility. Instead, it lay in her middle console. Tapping the screen, she saw missed call and text notifications. Most of them from Hollis.

Her heart rate quickened as she listened to his voicemail. "Mallory, please call me back when you get this. I need to explain… I'm so sorry."

She thought about the play and all the work she'd put in, and about how Evan had stepped into Hollis's role to make up for his absence. Evan didn't want to, of course. He wasn't prepared. But he'd said yes because he was a loyal friend—to Hollis and to Mallory.

Despite everything, a part of her longed to hear Hollis's voice, to check on him and make sure he was okay. It was too risky right now though, with the play opening its curtains in under an hour. All her energy needed to be directed toward that. *Sorry, Hollis.*

Whatever Hollis had to say, it would have to wait until after the performance.

There was no time for games tonight. She had a play to put on, with or without him.

Mallory typed out a quick message:

Mallory: I'll call you after the show.

As she hit send, Mallory took a deep breath. Then she tossed her phone onto the passenger seat and put the car in drive.

As she drove back to the barn theater, she found herself humming the song that opened the show. Whatever the future held, with Hollis, her career, and with her grandmother, she knew one thing for certain: Tonight, she would make Nan proud.

Mallory stood inside a tent, which served as the dressing area of the barn theater, her heart racing. The air was thick with the scent of hairspray and the buzz of preshow jitters. She smoothed down her costume, a vintage-inspired dress that sparkled under the lights, and took a deep breath.

"All right, everyone," she called out, her voice carrying over the chatter. "Gather round, please!"

The cast members, all in various states of costume and makeup, huddled around her. Evan stood at the edge of the group, a serious look on his face, which let her know that he was all nerves. The kind of nerves that came with not being prepared enough.

"Evan," Mallory said, meeting his eyes, "you ready?"

He tapped the small earpiece he wore. "All set. I've got the lines if I need them, but I stayed up half the night. I think I've got most of my part down."

"You'll do great. We all will." She looked around at the faces of her castmates, seeing anxious excitement reflected at her. "I know we've had some last-minute changes," she continued, carefully avoiding mentioning Hollis by name, "but we've worked hard, and we're ready for this. Remember, this play isn't just about us. It's about Nan, about this town, about the magic of Christmas and theater..." She took a cleansing breath, feeling a rush of theater nerves. "Okay, everyone. Let's make Bloom proud."

A chorus of agreement rose from the group, and Mallory felt a surge of affection for her fellow actors. They'd rallied around her, adapting to the changes without complaint. All the complainers had dropped off early in the process. Growing pains, Nan would have said.

"Places in five minutes," called Savannah, who was serving as stage manager.

The group dispersed.

Mallory made her way to the makeshift wings, which were basically some boards of plywood standing vertically. She peeked out at the audience filing in. The barn was transformed, twinkling lights strung across the rafters and the scent of pine and cinnamon filling the air. Her heart swelled with pride at what they'd accomplished.

At what would not have been possible without Hollis.

She swallowed hard, wishing he were here. She wished Nan were here too. And Maddie. Scanning the crowd, she blinked and wondered if she was hallucinating. But no, there in the back of the barn was her sister, wheeling herself down the aisle with Sam at her side.

Mallory squealed softly and slipped out from behind the curtain to make her way to her sister before the show. "Maddie? I didn't think you'd be here."

Maddie offered back a hesitant smile. "That's my fault for letting you even think that. I've kind of been working my way out of a dark spot." She glanced at her husband. "Not alone. Sam and Renee have been helping me."

"So I hear. How are those big plans you were telling me about coming along?"

"Stalled. We're looking for a location. The one we had in mind fell through." She frowned momentarily. "But we'll figure it out. You aren't the only one with ambition," Maddie teased.

Mallory didn't think she had as much ambition as she once had, but that was okay. "Well, if you get some time, I want to tell you what I've learned from reading Nan's journal."

Maddie nodded. "I'd like that." She held out a bouquet of flowers. "Now, go break a leg."

Mallory accepted the flowers. "Funny. Nan just said the same thing to me about an hour ago. You're a lot like her, you know."

"Me?" Maddie looked surprised. "I always thought it was you who had a special connection with Nan. She liked to say I reminded her of our mom." Maddie grimaced. "I'm not sure if that was an insult or a compliment."

"Compliment," Mallory assured Maddie, reaching out to touch her shoulder. "The best kind."

Mallory leaned down, enveloping her sister in a tight hug. She didn't want to let go because she missed Maddie so much these days, but she had to. It was almost time for the curtains to open. "I'll see you after?"

Maddie nodded. "Break two legs," she called as Mallory headed toward the backstage, her heart lighter than it'd been in days. "We can get matching wheelchairs for a while."

Mallory felt her eyes go wide.

"Laughter is better than tears."

"True." With a wave, Mallory headed back toward the side of the makeshift stage. "There's our leading lady," one of the cast called.

Mallory glanced around. Everyone was here except Hollis. A pang of sadness hit her, but she pushed it aside. "All right, everyone," she said, her voice steady and clear. "This is it. Nan wrote this play with love and laughter, and that's exactly what we're going to bring to the stage tonight. "Evan," she said, addressing the newest cast member, "you've stepped up in a big way, and we're all grateful. Just remember, we've got your back out there."

He nodded. "I'll do my best not to make a fool of myself."

"If you mess up, I solemnly promise to throw myself off the stage to divert the attention," she said, remembering when Hollis had said the same to her just a couple of weeks ago.

He looked horrified. "Don't do that. I'll survive any embarrassment."

She laughed. "We've all got your back. Right, everyone?"

The group agreed.

"Okay. Let's do this!" Mallory called, pulling in a deep breath.

As the curtain rose and the familiar opening notes of the opening song filled the air, Mallory stepped onto the stage. The lights were blindingly bright, but as she adjusted, she looked out at the audience, a sea of expectant faces. All of them were used to attending Nan's plays at the theater. Tonight would be different, but she hoped they'd all enjoy the show.

Taking a deep breath, she channeled the love and passion Nan had poured into this play, year after year.

Mallory's nerves settled as soon as she delivered her first line. The freedom of being onstage in front of a live audience reminded her just how exhilarating it was. Acting really did feel like flying. Then she blinked and her mind froze midsentence. Was that Hollis? Was this an illusion? Wishful thinking maybe?

No. He'd told her he wasn't coming, and she was pretty sure he'd meant it.

Chapter Twenty-Eight

Unless the theatre can ennoble you, make you a better person, you should flee from it.

—Constantin Stanislavski

Hollis was a jumble of nerves right now, but at the same time, he felt sure about what he was doing. Mallory had been ignoring his texts and calls, and he didn't blame her. He'd let her down.

Evan patted Hollis's back. "I gotta say, I'm relieved you came through, buddy. If Mallory is mad at me," Evan warned, "I'm going to tell her it's all your fault."

"You're afraid of Mal?" Hollis teased. Then he thought about it and gave a small nod. "Actually, I'm a little bit intimidated by her too." He always had been. She may be small, but she was mighty, and when people let her down, her thin skin thickened. The shackles around her heart went up, and he knew it wasn't easy to break them back down. Mallory didn't give her trust easily, but when she did, it meant you'd earned it.

Hollis had earned it over the years, especially recently, and then he'd gone and let his emotions get the best of him. To be fair, last night had been rough.

Evan handed Hollis an earpiece. "In case you forget your lines," Evan explained.

Hollis grunted, finding that humorous. "I know these lines. I was made for these roles."

"Yes, you were, bud, and after finishing up these first two acts tonight, I'm glad you're taking the third act back. I prefer to sit in the audience versus being onstage."

Hollis was glad too. Pulling on the red velvet Santa coat, he checked his reflection in the mirror and put on the iconic red hat. Then he hurriedly pulled on his heavy, black boots.

What if Mallory broke character when she saw him? That was unlikely because Mallory was a professional. When she was in the role of a nurse, she gave 100 percent. And here, in the role of the director and leading actress, she would give her all as well.

A little bell rang twice.

"That's your cue, bud." Evan nudged Hollis toward the stage. The sound meant Hollis was to enter stage left and approach Mrs. Claus. In the play, Santa had disappeared, overwhelmed by all the demands and expectations that came with being Santa. No relationship was perfect, and this play was basically a tribute to that. Even Mr. and Mrs. Claus had their ups and downs—they weren't always the jolly couple—but in the end, they returned to each other because that's where they belonged.

Santa couldn't exist without the backing of Mrs. Claus. And vice versa.

Hollis took a deep breath. Then he entered stage left ready to finish up tonight's play. As the audience cheered, he let out a booming "Ho, ho, ho!"

Mallory, staying in character, delivered her next line while facing the audience. Hollis didn't think she realized that he had replaced Evan. Folding her arms across her chest, she shook her head and lifted her chin stubbornly. "I'm not going to fall for that again," she told Santa. "You can't just leave with your sleigh and reindeer one night and expect to return home as if nothing happened. You can't expect me to have milk and cookies waiting for you every time you decide to go back to being your jolly self."

Hollis continued walking toward her, his boots clicking loudly on the stage. Then he lifted his arm and tapped her shoulder, as was written in the stage directions. He softened his voice, but the audience could still hear him through the microphone. "I don't expect milk and cookies, Mrs. Claus. And I don't expect you to put up with my mood swings."

Mallory must've understood that it was Hollis's voice because, when she turned to look at him, her lips parted and her eyes widened just a touch. She had a line to deliver, but she appeared momentarily speechless.

Hollis delivered the line for her, changing it around so that it made sense coming from him. "I wouldn't be so moody if I didn't carry all this responsibility on my shoulders three hundred and sixty-five days a year. We're a team, and I understand that now. You're always offering to help me and I'm always telling you I can do it myself."

Mallory cleared her throat. "I guess I have those same tendencies."

"We should be leaning on each other when we get frustrated and upset," Hollis said. It wasn't exactly the way the script was written. But it fit for both the play and for his relationship. "I lean on you, you lean on me." Hollis's eyes searched hers. "It's possible that we just fall over on the ground with all that leaning."

Mallory lifted a brow, and he couldn't tell if she was in character or being Mallory, the woman he knew and undeniably loved. "We could promise to catch each other when we fall," she suggested. "Because with all those cookies you're eating, I'm not sure that I won't fall over if you lean on me too hard."

Hollis belted out a "Ho, ho, ho, ha, ha, ha" for the audience, and laughter broke out in the barn.

The final notes of the *Santa, Baby* theme song faded away as Hollis pulled Mallory close. The red sequins of her costume sparkled under the stage lights as they shared a tender kiss, bringing Nan's Christmas play to a heartwarming close.

Then the audience erupted in applause and rose to their feet in a standing ovation.

As the curtain fell, Hollis felt a surge of elation. He'd made it. Despite everything, he'd shown up. He'd honored his commitment to the play, to the community, to Nan, and most importantly, to Mallory.

The cast hugged and congratulated each other, riding high on the success of tonight's performance. But Hollis only had one goal in mind. His eyes searched for Mallory, finding her surrounded by well-wishers. He waited patiently, his chest tight, wondering how this would go. There were two options. She'd either yell and scream or she'd hug him. Kiss him. He liked the sound of that last option.

He held his breath as the crowd thinned, and then he approached her. "Mal."

She turned to him with a guarded expression.

"You were amazing out there," he said softly.

"Thanks, Hollis." Her voice was polite but distant. "You did a great job too."

They stared at each other for a long moment. "I, uh, thought maybe we could talk," he finally said, resisting the urge to reach for her hand. "I want to explain—"

Mallory took a step backward. "Actually, I'm exhausted, Hol. It's been a long night… Can we talk tomorrow?"

Hollis's heart dropped with a heavy thud in the bottom of his stomach. Looking into Mallory's eyes, he realized the hurt ran deep. He was a fool to think this would be fixed with one grand gesture. He'd have to work harder to win back her trust, her heart. "Yeah. Yeah, of course. Tomorrow. Take care, Mal."

As Mallory turned her back to him and walked away, Savannah and Evan approached. Evan clapped a hand along Hollis's back, relief evident in his voice. "Man, am I glad you showed up for the final act. I was sweating bullets up there onstage."

Hollis managed a humorless chuckle, his chest still aching from disappointment. "Thanks for stepping in though."

Savannah gave Hollis a knowing look, her eyes darting to Mallory's retreating figure. "Give her time. Just be patient." She narrowed her eyes. "Same advice I gave you before."

Hollis nodded. "I've never been good at having patience." But for Mallory, he was willing to wait as long as it took.

As he made his way to the parking lot, Sandy and Matt intercepted him. "Hollis, you were wonderful up there!" Sandy pulled him into a big hug.

"You really were, son. I'm proud of you." Matt reached out and shook Hollis's hand.

Hollis looked at the couple. "Thanks for coming tonight."

Sandy squeezed his arm. "Of course. You're coming to the house for Christmas Eve dinner on Sunday, right? Matt will be checking Pop out of Memory Oaks for the day, so he'll be there too."

A lump formed in Hollis's throat at the thought of having Pop home for Christmas.

"And, of course, you're welcome to bring Mallory," Matt added. "Tell her to spring Nan from Memory Oaks as well. Our table can always fit one more."

"I'll ask her," he promised, though he wasn't sure Mallory would accept an invitation from him right now.

As he drove home, passing the darkened Christmas tree farm, Hollis felt a pang of sadness. Duke wouldn't be there to greet him with his usual enthusiasm. But Buster would be waiting, a reminder that second chances were possible.

Pulling into his driveway, Hollis's mind raced with ideas on how to win back Mallory's trust. Tonight, he'd made the first step by showing up for the play. That wasn't enough though. Not nearly. What more could he do?

As he unlocked his front door and Buster's excited barks greeting him, Hollis felt a renewed sense of purpose. He'd made mistakes, let his fears and insecurities get the best of him, but he was ready to fight for what mattered—for Mallory, for their potential future together, for the life he wanted to build in his hometown.

He poured himself a glass of water and settled onto the couch with Buster curling up beside him.

Buster whined softly.

"You miss Duke?" Hollis asked quietly. "Me too, buddy. But I'm glad you're here. You're a hero, you know." He petted the dog's head and met the dog's deep brown eyes. "This is your forever home. I want you to know that. Other dogs may come and go in the future, but not you. You're stuck with me and Duke. We're your forever family." What every dog deserved. Every kid too.

In the silence of the night, he knew in his heart of hearts that he was a good man. The kind of good man that was deserving of a woman like Mallory.

For the first time in his life, he knew that he was worthy. He felt it. He hadn't liked himself when he was growing up. But he liked who he was these days, loved himself even, which felt odd but true. Maybe that was what was missing until now. In order to truly love another, you had to love yourself. A dozen different therapists and counselors from foster care and juvenile detention had told him that over the years, but they were just words that suddenly rang true as he sat here with Buster. And he'd never believe the lie that he wasn't good enough ever again.

Early the next morning, Hollis's phone woke him up. A thousand things ran through his head before he even glanced at his screen. A list of the possibilities of who could be trying to message him.

Maybe it was Mallory.

Or Pop.

Instead, Hollis noticed Dr. Lynch's name on his screen. He

connected the call and quickly held the phone to his ear, hoping it was good news. Last he heard, Duke was out of the woods, but life had taught him that things flipped on a dime. "Hello? How's Duke?"

"That's why I'm calling you." Dr. Lynch's voice was cheerful, which gave Hollis hope. "Duke had a great night, and I think he's ready to go home. If you're ready for him to come back, that is." The veterinarian knew Hollis was ready. In fact, Hollis never wanted to be without his dog ever again.

Hollis sat up quickly on the edge of his bed and was already pulling on a pair of jeans. "I'll be there as soon as the clinic opens."

"We don't technically open until eight, but message me when you get here and I'll open the door for you. I don't want to delay the happy reunion any longer. Consider it my Christmas present to you." She laughed quietly.

They said good-bye, and Hollis disconnected the call. *Christmas present*, he thought realizing that he hadn't bought even one gift for anyone, and the holiday was only three days away. Granted it'd been a busy month, but how had he been so negligent?

He needed presents for Sandy, Matt, Evan, and Savannah. He also needed one for Mallory, which she might just throw in his face. Buster thumped his tail on the floor, demanding his attention. "You get a present too. And Duke."

Hollis quickly brushed his teeth and ran a comb through his hair. Then he put Buster in his crate and headed out the door on his way to Dr. Lynch's clinic. As soon as he parked in the veterinarian's lot, he texted, and she unlocked the door for him.

"Come on in. Duke is eager to see you."

Hollis wasn't sure what to expect as he walked down the hall to the kennels, but as he stepped inside the room, Duke rose to his feet and let out a happy bark.

"Well, hello to you too." Hollis reached out to run his hand through his dog's fur and scratched behind his ear.

"I enjoyed the play last night," Dr. Lynch told Hollis as he opened the crate and pulled Duke into his arms.

"You were there?" Hollis asked.

"I never miss the holiday play. Even when I was in college, I would come home to Bloom every Christmas just to watch the show. It just didn't feel like the holidays without *Santa, Baby* on my calendar."

Hollis understood exactly what she meant.

"I was a little worried that it might not be the same without Nan at the helm, but Mallory did a fantastic job, in my opinion."

Hollis wasn't sure if Dr. Lynch knew he and Mallory were dating. Were. Past tense. He was pretty sure whatever they'd had was over. "Thank you, Dr. Lynch. For everything," he said one more time. "I know it's late in the season, but if you need a tree, let me know. You can pick out any tree on the lot, and I'll deliver it myself."

Dr. Lynch looked thoughtful as she tilted her head to the side. "Actually, I don't have a Christmas tree yet."

"No? Why not?"

The vet shrugged her narrow shoulders. "My boyfriend and I just broke up, and he's the only reason I was in Bloom to begin with." She lowered her gaze and shrugged. "We broke up right after Thanksgiving, so we didn't even get a Christmas tree, and I haven't really felt the Christmas spirit. At least until now. I have to say, seeing Duke recover and attending *Santa, Baby* last night has cheered me up."

"Well, I meant what I said. Come to the farm and pick out any tree you want. I'll deliver it myself."

"What's the point with only a few days left before Christmas?" the veterinarian asked.

"The point is that there's always something to be grateful for. There's always a bright spot even in the darkness. Pop says that," Hollis told her. "Even when the skies are dark, there's always the North Star to guide you. I used to think it was cheesy, but now"—he shrugged—"not so much."

"We'll see," Dr. Lynch said. "Maybe I'll take you up on that offer."

As Hollis stepped out of the clinic with Duke on a leash, he wondered if Mallory was feeling the same sadness that Dr. Lynch was. A breakup at Christmas stung. He and Mallory had never actually made things official, so maybe it didn't hurt as much for her. It sure hurt him though.

They'd been official in his head. He'd thought that he and Mallory were going to last until next Christmas. And the one after that. They would be like Mr. and Mrs. Claus, overcoming the hurdles and growing old together. Wasn't that the dream?

Hollis helped Duke into the passenger seat and climbed behind the steering wheel. Then he pulled out his cell phone and tapped on Evan's contact, listening to the ring and waiting for his best friend to answer.

"It's awfully early in the morning for you to be calling," Evan finally said, breaking into a loud yawn.

"You win the bet," Hollis replied. "I'm thinking cheesy things, and next thing you know I'll be saying even cheesier things."

"What was the bet again?" Evan asked. "One million dollars, right?"

"You wish, buddy," Holla said on a laugh. "I just left the vet's office. Duke's going to be fine."

"That's great news. And what about you and Mal?"

Hollis put the truck in motion and pulled onto the main road. "It's only seven thirty in the morning. Give me time. I'm working on it. Also, I kind of need to go Christmas shopping. You up for a guys' day?"

Silence answered on the other line. "A guys' day of shopping?" Evan's tone was thick with disbelief.

"I have my list, and I'm checking it twice. What do you say?"

"I say…heck yeah," Evan answered. "I haven't finished my shopping either. We're in the same boat, and we'll be in the same doghouse if we don't get some presents under those Christmas trees of ours."

Hollis was already in the doghouse. If he played his cards right, though, maybe he'd find his way out.

The Memory Tree Ornament

The Memory Tree Ornament is actually just a tiny blue bear like you might win in one of those claw machines. With two beady black eyes and a threaded nose and mouth.

Here's the story.

I worried that the worst thing that could happen by me casting Hollis alongside Mallory was that she'd fall head over heels for him. I've been accused of always worrying about the worst-case scenario. There was a scenario I hadn't considered though.

I hadn't accounted for the possibility that Hollis would be a no-show on opening night. There was an understudy, of course. There should always be a good understudy for every role, but the boy I assigned didn't know the lines. He wasn't ready, and his lack of preparation would erase all the hard work that Mallory had put into this role that she was so excited about.

I wish Hollis being a no-show was even the worst part, but there's more. While he didn't show up for the stage, he did come to the theater. Instead of entering stage left, he made his grand entrance from the back of the theater, drunk as a skunk and ranting like a rebellious teen boy who only knew rejection and pain. I wanted to feel sorry for him, but the fact that he was hurting my granddaughter made me angry. So angry.

As Mallory delivered her lines, a loud "booooooo" rang out. Not just once, but again and again. Each boo was louder than the last until the audience started laughing and Mallory fled the stage in tears. Afterward, law enforcement hauled him off to juvenile detention. He'd caused some more commotion prior to coming to the theater that night, but, as mad as I was at Hollis, I also felt responsible. I knew he wasn't ready. I knew he was just as fragile, if not more so, than Mallory.

Some people can't accept kindness. Not when all they've ever known is the opposite.

Mallory refused a role the next year. Then she turned away from theater altogether, deciding that she wanted to study nursing instead. Mallory leaned into the straight and narrow. Nursing was practical, respectable, and safe. Mallory became more serious than ever. She rarely laughed, except with her friend Savannah, who came every summer and brought out the light in her.

Eventually, Mickey and I were empty nesters. Mallory went away to college, pursuing a degree that seemed fitting for the child who'd taken care of her younger sister all through growing up. Maddie had never enjoyed theater life. I wasn't a bit surprised when she reached eighteen and turned down a college scholarship to backpack along the Appalachian Trail. It did surprise me when she fearlessly climbed a few mountains. Strong and brave.

"They're grown now. All of them. What if I didn't do a good enough job?" I asked Mickey one night.

"Nan, they're fine. Mallory is a nurse. Maddie is an adventurer. She's exploring the great, big world. Even our Daisy is a success."

We'd been following Daisy's career. She got sober on her own. And every Christmas, she sent a card. You know, the kind that encapsulates the year in a letter, telling us about all her accomplishments. She was the lead actress in an off-Broadway play that ran for years. She had small roles on TV and even one on the big screen! Imagine that. My daughter. Your mother. We were proud. We even watched a few TV performances together.

"Our girls are all living their lives," Mickey said. "It's time for us to do the same." He leveled his gaze with mine. "Now we get to focus on us."

He was right. I knew it. I'd played the role of mother too long, neglecting the role of wife. He'd been so patient, as always.

For a while, maybe a decade, it was good. Then I noticed that I couldn't remember the lines of the play I'd been performing for so many years. My mother had dementia toward the end of her life. In the back of my mind, I wondered if I was following in her footsteps.

When our wedding anniversary came, Mickey gave me a little gift in honor of Michael, as had been his tradition since the beginning. It was a little blue stuffed bear, no bigger than my palm.

"Michael," I whispered. "Our baby." My brain must have shifted to a place I only went to in my imagination. "Oh, Ralph. Our baby boy."

When I looked up from the bear, expecting to see Ralph, however, I saw Mickey. In his expression, I saw the confusion. The horrible realization.

A panic crashed over me. It was two parts. The first being that I'd somehow disappeared into a false reality. The second being that I had revealed my big secret. The baby wasn't from a one-night stand in New York. The baby had been Ralph's. Part of me wanted to immediately play it off, but Mickey deserved better than a lie.

"Thank you for remembering him," I said instead, clutching that little blue bear and feeling like I was holding on to all my memories now, wondering if they'd fall out from under me. I later carried that bear to my keepsake box, my eyes scanning over all the tiny treasures that held my most precious memories. I held each one, ensuring that I knew its significance. It was Christmas and I had a small tree set up, not even decorated. That's when I started putting the items on the tree, choosing them by order, ensuring my time line was accurate.

That was the first time I put up my Memory Tree.

Mickey never wavered in how he treated me, and some part of me believes he knew all along and loved me anyway. He loved me for all my beauty, but for my flaws too. Truth be told, the flaws are what makes life, and love, more beautiful.

I put the Memory Tree up again the next year. And that time I wrote the stories down. For some reason, I wrote the stories as if I was telling them to you, my sweet granddaughters. As I wrote it all down, I was telling you the stories because in playwriting and theater, POV can change the entire story. The storyteller is the one who determines how history is ultimately remembered.

I realize that you girls may remember me as the stern grandmother who made you eat your vegetables, do your chores, and memorize your lines (Mallory). But you never met the me who made monumental mistakes. I wanted you to meet that girl. That woman. I wanted you to have the answers when your loved ones asked you one day.

So here we are. All my memories, my life, comes down to a box full of mysterious keepsakes that may look like someone's trash. They were my treasure though.

Take out those most special memories every so often,

like ornaments on a tree. Admire them. Reflect on what they meant to you. Then put them away just like your box of ornaments, because the future lies ahead, like the New Year after Christmas.

Oh, and make sure you choose love. Yes, love is a choice. It's more than a feeling, it's an action. A messy, painful, beautiful action that is worth it all in the end... And always use a live tree.

With my greatest love and sweetest memories,

Nan

Chapter Twenty-Nine

Acting is in everything but the words.

—Stella Adler

As first light spilled through her bedroom window, Mallory restlessly tossed around in her sheets, her mind racing with the revelations from Nan's journal. Pop, the gentle soul who'd run Popadine's Christmas Tree Farm all these years, who had become Hollis's adoptive grandfather, was Ralph. The same Ralph who had stolen Nan's heart all those years ago in a high school Christmas play. Who'd unknowingly fathered a child with Nan that had tragically passed away.

Ralph Popadine was Pop?

The pieces had fallen into place like a bittersweet puzzle. Every interaction Mallory had witnessed between Nan and Pop at Memory Oaks now carried new meaning, weighted with decades of unspoken history. History that Nan might not even remember at this point. In fact, Mallory felt certain she didn't.

Rolling onto her side, Mallory hugged her pillow close as she imagined young Nan and Ralph, their love blooming in simpler times. The way Nan wrote about Ralph was different from how she described Mallory's grandfather Mickey. Both loves were real, but first love had a magic all its own, an innocence that could never quite be recaptured.

Another thing that had kept Mallory tossing last night was a final note from Nan, along with a collection of her mother's letters, an envelope with a substantial amount of money, and Daisy's contact information.

> *Dearest Granddaughters,*
>
> *It's not an ornament but I saved all the Christmas letters your mother sent after that last visit. Read them and you'll see that she was following both of you every step of the way along your journey to this point. You'll find her address on the letters. It hasn't changed. If you should want to reach out, she'd be thrilled, but if you choose not to, Daisy will never hold that against you. Like love, it's a choice that is yours to make.*
>
> *P.S Daisy sent a savings bond for each of you every year since the last time you saw her. Consider the money like the rainy day fund that my mother used when I came home from New York, pregnant and scared. Everyone should have one, and you'll know when it's time to use it.*

Mallory had been too stunned and tired to even consider what this final keepsake meant. She would need to talk to Maddie before doing anything. She didn't know exactly how much, but the rainy day fund that Daisy had created for them was substantial. Maybe even enough to solve all the concerns of Nan's care and the upkeep for the theater. Wow.

On a yawn, Mallory sat up in bed and glanced over at the night-stand clock. She'd already planned to see Nan this morning, like she did any morning when she didn't have to work at the hospital.

I wish I could tell Nan that I finished her journal. There were so many questions Mallory still had left to ask. Most, however, were now answered. All that was left for Mallory to do was decide what the revelations meant in relation to her own life.

Hurrying, she showered, dressed, and made her cup of coffee to go, and then stepped out into the chilly morning. As she drove, frost sparkled on bare tree branches, and Christmas lights twinkled from nearby houses, reminding her of the season's magic—and of Hollis. Always of Hollis these days. Was he working the tree farm this morning? She envisioned him walking his dogs along the rows of trees, talking to them and himself, his boots making fresh footprints in the new fallen snow. Or walking one dog and pulling the other in a wagon. Even dogs could use a little fresh air for healing, right?

After parking, Mallory hugged her heavy coat tighter across her chest and walked briskly toward the front entrance of Memory Oaks, the cold air nipping her cheeks and nose.

"There's our star director!" Francis cheered from the front desk. "The play was absolutely magical last night. You've done your grandmother proud, keeping her tradition."

"Thanks." Mallory managed a tired smile.

Francis's expression softened. "Everything okay? You look like you've been carrying some heavy thoughts."

"Just… I don't know. I guess I'm processing some family history," Mallory answered carefully.

"Mm. I'm processing some things this morning too." Francis sighed. "Margaret put in her retirement notice earlier. She'll be leaving us next month. We're happy for her, of course. She's earned her rest. But it's a real loss for Memory Oaks. She's one of our best."

"She's been so great with Nan. It must be hard finding qualified nurses in a town this size."

"Like finding a needle in a haystack," Francis agreed. "You wouldn't happen to know anyone looking for work, would you?"

Mallory shook her head, her mind already drifting toward Nan's room. "I'll let you know if I think of anyone."

"I'd appreciate it."

Mallory continued down the hallway, watching her feet as she walked. Outside Nan's door, she heard something that stopped her in her tracks—laughter. Rich, genuine laughter that transported her back to her childhood, when Nan's joy had been a constant presence.

"Nan?" Mallory knocked softly and entered to find Pop seated beside Nan's chair, both caught in the afterglow of shared amusement. The sight struck Mallory with such force that she had to grip the doorframe. Here they were, two people who might have spent a lifetime together, finding each other again in the winter of their lives. It was beautiful and heartbreaking all at once.

"Mallory!" Pop's face creased with genuine pleasure. He turned to Nan, his voice gentle. "Look who's come to visit."

Nan's eyes held that familiar mix of confusion and polite interest as she studied Mallory's face. The lack of recognition still hurt, but Mallory had learned to find joy in each moment rather than mourning what was lost. "Who are you?"

"Just a friend of Pop's. Hi, Pop," Mallory said, glancing in his direction and sharing a look.

Settling into a nearby chair, she watched how naturally Pop and Nan interacted, how their shoulders angled toward each other without conscious thought. "The play was wonderful last night," she told them. "We performed it in your barn, Pop."

"Hollis told me. It's not my barn anymore though. It's his. I know he'll take care of the place."

Mallory knew that too.

"A play in a barn? How unusual," Nan commented. "Was there hay everywhere?"

"A little here and there," Mallory said. "It added charm."

"You'll have to take me next time," Nan said. Then she looked at Pop. "Or maybe you could take me. We're friends, aren't we?"

Pop reached for Nan's hand and gave it a squeeze, causing Mallory's heart to squeeze too. "We're good friends."

Nan's cheeks flushed.

"Actually, Nan," Mallory said, "we're planning to perform the play here next weekend." Francis had agreed to host, and the cast had all agreed as well.

Nan drew a hand to her chest. "A play? Here?" She looked at Pop and reached for his hand. "Ralph, did you hear that?"

Pop slid his gaze to meet Mallory's, maybe wondering if she knew his shared history with Nan. Mallory hadn't, but she did now. And she was so grateful. "I did hear it, Nan," he said. "Want to be my date?"

Nan looked pleased by the invitation.

Mallory felt like she was eavesdropping on two young lovebirds. "I, um, need to go. I was only dropping in to say hello." As she rose to leave, Nan caught her hand with surprising strength. "You should visit more often, dear. Every day if you can. This is a wonderful place to be."

The words resonated through Mallory like a struck bell. Nan was always right, even when lost in her current fog. Memory Oaks wasn't an ending place. It was where life continued to unfold, where connections deepened, where love persisted against all odds. Where memories settled like old friends.

Mallory's pace picked up along with her resolution as she approached the front desk again. "Francis? I think I do know someone who may be interested."

Francis looked up from her paperwork. "You do? Who?"

Mallory's heart raced with sudden certainty. "Me."

Francis's eyebrows shot up. "You?"

"I'll bring my résumé by later today," Mallory promised. "But first, I need to see a man about a Christmas tree."

Back in her car, Mallory gripped the steering wheel as emotions crashed over her. Her grandmother's story had taught her so much—about love, about timing, about courage. When you find real love, you don't let it slip away. You grab it with both hands. You fight for it with everything you have.

Yes, Hollis had let Mallory down once. Or twice. But no one else challenged her the way he did or supported her dreams as fiercely. No one else saw straight through her defenses to the person she truly was—and loved her anyway. No one else made her feel so completely herself.

She turned her car toward Popadine's Christmas Tree Farm, her grandmother's journal entries echoing in her mind. Life was too short for holding back, too precious for pride. The past had given her its lessons. Now it was time for Mallory to write her own love story.

As she drove, more snowflakes began to fall, dusting the world in possibilities. Mallory's excitement grew, her assuredness, leaving her more certain with every mile. Sometimes the greatest Christmas gifts weren't wrapped in paper and bows. The best ornaments weren't store bought, but instead little sentimental trinkets. Sometimes the best roles weren't played out onstage, but in a barn, in real life. At least that's what Mallory was hoping as she cut the engine and stepped out of her car.

Buster darted in her direction first. Trained, Duke waited for Hollis to give him the okay. Duke was slower than normal, still healing from his injuries. Both dogs greeted Mallory with tail wags, sniffing her hands and legs as she stood there, waiting for Hollis to slowly approach.

"I'm so sorry, Mal," he began.

She raised a hand to stop him. "Here's the deal. Next time life goes sideways, you need to promise to turn to me, okay?"

"I promise." He reached for her hand and held it in his. "You can lean on me and vice versa. Just like Santa and Mrs. Claus."

Mallory liked the sound of that. "Did you know that *Santa, Baby* was really about Nan and her first love?"

Hollis crinkled his forehead in a thoughtful expression. "I didn't know that."

"Mm-hmm. This holiday season has brought quite the revelations."

He stared at her. "I have a revelation of my own. I love you, Mal."

Her lips parted. "Hey, that's my line."

The corners of his lips curved. "I thought maybe you forgot it."

"Well, I didn't." Leaning into him, she hoped he'd keep his promise to catch her if she truly let herself fall, because that was the plan from here on out. Part of the plan. She also planned to leave the hospital, work at Memory Oaks, and reinvent Nan's theater for someone else's dream—Maddie's. Wouldn't the theater make a great location for the Adaptive Sports Center? Why hadn't that occurred to her before?

And maybe, just maybe, Mallory and Maddie would extend an olive branch to their mom.

The future was full of possibilities and plans to make. But right now, Mallory's only plan was getting Hollis to kiss her for a third time. Three's a charm. "I love you too, Hollis Franklin," she whispered, looking up into his dark brown eyes.

He didn't budge. Instead, he held her gaze, looking at her like no one ever had. "You do realize I'm just a small-town guy who's going to raise trees and rescue dogs, don't you?"

She narrowed her eyes. "What do you mean 'just.' That's more than enough for me."

Her words seemed to satisfy any hesitation he had left. Now he dipped low, his beard tickling her skin as he brushed his lips to hers. And just like being onstage, she felt like the ground was slipping from beneath her feet and she was flying.

As he pulled back, she flashed him a grin, her heart so full that it could burst. Not everyone got to live out their happily-ever-after with their one true love. Mallory didn't doubt that Nan and Mickey had loved each other in their own way, different from the once-in-a-lifetime way that Nan had loved Ralph. Still loved Ralph.

Mallory wouldn't take this chance with Hollis for granted.

"*Santa, Baby* is about Nan?" Hollis asked.

"It's a long story," Mallory said with a laugh. "All I care about now is our story."

"Ditto, Mrs. Claus." Wrapping his arm around her shoulders, he led her toward the trees, with Buster and Duke at their heels and snowflakes landing on their hair and dusting their shoulders. Stopping short, Hollis bent and grabbed a bright red cardinal's feather from the top of the freshly fallen snow. He turned and positioned it, along with a lock of hair, behind her ear.

This was a perfect moment, she thought, deserving of an ornament—the very first on her own Memory Tree.

Epilogue

As Mallory finished her shift at Memory Oaks, typing out the last note of the day, she glanced out the window of the carefully maintained grounds, admiring crepe myrtles in full bloom, their pink and purple blossoms adding splashes of color against a field of green. When she'd worked at the hospital all those years, the only view she'd gotten was... well, none. The blinds were always closed for patient privacy. There was no natural light. No glimpses of nature. And she rarely had time when she'd worked at the hospital to sit and admire anything.

It wasn't just the view and the moments of rest throughout her day though. Every day brought new challenges: helping residents navigate their confusion, supporting families through difficult transitions, celebrating small victories. But the greatest reward was seeing Nan daily. Though her grandmother rarely recognized her as family anymore, their relationship had evolved into something equally meaningful. Now they shared the special bond between a patient and a nurse who carried Nan's history in her heart.

Heading toward Nan's room for her customary good-bye, Mallory's shoes squeaked softly against the polished floors. She stopped short at the doorway, her heart warming at the scene before her. Inside, Pop sat with Nan, their laughter floating out into the hallway like music. The afternoon sun streamed through the open blinds, casting a golden glow around them, and for a moment, Mallory could almost see their younger selves superimposed over their present-day forms. Nan with her soft, auburn hair and bright eyes. Ralph with his strong shoulders and gentle smile.

Even with their memories fading, their connection remained. Over her brief time here at Memory Oaks, Mallory had witnessed countless moments that proved what she now knew to be true—the heart remembers what the mind forgets. Love persists beyond the boundaries of memory, living in shared laughter, in familiar gestures, in the comfort of presence even when names and faces blur.

She turned away quietly, not wanting to interrupt their time together. Besides, Mallory had somewhere important to be. Tonight marked the grand opening of Adaptive Outdoor Adventures, and Mallory's chest tightened with anticipation. She was so happy for her little sister. So proud of Maddie.

"See you tomorrow, Francis!" Mallory called to the facility manager as she headed toward the exit.

Francis looked up and nodded. "Have I told you how glad I am to have you here?"

"Every day for the past six months," Mallory said with a grin. She stopped short of the door. "But I think I may have failed to tell you just how glad I am you hired me. Thank you."

"I knew you'd fit in here. It takes a special person to work with our patient population. A true caregiver."

Mallory let that description sink in. Yeah. She'd been caring for her younger sister since their mom left. She'd cared for countless patients at the hospital. Nan. When she'd been in the thick of her burnout, she'd lost the joy of doing for others, but it was back. "I'm heading to the grand opening of Maddie's new business."

"Oh, wow. I haven't heard about a grand opening."

"It's just a family celebration. The community opening is this weekend," Mallory said, reaching for her car keys from her bag.

"Well, tell Maddie I'll be there. I think it's great what she and Renee Callister are doing."

The business was for everyone, inclusive in every way. People at all levels of ability were breaking through limitations and climbing their own "mountains," regardless of how big or how small.

Mallory pushed through the exit doors and crossed the parking lot toward her car. As she drove through Bloom, she rolled down her windows despite the heat, letting the scent of magnolia blossoms and freshly cut grass fill her senses. The downtown streets were quiet this afternoon. As she approached the old community theater, her breath caught.

The transformation really was stunning. The original structure remained, the weathered surface telling stories of decades past, but everything else had been thoughtfully reimagined. Wide, gently sloping ramps with elegant handrails led to the entrance, their design so seamlessly integrated that they looked like they'd always been there. The large windows, cleaned and restored to their original glory, offered glimpses of the interior where adaptive equipment waited to open new possibilities for those who thought certain adventures were beyond their reach because of their disabilities.

The building that had once housed Nan's theater now promised new kinds of performances, ones where people rediscovered their strength, their courage, and their joy in movement. The interior had been opened to create a bright, welcoming space. Kayaks hung on the walls, modified with special seating systems. Adaptive mountain bikes stood in racks, their specialized designs promising freedom to those who thought they'd never ride again. Rock climbing walls featured innovative harness systems, and the state-of-the-art fitness area boasted equipment designed to accommodate various abilities. Not just people with disabilities though. Everyone was invited to "play."

Maddie's face glowed as she sat on the wide front porch in her wheelchair, surrounded by potted ferns and hanging baskets of lantana, which thrived in the Carolina heat. There was a light in her eyes that Mallory recognized. The rare kind that people had when they were living out their purpose. Hollis had the same light. And, lately, Mallory had caught that light in her own reflection when she looked herself in the eye.

Maddie waved excitedly when she saw Mallory. Then she wheeled herself down the ramp with controlled speed and grace. "Everyone's finally here!" she called out, her voice carrying across the parking lot. "We can finally get this party started!"

"Not quite everyone," Mallory replied, biting her lower lip to contain her nerves as she watched Maddie's gaze sharpen on an SUV that was pulling into the parking lot.

This could go one of two ways. Good. Or bad. Very bad.

"Mom?" Maddie's voice caught on the word as she looked up at Mallory. "Is that…?"

Daisy stepped out of the vehicle, her hesitation visible in the way she gripped the car door before straightening her shoulders. Daisy was a beautiful woman, no question. She had long, shiny brown hair, streaked by the sun. A golden tan and delicate features. Looking at her, one wouldn't know the hardships she'd had along the way to this point. She'd lost the man she loved—Mallory's father. She'd gotten pregnant young and had chosen to give up her babies, which couldn't have been an easy choice.

Mallory's gaze pinged from her mom to her sister. She held her breath, waiting to see how this would go.

Suddenly, Maddie's squeal of delight broke the tension, sending relief flooding through Mallory's veins. She'd taken a risk in not telling her sister about inviting their estranged mom, but their recent conversations about reaching out with no expectations or pressure had given Mallory hope.

As they took turns hugging one another, years of distance seemed to dissolve. Mallory felt Daisy tremble as they embraced. There was an urgency to her hug, as if she'd been waiting for this very moment for who knew how long.

Time suspended as their tears fell. They only stopped when they heard the heavy footsteps coming down the wooden ramp, announcing Hollis's approach. He and Sam had been working the outdoor grill for hours, perfecting the art of barbecue. As he drew closer, the scent of smoking hickory wood and marinated chicken followed him. Slipping an arm around Mallory's shoulders, he pressed a kiss to her cheek before turning to Daisy.

"So you're the man who thinks he's going to ride off into the sunset with my baby girl?" Daisy's tone carried a playful edge, but Mallory thought she sensed something more. Or maybe she wanted to believe there was more. Perhaps maternal protectiveness and a deep love for the daughter that she'd missed.

No expectations, Mallory. No strings. That was the only way to ensure that no one got hurt, including Daisy. They were adults now. It was better to have a little bit of Daisy than to not have her at all. At least, that's what Mallory had decided for herself.

Mallory felt Hollis tense slightly beside her, but then Daisy's face softened into a genuine smile. "Take care of her. She's been through it because of me. She deserves the best." Her eyes narrowed slightly as she studied Hollis, seeing past the surface to the heart of him. "Something tells me, that's you."

Daisy's words had a visible effect on Hollis. Knowing how much Hollis had always struggled to feel worthy, Mallory reached for his hand and gave a small squeeze. She also met her mother's gaze and smiled. They had a long road of healing ahead, but making the man that Mallory loved feel good about himself won Daisy points for sure.

As they followed the smell of barbecue toward the back of the building, Mallory touched her mother's arm. "I'm happy you're here."

Daisy's eyes glistened with a sheen of tears. "Nowhere else I'd rather be."

Mallory felt the same. Surrounded by her family, including Nan and Pop, and the fireflies that began to twinkle in the fading sunlight, she was warmed by an all-encompassing peace, something she'd been missing last year and hadn't even realized. Sandy and Matt were here as well because Hollis was a huge part of Mallory's life these days and, as Hollis's family, so were Sandy and Matt.

Maddie's voice got Mallory's attention, carrying across the gathering as she proudly showed their mother the adaptive equipment and explained how each piece would help someone rediscover their love of outdoor adventure. The community had pooled together to fund what was an expensive venture. There was a lot of "old money" in small towns and generous folks who wanted to support the dreams of others.

Hollis caught Mallory's eye in the small crowd. She didn't have to remind herself not to hold expectations with him. She didn't have to avoid strings or worry about having her heart broken. He was a safe place to fall, and boy, had she fallen. In his eyes, she saw more holiday plays at The Barn, which had become the event location's official name. She also saw more gatherings with both of their families and quiet evenings visiting Nan and Pop at Memory Oaks.

Life rarely followed the script you expected. Sometimes it took unexpected turns, leading you down paths you would never have chosen. But if you kept your heart open, if you were brave enough to try again, to forgive, to love, those serendipitous detours could lead you exactly where you were meant to be.

Nan always said that love was the greatest adventure of all, and knowing the story behind that wisdom made Mallory realize it was true for Nan, and it would also be true for her. Looking at the family gathered around her, some by blood, some by choice, all by love, Mallory knew just how right she'd been. Now that she'd found her life partner, Mallory's adventure seemed to just be getting started, full of promise and possibility, and those rare and special memories worthy of capturing in a Christmas keepsake.

Acknowledgments

First and foremost, my deepest gratitude goes out to my husband and children—your unwavering support, patience, and love carried me through the long nights and uncertain moments when this book felt like a messy jumble of words. You are my foundation. Without you, I would crumble. With you, I'm able to keep going and achieve my dream. Sonny, Ralphie, Doc, and Lydia, you are my inspiration.

To my literary agent, Sarah—thank you for believing in this story from the first seed of an idea to the final, polished draft. Your guidance is and always has been invaluable.

I'm profoundly grateful to my publishing team at Forever/Grand Central: my brilliant editor Alex, whose keen eye and thoughtful suggestions transformed these pages; the talented cover artist who captured the essence of this story so beautifully; the meticulous copy editor and proofreader who polished every sentence; and the dedicated publicist at Forever who champions my books with contagious enthusiasm.

A special thank-you goes out to my assistant, Kimberly, who somehow manages to keep my author life organized while I'm lost in fictional worlds—your efficiency and support make it possible for me to focus on what I love most, which is creating.

To Rachel, my critique partner and first reader—your honesty, insight, and encouragement have shaped not just this book but also my growth as a writer. We've been on this journey from the start, and I hope we'll always walk this author path together. Thank you for always telling me what I need to hear, not just what I want to hear. That's the true sign of a great critique partner. Thank you to Tif, April, and Jeanette as well. #Girlswritenight forever!

And finally, to my readers—you who take time from your busy lives to spend hours with the characters and worlds I create—you give purpose to every word I write. Your enthusiasm, messages, and support remind me daily why I tell the stories I do. This book exists because of you, and for that, I am eternally grateful! To my MVPs—DeeAnn, Elaine, Vickie, Patricia, and so many more—there are no words for how much I appreciate you (and it's rare to make an author speechless).

About the Author

Annie Rains is a *USA Today* bestselling author of small-town contemporary stories full of hope and heart. After years of dreaming about becoming an author, Annie published her first book in 2015 and has been chasing deadlines and creating happily-ever-afters for her characters ever since. When she isn't writing, Annie is usually spending time with her family or reading a book by one of her favorite authors. Annie also enjoys spending time with her three attention-hungry and mischievous rescues, which inspire the lovable pets in her books.

You can learn more at:
AnnieRains.com
X @AnnieRainsBooks
Facebook.com/AnnieRainsBooks
Instagram @AnnieRainsBooks
TikTok @AnnieRainsBooks

RAISING READERS
Books Build Bright Futures

Thank you for reading this book and for being a reader of books in general. As an author, I am so grateful to share being part of a community of readers with you, and I hope you will join me in passing our love of books on to the next generation of readers.

Did you know that reading for enjoyment is the single biggest predictor of a child's future happiness and success?

More than family circumstances, parents' educational background, or income, reading impacts a child's future academic performance, emotional well-being, communication skills, economic security, ambition, and happiness.

Studies show that kids reading for enjoyment in the US is in rapid decline:

- In 2012, 53% of 9-year-olds read almost every day. Just 10 years later, in 2022, the number had fallen to 39%.
- In 2012, 27% of 13-year-olds read for fun daily. By 2023, that number was just 14%.

Together, we can commit to **Raising Readers** and change this trend. How?

- Read to children in your life daily.
- Model reading as a fun activity.
- Reduce screen time.
- Start a family, school, or community book club.
- Visit bookstores and libraries regularly.
- Listen to audiobooks.
- Read the book before you see the movie.
- Encourage your child to read aloud to a pet or stuffed animal.
- Give books as gifts.
- Donate books to families and communities in need.

BOB1217

Books build bright futures, and **Raising Readers** is our shared responsibility.

For more information, visit **JoinRaisingReaders.com**

Sources: National Endowment for the Arts, National Assessment of Educational Progress, WorldBookDay.org, Nielsen BookData's 2023 "Understanding the Children's Book Consumer"